MAGIC'S CALL

Kethry felt the room drop away from under her, a wash of anger threaten to overwhelm her, and a surge of nameless emotions hit her with a force that made her gasp. Unconsciously, she braced herself on the table, as her family turned to stare at her with varying degrees of surprise and concern.

And for a moment, she didn't recognize what had hit her, it had been so long—

"*Need*," she gasped, when she got her breath back. "It's Need! Something's wrong, something horrible has happened—"

"To whom?" Tarma demanded. "Can you tell?"

Kethry shook her head, both in negation and to clear the tears of shock from her eyes. "But it can't be too far away, not more than a day's ride at most, or it wouldn't be this *strong*—"

MERCEDES LACKEY
OATHBLOOD

DAW BOOKS, INC.
DONALD A. WOLLHEIM, FOUNDER
375 Hudson Street, New York, NY 10014

ELIZABETH R. WOLLHEIM
SHEILA E. GILBERT
PUBLISHERS

DAW TRADEMARK REGISTERED
U.S. PAT. OFF. AND FOREIGN COUNTRIES
—MARCA REGISTRADA
HECHO EN U.S.A.

PRINTED IN THE U.S.A.

This book is dedicated to everyone
who kept asking if we'd do it,
especially my dad.

CONTENTS

TARMA AND KETHRY
An Introduction

Tarma and Kethry were created because heroic fantasy was finally "coming of age," not the least because of people like Marion Zimmer Bradley and her *Sword and Sorceress* anthologies, but I saw two problems.

The first—most of the stories were about brawny C*n*n types, strong like bull, dumb like ox, iron-thewed and not something you'd invite to a nice restaurant. The remainder were equally divided between the incredibly depressing eternally doomed hero type, and the female counterpart to the C*n*n type. Trouble was, the latter seemed to share her male counterpart's taste in women.

Mind you, I have no personal objection to this, but I thought it would be *nice* to have at least one token heterosexual female hero. And hey, not every fantasy hero or heroine has to be as highly sexed as most of the then-current crop seemed to be!

So I invented Tarma and Kethry. Tarma is celibate, chaste, and altogether asexual; Kethry isn't, and though she doesn't think with her hormones, she definitely is fond of men.

Two books (three if you count the beginning of *By the Sword*) and many short stories later, things have changed for the better, insofar as there is now a vast cornucopia of books and stories in heroic fantasy, which incorporate a vast spectrum of heroes and heroines, but I'm still glad I invented Tarma and Kethry. Figuring out ways to get them in trouble and getting them out again has been highly entertaining for all concerned.

SWORD-SWORN

This is the very first appearance of Tarma and Kethry, and how they met. I distinctly remember presenting this and a second Tarma and Kethry story to Marion in person. The occasion was just before one of her Fantasy Worlds Festival conventions, and I had volunteered to be "go-fer mom"—I was going to see to it that all her eager young volunteers ate and slept regularly. Which I did, with a hammer, when necessary. But beforehand, Marion had invited me to come to her home; I had already sold her my first professional sale (a Darkover story), and I wanted very much to be accepted into the *Sword and Sorceress* anthologies. I brought both manuscripts with me—after first asking permission!—and presented them to her with much trepidation.

"I don't know about the first one," I said hesitantly. "It's kind of 'rape and revenge,' and I know you're tired of that." She just waved me off and took possession of the manuscripts.

Lisa Waters (her secretary and protegée) and I were making tea in the kitchen when *"Damn you, Misty!"* rang out from the living room. Certain that I had somehow offended her, I ran to find out what it was I had done wrong so I could try to make amends.

As it turned out, what I had done was not wrong, but I had presented her with a dilemma. She liked *both* stories, and wanted *both* of them, and could only publish one!

Giddily I told her to hang on to the second one; I was

certain there would be a *Sword and Sorceress IV.* Since the volume numbers are now up in the high teens, you can see that I was right. The second story was published in Volume IV, and I later sold two Tarma and Kethry books to DAW.

But this is how the two met in the first place.

The air inside the gathering-tent was hot, although the evening breeze that occasionally stole inside the closed tent flap and touched Tarma's back was chill, like a sword's edge laid along her spine. This high-desert country cooled off quickly at night, not like the Clan's grazing grounds down in the grass plains. Tarma shivered; for comfort's sake she'd long since removed her shirt and now, like most of the others in the tent, was attired only in her vest and breeches. In the light of the lamps Tarma's Clansfolk looked like living versions of the gaudy patterns they wove into their rugs.

Her brother-uncle Kefta neared the end of his sword-dance in the middle of the tent. He performed it only rarely, on the most special of occasions, but this occasion warranted celebration. Never before had the men of the Clan returned from the Summer Horsefair laden with so much gold—it was nearly three times what they'd hoped for. There was war a-brewing somewhere, and as a consequence horses had commanded more than prime prices. The Shin-'a'in hadn't argued with their good fortune. Now their new wealth glistened in the light of the oil lamps, lying in a shining heap in the center of the tent for all of the Clan of the Stooping Hawk to rejoice over. Tomorrow it would be swiftly converted into salt and herbs, grain and leather, metal weapons and staves of true, straight-grained wood for looms and arrows (all things the Shin'a'in did not produce themselves) but for this night, they would admire their short-term wealth and celebrate.

Not all that the men had earned lay in that shining heap. Each man who'd undertaken the journey had earned a special share, and most had brought back gifts. Tarma stroked the necklace at her throat as she breathed in the scent of clean sweat, incense, and the sentlewood perfume most of her Clan had anointed themselves with. She glanced to her right as she did so, surprised at her flash of shyness. Dharin seemed to have all his attention fixed on the whirling figure of the dancer, but he intercepted her glance as if he'd been watching for it, and his normally solemn expression vanished as he smiled broadly. Tarma blushed, then made a face at him. He grinned even more, and pointedly lowered his eyes to the necklace of carved amber she wore, curved claws alternating with perfect beads. He'd brought that for her, evidence of his trading abilities, because (he said) it matched her golden skin. That she'd accepted it and was wearing it tonight was token that she'd accepted him as well. When Tarma finished her sword-training, they'd be bonded. That would be in two years, perhaps less, if her progress continued to be as rapid as it was now. She and Dharin dealt with each other very well indeed, each being a perfect counter for the other. They were long-time friends as well as lovers.

The dancer ended his performance in a calculated sprawl, as though exhausted. His audience shouted their approval, and he rose from the carpeted tent floor, beaming and dripping with sweat. He flung himself down among his family, accepting with a nod of thanks the damp towel handed to him by his youngest son. The plaudits faded gradually into chattering; as last to perform he would pick the next.

After a long draft of wine he finally spoke, and his choice was no surprise to anyone. "Sing, Tarma," he said.

His choice was applauded on all sides as Tarma rose, brushed back her long ebony hair, and picked her way through the crowded bodies of her Clansfolk to take her place in the center.

Tarma was no kind of beauty; her features were too sharp and hawklike, her body too boyishly slender; and well she knew it. Dharin had often joked when they lay together that he never knew whether he was bedding her or her sword. But the Goddess of the Four Winds had granted her a voice that was more than compensation, a voice that was un-matched among the Clans. The Shin'a'in, whose history was mainly contained in song and story, valued such a voice more than precious metals. Such was her value that the shaman had taught her the arts of reading and writing, that she might the more easily learn the ancient lays of other peoples as well as her own.

Impishly, she had decided to pay Dharin back for making her blush by singing a tale of totally faithless lovers, one that was a Clan favorite. She had only just begun it, the musicians picking up the key and beginning to follow her, when unlooked-for disaster struck.

Audible even over the singing came the sound of tearing cloth; and armored men, seemingly dozens of them, poured howling through the ruined tent walls to fall upon the stunned nomads. Most of the

Clan were all but weaponless—but the Shin'a'in were warriors by tradition as well as horsebreeders. There was not one of them above the age of nine that had not had at least some training. They shook off their shock quickly, and every member of the Clan that could seized whatever was nearest and fought back with the fierceness of any cornered wild thing.

Tarma had her paired daggers and a throwing spike in a wrist sheath—the last was quickly lost as she hurled it with deadly accuracy through the visor of the nearest bandit. He screeched, dropped his sword, and clutched his face, blood pouring between his fingers. One of her cousins snatched up the forgotten blade and gutted him with it. Tarma had no time to see what other use he made of it; another of the bandits was bearing down on her and she had barely enough time to draw her daggers before he closed with her.

A dagger, even two of them, rarely makes a good defense against a longer blade, but fighting in the tent was cramped, and the bandit found himself at a disadvantage in the close quarters. Though Tarma's hands were shaking with excitement and fear, her mind stayed cool and she managed to get him to trap his own blade long enough for her to plant one of those daggers in his throat. He gurgled hoarsely, then fell, narrowly missing imprisoning her beneath him. She wrenched the sword from his still-clutching hands and turned to find another foe.

She saw with fear that the invaders were easily winning the unequal battle; that despite a gallant defense with such improvised weapons as rugs and hair ornaments, despite the fact that more than one of the bandits was wounded or dead, her people were rapidly falling before their enemies. The bandits were armored; the Shin'a'in were not. That was making a telling difference. Out of the corner of one eye she could see a pair of them dropping their weapons and seizing women—and around her she could hear the shrieks of children, the harsher cries of adults—

But there was another fighter facing her now, his face blood- and sweat-streaked, and she forced herself not to hear, to think only of the moment and her opponent as she'd been taught.

She parried his thrust with the dagger she still held and made a slash at his neck. The fighting had thinned now, and she couldn't hope to use the same tactics that had worked before. He countered it in a leisurely fashion and turned the counter into a return stroke with careless ease that sent her writhing out of the way of the blade's edge. She wasn't quite fast enough—he left a long score on her ribs. The cut wasn't deep or dangerous, but it hurt and bled freely. She stumbled over a body—friend or foe, she didn't notice, and only barely evaded his blade a second time. He toyed with her, his face splitting in an ugly grin as he saw how tired she was becoming. Her hands were shaking now, not with fear, but with exhaustion. She was so weary she failed to notice the little circle of three or four bandits that had formed around her, and that she was the only Shin'a'in still fighting. He made a pass; before she had time to realize it was merely a feint, he'd gotten inside her guard and swatted her to the ground as the flat of his blade connected with the side of her head, the edges cutting into her scalp, searing like hot irons. He'd swung the blade full-force—she fought off unconsciousness as her hands reflexively let her weapons fall and she collapsed. Half-stunned, she tried to punch, kick, and bite (in spite of nausea and a dizziness that kept threatening to overwhelm her): he began battering at her face and head with heavy, massive fists.

He connected one time too many, and she felt her legs give out, her arms fall helplessly to her sides. He laughed, then threw her to the floor of the tent, inches away from the body of one of her brothers. She felt his hands tearing off her breeches; she tried to get her knee into his groin, but the last of her strength was long gone. He laughed again and settled his hands almost lovingly around her neck and began to squeeze. She clawed at the hands, but he was too strong; nothing she did made him release that ever-tightening grip. She began to thrash as her chest tightened and her lungs cried out for air. Her head seemed about to explode, and reality narrowed to the desperate struggle for a single breath. At last, mercifully, blackness claimed her even as he began to thrust himself brutally into her.

The only sound in the violated tent was the steady droning of flies. Tarma opened her right eye—the left one was swollen shut—and stared dazedly at the ceiling. When she tried to swallow, her throat howled in protest, she gagged, and nearly choked. Whimpering, she rolled onto one side. She found she was staring into the sightless eyes of her baby sister, as flies fed greedily at the pool of blood congealing beneath the child's head.

She vomited up what little there was in her stomach, and nearly choked to death in the process. Her throat was swollen almost completely shut.

She dragged herself to her knees, her head spinning dizzily, her stomach threatening to empty itself again of what it didn't contain. As she looked around her, and her mind took in the magnitude of disaster, something within her parted with a nearly audible snap.

Every member of the Clan, from the oldest grayhair to the youngest infant, had been brutally and methodically slaughtered. The sight was more than her dazed mind could bear. Most of her ran screaming to hide in a safe, dark, mental corner; what was left coaxed her body to its feet.

A few rags of her vest hung from her shoulders; there was blood running down her thighs and her loins ached sharply, echoing the pounding pain in her head. More blood had dried all down one side, some of it from the cut along her ribs, some that of her foes or her Clansfolk. Her hand rose of its own accord to her temple and found her long hair sticky and hard with dried blood matting it into clumps. The pain of her head and the nausea that seemed linked with it overwhelmed any other hurt, but as her hand drifted absently over her face, it felt strange, swollen and puffy. Had she been able to see it, she would not have recognized even her own reflection, her face was so battered. The part of her that was still thinking sent her body to search for something to cover her nakedness. She found a pair of breeches—not her own, they were much too big— and a vest, both flung into corners as worthless. Her eyes slid unseeing over the huddled, nude bodies that might have been the previous wearers. Then the thread of direction sent her to retrieve the clan banner from where it still hung on the centerpole.

Clutching it in one hand, she found herself outside the gathering-tent. She stood dumbly in the sun for several long moments, then moved trancelike toward the nearest of the family tents. They, too, had been ransacked, but at least there were no bodies in them. The raiders had found little to their taste there, other than the odd bit of jewelry. Only a Shin'a'in would be interested in the kinds of tack and personal gear of a Shin'a'in—and anyone not of the Clans found trying to sell such would find himself with several inches of Shin'a'in steel in his gut. Apparently the bandits knew this.

She found a halter and saddlepad in one of the nearer tents. The rest of her crouched in its mind-corner and gibbered. She wept soundlessly when it recognized the tack by its tooling as having been Dharin's.

The brigands had not been able to steal the horses—the Shin'a'in let them run free and the horses were trained nearly from birth to come only to their riders. The sheep and goats had been scattered, but the goats were guardian enough to reunite the herds and protect them in the absence of shepherds—and in any case, it was the horses that concerned her now, not the other animals. Tarma managed a semblance of her whistle with her swollen, cracked lips; Kessira came trotting up eagerly, snorting with distaste at the smell of blood on her mistress. Her hands, swollen, stiff, and painful, were clumsy with the harness, but Kessira was patient while Tarma struggled with the straps, not even tossing her gray head in an effort to avoid the hackamore as she usually did.

Tarma somehow dragged herself into the saddle; there was another Clan camped less than a day's ride away. She lumped the banner in front of her, pointed Kessira in the right direction, and gave her the set of signals that meant that her mistress was hurt and needed help. That accomplished, the dregs of directing intelligence receded into hiding with the rest of her, and the ghastly ride was endured in a complete state of blankness.

She never knew when Kessira walked into the camp with her broken, bleeding mistress slumped over the Clan banner. No one there recognized her—they only knew she was Shin'a'in by her coloring and costume. She never realized that she led a would-be rescue party all the way back to the ruined camp before collapsing over Kessira's neck. The shaman and Healers eased her off the back of her mare, and she never felt it, nor did she feel their ministrations. For seven days and nights she lay silent, never moving, eyes either closed or staring fixedly into space. The Healers feared for her life and sanity, for a Shin'a'in Clanless was one without purpose.

But on the morning of the eighth day, when the Healer entered the tent in which she lay, her head turned and the eyes that met his were once again bright with intelligence.

Her lips parted. "Where—?" she croaked, her voice uglier than a raven's cry.

"Liha'irden," he said, setting down his burden of broth and medicine. "Your name? We could not recognize you, only the banner—" he hesitated, unsure of what to tell her.

"Tarma," she replied. "What of—my Clan—Deer's Son?"

"Gone." It would be best to tell it shortly. "We

gave them the rites as soon as we found them, and brought the herds and goods back here. You are the last of the Hawk's Children."

So her memory was correct. She stared at him wordlessly.

At this time of year the entire Clan traveled together, leaving none at the grazing-grounds. There was no doubt she was the sole survivor.

She was taking the news calmly—too calmly. He did not like it that she did not weep. There was madness lurking within her; he could feel it with his Healer's senses. She walked a thin thread of sanity, and it would take very little to cause the thread to break. He dreaded her next question.

It was not the one he had expected. "My voice— what ails it?"

"Something broken past mending," he replied regretfully—for he had heard her sing less than a month ago.

"So." She turned her head to stare again at the ceiling. For a moment he feared she had retreated into madness, but after a pause she spoke again.

"I cry blood-feud," she said tonelessly.

When the Healer's attempts at dissuading her failed, he brought the Clan Elders. They reiterated all his arguments, but she remained silent and seemingly deaf to their words.

"You are only one—how can you hope to accomplish anything?" the Clanmother said finally. "They are many, seasoned fighters, and crafty. What you wish to do is hopeless before it begins."

Tarma stared at them with stony eyes, eyes that

did not quite conceal the fact that her sanity was questionable.

"Most importantly," said a voice from the tent door, "You have called what you have no right to call."

The shaman of the Clan, a vigorous woman of late middle age, stepped into the healer's tent and dropped gracefully beside Tarma's pallet to sit cross-legged.

"You know well only one Sword Sworn to the Warrior can cry blood-feud," she said calmly and evenly.

"I know," Tarma replied, breaking her silence. "And I wish to take Oath."

It was a Shin'a'in tenet that no person was any holier than any other, that each was a priest in his own right. The shaman might have the power of magic, might also be more learned than the average Clansman had time to be, but when the time came that a Shin'a'in wished to petition the God or Goddess, he simply entered the appropriate tent-shrine and did so, with or without consulting the shaman beforehand.

So it happened that Tarma was standing within the shrine on legs that trembled with weakness.

The Wise One had not seemed at all surprised at Tarma's desire to be Sworn to the Warrior, and had supported her in her demand over the protests of the Elders. "If the Warrior accepts her," she had said reasonably, "who are we to argue with the will of the Goddess? And if she does not, then blood-feud cannot be called."

The tent-shrines of the Clans were always absolutely identical in their spartan simplicity. There were four tiny wooden altars, one against each wall of the tent. In the East was that of the Maiden; on it was her symbol, a single fresh blossom in spring and summer, a stick of burning incense in winter and fall. To the South was that of the Warrior, marked by an ever-burning flame. The West held the Mother's altar, on it a sheaf of grain. The North was the domain of the Crone or Ancient One. The altar here held a smooth black stone.

Tarma stepped to the center of the tent. What she intended to do was nothing less than self-inflicted torture. All prayers among the Shin'a'in were sung, not spoken; further, all who came before the Goddess must lay all their thoughts before her. Not only must she endure the physical agony of trying to shape her ruined voice into a semblance of music, but she must deliberately call forth every emotion, every too-recent memory; all that caused her to be standing in this place.

She finished her song with her eyes tightly closed against the pain of those memories; her eyes burned and she ached with stubborn refusal to give in to tears.

There was a profound silence when she'd done; after a moment she realized she could not even hear the little sounds of the encampment on the other side of the thin tent walls. Just as she'd realized that, she felt the faint stirrings of a breeze—

It came from the East, and was filled with the scent of fresh flowers. It encircled her, and seemed to blow right through her very soul. It was soon joined by a second breeze, out of the West; a robust and strong little wind carrying the scent of ripening grain. As the first had blown through her, emptying her of pain, the second filled her with strength. Then it, too, was joined; a bitterly cold wind from the North, sharp with snow-scent. At the touch of this third wind her eyes opened, though she remained swathed in darkness born of the dark of her own spirit. The wind chilled her, numbed the memories until they began to seem remote; froze her heart with an icy armor that made the loneliness bearable. She felt now as if her soul were swathed in endless layers of soft, protecting bandages. The darkness left her sight—she saw through eyes grown distant and withdrawn to view a world that seemed to have receded to just out of reach.

The center of a whirlwind now, she stood unmoving while the physical winds whipped her hair and clothing about and the spiritual ones worked their magics within her.

But the Southern wind, the Warrior's Wind, was not one of them.

Suddenly the winds died to nothing. A voice that held nothing of humanity, echoing, sharp-edged as a fine blade yet ringing with melody, spoke one word. Her name.

Tarma obediently turned slowly to her right. Before the altar in the South stood a woman.

She was raven-haired and tawny-skinned, and the lines of her face were thin and strong, like all the Shin'a'in. She was arrayed all in black, from her boots to the headband that held her shoulder-length tresses out of her eyes. Even the chainmail hauberk she wore was black, as well as the sword she wore slung across her back and the daggers in her belt. She raised her eyes to meet Tarma's, and they had no whites, irises or pupils; her eyes were reflections of a cloudless night sky, black and star-strewn.

The Goddess had chosen to answer as the Warrior, and in Her own person.

When Tarma stepped through the tent flap, there was a collective sigh from those waiting. Her hair was shorn just short of shoulder length; the Clansfolk knew they would find the discarded locks lying across the Warrior's altar. Tarma had carried nothing into the tent, there was nothing within the shrine that she would have been able to use to cut it. Tarma's Oath had been accepted. There was an icy calm about her that was unmistakable, and completely unhuman.

No one in this Clan had been Swordsworn within living memory, but all knew what tradition demanded of them. No longer would the Sworn One wear garments bright with the colors the Shin'a'in loved; from out of a chest in the Wise One's tent, carefully husbanded against such a time, came clothing of dark brown and deepest black. The brown was for later, should Tarma survive her quest. The black was for now, for ritual combat, or for one pursuing blood-feud.

They clothed her, weaponed her, provisioned her. She stood before them when they had done, looking much as the Warrior herself had, her weapons about her, her provisions at her feet. The light of the dying sun turned the sky to blood as they brought the youngest child of the Clan Liha'irden to receive her blessing, a toddler barely ten months old. She placed her hands on his soft cap of baby hair without really seeing him—but this child had a special significance.

The herds and properties of the Hawk's Children would be tended and preserved for her, either until Tarma returned, or until this youngest child in the Clan of the Racing Deer was old enough to take his own sword. If by then she had not returned, they would revert to their caretakers.

Tarma rode out into the dawn. Tradition forbade anyone to watch her departure. To her own senses it seemed as though she rode still drugged with one of the healer's potions. All things came to her as if filtered through a gauze veil, and even her memories seemed secondhand—like a tale told to her by some gray-haired ancient.

She rode back to the scene of the slaughter; the pitiful burial mound aroused nothing in her. Some force outside of herself showed her eyes where to catch the scant signs of the already cold trail. It was not an easy trail to follow, despite the fact that no attempt had been made to conceal it. She rode until the fading light made tracking impossible, but was unable to make more than a few miles.

She made a cold camp, concealing herself and her horse in the lee of a pile of boulders. Enough moisture collected on them each night to support some meager grasses, which Kessira tore at eagerly. Tarma made a sketchy meal of dried meat and fruit, still wrapped in that strange calmness, then rolled herself into her blanket intending to rise with the first light of morning.

She was awakened before midnight.

A touch on her shoulder sent her scrambling out of her blanket, dagger in hand. Before her stood a figure, seemingly a man of the Shin'a'in, clothed as one Swordsworn. Unlike her, his face was veiled.

"Arm yourself, Sworn One," he said, his voice having an odd quality of distance to it, as though he were speaking from the bottom of a well.

She did not pause to question or argue. It was well that she did not, for as soon as she had donned her arms and light chain shirt, he attacked her.

The fight was not a long one; he had the advantage of surprise, and he was a much better fighter than she. Tarma could see the killing blow coming, but was unable to do anything to prevent it from falling. She cried out in agony as the stranger's sword all but cut her in half.

She woke staring up at the stars. The stranger interposed himself between her eyes and the sky. "You are better than I thought—" he said, with grim humor, "but you are still as clumsy as a horse in a pottery shed. Get up and try again."

He killed her three more times—with the same nonfatal result. After the third, she woke to find the sun rising, herself curled in her blanket and feeling completely rested. For one moment, she wondered if the strange combat of the night had all been a nightmare—but then she saw her arms and armor stacked neatly to hand. As if to mock her doubts, they were laid in a different pattern than she had left them.

Once again she rode as in a dream. Something controlled her actions as deftly as she managed Kessira, keeping the raw edges of her mind carefully swathed and anesthetized. When she lost the trail, her controller found it again, making her body pause long enough for her to identify how it had been done.

She camped, and again she was awakened before midnight.

Pain is a rapid teacher; she was able to prolong the bouts this night enough that he only killed her twice.

It was a strange existence, tracking by day, training by night. When her track ended at a village, she found herself questioning the inhabitants shrewdly. When her provisions ran out, she discovered coin in the pouch that had held dried fruit—not a great deal, but enough to pay for more of the same. When, in other towns and villages, her questions were met with evasions, her hand stole of itself to that same pouch, to find therein more coin, enough to loosen the tongues of those she faced. She learned that all her physical needs were cared for—always when she needed something, she either woke with it to hand, or discovered more of the magical coins appearing to pay for it, and always just enough, and no more. Her nights seemed clearer and less dreamlike than her days, perhaps because the controls over her were thinner then, and the skill she fought with was all her own. Finally one night she "killed" her instructor.

He collapsed exactly as she would have expected a man run through the heart to collapse. He lay unmoving—

"A good attack, but your guard was sloppy," said a familiar voice behind her. She whirled, her sword ready.

He stood before her, his own sword sheathed. She risked a glance to her rear; the body was gone.

"Truce; you have earned a respite and a reward," he said. "Ask me what you will, I am sure you have many questions. I know *I* did."

"Who are you?" she cried eagerly. "*What* are you?"

"I cannot give you my name, Sworn One. I am

only one of many servants of the Warrior; I am the first of your teachers—and I am what you will become if you should die while still under Oath. Does that disturb you? The Warrior will release you at any time you wish to be freed. She does not want the unwilling. Of course, if you are freed, you must relinquish the blood-feud."

Tarma shook her head.

"Then ready yourself, Sworn One, and look to that sloppy guard."

There came a time when their combats always ended in draws or with his "death." When that had happened three nights running, she woke the fourth night to face a new opponent—a woman, and armed with daggers.

Meanwhile she tracked her quarry, by rumor, by the depredations left in their wake, by report from those who had profited or suffered in their passing. It seemed that what she tracked was a roving band of freebooters, and her Clan was not the only group to have been made victims. They chose their quarry carefully, never picking anyone the authorities might feel urged to avenge, nor anyone with friends in power. As a result, they managed to operate almost completely unmolested.

When she had mastered the use of sword, dagger, bow, and staff, her trainers appeared severally rather than singly; she learned the arts of the single combatant against many.

Every time she gained a victory, they instructed her further in what her Oath meant.

One of those things was that her body no longer felt the least stirrings of sexual desire. The Swordsworn were as devoid of concupiscence as their weapons.

"The gain outweighs the loss," the first of them told her. After being taught the disciplines and rewards of the meditative trance they called "The Moonpaths," she agreed. After that, she spent at least part of every night walking those paths, surrounded by a curious kind of ecstasy, renewing her strength and her bond with her Goddess.

Inexorably, she began to catch up with her quarry. When she had begun this quest, she was months behind them; now she was only days. The closer she drew, the more intensely did her spirit-trainers drill her.

Then one night, they did not come. She woke on her own and waited, waited until well past midnight, waited until she was certain they were not coming at all. She dozed off for a moment, when she felt a presence. She rose with one swift motion, pulling her sword from the scabbard on her back.

The first of her trainers held out empty hands. "It has been a year, Sworn One. Are you ready? Your foes lair in the town not two hours' ride from here, and the town is truly their lair, for they have made it their own."

So near as that? His words came as a shock, ripping the protective magics that veiled her mind and heart, sending her to her knees with the shrilling pain and raging anger she had felt before the winds of the Goddess answered her prayers. No longer was she protected against her own emotions, and the wounds were as raw as they had ever been.

He regarded her thoughtfully, his eyes pitying above the veil. "No, you are *not* ready. Your hate will undo you, your hurt will disarm you. But you have little choice, Sworn One. This task is one you bound *yourself* to, you cannot free yourself of it. Will you heed advice, or will you throw yourself uselessly into the arms of Death?"

"What advice?" she asked dully.

"When you are offered aid unlooked for, do not cast it aside," he said and vanished.

She could not sleep; she set out at first light for the town , and then hovered about outside the walls until just before the gates were closed for the night. She soothed the ruffled feathers of the guard with a coin, offered as "payment" for directions to the inn.

The inn was noisy, hot, and crowded. She wrinkled her nose at the unaccustomed stench of old cooking smells, spilled wine, and unwashed bodies. Another small coin bought her a jug of sour wine and a seat in a dark corner, from which she could hear nearly everything said in the room. It did not take long to determine from chance-dropped comments that the brigand-troop made their headquarters in the long-abandoned mansion of a merchant who had lost everything he had to their depredations, including his life. Their presence was very unwelcome. They seemed to regard the townsfolk as their lawful prey; having been freed from their attentions for the past year, their "chattels" were not pleased with their return.

Tarma burned with scorn for these soft townsmen. Surely there were enough able-bodied adults in the place to outnumber the bandit crew several times over. If by nothing else, by sheer numbers the townsmen could probably defeat them, if they'd try.

She turned her mind toward her own quest, trying

to develop a plan that would enable her to take as many of the enemy down into death with her as she could manage. She was under no illusion that she could survive this. The kind of frontal assault she planned would leave her no path of escape.

A shadow came between Tarma and the fire.

She looked up, startled that the other had managed to come so close without her being aware of it. The silhouette was that of a woman, wearing the calf-length, cowled brown robe of a wandering sorceress. There was one alarming anomaly about this woman— unlike any other magic-worker Tarma had ever seen, this one wore a sword belted at her waist.

She reached up and laid back the cowl of her robe, but Tarma still was unable to make out her features; the firelight behind her hair made a glowing nimbus of amber around her face.

"It won't work, you know," the stranger said very softly, in a pleasant, musical alto. "You won't gain anything by a frontal assault but your own death."

Fear laid an icy hand on Tarma's throat; to cover her fear she snarled. "How do you know what I plan? Just who are you?"

"Lower your voice, Sworn One." The sorceress took a seat on the bench next to Tarma, uninvited. "Anyone with the Talent and the wish to do so can read your thoughts. Your foes number among them a sorcerer; I know he is responsible for the deaths of many a sentry that otherwise would have warned their victims in time to defend themselves. I judge him to be at least as capable as I; rest assured that if *I* can read your intentions, *he* will be able to do the same should he care to cast his mind in this direction. I want to help you. My name is Kethry."

"Why help me?" Tarma asked bluntly, knowing that by giving her name the sorceress had given Tarma a measure of power over her.

Kethry stirred in her seat, bringing her face fully into the light of the fire. Tarma saw then that the woman was younger than she had first judged; they were almost of an age. Had she seen only the face, she would have thought her to be in the same class as the townsmen; the sorceress was doll-like in her prettiness. But Tarma had also seen the way she moved, like a wary predator; and the too-wise expression in those emerald eyes sat ill with the softness of the face. Her robe was worn to the point of shabbiness, and though clean, was much travel-stained. It was evident from that, that whatever else this woman was, she was not one who was overly concerned with material wealth. That in itself was a good sign to Tarma—since the only real wealth in this town was to be had by serving with the brigands.

But why did she wear a sword?

"I have an interest in dealing with these robbers myself," she said, "and I'd rather that they weren't set on their guard. And I have another reason as well—"

"So?"

She laughed deprecatingly. "You could say I am under a kind of geas, one that binds me to help women in need. I am bound to help you, whether or not either of us are pleased with the fact. Will you have that help unforced?"

Tarma's initial reaction had been to bristle with hostility—then, unbidden, into her mind came the

odd, otherworldly voice of her trainer, warning her
not to cast away unlooked-for aid.

"As you will," she replied curtly.

The other did not seem to be the least bit discom-
fited by her antagonism. "Then let us leave this
place," she said, standing without haste. "There are
too many ears here."

She waited while Tarma retrieved her horse, and
led her down tangled streets to a dead-end alley lit
by gay red lanterns. She unlocked a gate on the left
side and waved Tarma and Kessira through it. Tarma
waited as she relocked the gate, finding herself in a
cobbled courtyard that was bordered on one side by
an old but well-kept stable. On the other side was a
house, all its windows ablaze with lights, also fes-
tooned with the red lanterns. From the house came
the sound of music, laughter, and the voices of many
women. Tarma sniffed; the air was redolent with
cheap perfume and an animal muskiness.

"Is this place what I think it is?" she asked, finding
it difficult to match the picture she'd built in her
mind of the sorceress with the house she'd led
Tarma to.

"If you think it's a brothel, you're right," Kethry
replied. "Welcome to the House of Scarlet Joys,
Sworn One. Can you think of a *less* likely place to
house two such as we?"

"No." Tarma almost smiled.

"The better to hide us. The mistress of this place
and her charges would rejoice greatly at the conquer-
ing of our mutual enemies. Nevertheless, the most
these women will do for us is house and feed us.
The rest is all in our four hands. Now, let's get your

weary beast stabled, and we'll adjourn to my rooms.
We have a great deal of planning to do."

Two days after Tarma's arrival in the town of
Brether's Crossroads, one of the brigands (drunk
with liquor and drugs far past his capacity) fell into
a horsetrough, and (bizarrely enough) drowned trying to get out. His death signaled the beginning of a
streak of calamities that thinned the ranks of the bandits as persistently as a plague.

One by one they died, victims of weird accidents,
overdoses of food or drugs, or ambushes by preter-
naturally clever thieves. No two deaths were alike—
with one exception. He who failed to shake out his
boots of a morning seldom survived the day, thanks
to the scorpions that had taken to invading the place.
Some even died at each other's hands, goaded into
fights.

("I dislike this skulking in corners," Tarma
growled, sharpening her swordblade. "It's hardly
satisfactory, killing these dogs at a distance with poison and witchery."

"Be patient, my friend," Kethry said without rancor. "We're better off thinning them down somewhat
before we engage them at sword's point. There will
be time enough for that later.")

When the deaths were obviously at the hands of
enemies, there were no clues. Those arrow-slain were
found pierced by several makes; those dead by
blades seemed to have had their own used on them.

(Tarma found herself coming to admire the sorceress more with every passing day. Their arrangement
was a partnership in every sense of the word, for
when Kethry ran short of magical ploys she turned

without pride to Tarma and her expertise in weaponry. Even so, the necessary restrictions that limited them to the ambush and the skills of the assassin chafed at her.

"It will not be much longer," Kethry counseled. "They'll come to the conclusion soon enough that this has been no series of coincidences. *Then* will be the time for frontal attack.")

The leader, so it was said, ordered that no man go out alone, and all must wear talismans against sorcery.

("See?" Kethry said then. "I told you you'd have your chance.")

A pair of swaggering bullies swilled ale, unpaid for, in the inn. None dared speak in their presence; they'd already beaten one farmer senseless who'd given some imagined insult. They were spoiling for a fight, and the sheeplike timidity of the people trapped with them in the inn was not to their liking. So when a slender young man, black-clad and wearing a sword slung across his back entered the door, their eyes lit with savage glee.

One snaked out a long arm, grasping the young man's wrist. Some of those in the inn marked how his eyes flashed with a hellish joy before being veiled with cold disdain.

"Remove your hand," he said in a harsh voice, "dog-turd."

That was all the excuse the brigands needed. Both drew their weapons; the young man unsheathed his in a single fluid motion. Both moved against him in a pattern they had long found successful in bringing down a single opponent.

Both died within heartbeats of each other.

The young man cleaned his blade carefully on their cloaks before sheathing it. (Some sharp eyes may have noticed that when his hand came in contact with one of the brigand's talismans, the young man seemed to become, for a fleeting second, a harsh-visaged young *woman*). "This is no town for a stranger," he said to no one and everyone. "I will be on my way. Let him follow me who desires the embrace of the Lady Death."

Predictably, half-a-dozen robbers followed the clear track of his horse into the hills. None returned.

The ranks of his men narrowed to five including himself and the sorcerer, the bandit leader shut them all up in their stronghold.

("Why are these—ladies—sheltering us?" Tarma demanded one day, when forced idleness had her pacing the confines of Kethry's rooms like a caged panther.

"Madam Isa grew tired of having her girls abused, and they were more than tired of being abused."

Tarma snorted with scorn. "I should have thought one would learn to expect abuse in such a profession."

"It is one thing when a customer expresses a taste for pain and is willing to pay to inflict it. It is quite another when he does so without paying," Kethry answered with wry humor. Tarma replied to this with something almost like a smile. There was that about her accomplice—fast becoming her friend—that could lighten even her grimmest mood. Occasionally the sorceress was even able to charm the Shin'a'in into forgetfulness for hours at a time. And yet—and yet—there was never a time she could entirely forget what had driven her here. . . .)

At the end of two months, there were rumors that the chieftain had begun recruiting new underlings, the information passed to other cities via the arcane methods of his sorcerer.

("We'll have to do something to flush at least one of them out," Kethry said at last. "The sorcerer has transported at least three more people into that house. He may have done more—I couldn't tell if the spell brought one or several at a time, only that he definitely brought people in.")

A new courtesan, property of none of the three Houses, began to ply her trade among those who still retained some of their wealth. One had to be wealthy to afford her services—but those who spent their hours in her skillful embraces were high in their praise.

("I thought your vows kept you sorcerers from lying," Tarma said, watching Kethry's latest client moaning with pleasure in the dream-trance she'd conjured for him.

"I didn't lie," she answered, eyes glinting green with mischief. "I promised him—all of them—an hour to match their wildest dreams. That's *exactly* what they're getting. Besides, nothing I'd be able to do could ever match what they're conjuring up for themselves!")

The chieftain's sergeant caught a glimpse of her spending an idle hour in the marketplace. He had been without a woman since his chief had forbidden the men to go to the Houses. He could see the wisdom in that: *someone* was evidently out after the band's hearts, and a House would be far too easy a place in which to set a trap. But this whore was alone but for her pimp, a thin beardless boy who did not even wear a sword, only paired daggers. She should be safe enough. Nor would he need to spend any of his stored coin, though he'd bring it to tempt her. When he'd had his fill of her, he'd teach her that it was better to *give* her wares to *him*.

She led him up the stairs to her room above the inn, watching with veiled amusement as he carefully bolted the door behind him. But when he began divesting himself of his weaponry and garments, she halted him, pinioning his arms gently from the rear and breathing enticingly on the back of his neck as she whispered in his ear.

"Time enough, and more, great warrior—I am sure you have not the taste for common tumblings that are all you can find in *this* backward place." She slid around to the front of him, urging him down onto the room's single stool, a water-beaded cup in her hand. "Refresh yourself first, great lord. The vintage is of mine own bringing—you shall not taste its like here—"

It was just Kethry's bad luck that he had been the official "taster" to a high lordling during his childhood of slavery. He sipped delicately out of habit, rather than gulping the wine down, and rolled the wine carefully on his tongue—and so detected in the cup what he should not have been able to sense.

"Bitch!" he roared, throwing the cup aside and seizing Kethry by the throat.

Kethry's panic-filled scream warned Tarma that the plan had gone awry. She wasted no time in battering at the door—the man was no fool and would have bolted it behind him. It would take too long to break it down. Instead, she sprinted through the crowded inn and out the back through the kitchen. A second cry—more like a strangled gurgle than a scream, which recalled certain things sharply to her and gave her strength born of rage and hatred—fell into the stableyard from the open window of Kethry's room. Tarma swarmed up the stable door onto the roof of the building, and launched herself from there in through that window. Her entrance was as unexpected as it was precipitate.

Kethry slowly regained consciousness in her bed in the rented room. She hurt from top to toe—her assailant had been almost artistic, if one counted the ability to evoke pain among the arts. Oddly enough, he hadn't raped her—she would have expected that, been able to defend herself arcanely. He'd reacted to the poisoned drink instead by throwing her to the floor and beating her with no mercy. She'd had no chance to defend herself with magic, and her sword had been left back at the brothel at Tarma's insistence.

Tarma was bathing and tending her hurts. One look at her stricken eyes, and any reproaches she might have uttered died on Kethry's tongue.

"It's all right," she said as gently as she could with swollen lips. "It wasn't your fault."

Tarma's eyes said that she thought otherwise, but she replied gruffly, "Looks like you need a keeper more than I do, lady-mage."

It hurt to smile, but Kethry managed. "Perhaps I do, at that."

Four evenings later, all but three of the bandits marched in force on the inn, determined to take revenge on the townsfolk for the acts of the invisible enemy in their midst. Halfway there, they were met by two women blocking their path. One was an amber-haired sorceress with a bruised face and a blackened eye. The other was a Shin'a'in swordswoman.

Only those two survived the confrontation.

"We have no choice now," Kethry said grimly. "If we wait, they'll only be stronger—and I'm certain that sorcerer has been watching. They're warned, they know who and what we are."

"Good," Tarma replied. "Then let's bring the war to *their* doorstep. We've been doing things in secret long enough, and it's more than time that this thing was finished. Now. Tonight." Her eyes were no longer quite sane.

Kethry didn't like it but knew there was no other way. Gathering up her magics about her, and resting one hand on the comforting presence of he sword, she followed Tarma to the bandit stronghold.

The three remaining were waiting in the courtyard. At the forefront was the bandit-chief, a red-faced, shrewd-eyed bull of a man. To his right was his second in command, and Tarma's eyes narrowed as she recognized the necklace of amber claws he wore. He was as like to a bear as his leader was to a bull. To his left was the sorcerer, who gave a mocking bow in Kethry's direction.

Kethry did not return the bow, but launched an immediate magical attack. Something much like red lightning flew from her outstretched hands.

He parried it—but not easily. His eyes widened in surprise; her lips thinned in satisfaction. They settled down to duel in deadly earnest. Colored lightnings and weird mists swirled about them, sometimes the edges of their shields could be seen, straining against the impact of the sorcerous bolts. Creatures out of insane nightmares formed themselves on his side, and flung themselves raging at the sorceress, before being attacked and destroyed by enormous eagles with wings of fire, or impossibly slim and delicate armored beings with no faces at their helm's openings, but only a light too bright to look upon.

Tarma meanwhile had flung herself at the leader with the war cry of her clan—the shriek of an angry hawk. He parried her blade inches away from his throat, and answered with a cut that took part of her sleeve and bruised her arm beneath the mail. His companion swung at the same time; his sword did no more than graze her leg. She twisted to parry his second stroke, moving faster than either of them expected her to. She marked him as well, a cut bleeding freely over his eyes, but not before the leader gashed her where the chainmail shirt ended.

There was an explosion behind her; she dared not turn to look, but it sounded as though one of the two mages would spin spells no more.

She parried a slash from the leader only barely in time, and at the cost of a blow from her other opponent that did not penetrate her armor, but surely broke a rib. Either of these men was her equal; at this rate they'd wear her down and kill her soon— and yet, it hardly mattered. *This* was the fitting end to the whole business, that the last of the Tale'sedrin should die with the killers of her Clan. For when they were gone, what else was there for her to do? A Shin'a'in Clanless was a Shin'a'in with no purpose in living. And no wish to live.

Suddenly she found herself facing only one of

them, the leader. The other was battling for his life against Kethry, who had appeared out of the mage-smokes and was wielding her sword with all the skill of one of Tarma's spirit-teachers.

Tarna had just enough thought to spare for a moment of amazement. *Everyone* knew sorcerers had no skill with a blade—they had not the time to spare to learn such crafts.

Yet—there was Kethry, cutting the man to ribbons.

Tarma traded blows with her opponent; then saw her opening. To take advantage of it meant she must leave herself wide open, but she was far past caring. She struck—her blade entered his throat in a clean thrust. Dying, he swung; his sword caving in her side. They fell together.

Grayness surrounded Tarma, a gray fog in which the light seemed to come from no particular direction, the grayness of a peculiarly restful quality. She found her hurts had vanished, and that she felt no particular need to move from where she was standing. Then a warm wind caressed her, the fog parted, and she found herself facing the first of her instructors.

"So—" he said, hands (empty, for a change, of weapons) on hips, a certain amusement in his eyes. "Past all expectation, you have brought down your enemies. Remarkable, Sworn One, the more remarkable as you had the sense to follow my advice."

"You came for me, then?" It was less a question than a statement.

"I, come for you?" He laughed heartily behind his veil. "Child, child, against all prediction you have not only won, but *survived!* No, I have come to tell you that your aid-time is over, though we shall continue to train you as we always have. From this moment, it is your actions alone that will put food in your mouth and coin in your purse. I would suggest you follow the path of the mercenary, as many another Sworn One has done when Clanless. And—" he began fading into the mist, "—remember that one can be Shin'a'in without being born into the Clans. All it requires is the oath of *she'enedran*."

"Wait!" she called after him—but he was gone.

There was the sound of birds singing, and an astringent, medicinal tang in the air. Tarma opened eyes brimming with amazement and felt gingerly at the bandages wrapping various limbs and her chest. Somehow, unbelievable as it was, she was still alive.

"It's about time you woke up." Kethry's voice came from nearby. "I was getting tired of spooning broth down your throat. You've probably noticed this *isn't* the House of Scarlet Joys. Madame wasn't the only one interested in getting rid of the bandits; the whole town hired me to dispose of them. My original intention was to frighten them away, but then *you* came along and ruined my plans! By the way, you happen to be lying in the best bed in the inn. I hope you appreciate the honor. You're quite a heroine now. These people have far more appreciation of good bladework than good magic."

Tarma slowly turned her head; Kethry was perched on the side of a second bed a few paces from hers and nearer the window. "Why did you save me?" she whispered hoarsely.

"Why did you want to die?" Kethry countered.

Tarma's mouth opened, and the words spilled out. In the wake of this purging of her pain, came peace;

not the numbing, false peace of the North Wind's icy armor, but the true peace Tarma had never hoped to feel. Before she had finished, they were clinging to each other and weeping together.

Kethry had said nothing—but in her eyes Tarma recognized the same unbearable loneliness that she was facing. And she was moved by something outside herself to speak.

"My friend—" Tarma startled Kethry with the phrase; their eyes met, and Kethry saw that loneliness recognized like, "—we are both Clanless; would you swear bloodoath with me?"

"Yes!" Kethry's eager reply left nothing to be desired.

Without speaking further, Tarma cut a thin, curving line like a crescent moon in her left palm; she handed the knife to Kethry, who did likewise. Tarma raised her hand to Kethry, who met it, palm to palm—

Then came the unexpected; their joined hands flashed briefly, incandescently; too bright to look on. When their hands unjoined, there were silver scars where the cuts had been.

Tarma looked askance at her *she'enedra*—her blood sister.

"Not of my doing," Kethry said, awe in her voice.

"The Goddess' then." Tarma was certain of it; with the certainty came the filling of the empty void within her left by the loss of her Clan.

"In that case, I think perhaps I should give you my last secret," Kethry replied, and pulled her sword from beneath her bed. "Hold out your hands."

Tarma obeyed, and Kethry laid the unsheathed sword across them.

"Watch the blade," she said, frowning in concentration.

Writing, as fine as any scribe's, flared redly along the length of it. To her amazement it was in her own tongue.

"If *I* were holding her, it would be in my language," Kethry said, answering Tarma's unspoken question. " 'Woman's Need calls me/As Woman's Need made me/Her Need must I answer/As my maker bade me.' My geas, the one I told you of when we first met. She's the reason I could help you after my magics were exhausted, because she works in a peculiar way. If you were to use her, she'd add nothing to your sword skill, but she'd protect you against almost any magics. But when I have her—"

"No magic aid, but you fight like a sand-demon," Tarma finished for her.

"But only if I am attacked first, or defending another. And last, her magic only works for women. A fellow journeyman found that out the hard way."

"And the price of her protection?"

"While I have her, I cannot leave any woman in trouble unaided. In fact, she's actually taken me miles out of my way to help someone." Kethry looked at the sword as fondly as if it were a living thing—which, perhaps, it was. "It's been worth it—she brought us together."

She paused, as though something had occurred to her. "I'm not sure how to ask this—Tarma, now that we're *she'enedran*, do I have to be Swordsworn, too?" She looked troubled. "Because if it's all the same to you, I'd rather not. I have very healthy appetites that I'd rather not lose."

"Horned Moon, no!" Tarma chuckled, her facial

muscles stretching in an unaccustomed smile. It felt good. "In fact, *she'enedra*, I'd rather you found a lover or two. You're all the Clan I have now, and my only hope of having more kin."

"Just a Shin'a'in brood mare, huh?" Kethry's infectious grin kept any sting out of the words.

"Hardly," Tarma replied, answering the smile with one of her own. "However, *she'enedra*, I am going to make sure you—we—get paid for jobs like these in good, solid coin, because that's something I think, by the look of you, you've been too lax about. After all, besides being horsebreeders, Shin'a'in have a *long* tradition of selling their swords—or in your case, magics! And are we not partners by being bloodsisters?"

"True enough, oh, my keeper and partner," Kethry replied, laughing—laughter in which Tarma joined. "Then mercenaries—and the very best!—we shall be."

TURNABOUT

This was the original story I sent Marion which was rejected; I later broke it into "Sword-sworn" and this one, and sold this one to *Fantasy Book Magazine*. It was my very first piece to appear in print!

The verses are also part of an original song published by Firebird Arts and Music of Portland, Oregon, which actually predated the story. Can I recycle, or what?

By the way, the song doesn't exactly match the story; that was because I had left the only copy I had of the song with the folks at Firebird and I couldn't remember who did what to whom. So, to cover the errors, I blamed them on the Bard Leslac, who began following the pair around to make songs about them—but kept getting the details wrong!

> *"Deep into the stony hills*
> *Miles from keep or hold,*
> *   A troupe of guards comes riding*
> *With a lady and her gold.*
> *   Riding in the center,*
> *Shrouded in her cloak of fur*
> *Companioned by a maiden*
> *And a toothless, aged cur."*

"And every packtrain we've sent out since has vanished without a trace—and without survivors," the merchant Grumio concluded. "And yet the decoy trains were allowed to reach their destinations unmolested."

In the silence that followed his words, he studied the odd pair of mercenaries before him, knowing they knew he was doing so. Neither of the two women seemed in any great hurry to reply to his speech, and the crackle of the fire behind him in this tiny private eating room sounded unnaturally loud in the absence of conversation. So, too, did the steady whisking of a whetstone on blade-edge, and the muted murmur of voices from the common room of the inn beyond their closed door.

The whetstone was being wielded by the swordswoman, Tarma by name, who was keeping to her self-appointed task with an indifference to Grumio's words that might—or might not—be feigned. She sat straddling her bench in a position that left him mostly with a view of her back and the back of her head, what little he might have been able to see of her face screened by her unruly shock of coarse black hair. He was just as glad of that; there was something about that expressionless, hawklike face with its ice-cold blue eyes that sent shivers up his spine.

The other partner cleared her throat, and gratefully he turned his attention to her. Now *there* was a face a man could easily rest his eyes on! She faced him squarely, this sorceress called Kethry, leaning on her folded arms that rested on the table between them. The light from the fire and the oil lamp on their table fell fully on her. A less canny man than Grumio might be tempted to dismiss her as being very much the inferior of the two; she was always soft of speech, her demeanor refined and gentle. She was sweet-faced and quite conventionally pretty, with hair like the finest amber and eyes of beryl-green, and it would have been easy to think of her as being the swordswoman's vapid tagalong. But as he'd spoken, Grumio had now and then caught a disquieting glimmer in those calm eyes—nor had he missed the fact that she, too, bore a sword, and one with the marks of frequent use and a caring hand on it. That in itself was an anomaly; most sorcerers never wore more than an eating knife. They simply hadn't the time— or the inclination—to attempt studying the art of the blade. To Grumio's eyes the sword looked very odd slung over the plain, buff-colored, calf-length robe of a wandering sorceress.

"I presume," Kethry said when he turned to face her, "that the road patrols have been unable to find your bandits."

She had been studying the merchant in turn; he interested her. There was muscle beneath the fat of good living, and old sword-calluses on his hands. Unless she was wildly mistaken, there was also a sharp mind beneath that balding skull. He knew they didn't come cheaply—it followed then that there was something more to this tale of banditry than he was telling. Certain signs seemed to confirm this; he looked as though he had not slept well of late, and there seemed to be a shadow of deeper sorrow upon him than the loss of mere goods would account for.

Grumio snorted his contempt for the road patrols. "They rode up and down for a few days, never venturing off the trade road, and naturally found nothing. Overdressed, overpaid, underworked arrogant idiots!"

Kethry toyed with a fruit left from their supper,

and glanced up at the hound-faced merchant through long lashes that veiled her eyes and her thoughts.

Tarma answered right on cue. "Then guard your packtrains, merchant, if guards keep these vermin hidden." He started; her voice was as harsh as a raven's, and startled those not used to hearing it.

Grumio saw at once the negotiating ploy these two were minded to use with him. The swordswoman was to be the antagonizer, the sorceress the sympathizer. His respect for them rose another notch. Most freelance mercenaries hadn't the brains to count their pay, much less use subtle bargaining tricks. Their reputation was plainly well-founded.

However he had no intention of falling for it. "Swordlady, to hire sufficient force requires we raise the price of goods above what people are willing to pay."

Odd—there was a current of communication and understanding running between these two that had him thoroughly puzzled. He dismissed without a second thought the notion that they might be lovers—the signals between them were all wrong for that. No, it was something else, something that you wouldn't expect between a Shin'a'in swordswoman and an outClansman—

Tarma shook her head impatiently. "Then cease your interhouse rivalries, *kadessa*, and send all your trains together under a single large force."

Now she was trying to get him off-guard by insulting him, calling him after a little grasslands beast that only the Shin'a'in ever saw, a rodent so notoriously greedy that it would, given food enough, eat itself to death; and one that was known for hoarding anything and everything it came across in its nest-tunnels. He refused to allow the insult to distract him. "Respect, swordlady," he replied patiently, "but we tried that, too. The beasts of the train were driven off in the night, and the guards and traders were forced to return afoot. This is desert country, most of it, and all they dared burden themselves with was food and drink."

"Leaving the goods behind to be scavenged. Huh. Your bandits are clever, merchant," the swordswoman replied thoughtfully. Grumio thought he could sense her indifference lifting.

"You mentioned decoy trains—?" Kethry interjected.

"Yes, lady." Grumio's mind was still worrying away at the puzzle these two presented. "Only I and the men in the train knew which were the decoys and which were not, yet the bandits were never deceived, not once. We had taken extra care that all the men in the train were known to us, too."

A glint of gold on the smallest finger of Kethry's left hand gave him the clue he needed, and the crescent scar on the palm of that hand confirmed his surmise. He knew without looking the swordswoman would have an identical scar and ring. These two had sworn Shin'a'in bloodoath, the strongest bond known to that notoriously kin-conscious race. The bloodoath made them closer than sisters, closer than lovers—so close they sometimes would think as one.

"So who was it that passed judgement on your estimable guards?" Tarma's voice was heavy with sarcasm.

"I did, or my fellow merchants, or our own personal guards. No one was allowed on the trains but those who had served us in the past or were known to those who had."

Tarma held her blade up to catch the firelight and examined her work with a critical eye. Satisfied, she drove it home in the scabbard slung across her back with a fluid, unthinking grace, then swung one leg back over the bench to face him as her partner did. Grumio found the unflinching chill of her eyes disconcertingly hard to meet for long.

In an effort to find something else to look at, he found his gaze caught by the pendant she wore, a thin silver crescent surrounding a tiny amber flame. That gave him the last bit of information he needed to make everything fall into place—although now he realized that her plain brown clothing should have tipped him off as well, since most Shin'a'in favored garments heavy with bright embroideries. Tarma was a Sworn One, pledged to the service of the Shin'a'in Warrior, the Goddess of the New Moon and the South Wind. Only two things were of any import to her at all—her Goddess and her clan (which, of course, would include her "sister" by bloodoath). The Sworn Ones were just as sexless and deadly as the weapons they wore.

"So why come to us?" Tarma's expression indicated she thought their time was being wasted. "What makes you think that *we* can solve your bandit problem?"

"You—have a certain reputation," he replied guardedly.

A single bark of contemptuous laughter was Tarma's reply.

"If you know our reputation, then you also know that we only take those jobs that—shall we say—

interest us," Kethry said, looking wide-eyed and innocent. "What is there about your problem that could possibly be of any interest to *us*?"

Good—they were intrigued, at least a little. Now, for the sake of poor little Lena, was the time to hook them and bring them in. His eyes stung a little with tears he would not shed—not now—

"We have a custom, we small merchant houses. Our sons must remain with their fathers to learn the trade, and since there are seldom more than two or three houses in any town, there is little in the way of choice for them when it comes time for marriage. For that reason, we are given to exchanging daughters of the proper age with our trade allies in other towns, so that our young people can hopefully find mates to their liking." His voice almost broke at the memory of watching Lena waving good-bye from the back of her little mare—but he regained control quickly. It was a poor merchant that could not school his emotions. "There were no less than a dozen sheltered, gently-reared maidens in the very first packtrain they took. One of them was my niece. My only heir."

Kethry's breath hissed softly, and Tarma swallowed an oath.

"Your knowledge of what interests us is very accurate, merchant," Tarma said after a long pause. "I congratulate you."

"You—you accept?" Discipline could not keep hope out of his voice.

"I pray you are not expecting us to rescue your lost ones," Kethry said as gently as she could. "Even supposing that the bandits were more interested in slaves to be sold than their own pleasure—which in my experience is *not* likely—there is very, very little chance that any of them still live. The sheltered, the gentle, well, they do not survive—shock—successfully."

"When we knew they had not reached their goal, we sent agents to comb the slave markets. They returned empty-handed," he replied with as much stoicism as he could muster. "We will not ask the impossible of you; we knew when we sent for you there was no hope for them. No, we ask only that you wipe out this viper's den, to ensure that this can *never* happen to us again—and that you grant us revenge for what they have done to us!"

His words—and more, the tight control of his voice—struck echoes from Tarma's own heart. And she did not need to see her partner to know *her* feelings in the matter.

"You will have that, merchant-lord," she grated, giving him the title of respect. "We accept your job—but there are conditions."

"Swordlady, any conditions you would set, I would gladly meet. Who am I to contest the judgement of those who destroyed Tha—"

"Hush!" Kethry interrupted him swiftly, and cast a wary glance over her shoulder. "The less that is said on *that* subject, the better. I am still not altogether certain that what you were about to name was truly destroyed. It may have been merely banished, and perhaps for no great span of time. If the second case is true, it is hardly wise to call attention to one's self by speaking Its name."

"Our conditions, merchant, are simple," Tarma continued unperturbed. "We will, to all appearances, leave on the morrow. You will tell all, including your fellow merchants, that you could not convince us. Tomorrow night, you—and you *alone*, mind—will bring us, at a meeting place of your choosing, a cart and horse . . ." Now she raised an inquiring eyebrow at Kethry.

"And the kind of clothing and gear a lady of wealth and blood would be likely to have when traveling. The clothing should fit me. I will be weaving some complicated illusions, and anything I do not have to counterfeit will be of aid to me and make the rest stronger. You might include lots of empty bags and boxes," Kethry said thoughtfully.

Tarma continued: "The following morning a fine lady will ride in and order you to include her with your next packtrain. You, naturally, will do your best to dissuade her, as loudly and publicly as possible. Now your next scheduled trip was—?"

"Coincidentally enough, for the day after tomorrow." Grumio was impressed. These women were even cleverer than he'd thought.

"Good. The less time we lose, the better off we are. Remember, only *you* are to be aware that the lady and the packtrain are not exactly what they seem to be. If you say one word otherwise to anyone—"

The merchant found himself staring at the tip of a very sharp dagger a scant inch from his nose.

"—I will *personally* remove enough of your hide to make both of us slippers." The dagger disappeared from Tarma's hand as mysteriously as it had appeared.

Grumio had been startled, but had not been particularly intimidated; Tarma gave him high marks for that.

"I do not instruct the weaver in her trade," he

replied with a certain dignity, "nor do I dictate the setting of a horseshoe to a smith. There is no reason why I should presume to instruct you in your trade either."

"Then you are a rare beast indeed, merchant." Tarma graced him with one of her infrequent smiles. "Most men—oh, not fellow mercenaries, they know better; but most men we deal with—seem to think they know our business better than we simply by virtue of their sex."

The smile softened her harsh expression, and made it less intimidating, and the merchant found himself smiling back. "You are not the only female hire-swords I have dealt with," he replied. "Many of my trade allies have them as personal retainers. It has often seemed to me that many of those I met have had to be twice as skilled as their male counterparts to receive half the credit."

"A hit, merchant-lord," Kethry acknowledged with open amusement. "And a shrewd one at that. Now, where are we to meet you tomorrow night?"

Grumio paused to think. "I have a farmstead— deserted now that the harvest is in—which is at the first lane past the crossroad at the south edge of town. No one would think it odd for me to pay a visit to it, and the barn is a good place to hide horses and gear."

"Well enough," Tarma replied. All three rose as one—Grumio caught the faint clink of brigandine mail from Tarma's direction, though there was no outward sign that she wore any such thing beneath her worn leather tunic, brown shirt, and darker breeches.

"Merchant—" Tarma said suddenly.

He paused halfway through the door.

"I, too, have known loss. You *will* have your revenge." He shivered at the look in her eyes, and left.

"Well?" Tarma asked, shutting the door behind him and leaning her back up against it.

"Magic's afoot here. It's the only answer to what's been going on. I don't think it's easy to deceive this merchant—he caught on to our 'divide and conquer' trick right away. He's no soft money-counter either."

"I saw the sword-calluses." Tarma balanced herself on one foot and folded her arms. "Did he tell us all he knew?"

"I think so. I don't think he held anything back after he played his high card."

"The niece? He also didn't want us to know how much he valued her. Damn. This is a bad piece of business."

"He'd rather we thought the loss of goods and trade meant more to him," Kethry replied. "They're a secretive lot in many ways, these traders."

"Almost as secretive as sorceresses, no?" One corner of Tarma's thin lips quirked up in a half-smile. The smile vanished as she thought of something else. "*Is* there any chance that any of the women survived?"

"Not to put too fine a point upon it, no. *This*—" Kethry patted the hilt of her sword, "—would have told me if any of them had. The pull is there, but without the urgency there'd be if there was anyone needing rescue. Still, we need more information, so I might as well add that to the set of questions I intend to ask."

Concern flickered briefly in Tarma's eyes. "An unprepared summoning? Are you sure you want to risk it? If nothing else, it will wear you down, and you have all those illusions to cast."

"I think it's worth it. There aren't that many hostile entities to guard against in this area, and I'll have all night to rest afterward—most of tomorrow as well, once we reach that farmstead."

"You're the magic-worker." Tarma sighed. "Since we've hired this room for the whole evening, want to make use of it? It's bigger than our sleeping room."

At Kethry's nod, Tarma pushed the table into a corner, stacking the benches on top of it, while Kethry set the oil lamp on the mantelpiece. Most of the floor space was now cleared.

"I'll keep watch on the door." Tarma sat on the floor with her back firmly braced against it. Since it opened inward, the entrance was now solidly guarded against all but the most stubborn of intruders.

Kethry inscribed a circle on the floor with powders from her belt-pouch, chanting under her breath. She used no dramatic or spectacular ceremonies, for she had learned her art in a gentler school than the other sorcerers Tarma had seen. Her powers came from the voluntary cooperation of other-planar entities, and she never coerced them into doing her bidding.

There were advantages and disadvantages to this. She need not safeguard herself against the deceptions and treacheries of these creatures—but the cost to her in terms of her own energies expended was correspondingly higher. This was particularly true at times when she had no chance to prepare herself for a summoning. It took a great deal of power to attract a being of benign intent—particularly one that did not know her—and more to convince it that her intent was good. Hence, the circle—meant not to protect her, but to protect what she would call, so that it would know itself unthreatened.

As she seated herself within the circle, Tarma shifted her own position until she, too, was quite comfortable. Then she removed one of her hidden daggers and began honing it with her sharpening-stone.

Kethry had removed her sword and placed it outside the circle—something she did only when working summonings. Tarma regarded the blade, as it lay between her and her bloodsister, with a thoughtful eye.

Kethry's sword was no ordinary blade—it held a powerful and strange magic. "Need" was the name of the blade, and it bound its bearer to the aid of other women. To a fighter, it granted near immunity to any magics. To a magician, it conferred expertise in the wielding of it, but only to defend herself or another woman. *Herself*—for only a woman could use it. It had other properties as well, such as being able to speed healing or hold off death for a limited time, but those were the main gifts the blade bestowed.

Tarma wondered how many of those arcane gifts they'd be using this time.

There was a stirring in the circle Kethry had inscribed, and Tarma pulled her attention back to the present. Something was beginning to form mistily in front of the seated sorceress.

The mist began to form into a miniature whirlpool, coalescing into a figure as it did so. As it solidified, Tarma could see what seemed to be a jewel-bright desert lizard, but one that stood erect, like a man. It was as tall as a man's arm is long, and had a cranium far larger than any lizard Tarma had ever seen. Fire-light winked from its scales in bands of shining colors, topaz and ruby predominating. It was regarding Kethry with intelligence and wary curiosity.

"Sa-asartha, n'hellan?" it said, tilting its head to one side and fidgeting from one foot to the other. Its voice was shrill, like that of a very young child.

"Vede, sa-asarth," Kethry replied in the same tongue.

The little creature relaxed and stopped fretting. It appeared to be quite eager to answer all of Kethry's questions. Now that the initial effort of calling it was done with, she had no trouble in obtaining all the information she wanted. Finally she gave the little creature the fruit she'd been toying with after supper. It snatched the gift greedily, trilled what Tarma presumed to be thanks, and vanished into mist again.

Kethry rose stiffly and began to scuff the circle into random piles of dirt with the toe of her boot. "It's about what I expected," she said. "Someone—some-one with 'a smell of magic about him' according to the khamsin—has organized what used to be several small bands of marauders into one large one of rather formidable proportions. They have no set camp, so we can't arrange for the camp to be attacked while they're ambushing us, I'm sorry to say. They have no favored ambush point, so we won't know when to expect them. And none of the women—girls, really—survived for more than a day."

"Damn." Tarma's eyes were shadowed. "Well, we didn't really expect anything different."

"No, but you know damn well we both hoped." Kethry's voice was rough with weariness. "It's up to you now, *she'enedra*. You're the tactician."

"Then as the tactician, I counsel rest for you."
Tarma caught Kethry's shoulders to steady her as she
stumbled a little from fatigue. The reaction to spellcasting was setting in fast now. Kethry had once de-
scribed summoning as being "like balancing on a
rooftree while screaming an epic poem in a foreign
language at the top of your lungs." Small wonder
she was exhausted afterward.

The sorceress leaned on Tarma's supporting shoulder with silent gratitude as her partner guided her
up the stairs to their rented sleeping room.

"It's us, Warrl," Tarma called softly at the door. A
muted growl answered her, and they could hear the
sound of the bolt being shoved back. Tarma pushed
the door open with one foot, and picked up one of
the unlit tallow candles that waited on a shelf just
inside with her free hand. She lit it at the one in the
bracket outside their door, and the light from it fell
on the head and shoulders of a huge black wolf. He
stood, tongue lolling out in a lupine grin, just inside
the room. His shoulders were on a level with Tarma's
waist. He sniffed inquisitively at them, making a
questioning whine deep in his throat.

"Yes, we took the job—that's our employer you
smell, so don't mangle him when he shows up tomorrow night. And Kethry's been summoning, of
course, so as usual she's half dead. Close the door
behind us while I put her to bed."

By now Kethry was nearly asleep on her feet; after
some summonings Tarma had seen her pass into unconsciousness while still walking. Tarma undressed
her with the gentle and practiced hands of a nurse-
maid and got her safely into bed before she had the
chance to fall over. The wolf, meanwhile, had butted

the door shut with his head and pushed the bolt home with his nose.

"Any trouble?" Tarma asked him.

He snorted with derision.

"Well, I didn't really expect any either. This is the *quietest* inn I've been in for a long time. The job is bandits, hairy one, and we're all going to have to go disguised. That includes you."

He whined in protest, ears down.

"I know you don't like it, but there's no choice. There isn't enough cover along the road to hide a bird, and I want you close at hand, within a few feet of us at all times, not wandering out in the desert somewhere."

The wolf sighed heavily, padded over to her, and laid his heavy head in her lap to be scratched.

"I know. I know," she said, obliging him. "I don't like it any more than you do. Just be grateful that all we'll be wearing is illusions, even if they *do* make the backs of our eyes itch. Poor Kethry's going to have to ride muffled head-to-toe like a fine lady."

Warrl obviously didn't care about poor Kethry.

"You're being very unfair to her, you know. And you're *supposed* to have been her familiar, not mine."

She and Kethry had gone deep into the Pelagir Hills, the site of ancient magical wars, and a place where traces of old magic had changed many of the animals living there into something more than dumb creatures. Kethry had intended to attract a familiar, and she'd done everything perfectly, had gone through a day and a night of complicated spellcasting—only to have Warrl appear, then choose Tarma instead.

"You're a magic beast; born out of magic. You belong with a spell-caster, not some clod with a sword."

Warrl was not impressed with Tarma's logic.

:She *doesn't need me,*: he spoke mind-to-mind with the swordswoman. :*She has the spirit-sword.* You *need me.*: And that, so far as Warrl was concerned, was that.

"Well, I'm not going to argue with you. I never argue with anyone with as many sharp teeth as you've got. Maybe being Swordsworn counts as being magic."

She pushed Warrl's head off her lap and went to open the shutters to the room's one window. Moonlight flooded the room; she seated herself on the floor where it would fall on her, just as she did every night when there was a moon and she wasn't ill or injured. Since they were within the walls of a town and not camped, she would not train this night—but the Moonpaths were there, as always, waiting to be walked. She closed her eyes and found them. Walking them was, as she'd often told Kethry, impossible to describe.

When she returned to her body, Warrl was lying patiently at her back, waiting for her. She ruffled his fur with a grin, stood, stretched stiffened muscles, then stripped to a shift and climbed in beside Kethry. Warrl sighed with gratitude and took his usual spot at her feet.

> "Three things see no end—
> A flower blighted ere it bloomed,
> A message that was wasted
> And a journey that was doomed."

The two mercenaries rode out of town in the morning, obviously eager to be gone. Grumio watched them leave, gazing sadly at the cloud of dust they raised, his houndlike face clearly displaying his disappointment. His fellow merchants were equally disappointed when he told them of his failure to persuade them; they had all hoped the women would have solved their problem.

After sundown Grumio took a cart and horse out to his farmstead, a saddled riding beast tied to the rear of it. After making certain that no one had followed him, he drove directly into the barn, then peered around in the hay-scented gloom. A fear crossed his mind that the women had tricked him and had *truly* left that morning.

"Don't fret yourself, merchant," said a gravelly voice just above his head. He jumped, his heart racing. "We're here."

A vague figure swung down from the loft; when it came close enough for him to make out features, he started at the sight of a buxom blonde wearing the swordswoman's clothing.

She grinned at his reaction. "Which one am I? She didn't tell me. Blonde?"

He nodded, amazed.

"Malebait again. Good choice, no one would ever think I knew what a blade was for. You don't want to see my partner." The voice was still in Tarma's gravelly tones; Grumio assumed that *that* was only so he'd recognize her. "We don't want you to have to strain your acting ability tomorrow. Did you bring everything we asked for?"

"It's all here," he replied, still not believing what

his eyes were telling him. "I weighted the boxes with sand and stones so that they won't seem empty."

"You've got a good head on you, merchant." Tarma saluted him as she unharnessed the horse. "That's something I didn't think of. Best you leave now, though, before somebody comes looking for you."

He jumped down off the wagon, taking the reins of his riding beast.

"And merchant—" she called as he rode off into the night, "—wish us luck."

That was one thing she didn't have to ask for.

He didn't have to act the next morning, when the delicate and aristocratically frail lady of obvious noble birth accosted him in his shop, and ordered him (although it was framed as a request) to include her in his packtrain. In point of fact, had he not recognized the dress and fur cloak she was wearing, he would have taken her for a *real* aristo—one who, by some impossible coincidence, had taken the same notion into her head that the swordswoman had proposed as a ruse. This sylphlike, sleepy-eyed creature with her elaborately coiffed hair of platinum silk bore no resemblance at all to the very vibrant and earthy sorceress he'd hired.

And though he was partially prepared by having seen her briefly the night before, Tarma (posing as milady's maid) still gave him a shock. He saw why she called the disguise "malebait"—this amply-endowed blonde was a walking invitation to impropriety, and nothing like the sexless Sworn One. All that remained of "Tarma" were the blue eyes, one of which winked cheerfully at him, to bring him out of his shock.

Grumio argued vehemently with the highborn dame for the better part of an hour, and all to no avail. Undaunted, he carried his expostulations out into the street, still trying to persuade her to change her mind even as the packtrain formed up in front of his shop. The entire town was privy to the argument by that time.

"Lady, I beg you—reconsider!" he was saying anxiously. "Wait for the King's Patrol. They have promised to return soon and in force, since the bandits have not ceased raiding us, and I'm morally certain they'll be willing to escort you."

"My thanks for your concern, merchant," she replied with a gentle and bored haughtiness, "but I fear my business cannot wait on their return. Besides, what is there about me that could possibly tempt a bandit?"

Those whose ears were stretched to catch this conversation could easily sympathize with Grumio's silent—but obvious—plea to the gods for patience, as they noted the lady's jewels, fine garments, the weight of the cart holding her possessions, and the well-bred mares she and her maid rode.

The lady turned away from him before he could continue; a clear gesture of dismissal, so he held his tongue. In stony silence he watched the train form up, with the lady and her maid in the center. Since they had no driver for the cart—though he'd offered to supply one—the lead-rein of the carthorse had been fastened to the rear packhorse's harness. Surmounting the chests and boxes in the cart was a toothless old dog, apparently supposed to be guarding her possessions and plainly incapable of guarding anything anymore. The leader of the train's six guards took his final instructions from his master, and the train lurched off down the trade road. As Grumio watched them disappear into the distance, he could be seen to shake his head in disapproval.

Had anyone been watching very closely—though no one was—they might have noticed the lady's fingers moving in a complicated pattern. Had there been any mages present—which wasn't the case—said mage might have recognized the pattern as belonging to the Spell of True Sight. If illusion was involved, it would not be blinding Kethry.

> "One among the guardsmen
> Has a shifting, restless eye
> And as they ride, he scans the hills
> That rise against the sky.
> He wears a sword and bracelet
> Worth more than he can afford
> And hidden in his baggage
> Is a heavy, secret hoard."

One of the guards was contemplating the lady's assets with a glee and greed that equaled his master's dismay. His expression, carefully controlled, seemed to be remote and impassive—only his rapidly shifting gaze and the nervous flicker of his tongue over dry lips gave any clue to his thoughts. Behind those remote eyes, a treacherous mind was making a careful inventory of every jewel and visible possession and calculating their probable values.

When the lady's skirt lifted briefly to display a tantalizing glimpse of white leg, his control broke enough that he bit his lip. *She* was one prize he intended to reserve for himself; he'd never been this

close to a highborn woman before, and he intended
to find out if certain things he'd heard about bedding
them were true. The others were going to have to be
content with the ample charms of the serving maid,
at least until he'd tired of the mistress. At least there
wouldn't be all that caterwauling and screeching
there'd been with the merchant wenches. That maid
looked as if she'd had a man twixt her legs plenty
of times before, and enjoyed it, too. She'd probably
thank him for livening up her life when he turned
her over to the men!

He had thought at first that this was going to be
another trap, especially after he'd heard that old
Grumio had tried to hire a pair of highly-touted mercenary women to rid him of the bandits. One look
at the lady and her maid, however, had convinced
him that not only was it absurd to think that they
could be wary hire-swords in disguise, but that they
probably didn't even know which end of a blade to
hold. The wench flirted and teased each of the men
in turn. Her mind was obviously on something other
than ambushes and weaponry—unless those ambushes were amorous, and the weaponry of flesh.
The lady herself seemed to ride in a half-aware
dream, and her maid often had to break off a flirta-
tion in order to ride forward and steady her in the
saddle.

Perhaps she was a *tran*-dust sniffer, or there was
faldis-juice mixed in with the water in the skin on her
saddlebow. That would be an unexpected bonus—
she was bound to have a good supply of it among
her belongings, and drugs were worth more than
jewels. And it would be distinctly interesting—his
eyes glinted cruelly—to have her begging on her

knees for her drugs as withdrawal set in. Assuming, of course, that she survived that long. He passed his tongue over lips gone dry with anticipation. Tomorrow he would give the scouts trailing the packtrain the signal to attack.

> *"Of three things be wary—*
> *Of a feather on a cat,*
> *The shepherd eating mutton,*
> *And the guardsman that is fat."*

The lady and her companion made camp a discreet distance from the rest of the caravan, as was only to be expected. She would hardly have a taste for sharing their rough camp, rude talk, or coarse food.

Kethry's shoulders sagged with fatigue beneath the weight of her heavy cloak, and she was chilled to the bone in spite of its fur lining.

"Are you all right?" Tarma whispered sharply when she hadn't spoken for several minutes.

"Just tired. I never thought that holding up five illusions would be so *hard*. Three aren't half so difficult to keep intact." She leaned her forehead on one hand, rubbing her temples with cold fingers. "I wish it was over."

Tarma pressed a bowl into her other hand. Dutifully, she tried to eat, but the sand and dust that had plagued their progress all day had crept into the food as well. It was too dry and gritty to swallow easily, and after one attempt, Kethry felt too weary to make any further effort. She laid the bowl aside, unobtrusively—or so she hoped.

Faint hope. "Sweeting, if you don't eat by yourself, I'm going to pry your mouth open and *pour* your dinner down your throat." Tarma's expression was cloyingly sweet, and the tone of her shifted voice dulcet. Kethry was roused enough to smile a little. When she was this wearied with the exercise of her magics, she had to be bullied into caring for herself. When she'd been on her own, she'd sometimes had to spend days recovering from the damages she'd inflicted on her body by neglecting it. It was at moments like this that she valued Tarma's untiring affection and aid the most.

"What, and ruin our disguises?" she retorted with a little more life.

"There's nothing at all out of the ordinary in an attentive maid helping her poor, sick mistress to eat. They already think there's something wrong with you. Half of them think you're ill, the other half think you're in a drug daze," Tarma replied. "They *all* think you've got nothing between your ears but air."

Kethry capitulated, picked up her dinner, and forced it down, grit and all.

"Now," Tarma said, when they'd both finished eating, "I know *you've* spotted a suspect. I can tell by the way you're watching the guards. Tell me which one it is; I'd be very interested to see if it's the same one I've got *my* eye on."

"It's the one with the mouse-brown hair and ratty face that rode tail-guard this morning."

Tarma's eyes widened a little, but she gave no other sign of surprise. "Did you say *brown* hair? And a ratty face? Tail-guard this morning had *black* hair and a pouty, babyish look to him."

Kethry revived a bit more. "Really? Are you talking about the one walking between us and their fire right now? The one with all the jewelry? And does he seem to be someone you know very vaguely?"

"Yes. One of the hire-swords with the horse traders my clan used to deal with—I think his name was Tedric. Why?"

Kethry unbuckled a small ornamental dagger from her belt and passed it to Kethry with exaggerated care. Tarma claimed it with the same caution—caution that was quite justified, since the "dagger" was in reality Kethry's sword Need, no matter what shape it wore at the moment. Beneath the illusion, it still retained its original mass and weight.

"Now look at him."

Tarma cast a surreptitious glance at the guard again, and her lips tightened. Even when it was done by magic, she didn't like being tricked. "Mouse-brown hair and a ratty face," she said. "He changed." She returned the blade to Kethry.

"And now?" Kethry asked, when Need was safely back on her belt.

"Now *that's* odd," Tarma said thoughtfully. "If he were using an illusion, he should have gone back to the way he looked before, but he didn't. He's still mousy and ratty, but my eyes feel funny—like something's pulling at them—and he's blurred a bit around the edges. It's almost as if his face was trying to look different from what I'm seeing."

"Mind-magic," Kethry said with satisfaction. "So that's why I wasn't able to detect any spells! It's not a true illusion like I'm holding on us. They practice mind-magic a lot more up north, and I'm only marginally familiar with the way it works since it doesn't operate quite like what I've learned. If what I've been told is true, his mind is telling your mind that you know him, and letting your memory supply an acceptable face. He could very well look like a different person to everyone in the caravan, but since he always looks familiar, any of them would be willing to vouch for him."

"Which is how he keeps sneaking into the pack-trains. He looks different each time, since no one is likely to 'see' a man they know is dead. Very clever. You say this isn't a spell?"

"Mind-magic depends on inborn abilities to work; if you haven't got them, you can't learn it. It's unlike *my* magic, where it's useful to have the Gift, but not necessary. Was he the same one you were watching?"

"He is, indeed. So your True Sight spell works on this 'mind-magic,' too?"

"Yes, thank the gods. What tipped you off to him?"

"Nothing terribly obvious, just a lot of little things that weren't quite right for the ordinary guard he's pretending to be. His sword is a shade too expensive. His horse has been badly misused, but he's got very good lines; he's of much better breeding than a common guard should own. And lastly, he's wearing jewelry he can't afford."

Kethry looked puzzled. "Several of the other guards are wearing just as much. I thought most hire-swords wore their savings."

"So they do. Thing is, of the others, the only ones with as much or more are either the guard-chief, or ones wearing mostly brass and glass; showy, meant to impress village tarts, but worthless. His is all real, and the quality is high. Too damned high for the likes of him."

"Now that we know who to watch, what do we do?"

"We wait," Tarma replied with a certain grim satisfaction. "He'll have to signal the rest of his troupe to attack us sooner or later, and one of us should be able to spot him at it. With luck and the Warrior on our side, we'll have enough warning to be ready for them."

"I hope it's sooner." Kethry sipped at the wellwatered wine which was all she'd allow herself when holding spells in place. Her eyes were heavy, dry, and sore. "I'm not sure how much longer I can hold up my end."

"Then go to sleep, dearling." Tarma's voice held an unusual gentleness, a gentleness only Kethry, Warrl, and small children ever saw. "Furface and I can take turns on nightwatch; you needn't take a turn at all."

Kethry did not need further urging, but wrapped herself up in her cloak and a blanket, pillowed her head on her arm, and fell asleep with the suddenness of a tired puppy. The illusions she'd woven would remain intact even while she slept. Only three things could cause them to fail. They'd break if she broke them herself, if the pressure of spells from a greater sorcerer than she were brought to bear on them, or if she died. Her training had been arduous and quite thorough; as complete in its way as Tarma's sword training had been.

Seeing her shiver in her sleep, Tarma built up the fire with a bit more dried dung (the leavings of previous caravans were all the fuel to be found out here) and covered her with the rest of the spare blankets. The illusions were draining energy from Kethry;

Tarma knew she'd be quite comfortable with one blanket and her cloak, and if that didn't suffice, Warrl made an excellent "bedwarmer." The night passed uneventfully.

Morning saw them riding deeper into the stony hills that ringed the desert basin they'd spent the day before passing through. The road was considerably less dusty now, but the air held more of a chill. Both Tarma and Kethry tried to keep an eye on their suspect guard, and shortly before noon their vigilance was rewarded. Both of them saw him flashing the sunlight off his armband in what could only be a deliberate series of signals.

> *"From ambush, bandits screaming*
> *Charge the packtrain and its prize,*
> *And all but four within the train*
> *Are taken by surprise,*
> *And all but four are cut down*
> *Like a woodsman fells a log,*
> *The guardsman, and the lady,*
> *And the maiden, and the dog.*
> *Three things know a secret—*
> *First; the lady in a dream;*
> *The dog that barks no warning*
> *And the maid that does not scream."*

Even with advance warning, they hadn't much time to ready themselves.

Bandits charged the packtrain from both sides of the road, screaming at the tops of their lungs. The guards were taken completely by surprise. The three apprentice traders accompanying the train flung themselves down on their faces as their master

Grumio had ordered them to do in hopes that they'd be overlooked. To the bandit-master at the rear of the train, it seemed that once again all had gone completely according to plan.

Until Kethry broke her illusions.

> *"Then off the lady pulls her cloak—*
> *In armor she is clad,*
> *Her sword is out and ready*
> *And her eyes are fierce and glad.*
> *The maiden gestures briefly,*
> *And the dog's a cur no more.*
> *A wolf, sword-maid, and sorceress*
> *Now face the bandit corps!*
> *Three things never anger,*
> *Or you will not live for long—*
> *A wolf with cubs, a man with power,*
> *And a woman's sense of wrong."*

The brigands at the forefront of the pack found themselves facing something they hadn't remotely expected. Gone were the helpless, frightened women on high-bred steeds too fearful to run. In their place sat a pair of well-armed, grim-faced mercenaries on schooled warbeasts. With them was an oversized and very hungry-looking wolf.

The pack of bandits milled, brought to a halt by this unexpected development.

Finally one of the bigger ones growled a challenge at Tarma, who only grinned evilly at him. Kethry saluted them mockingly—and the pair moved into action explosively.

They split up and charged the marauders, giving them no time to adjust to the altered situation. The bandits had hardly expected the fight to be carried to *them*, and reacted too late to stop them. Their momentum carried them through the pack and up onto the hillsides on either side of the road. Now *they* had the high ground.

Kethry had drawn Need, whose magic was enabling her to keep herself intact long enough to find a massive boulder to put her back against. The long odds were actually favoring the two of them for the moment, since the bandits were mostly succeeding only in getting in each other's way. Obviously they had not been trained to fight together, and had done well so far largely because of the surprise with which they'd attacked and their sheer numbers. Once Kethry had gained her chosen spot, she slid off her horse, and sent it off with a slap to its rump. The mottled, huge-headed beast was as ugly as a piece of rough granite, and twice as tough, but she was a Shin'a'in-bred-and-trained warsteed, and worth the weight in silver of the high-bred mare she'd been spelled to resemble. Now that Kethry was on the ground, she'd attack anything whose scent she didn't recognize—and quite probably kill it.

Warrl came to her side long enough to give her the time she needed to transfer her sword to her left hand and begin calling up her more arcane offensive weaponry.

In the meantime, Tarma was in her element, cutting a bloody swath through the bandit horde with a fiercely joyous gleam in her eyes. She clenched her mare's belly with viselike legs; only one trained in Shin'a'in-style horse-warfare from childhood could possibly have stayed with the beast. The mare was laying all about her with iron-shod hooves and enormous yellow teeth; neither animal nor man was likely to escape her once she'd targeted him. She had an uncanny sense for anyone trying to get to her rider by disabling her; once she twisted and bucked like a cat on hot metal to simultaneously crush the bandit in front of her while kicking in the teeth of the one that had thought to hamstring her from the rear. She accounted for at least as many of the bandits as Tarma did.

Tarma saw Kethry's mare rear and slash out of the corner of her eye; the saddle was empty, but she wasn't worried. The bond of *she'enedran* made them bound by spirit, and she'd have *known* if anything was wrong. Since the mare was fighting on her own, Kethry must have found someplace high enough to see over the heads of those around her.

As if to confirm this, things like ball-lightning began appearing and exploding, knocking bandits from their horses, clouds of red mist began to wreathe the heads of others (who clutched their throats and turned interesting colors), and oddly formed creatures joined Warrl at harrying and biting at those on foot.

When *that* began, especially after one spectacular fireball left a pile of smoking ash in place of the bandit's second-in-command, it was more than the remainder of the band could stand up to. Their easy prey had turned into Hellspawn, and there was *nothing* that could make them stay to face anything more. The ones that were still mounted turned their horses out of the melee and fled for their lives. Tarma and the three surviving guards took care of the rest.

As for the bandit chief, who had sat his horse in stupefied amazement from the moment the fight turned against them, he suddenly realized his own peril and tried to escape with the rest. Kethry, however, had never once forgotten him. Her bolt of power—intended this time to stun, not kill—took him squarely in the back of the head.

> *"The bandits growl a challenge,*
> *But the lady only grins.*
> *The sorceress bows mockingly,*
> *And then the fight begins.*
> *When it ends, there are but four*
> *Left standing from that horde—*
> *The witch, the wolf, the traitor,*
> *And the woman with the sword.*
> *Three things never trust in—*
> *The maiden sworn as pure,*
> *The vows a king has given*
> *And the ambush that is 'sure.'"*

By late afternoon the heads of the bandits had been piled in a grisly cairn by the side of the road as a mute reminder to their fellows of the eventual reward of banditry. Their bodies had been dragged off into the hills for the scavengers to quarrel over. Tarma had supervised the cleanup, the three apprentices serving as her work force. There had been a good deal of stomach purging on their part at first—especially after the way Tarma had casually lopped off the heads of the dead or wounded bandits—but they'd obeyed her without question. Tarma had had to hide her snickering behind her hand, for they looked at her whenever she gave them a command as though they feared that *their* heads might well adorn the cairn if they lagged or slacked.

She herself had seen to the wounds of the surviving guards, and the burial of the two dead ones.

One of the guards could still ride; the other two were loaded into the now-useless cart after the empty boxes had been thrown out of it. Tarma ordered the whole caravan back to town; she and Kethry planned to catch up with them later, after some unfinished business had been taken care of.

Part of that unfinished business was the filling and marking of the dead guards' graves.

Kethry brought her a rag to wipe her hands with when she'd finished. "Damn. I wish— Hellspawn, they were just honest hire-swords," she said, looking at the stone cairns she'd built with remote regret. "It wasn't *their* fault we didn't have a chance to warn them. Maybe they shouldn't have let themselves be surprised like that, not with what's been happening to the packtrains lately—but still, your life's a pretty heavy price to pay for a little carelessness. . . ."

Kethry, her energy back to normal now that she was no longer being drained by her illusions, slipped a sympathetic arm around Tarma's shoulders. "Come on, *she'enedra.* I want to show you something that might make you feel a little better."

When Tarma had gone to direct the cleanup, Kethry had been engaged in stripping the bandit chief down to his skin and readying his unconscious body for some sort of involved sorcery. Tarma knew she'd had some sort of specific punishment in mind from the time she'd heard about the stolen girls, but she'd had no idea of what it was.

> "They've stripped the traitor naked
> And they've whipped him on his way

Into the barren hillsides,
Like the folk he used to slay.
They take a thorough vengeance
For the women he's cut down,
And then they mount their horses
And they journey back to town.
Three things trust and cherish well—
The horse on which you ride,
The beast that guards and watches
And your shield-mate at your side!"

Now before her was a bizarre sight. Tied to the back of one of the bandit's abandoned horses was— apparently—the unconscious body of the high-born lady Kethry had spelled herself to resemble. She was clad only in a few rags, and had a bruise on one temple, but otherwise looked to be unharmed.

Tarma circled the tableau slowly. There was no flaw in the illusion—if indeed it was an illusion.

"Unbelievable," she said at last. "That *is* him, isn't it?"

"Oh, yes, indeed. One of my best pieces of work."

"Will it hold without you around to maintain it?"

"It'll hold, all right," Kethry replied with deep satisfaction. "That's part of the beauty and the justice of the thing. The illusion is irretrievably melded with his own mind-magic. He'll never be able to break it himself, and no reputable sorcerer will break it for him. And I promise you, the only sorcerers for weeks in any direction are quite reputable."

"Why wouldn't he be able to get one to break it for him?"

"Because I've signed it." Kethry made a small gesture, and two symbols appeared for a moment above the bandit's head. One was the symbol Tarma knew to be Kethry's sigil, the other was the glyph for "Justice." "Any attempt to probe the spell will make *those* appear. I doubt that anyone will ignore the judgment sign, and even if they were inclined to, I think my reputation is good enough to make most sorcerers think twice about undoing what I've done."

"You really didn't change him, did you?" Tarma asked, a horrible thought occurring to her. "I mean, if he's *really* a woman now—"

"Bright Lady, what an awful paradox we'd have!" Kethry laughed, easing Tarma's mind considerably. "We punish him for what he's done to women by turning him into a woman—but as a woman, we'd now be honor-bound to protect him! No, don't worry. Under the illusion—and it's a *very* complete illusion, by the way, it extends to all senses—he's still quite male."

She gave the horse's rump a whack, breaking the light enchantment that had held it quiet, and it bucked a little, scrabbling off into the barren hills.

"The last of the band went that way," she said, pointing after the beast, "And the horse he's on will follow their scent back to where they've made their camp. Of course, none of his former followers will have any notion that he's anything other than what he appears to be."

A wicked smile crept across Tarma's face. It matched the one already curving Kethry's lips.

"I wish I could be there when he arrives," Tarma said with a note of viciousness in her harsh voice. "It's *bound* to be interesting."

"He'll certainly get *exactly* what he deserves." Kethry watched the horse vanish over the crest of the hill. "I wonder how he'll like being on the receiving end?"

"I know somebody who *will* like this—and I can't wait to see his face when you tell him."

"Grumio?"

"Mm-hmm."

"You know—" Kethry replied thoughtfully, "—this was almost worth doing for free."

"*She'enedra!*" Tarma exclaimed in mock horror. "Your misplaced honor will have us starving yet! We're *supposed* to be mercenaries!"

"I said *almost.*" Kethry joined in her partner's gravelly laughter. "Come on. We've got pay to collect. You know—this just might end up as some bard's song."

"It might at that," Tarma chuckled. "And what will you bet me that he gets the tale all wrong?"

THE MAKING OF A LEGEND

Speaking of Leslac, here he is, in *his* debut, making life miserable for the ladies. It's kind of interesting that the more I write about Tarma and Kethry, the more often there's humor in the stories. The first one was rather grim, but they've gradually lightened up.

By the way, if you've noticed that the ladies often swtich horses, it's not a mistake. As explained in *By the Sword*, since they *are* partners, the battlesteeds are trained to accept either rider, so they often switch off just to keep the mares in training, just as one can have a guard dog that accepts more than one handler, but eats anyone who *isn't* a designated handler. It would be a real problem if Tarma happened to need a horse that was all the way across a battlefield, and Kethry's happened to be right at hand but wouldn't let her mount. . . .

Brown-gray and green-brown landscape, and a coating of dust all over everything, a haze of dust in the air, a cloud of dust hanging behind them where Tarma and Kethry's tired mares had kicked it up. Fields, farmholdings, trees. More fields, more farmholdings, more trees. Not wild trees either; trees tamed, planted in neat little orchards or windbreaks, as orderly and homebound as the farmers who husbanded them. A tidy land this; carefully ruled. No calling *here* for outland mercenaries.

All the more reason to get through it as fast as Hellsbane and Ironheart could manage.

On the other hand, the White Winds sorceress Kethry reflected, there was no use in night-long riding when they were in civilized lands. No telling when they might see a real bed once they got into territory that *did* need their spells and swords.

Kethry wiped her forehead with her sleeve, adjusted the geas-blade Need on her back, and blinked the road dust out of her sore eyes. The sun sat on the horizon like a fat red tomato, seemingly as complacent as the farmers it shone down on. "How far to the next town?" she asked over the dull clopping of hooves on flint-hard earth.

"Huh?" Her companion, the Shin'a'in Swordsworn Tarma, started up out of a doze, blinking sleepy, ice-blue eyes. Her granite-gray mare snorted and sneezed as the thin swordswoman jerked alert.

"I asked you how far it was to the next town," Kethry repeated, raking sweat-damp amber hair with her fingers, trying to get it tucked behind her ears. In high-summer heat like this, she envied Tarma's chosen arrangement of tiny, tight-bound braids. It may not have *been* cooler, but it *looked* cooler. And Tarma's coarse black hair wasn't always coming loose and getting into her eyes and mouth, or making the back of her neck hot.

"Must've nodded off; sorry about that, Greeneyes," Tarma said sheepishly, extracting the map from the waterproof pocket on the saddle skirting in front of her. "Hmm—next town's Viden; we'll hit there just about dusk."

"Viden? Oh, hell—" Kethry replied in disgust, rolling the sleeves of her buff sorcerer's robe a little higher. "It *would* be Viden. I was hoping for a bath and a bed."

"What's wrong with Viden?" Tarma asked. To Kethry's further disgust she didn't even look *warm;* there was no sheen of sweat on that dark-gold skin, and that despite the leather tunic and breeches she wore. Granted, she *was* from the Dhorisha Plains where it got a lot hotter than it was here, but—

Well, it wasn't fair.

"Viden's overlord is what's wrong," she answered. "A petty despot, Lord Gorley; hired a gang of prison scum to enforce things for him." She made a sour face. "He manages to stay just on the right side of tolerable for the Viden merchants, so they pay his fees and ignore him. But outsiders find themselves a lot lighter in the pocket if they overnight there. Doesn't even call it a tax, just sends his boys after you to shake you down. Hell*fire*."

"Oh, well," Tarma shrugged philosophically. "At least we were warned. Figure we'd better skirt the place altogether, or is it safe enough to stop for a meal?"

:For a short stop I misdoubt a great deal of trouble with me at your side,: the lupine *kyree* trotting at Ironheart's side mindspoke to both of them. Kethry grinned despite her disappointment. Seeing as Warrl's shoulders came as high as Tarma's waist, and he had a head the size of a large melon with teeth of a length to match, it was extremely doubtful that any one— or even three—of the Viden-lord's toughs would care to chance seeing what the *kyree* was capable of.

"Safe enough for that," Kethry acknowledged. "From all I heard they don't bestir themselves more than they can help. By the time they manage to get themselves organized into a party big enough to give us trouble, we'll have paid for our meal and gone."

The dark, stone-walled common room of the inn was *much* cooler than the street outside. Bard Leslac lounged in the coolest, darkest corner, sipped his tepid ale, and congratulated himself smugly on his foresight. There was only one inn—his quarry would *have* to come here to eat and drink. He'd beaten them by nearly half a day; he'd had plenty of time to choose a comfortable, out-of-the-way corner to observe what *must* come.

For nearly two years now, he had been following the careers of a pair of freelance mercenaries, both of them women (which was unusual enough), one a sorceress, the other one of the mysterious Shin'a'in out of the Dhorisha Plains (which was unheard of). He had created one truly masterful ballad out of the stories he'd collected about them—masterful enough that he was no longer being pelted with refuse in village squares, and was now actually welcome in taverns.

But he wanted more such ballads. And there was one cloud on his success.

Not once in all that time had he ever managed to actually catch sight of the women.

Oh, he'd *tried*, right enough—but they kept making unexpected and unexplained detours—and by the time he found out where they'd gone, it was too late to do anything but take notes from the witnesses and curse his luck for not being on the scene. No bard worth his strings would ever take secondhand accounts for the whole truth. Especially not when those secondhand accounts were so—unembellished. No

impassioned speeches, no fountains of blood—in fact,
by the way these stupid peasants kept telling the
tales, the women seemed to go out of their way to
avoid fights. And that was plainly *not* possible.

But *this* time he had them. There was no place for
them to go now except Viden—and Viden boasted a
wicked overlord.

Leslac was *certain* they'd head here. How could
they not? Hadn't they made a career out of righting
the wrongs done to helpless women? Surely some of
the women in Viden had been abused by Lord Gorley. Surely Gorley's Lady was in dire need of rescue.
He could just imagine it—Tarma facing down a
round dozen of Gorley's men, then dispatching them
easily with a triumphant laugh. Kethry taking on
Lord Gorley's sorcerer (surely he had one) in a mage-
duel of titanic proportions. The possibilities were
endless. . . .

And Leslac would be on hand to record *everything*.

Tarma sagged down onto the smooth wooden
bench with a sigh. *Damn, but I wish we could overnight
it. One more day in this heat and folks'll smell us coming
a furlong away. Wish I just dared to take my damned
boots off. My feet feel broiled.*

She propped both elbows on the wooden table and
knuckled the dust out of her eyes.

Footsteps approaching. Then, "What'll it be,
miladies?"

The deep voice to her right sounded just a shade
apprehensive. Tarma blinked up at the burly innkeeper standing a respectful distance away.

*Apron's clean—hands're clean. Table's clean. Good
enough. We can at least have a meal before we hie out.*

"No ladies here, Keeper," she replied, her hoarse
voice even more grating than usual because of all the
dust she'd eaten today. "Just a couple of tired mercs
wanting a meal and a *quiet* drink."

The slightly worried look did not leave the innkeeper's shiny, round face. "And *that?*" he asked,
nodding at Warrl, sprawled beside her on the stone
floor, panting.

"All *he* wants is about two tradeweight of meat
scraps and bones—more meat than bone, please, and
no bird bones. A big bowl of cool water. And half a
loaf of barley bread."

:With honey,: prompted the voice in her head.

You want honey in this *heat?*

:Yes,: Warrl said with finality.

"With honey," she amended. "Split the loaf and
pour it down the middle."

*You're going to get it in your fur, and who's going to
have to help you get it out?*

:I will not!: Warrl gave her an offended glance from
the floor.

The innkeeper smiled a little. Tarma grinned back.
"Damn beast's got a sweet tooth. What's on the
board tonight?"

"Mutton stew, chicken fried or stewed, egg'n'onion
pie. Cheese bread or barley bread. Ale or wine."

"Which's cooler?"

The innkeeper smiled a little more. "Wine. More
expensive and goes bad quicker, so we keep it deeper
in cellar."

"Egg pie, cheese bread, and wine." Tarma looked
across the tiny table at Kethry, who was trying to

knot her amber hair up off her neck and having no great success. Kethry nodded shortly. "White wine, if you've got it. For two."

"You be staying?" The apprehensive look was back.

"No," Tarma raised an eyebrow at him. "I don't like to slander a man's homeplace, but your town's got a bad name for travelers, Keeper. I don't doubt we could take care of anyone thinking to shake us down, but it would make an almighty mess in your clean inn."

The innkeeper heaved a visible sigh of relief. "My mind exactly, swordlady. I seen a few mercs in my time—and you two look handier than most. But you dealin' with Gorley's bullyboys would leave *me* out of pocket for things broke—more than losin' your night's lodging is gonna cost me."

Tarma looked around the common room, and was mildly surprised to see that they were the only occupants other than a scruffy, curly-pated minstrel-type tucked up in one corner. She dismissed that one without a second thought. Too skinny to be any kind of fighter, so he wasn't one of Gorley's enforcers; dark of hair and dusky of skin, so he wasn't local. And he blinked in a way that told her he was just a tad shortsighted. No threat.

"That why you're a bit short on custom?" she asked. "Not having travelers?"

"Nah—it ain't market-day, that's all. We never was much on overnighters anyway, only got three rooms upstairs. Most folk stop at Lyavor or Grant's Hold. Always made *our* way on local custom. I bring you your wine, eh? You want that pie cold or het up?"

Tarma shuddered. "Cold, cold—I've had enough heat and dust today."

"Then it won't be but a blink—"

The innkeeper hurried through the open door in the far wall that presumably led to the kitchen. Tarma sagged her head back down to her hands and closed her eyes.

Leslac frowned. This was *not* going as he'd expected.

The women—he'd expected them to be taller, somehow, especially the swordswoman. Cleaner, not so—shabby. Aristocratic. Silk for the sorceress, and shining steel armor for the swordswoman, not a dull buff homespun robe and a plain leather gambeson. And in his mental image they had always held themselves proudly, challengingly—shining Warriors of the Light—

Not two tired, dusty, slouching, *ordinary* women; not women who rubbed their red-rimmed eyes or fought with their hair.

Not women who avoided a confrontation.

He studied them despite his disappointment—surely, surely there was *some* sign of the legend they were becoming—the innkeeper had seen it. He'd been concerned that they *could* take on Lord Gorley's men and win—and wreck the inn in the process.

After long moments of study, as the innkeeper came and went with food and drink, Leslac began to smile again. No, these weren't Shining Warriors of the Light—these women were something even better.

Like angels who could put on human guise, Tarma and Kethry hid their strengths—obviously to put their targets off-guard. But the signs were there, and the innkeeper had read them before Leslac had even guessed at them. But—it showed; in the easy way they moved, in the hands that never strayed too far from a hilt, in the fact that they had not put off their weapons. In the way that *one* of them was always on guard, eyes warily surveying the room between bites. In the signs of wear that only hard usage could put on a weapon.

Undoubtedly they were *intending* to remain here—but they didn't want Lord Gorley alerted by staying in the inn.

Leslac mentally congratulated them on their subtlety.

Even as he did so, however, there was a commotion at the inn door—and red-faced and besotted with drink, Lord Gorley himself staggered through it after colliding with both of the doorposts.

Leslac nearly crowed with glee and pressed himself back into the rough stone of the corner wall. *Now* he'd have what he'd come so far to witness! There would be no way now for the women to avoid a confrontation!

Tarma was sipping the last of her wine when the drunk stumbled in through the door and tripped over Warrl's tail.

Warrl yelped and sent out a Mindshriek that was comprised of more startlement than pain. But it left Tarma stunned and deafened for a moment—and when her eyes cleared, the sot was looming over her, enveloping her in a cloud of stale wine fumes.

Oh, Lady of the Sunrise, I do not need this—

"Ish zhish yer dog?" The man was beefy, muscle running to fat, nose a red lacework of broken veins that told a tale of far too many nights like this one—nights spent drunk on his butt before the sun was

scarcely below the horizon. His wattled face was
flushed with wine and anger, his curly brown hair
greasy with sweat.

Tarma sighed. "Insofar as anyone can claim him,
yes, he's mine," she said placatingly. "I'm sorry he
was in your way. Now why don't you let me buy
you a drink by way of apology?"

The innkeeper had inexplicably vanished, but there
was a mug or three left in their bottle—

The man would not be placated. "I don' like yer
dog," he growled, "an' I don' like yer ugly face!"

He stumbled back a pace or two—then, before
Tarma had a chance to blink, he'd drawn his sword
and was swinging at her.

Wildly, of course. She didn't have to move but a
hand's breadth to dodge out of his way—but that
only served to anger him further, and he came at her,
windmilling his blade fit to cut the air into ribbons.

She rolled off the bench and came up on her toes.
He followed so closely on her heels that she had only
time to dodge, drop to her shoulder and roll out of
his way again, under the shelter of another bench.

As he kicked at her shelter, she could see that
Warrl was beneath the table, grinning at her.

You mangy flea-monger, you started *this!* she thought
at him, avoiding the drunk's kick, but losing her
shield. She scrambled to her feet again, dodging another swing.

:I did no such thing,: Warrl replied coolly. *:It was
purely accident—:*

She got a table between herself and the sot—but
the drunk swung, split the table in two, and kept
coming.

Lady's teeth, I daren't use a blade on him, I'll kill him

by accident, she thought. *And then I'll have the townsfolk or his friends on our backs.*

She looked about her in a breath between a duck and a dodge. In desperation she grabbed a broom that was leaning up in a corner by the kitchen door.

Since he was flailing away as much with the flat as with the edge, and since *she* could pick the angle with which she met his weapon, she was now effectively on equal footing. Mostly.

He was still drunk as a pig, and mad as a hornet's nest. And *he* wanted to kill her.

She countered, blocked, and countered again; blocked the blade high and slipped under it to end up behind him.

And swatted his ample rear with the business end of the broom.

That was a mistake; he was angered still more, and his anger was making him sober. His swings were becoming more controlled, and with a lot more force behind them—

Tarma looked around for assistance. Kethry was standing over in the sheltered corner beside the fireplace, laughing her head off.

"You might *help!*" Tarma snapped, dodging another blow, and poking the drunk in the belly with the end of the broom. Unfortunately, the straw end, or the contest would have finished right there.

"Oh, no, I wouldn't think of it!" Kethry howled, tears pouring down her face. "You're doing so well by yourself!"

Enough is enough.

Tarma blocked another stroke, then poked the sot in the belly again—but *this* time with the sharp end of the broom.

The man's eyes bulged and he folded over, dropping his sword and grabbing his ample belly.

Tarma ran around behind him and gave him a tremendous swat in the rear, sending him tumbling across the room—

—where he tripped and fell into the cold fireplace, his head meeting the andiron with a sickening *crack*.

Silence fell, thick as the heat, and Tarma got a sinking feeling in her stomach.

"Oh, hell—" Tarma walked over to the fallen drunk and poked him with her toe.

No doubt about it. He was stone dead.

"Oh, *hell*. Oh, *bloody* hell."

The innkeeper appeared at her elbow as silently and mysteriously as he'd vanished. He looked at the shambles of his inn—and took a closer look at the body.

"By the gods—" he gulped. "You've killed Lord Gorley!"

"Your husband may not have been much before, Lady, but I'm afraid right now he's rather less," Tarma said wearily. Somewhat to her amazement, the innkeeper had *not* summoned what passed for the law in Viden; instead he'd locked up the inn and sent one of his boys off for Lady Gorley. Tarma was not minded to try and make a run for it—unless they *had* to. The horses were tired, and so were they. It *might* be they could talk themselves out of this one.

Maybe.

The Lady had arrived attended by no one—which caused Kethry's eyebrow to rise. And she wasn't much better dressed than a well-to-do merchant's wife, which surprised Tarma.

It was too bad they'd had to meet under circumstances like this one; Tarma would have liked to get to know her. She held herself quietly, but with an air of calm authority like a Shin'a'in shaman. A square face and graying blonde hair held remnants of great beauty—not ruined beauty either, just transformed into something with more character than simple prettiness.

She gazed dispassionately down on the body of her former Lord for several long moments. And Tarma longed to know what was going on in her head.

"I'm afraid I have to agree with your assessment on all counts, Shin'a'in," she replied. "I shan't miss him, poor man. Neither will anyone else, to be frank. But this puts us all in a rather delicate position. I appreciate that you could have fled. I appreciate that you didn't—"

"No chance," Kethry answered, without elaborating. She'd signaled to her partner that her damned ensorcelled blade had flared up at her the heartbeat after Lord Gorley breathed his last. Plainly his Lady would be in danger from his death. Just as plainly, Need expected them to do something about this.

"Well." Lady Gorley turned away from the body as a thing of no importance, and faced Tarma. "Let me explain a little something. In the past several years Kendrik has been more and more addicted to the bottle, and less and less capable. The Viden-folk took to bringing *me* their business, and when Kendrik hired that gang of his and began extracting money from them, *I* began returning it as soon as it went into the treasury. No one was hurt, and no one was the wiser."

"What about—" Tarma coughed politely. "Begging your pardon milady, but that kind of scum generally is bothersome to young women—"

She smiled thinly. "The men satisfied their lust without rapine—Kendrik knew *I* wouldn't stand for that, and *I* was the one who saw to his comforts. One week of doing without proper food and without his wine taught him to respect my wishes in that, at least. And the one time Kendrik took it into his head to abscond with a Viden-girl—well, let us just say that his capabilities were not equal to his memories. I smuggled the girl out of his bed and back to her parents as virgin as she'd left."

"So that's why—"

"Why none of us cared to see things disturbed," the innkeeper put in, nodding so hard Tarma thought his head was going to come off. "Things was all right—we'd warn travelers, and if they chose to disregard the warnings—" he shrugged. "—sheep was meant to be sheared, they say, and fools meant to share the same fate."

"So what's the problem?" Tarma asked, then realized in the next breath what the problem was. "Ah— the bullyboys. Without Kendrik to pay 'em and to keep his hand on 'em—"

Lady Gorley nodded. "Exactly. They *won't* heed me. I would be in as much danger from them as my people. We're farm and tradesfolk here; *we* would be easy prey for them. It will be bad if I keep them, and worse if I discharge them."

Tarma pursed her lips thoughtfully. "Your respect, Lady, but I've got no wish to take on a couple dozen bad cases with just me and my partner and less than a day to take them out. But maybe if we put our heads together—"

"You've got until moonrise," Lady Gorley said, handing a pouch up to Tarma that chinked as she looked inside before stowing it away in her saddle-bag. Light streaming from the back door of the inn gave Tarma enough illumination to see that more than half the coins were gold. "That is really all the time we can give you. And I'm sorry I didn't have much to pay you for your discomfort."

"It'll be enough," Tarma assured her. "Now—you've got it all straight—at moonrise you raise the hue and cry after us; you offer fifty gold to the man who brings back our heads, and you turn the lads loose. They're going to hear the word 'gold' and they won't even stop to think—they'll just head out after us. You do realize this is going to cost you in horses—they'll take every good mount in your stables."

Lady Gorley shrugged. "That can't be helped, and better horses than lives. But can you lay a trail that will keep them following without getting caught yourselves?"

Tarma laughed. "You ask a *Shin'a'in* if she can lay a trail? No fear. By the time they get tired of follow-ing—those that I don't lose once their horses founder—they'll have had second and third thoughts about coming back to Viden. They'll know that *you'll* never keep them on. They'll think about the kings' men you've likely called in—and the good armsmen of your neighbors. And they'll be so far from here that they'll give it all up as a bad cause."

The innkeeper nodded. "She's right, Lady. They

drifted in; they drift out just the same with no easy pickings in sight."

"What about that little rhymester?" Tarma asked, nodding back at the tavern door. They hadn't noticed the minstrel trying to make himself a part of the wall until it was too late to do anything about him.

"I'll keep him locked up until it's safe to let him go," the innkeeper replied. "If I know musickers, he'll have a long gullet for wine. I'll just keep him too happy to move."

"Very well—and the gods go with you," Lady Gorley said, stepping away from the horses.

"Well, Greeneyes," Tarma smiled crookedly at her partner.

Kethry sighed, and smiled back. "All right, I'll geas them. But dammit, that means *we* won't be seeing beds for months!"

Tarma nudged Ironheart with her heels and the battlemare sighed as heavily as Kethry had, but moved out down the village street with a faint jingling of harness. "Greeneyes, I didn't say you should geas them to follow *us* now, did I?"

"Then who—"

"Remember that loudmouth, Rory Halfaxe? The one that kept trying to drag you into his bed? *He's* in Lyavor, and planning on going the direction opposite of this place. Now if we double back and come up on his backtrail—think you can transfer the geas?"

Leslac slumped, nearly prostrate with despair. His head pounded, and he downed another mug of wine without tasting it. *Oh, gods of fortune—do you hate me?*

He couldn't believe what he had seen—he just *couldn't!*

First—that—*farce* with the broomstick. He moaned and covered his eyes with his hand. How could *anyone* make a heroic ballad out of *that*? "Her broomstick flashing in her hands—"? Oh, gods, they'd laugh him out of town; they wouldn't *need* the rotten vegetables.

Then—that Lord Gorley died by *accident!* Gods, gods, gods—

"This can't be happening to me," he moaned into his mug. "This simply cannot be happening."

And as if that wasn't enough—the collusion between Gorley's widow and the other two to lure the gang of bullies away without so much as a single *fight!*

"I'm ruined," he told the wine. "I am utterly *ruined*. How could they *do* this to me? This is *not* the way heroes are supposed to behave—what am I going to *do*? Why couldn't things have happened the way they *should* have happened?"

Then—*the way they* should *have happened*—

The dawn light creeping in the window of his little cubby on the second floor of the inn was no less brilliant than the inspiration that came to him.

The way they should *have happened!*

Feverishly he reached for pen and paper, and began to write—

"The warrior and the sorceress rode into Viden-town, for they had heard of evil there and meant to bring it down—"

HEYS

I love locked-room mysteries, and I thought it would be fun to do one with a different setting—one in which magic was used in place of forensic detection, but magic itself was *not* used to create the mystery in the first place. And who better to take that setting than Tarma and Kethry?

She stood all alone on the high scaffold made of raw, yellow wood, as motionless as any statue. She was cold despite the heat of the summer sunlight that had scorched her without pity all this day; cold with the ice-rime of fear. She had begun her vigil as the sun rose at her back; now the last light of it flushed her white gown and her equally white face, lending her pale cheeks false color. The air was heavy, hot and scented only with the odor of scorched grass and sweating bodies, but she breathed deeply, desperately of it. Soon now, soon—

Soon the last light of the sun would die, and she would die with it. Already she could hear the men beneath her grunting as they heaved piles of oily brush and faggots of wood into place below her platform. Already the motley-clad herald was signaling to the bored and weary trumpeter in her husband's green livery that he should sound the final call. *Her* last chance for aid.

For the last time the three rising notes of a summoning rang forth over the crowd beneath her. For the last time the herald cried out his speech to a sea of pitying or avid faces. *They* knew that this was the last time, the last farcical call, and they waited for the climax of this day's fruitless vigil.

"Know ye all that the Lady Myria has been accused of the foul and unjust murder of her husband, Lord Corbie of Felwether. Know that she has called for trial by combat as is her right. Know that she names no champion, trusting in the gods to send forth one to fight in her name as token of her innocence. Therefore, if such there be, I do call, command, and summon him here, to defend her honor!"

No one looked to the gate except Myria. She, perforce, must look there, since she was bound to her platform with hempen rope as thick as her thumb. This morning she had strained her eyes toward that empty arch every time the trumpet sounded, but no savior had come—and now even she had lost hope.

The swordswoman called Tarma goaded her gray Shin'a'in warsteed into another burst of speed, urging her on with hand and voice (though not spur— *never* spur) as if she were pursued by the Jackals of Darkness. Her long, ebony braids streamed behind her; close enough to catch one of them rode her amber-haired partner, the sorceress Kethry; Kethry's mare a scant half a length behind her herd-sister.

Kethry's geas-blade, Need by name, had awakened her this morning almost before the sun rose, and had been driving the sorceress (and so her blood-oath sister as well) in this direction all day. At first it had been a simple pull, as she had often felt before. Both

Kethry and Tarma knew from experience that once Need called, Kethry had very little choice in whether or not she would answer that call, so they had packed up their camp and headed for the source. But the call had grown more urgent as the hours passed, not less so—increasing to the point where by mid-afternoon it was actually causing Kethry severe mental pain. They had gotten Tarma's companion-beast Warrl up onto his carry-pad and urged their horses first into a fast walk, then a trot, then as sunset neared, into a full gallop. Kethry was near-blind by the mental anguish it caused. Need *would* not be denied in this; Kethry was soul-bonded to it—it conferred upon her a preternatural fighting skill, it had healed both of them of wounds it was unlkikely they would have survived otherwise—but there was a price to pay for the gifts it conferred. Kethry (and thus Tarma) was bound to aid any woman in distress within the blade's sensing range—and it seemed there was one such woman in grave peril now. Peril of her life, by the way the blade was driving Kethry.

Ahead of them on the road they were following loomed a walled village; part and parcel of a manor-keep—a common arrangement in these parts. The gates were open; the fields around empty of workers. That was odd—very odd. It was high summer, and there should have been folk out in the fields, weeding and tending the irrigation ditches. There was no immediate sign of trouble—but as they neared the gates, it was plain just who the woman they sought was—

Bound to a scaffold high enough to be visible through the open gates, they could see a young, dark-haired woman dressed in white, almost like a sacrificial victim. The last rays of the setting sun touched her with color—touched also the heaped wood beneath the platform on which she stood, making it seem as if her pyre already blazed up. Lining the mud-plastered walls of the keep and crowding the square inside the gate were scores of folk of every class and station, all silent, all waiting.

Tarma really didn't give a fat damn about what they were waiting for, though it was a good bet that they were there for the show of the burning, and not out of sympathy for the woman. She coaxed a final burst of speed out of her tired mount, sending her shooting ahead of Kethry's as they passed the gates, and bringing her close in to the platform. Once there, she swung her mare Hellsbane around in a tight circle and drew her sword, placing herself between the woman on the scaffold and the men with the torches to set it alight.

She knew she was an imposing sight, even covered with sweat and the dust of the road; hawk-faced, intimidating, ice-blue eyes blazing defiance. Her clothing was patently that of a fighting mercenary; plain brown leathers and brigandine armor. Her sword reflected the dying sunlight so that she might have been holding a living flame in her hand. She said nothing; her pose said it all for her—

Nevertheless, one of the men started forward, torch in hand.

"I wouldn't—" Kethry said from behind him. She was framed in the arch of the gate, silhouetted against the fiery sky; her mount rock-still, her hands glowing with sorcerous energy. "If Tarma doesn't get you, *I* will."

"Peace—" a tired, gray-haired man in plain, dusty-black robes stepped forward from the crowd, holding his arms out placatingly, and motioned the torch-bearer to give way. "Ilvan, go back to your place. Strangers, what brings you here at this time of all times?"

Kethry pointed—a thin strand of glow shot from her finger and touched the ropes binding the captive on the platform. The bindings loosed and fell from her, sliding down her body to lie in a heap at her feet. The woman swayed and nearly fell, catching herself at the last moment with one hand on the stake she had been bound to. A small segment of the crowd—mostly women—stepped forward as if to help, but fell back again as Tarma swiveled to face them.

"I know not what crime you accuse this woman of, but she is innocent of it," Kethry said to him, ignoring the presence of anyone else. "*That* is what brings us here."

A collective sigh rose from the crowd at her words. Tarma watched warily to either side, but it appeared to be a sigh of relief rather than a gasp of anger. She relaxed the white-knuckled grip she had on her sword hilt by the merest trifle.

"The Lady Myria is accused of the slaying of her lord," the robed man said quietly. "She called upon her ancient right to summon a champion to her defense when the evidence against her became overwhelming. I, who am priest of Felwether, do ask you—strangers, will you champion the Lady and defend her in trial-by-combat?"

Kethry began to answer in the affirmative, but the priest shook his head negatively. "No, lady-mage, by ancient law *you* are bound from the field; neither sor-

cery nor sorcerous weapons such as I see you bear
may be permitted in trial-by-combat."

"Then—"

"He wants to know if I'll do it, *she'enedra*," Tarma
croaked, taking a fiendish pleasure in the start the
priest gave at the sound of her harsh voice. "I know
your laws, priest, I've passed this way before. I ask
you in my turn—if my partner, by her skills, can
prove to you the lady's innocence, will you set her
free and call off the combat, no matter how far it
has gotten?"

"I so pledge, by the Names and the Powers," the
priest nodded—almost eagerly.

"Then I will champion this lady."

About half the spectators cheered and rushed forward. Three older women edged past Tarma to bear
the fainting woman back into the keep. The rest, except for the priest, moved off slowly and reluctantly,
casting thoughtful and measuring looks back at
Tarma. Some of them seemed friendly—most did not.

"What—"

"Was that all about?" That was as far as Tarma
got before the priest interposed himself between the
partners.

"Your pardon, mage-lady, but you may not speak
with the champion from this moment forward—any
message you may have must pass through me—"

"Oh, no, not yet, priest." Tarma urged Hellsbane
forward and passed his outstretched hand. "I told
you I know your laws—and the ban starts at sundown—Greeneyes, pay attention, I have to talk fast.
You're going to have to figure out just who the real
culprit is—the best I can possibly do is buy you time.
This business is combat to the death for the cham-

pion—I can choose just to defeat my challengers, but they *have* to kill me. And the longer you take, the more likely that is—"

"Tarma, you're better than anybody here—"

"But not better than any twenty—or thirty." Tarma smiled crookedly. "The rules of the game, *she'enedra*, are that I keep fighting until nobody is willing to challenge me. Sooner or later they'll wear me out and I'll go down."

"*What?*"

"Shush, I knew what I was getting into. You're as good at your craft as I am at mine—I've just given you a bit of incentive. Take Warrl—" The tall, lupine creature jumped to the ground from behind Tarma where he'd been clinging to the special pad with his retractile claws. "—he might well be of some use. Do your best, *veshta'cha*; there're two lives depending on you—"

The priest interposed himself again. "Sunset, champion," he said firmly, putting his hand on her reins.

Tarma bowed her head, and allowed him to lead her and her horse away, Kethry staring dumbfounded after them.

"All right, let's take this from the very beginning."

Kethry was in the Lady Myria's bower—a soft and colorful little corner of an otherwise drab fortress. There were no windows—no drafts stirred the bright tapestries on the walls, or caused the flames of the beeswax candles to flicker. The walls were thick stone covered with plaster—warm by winter, cool by summer. The furnishings were of light yellow wood, padded with plump feather cushions. In one corner stood a cradle, watched over broodingly by the lady herself. The air was pleasantly scented with herbs and flowers. Kethry wondered how so pampered a creature could have gotten herself into such a pass.

"It was two days ago. I came here to lie down in the afternoon. I—was tired; I tire easily since Syrtin was born. I fell asleep."

Close up, the Lady proved to be several years Kethry's junior; scarcely past her mid-teens. Her dark hair was lank and without luster, her skin pale. Kethry frowned at that, and wove a tiny spell with a gesture and two whispered words while Myria was speaking. The creature of the ethereal plane who'd agreed to serve as their scout was still with her—it would have taken a far wilder ride than they had made to lose it. The answer to her question came quickly as a thin voice breathed whispered words into her ear.

Kethry grimaced angrily. "Lady's eyes, child, I shouldn't wonder that you tire—you're still torn up from the birthing! What kind of a miserable excuse for a Healer have you got here, anyway?"

"We have *no* Healer, lady." One of the three older women who had borne Myria back into the keep rose from her seat behind Kethry and stood between them, challenge written in her stance. She had a kind, but careworn face; her gray-and-buff gown was of good stuff, but old-fashioned in cut. Kethry guessed that she must be Myria's companion—an older relative, perhaps. "The Healer died before my dove came to childbed and her lord did not see fit to replace him. We had no use for a Healer, or so he claimed, since he kept no great number of men-at-arms, and birthing was a perfectly normal procedure and surely didn't require the expensive services of a Healer."

"Now, Katran—"

"It is no more than the truth! He cared more for his horses than for you! He replaced the farrier quickly enough when *he* left!"

"His horses were of more use to him—" the girl said bitterly, then bit her lip. "There, you see, *that* is what brought me to this pass—one too many careless remarks let fall among the wrong ears."

Kethry nodded, liking the girl; the child was *not* the pampered pretty she had first thought. No windows to this chamber—only the one entrance; a good bit more like a cell than a bower, it occurred to her. A comfortable cell, but a cell still. She stood, smoothed her buff-colored robe with an unconscious gesture, and unsheathed the sword that seldom left her side.

"Lady, what—" Katran stood, startled by the gesture.

"Peace; I mean no ill. Here—" Kethry said, bending over Myria and placing the blade in the startled girl's hands. "—hold this for a bit."

Myria took the blade, eyes wide, a puzzled expression bringing a bit more life to her face. "But—"

"Women's magic, child. For all that blades are a man's weapon, Need here is strong in the magic of women. She serves women only—it was her power that called me here to aid you—and given an hour of your holding her, she'll Heal you. Now, go on. You fell asleep."

Myria accepted the blade gingerly, then settled the sword across her knees and took a deep breath. "Something woke me—a sound of something falling,

I think. You can see that this room connects with My Lord's chamber—that in fact the only way in or out is through his chamber. I saw a candle burning, so I rose to see if he needed anything. He—he was slumped over his desk. I thought perhaps he had fallen asleep—"

"You thought he was drunk, you mean," the older woman said wryly.

"—does it *matter* what I thought? I didn't *see* anything out of the ordinary, because he wore dark colors always. I reached out my hand to shake him—and it came away bloody—"

"And she screamed fit to rouse the household," Katran finished.

"And when we came, she had to unlock the door for us," said the second woman, silent till now. "Both doors into that chamber were locked—hallside with the lord's key, seneschal's side barred from within this room. And the bloody dagger that had killed him was under her bed."

"Whose was it?"

"Mine, of course," Myria answered. "And before you ask, there was only one key to the hallside door; it could only be opened with the key, and the key was under his hand. It's an ensorcelled lock; even if you made a copy of the key, the copy would never unlock the door."

"Warrl?" The huge beast rose from the shadows where he'd been lying and padded to Kethry's side. Myria and her women shrank away a little at the sight of him.

"I may need to conserve my energies. You can detect what I'd need a spell for—see if there's magical residue on the bar on the other door, would you?

Then see if the spell on the lock's been tampered with."

The dark-gray, nearly black beast trotted out of the room on silent paws, and Myria shivered.

"I can see where the evidence against you is overwhelming, even without misheard remarks."

"I had no choice in this wedding," Myria replied, her chin rising defiantly, "but I have been a true and loyal wife to my lord."

"Loyal past his deserts, if you ask me," Katran grumbled. "Well, that's the problem, lady-mage. My Lady came to this marriage reluctant, and it's well known. It's well known that he didn't much value her. And there's been more than a few heard to say they thought Myria reckoned to set herself up as Keep-ruler with the Lord gone."

Warrl padded back into the room, and flopped down at Kethry's feet.

"Well, fur-brother?"

He shook his head negatively, and the women stared at this evidence of human-like intelligence.

"Not the bar nor the lock, hmm? And how do you get into a locked room without a key? Still—Lady, is all as it was in the other room?"

"Yes—the priest was one of the first in the door, and would not let anyone change so much as a dust mote. He only let them take the body away."

"Thank the Goddess!" Kethry looked curiously at the girl. "Lady, *why* did you choose to prove yourself as you did?"

"Lady-mage—" Kethry was surprised at the true expression of guilt and sorrow the child wore. "If I had guessed strangers would be caught in this web, I never would have—I—I thought that my kin would come to my defense. I came to this marriage of their will, I thought at least one of them might—at least try. I don't think anyone here would dare the family's anger by taking the chance of killing one of the sons—even if the daughter is thought worthless by most of them—" A slow tear slid down one cheek, and she whispered her last words. "—my youngest brother, I thought at least was fond of me—"

The spell Kethry had set in motion was still active; she whispered another question to the tiny air-entity she had summoned. This time the answer made her smile, albeit sadly.

"Your youngest brother, child, is making his way here afoot, having ridden his horse into foundering trying to reach you in time, and blistering the air with his oaths."

Myria gave a tiny cry and buried her face in her hands; Katran moved to comfort her as her shoulders shook with silent sobs. Kethry stood and made her way into the other room. Need's magic was such that the girl would hold the blade until she no longer required its power; it would do nothing to augment Kethry's magical abilities, so it was fine where it was. Right now there was a mystery to solve—and two lives hung in the balance until Kethry could puzzle it out.

As she surveyed the outer room, she wondered how Tarma was faring.

Tarma sat quietly beneath the window of a tiny, bare, rock-walled cell. In a few moments the light of the rising moon would penetrate it—first through the eastern window, then the skylight overhead. For now, the only light in the room was that of the oil-fed flame burning on the low table before her. There was something else on that table—the long, coarse braids of Tarma's hair.

She had shorn those braids off herself at shoulder-length, then tied a silky black headband around her forehead to confine what remained. That had been the final touch to the costume she'd donned with an air of robing herself for some ceremony—clothing that had long stayed untouched, carefully folded in the bottom of her pack. Black clothing; from low, soft boots to chainmail shirt, from headband to hose—the stark, unrelieved black of a Shin'a'in Swordsworn about to engage in ritual combat or on the trail of blood-feud.

Now she waited, patiently, seated cross-legged before the makeshift altar, to see if her preparations received an answer.

The moon rose behind her, the square of dim white light creeping slowly down the blank stone wall opposite her, until, at last, it touched the flame on the altar.

And without warning, without fanfare, *She* was there, standing between Tarma and the altar-place. Shin'a'in by her golden skin and sharp features, clad identically to Tarma—only Her eyes revealed Her as something not human. Those eyes—the spangled darkness of the sky at midnight, without white, iris or pupil—could belong to only one being; the Shin'-a'in Goddess of the South Wind, known only as the Star-Eyed, or the Warrior.

"Child." Her voice was as melodious as Tarma's was harsh.

"Lady," Tarma bowed her head in homage.

"You have questions, child? No requests?"

"No requests, Star-Eyed. My fate—does not interest me. I will live or die by my own skills. But Kethry's—"

"The future is not easy to map, child, not even for a goddess. Tomorrow might bring your life *or* your death; both are equally likely."

Tarma sighed. "Then what of my *she'enedra* should it be the second path?"

The Warrior smiled, Tarma felt the smile like a caress. "You are worthy of your blade, child; hear, then. If you fall tomorrow, your *she'enedra*—who has fewer compunctions than you and would have done this already had you not bound yourself to the trial— will work a spell that lifts both herself and the Lady Myria to a place leagues distant from here. And as she does this, Warrl will release Hellsbane and Ironheart and drive them out the gates. When Kethry recovers from that spell, they shall go to our people, to the Liha'irden; Lady Myria will find a mate to her liking there. Then, with some orphans of other clans, they shall go forth and Tale'sedrin will ride the plains again, as Kethry promised you. The blade will release her, and pass to another's hands."

Tarma sighed, and nodded. "Then, Lady, I am content, whatever my fate tomorrow. I thank you."

The Warrior smiled again; then between one heartbeat and the next, was gone.

Tarma left the flame to burn itself out, lay down upon the pallet that was the room's only other furnishing, and slept.

Sleep was the last thing on Kethry's mind.

She surveyed the room that had been Lord Corbie's; plain stone walls, three entrances, no windows.

One of the entrances still had the bar across the door, the other two led to Myria's bower and to the hall outside. Plain wooden floor, no hidden entrances there. She knew the blank wall held nothing either; the other side was the courtyard of the manor. Furnishings; one table, one chair, one ornate bedstead against the blank wall, one bookcase, half filled, four lamp. A few bright rugs. Her mind felt as blank as the walls.

"Start at the beginning," she told herself. "Follow what happened. The girl came in here alone—the man followed after she was asleep—then what?"

:He was found at his desk,: said a voice in her mind, startling her. *:He probably walked straight in and sat down. What's on the desk that he might have been doing?:*

Every time Warrl spoke to her mind-to-mind it surprised her. She still couldn't imagine how he managed to make himself heard when she hadn't a scrap of that particular Gift. Tarma seemed to accept it unquestioningly; how she'd ever gotten used to it, the sorceress couldn't imagine.

Tarma—time was wasting.

On the desk stood a wineglass with a sticky residue in the bottom, an inkwell and quill, and several stacked ledgers. The top two looked disturbed.

Kethry picked them up, and began leafing through the last few pages, whispering a command to the invisible presence at her shoulder. The answer was prompt—the ink on the last three pages of both ledgers was fresh enough to still be giving off fumes detectable only by a creature of the air. The figures were written no more than two days ago.

She leafed back several pages worth, noting that the handwriting changed from time to time.

"Who else kept the accounts besides your lord?" she called into the next room.

"The seneschal; that was why his room has an entrance on this one," the woman Katran replied, entering the lord's room herself. "I can't imagine why the door was barred—Lord Corbie almost never left it that way."

"That's a lot of trust to place in a hireling—"

"Oh, the seneschal isn't a hireling, he's Lord Corbie's bastard brother. He's been the lord's right hand since he inherited the lordship of Felwether."

The sun rose; Tarma was awake long before.

If the priest was surprised to see her change of outfit, he didn't show it. He had brought a simple meal of bread and cheese and watered wine; he waited patiently while she ate and drank, then indicated she should follow him.

Tarma checked all her weapons; made sure of all the fastenings of her clothing, and stepped into place behind him, as silent as his shadow.

He conducted her to a small tent that had been erected in one corner of the keep's practice ground, against the keep walls. The walls of the keep formed two sides, the outer wall the third; the fourth side was open. The practice ground was of hard-packed clay, and relatively free of dust. A groundskeeper was sprinkling water over the dirt to settle it.

Once they were in front of the little pavilion, the priest finally spoke.

"The first challenger will be here within a few minutes; between fights you may retire here to rest for as long as it takes for the next to ready himself, or one candlemark, whichever is longer. You will be brought food at noon and again at sunset—'' his expression plainly said that he did not think she would be needing the latter, ''—and there will be fresh water within the tent at all times. I will be staying with you.''

Now his expression was apologetic.

"To keep my partner from slipping me any magical aid?'' Tarma asked wryly. ''Hellfire, priest, *you* know what I am, even if these dirt-grubbers here don't!''

"I know, Swordsworn—this is for your protection as well. There are those here who would not hesitate to tip the hand of the gods somewhat.''

Tarma's eyes hardened. ''Priest, I'll spare who I can, but it's only fair to tell you that if I catch anyone trying an underhanded trick, I won't hesitate to kill him.''

"I would not ask you to do otherwise.''

She looked at him askance. ''There's more going on here than meets the eye, isn't there?''

He shook his head, and indicated that she should take her seat in the champion's chair beside the tent flap. There was a bustling on the opposite side of the practice ground, and a dark, heavily bearded man followed by several boys carrying arms and armor appeared only to vanish within another, identical tent on that side. Spectators began gathering along the open side and the tops of the walls.

"I fear I can tell you nothing, Swordsworn. I have only speculations, nothing more. But I pray your little partner is wiser than I—''

"Or I'm going to be cold meat by nightfall,'' Tarma finished for him, watching as her first opponent emerged from the challenger's pavilion.

* * *

Kethry had not been idle.

The sticky residue in the wineglass had been more than just the dregs of drink; there had been a powerful narcotic in it. Unfortunately, this just pointed back to Myria; she'd been using just such a potion to help her sleep since the birth of her son. Still—it wouldn't have been all that difficult to obtain, and Kethry had a trick up her sleeve—one the average mage wouldn't have known; one she would use *if* they could find the other bottle of potion.

More encouraging was what she had found perusing the ledgers. The seneschal had been siphoning off revenues; never much at a time, but steadily. By now it must amount to a tidy sum. What if he suspected Lord Corbie was likely to catch him at it?

Or even more—what if Lady Myria *was* found guilty and executed? The estate would go to her infant son—and who would be the child's most likely guardian but his half-uncle, the seneschal?

And children die so very easily.

Now that she had a likely suspect, Kethry decided it was time to begin investigating him.

The first place she checked was the barred door. And on the bar itself she found an odd little scratch, obvious in the paint. It looked new—her air-spirit confirmed that it was. She lifted the bar after examining it even more carefully, finding no other marks on it but those worn places where it rubbed against the brackets that held it.

She opened the door, and began examining every inch of the door and frame. And found, near the top, a tiny piece of hemp that looked as if it might have come from a piece of twine, caught in the wood of the door itself.

Further examination of the door yielded nothing, so she turned her attention to the room beyond.

It looked a great deal like the lord's room, with more books and a less ostentatious bedstead. She called Warrl in and sent him sniffing about for any trace of magic. That potion required a tiny bit of magicking to have full potency, and if there was another bottle of it anywhere about, Warrl would find it.

She turned her own attention to the desk.

Tarma's first opponent had been good, and an honest fighter. It was with a great deal of relief—especially after she'd seen an anxious-faced woman with three small children clinging to her skirt watching every move he made—that she was able to disarm him and knock him flat on his rump without seriously injuring him.

The second had been a mere boy; he had no business being out here at all. Tarma had the shrewd notion he'd been talked into it just so she'd have one more live body to wear her out. Instead of exerting herself in any way, she lazed about, letting him wear *himself* into exhaustion, before giving him a little tap on the skull with the pommel of her knife that stretched him flat on his back, seeing stars.

The third opponent was another creature altogether.

He was slim and sleek, and Tarma smelled "assassin" on him as plainly as if she'd had Warrl's clever nose. When he closed with her, his first few moves confirmed her guess. His fighting style was all feint and rush, never getting in too close. This was a real problem. If she stood her ground, she'd open herself to the poisoned dart or whatever other tricks he had secreted on his person. If she let him drive her all over the bloody practice ground he'd wear her down. Either way, she lost.

Of course, she might be able to outfox him—

So far she'd played an entirely defensive game, both with him and her first two opponents. If she took the offense when he least expected it, she might be able to catch him off his guard.

She let him begin to drive her; and saw at once that he was trying to work her around so that the sun was in her eyes. She snarled inwardly, let him think he was having his way, then turned the tables on him.

She came at him in a two-handed pattern-dance, one that took her back to her days on the plains and her first instructor; an old man she'd never *dreamed* could have moved as fast as he did. She hadn't learned that pattern then; hadn't learned it until the old man and her clan were four years dead and she'd been Kethry's partner for almost three. She'd learned it from one of Her Swordsworn, who'd died a hundred years before Tarma had ever been born—

It took her opponent off-balance; he backpedaled furiously to get out of the way of the shining circles of steel, great and lesser, that were her sword and dagger. And when he stopped running, he found himself facing into the sun.

Tarma saw him make a slight movement with his left hand; when he came in with his sword in an over-and-under cut, she paid his sword hand only scant attention. It was the other she was watching for.

Under the cover of his overt attack he made a strike for her upper arm with his gloved left. She avoided it barely in time; a circumstance that made her sweat when she thought about it later, and executed a spin-and-cut that took the hand off at the wrist at the end of the move. While he stared in shock at the spurting stump, she carried her blade back along the arc to take his head as well.

The onlookers were motionless, silent with shock. What they'd seen from her up until now had not prepared them for this swift slaughter. While they remained still, she stalked to where the gloved hand lay and picked it up with great care. Embedded in the fingertips of the gloves, retracted or released by a bit of pressure to the center of the palm, were four deadly little needles. Poisoned, no doubt.

She decided to make a grandstand move out of this. She stalked to the challenger's pavilion, where more of her would-be opponents had gathered, and cast the hand down at their feet.

"Assassin's tricks, 'noble lords'?" she spat, oozing contempt. "Is this the honor of Felwether? I'd rather fight jackals—at least they're honest in their treachery! Have you no trust in the judgment of the gods—and their champion?"

That should put a little doubt in the minds of the honest ones—and a little fear in the hearts of the ones that weren't.

Tarma stalked stiff-legged back to her own pavilion, where she threw herself down on the little cot inside it, and hoped she'd get her wind back before they got their courage up.

*   *   *

In the very back of one of the drawers Kethry found a very curious contrivance. It was a coil of hempen twine, two cords, really, at the end of which was tied a barbless, heavy fishhook—the kind sea-fishers used to take shark and the great sea-salmon. But the coast was weeks from here. What on earth could the seneschal have possibly wanted with such a curious souvenir?

Just then Warrl barked sharply; Kethry turned to see his tail sticking out from under the bedstead.

:There's a hidden compartment under the boards here,: he said eagerly in her mind. *:I smell gold, and magic— and fresh blood.:*

She tried to move the bed aside, but it was far too heavy—something the seneschal probably counted on. So she squeezed in beside Warrl, who pawed at the place on the board floor where he smelled strangeness.

Sneezing several times from the dust beneath the bed, she felt along the boards—carefully, carefully; it could be booby-trapped. She found the catch, and a whole section of the board floor lifted away. And inside—

Gold, yes; packed carefully into the bottom of it— but on top, a bloodstained, wadded-up tunic, and an empty bottle.

Now if she just had some notion how he could have gotten into a locked room without the proper key. There was no hint or residue of any kind of magic. And no key to the door with the bar across it.

How *could* you get into a locked room?

:Go before the door is locked,: Warrl said in her mind.

And suddenly she realized what the fishhook was for.

Kethry wriggled out from under the bed, leaving the hidden compartment untouched.

"Katran!" she called. A moment later Myria's companion appeared, quite nonplussed to see the sorceress covered with dust beside the seneschal's bed.

"Get the priest," Kethry told her, before she had a chance to ask any questions. "I know who the murderer is—and I know how and why."

Tarma was facing her first real opponent of the day; a lean, saturnine fellow who used twin swords like extensions of himself. He was just as fast on his feet as she was—and he was fresher. The priest had vanished just before the beginning of this bout, and Tarma was fervently hoping this meant Kethry had found something. Otherwise, this fight bid fair to be her last.

Thank the Goddess this one was an honest warrior; if she went down, it would be to an honorable opponent. Not too bad, really, if it came to it. Not even many Swordsworn could boast of having defeated twelve opponents in a single morning.

She had a stitch in her side that she was doing her best to ignore, and her breath was coming in harsh pants. The sun was punishing-hard on someone wearing head-to-toe black; sweat was trickling down her back and sides. She danced aside, avoiding a blur of sword, only to find she was moving right into the path of his second blade. Damn!

At the last second she managed to drop and roll, and came up to find him practically on top of her again. She managed to get to one knee and trap his first blade between dagger and sword—but the second was coming in—

"*Hold!*"

And miracle of miracles, the blade stopped mere inches from her unprotected neck.

The priest strode onto the field, robes flapping. "The sorceress has found the true murderer of our lord and proved it to my satisfaction," he announced to the waiting crowd. "She wishes to prove it to yours—"

Then he began naming off interested parties as Tarma sagged to the dirt, limp with relief, and just about ready to pass out with exhaustion.

"Swordsworn—shall I find someone to take you to your pavilion?" The priest was bending over her in concern. Tarma managed to find one tiny bit of unexpended energy.

"Not on your life, priest. I want to see this myself!"

There were perhaps a dozen nobles in the group that the priest escorted to lord's chamber. Foremost among them was the seneschal, the priest most attentive on him. Tarma was too tired to wonder about that—she saved what little energy she had to get her to the room and safely leaning up against the wall within.

"I trust you all will forgive me if I am a bit dramatic, but I wanted you all to see exactly how this deed was done." Kethry was standing behind the chair that was placed next to the desk; in that chair was an older woman in buff and gray. "Katran has kindly agreed to play the part of Lord Corbie; I am the murderer. The lord has just come into this chamber; in the next is his lady. She has taken a potion to relieve pain, and the accustomed sound of his footstep is not likely to awaken her."

She held up a wineglass. "Some of that same potion was mixed in with the wine that was in this glass, but it did *not* come from the batch Lady Myria was using. Here is Myria's bottle." She placed the wineglass on the desk, and Myria brought a bottle to stand beside it. "Here—" she produced a second bottle, "—is the bottle I found. The priest knows where, and can vouch for the fact that until he came, no hand but the owner's touched it."

The priest nodded. Tarma noticed that the seneschal was beginning to sweat.

"The spell I am going to cast now—as your priest can vouch, since he is no mean student of magic himself—will cause the wineglass and the bottle that contained the potion that was poured into it glow."

Kethry dusted something over the glass and the two bottles. As they watched, the residue in the glass and the fraction of potion in Kethry's bottle began to glow with an odd, greenish light.

"Is this a true casting, priest?" Tarma heard one of the nobles ask in an undertone.

He nodded. "As true as ever I've seen."

"Huh," the man replied, bemused.

"Now—Lord Corbie has just come in; he is working on the ledgers. I give him a glass of wine." Kethry handed the glass to Katran. "He is grateful; he thinks nothing of the courtesy, I am an old and trusted friend. He drinks it—I leave the room—presently he is asleep."

Katran allowed her head to sag down on her arms.

"I take the key from beneath his hand, and quietly lock the door to the hall. I replace the key. I know he will not stir, not even cry out, because of the strength of the potion. I take Lady Myria's dagger, which I obtained earlier—I stab him." Kethry mimed the murder; Katran did not move, though Tarma could see she was smiling sardonically. "I take the dagger and plant it beneath Lady Myria's bed—and I know that because of the potion, she will not wake either."

Kethry went into Myria's chamber and returned empty-handed.

"I've been careless—got some blood on my tunic; no matter, I will hide it where I plan to hide the bottle. By the way, the priest has that bloody tunic, and he knows that his hands alone removed it from its hiding place—just like the bottle. Now comes the important part—"

She took an enormous fishhook on a double length of twine out of her beltpouch.

"The priest knows where I found this—rest assured that it was *not* in Myria's possession. Now, on the top of this door, caught on a rough place in the wood, is another scrap of hemp. I am going to get it now. Then I shall cast another spell—and if that bit of hemp came from this twine, it shall return to the place it came from."

She went to the door and jerked loose a bit of fiber, taking it back to the desk. Once again she dusted something over the twine on the hook and the scrap—this time she chanted as well. A golden glow drifted down from her hands to touch first the twine, then the scrap—

And the bit of fiber shot across to the twine like an arrow loosed from a bow.

"Now you will see the key to entering a locked

room—now that I have proved that this was the mechanism by which the trick was accomplished."

She went over to the door to the seneschal's chamber. She wedged the hook under the bar on the door, and lowered the bar so that it was only held in place by the hook; the hook was kept where it was by the length of twine going over the door itself. The other length of twine Kethry threaded *under* the door. Then she closed the door—

The second piece of twine jerked; the hook came free, and the bar thudded into place. And the whole contrivance was pulled up over the door and through the upper crack by the first piece.

All eyes turned toward the seneschal—whose white face was confession enough.

"Lady Myria was certainly grateful enough—"

"If we'd let her, she'd have given us all the seneschal stole," Kethry replied, waving at the distant figures on the keep wall. "I'm glad you talked her out of it."

"Greeneyes, what she gave us was plenty. As it is, we'll have to send a good chunk of it back to Liha'irden to bank with the rest of the Clan possessions. I'm not really comfortable walking around with this much coin in my saddlebags."

"Will she be all right, do you think?"

"Now that her brother's here, I don't think she has a thing to worry about. She's gotten back all the loyalty of her lord's people and more besides. All she needed was a strong right arm to beat off unwelcome suitors, and she's got that now! Warrior's Oath—I'm glad *that* young monster wasn't one of the challengers—I'd never have lasted past the first round!"

"Tarma—"

The swordswoman raised an eyebrow at Kethry's unwontedly serious tone.

"If you—did all that because you think you owe me—"

"I 'did all that' because we're *she'enedran*," she replied, a slight smile warming her otherwise forbidding expression. "No other reason is needed."

"But—"

"No 'buts,' Greeneyes. Besides, I happen to know you'd have more than repaid anything I did. Puzzle *that* one out, oh, discoverer of keys!"

A WOMAN'S WEAPON

These Tarma and Kethry stories are not in any particular order, since I didn't write them chronologically. This one was inspired by the rather sexist comment that "poison is a woman's weapon," when I believe that police records show a poisoner is more likely to be a man.

On the other hand, since most women are still physically weaker and smaller than men, they tend to take revenge in an indirect fashion. While it is true that very few men will sneak up on you when you're asleep and chop important anatomical parts off, it is equally true that most men taking revenge blow large holes in their opponent, rendering the use of those anatomical parts moot. Which may or may not prove that, as Kipling asserted, "the female of the species is deadlier than the male."

The weather was usually more of a plague to a traveling freelance mercenary than something to be enjoyed, but today was different. Such a bright fall day, warm and sunny, should have been perfect. As Tarma and her partners rode over golden-grassed hill after undulating hill, even the warsteeds frisked a little, kicking up puffs of dust from the road with each hoofbeat, and they were at the end of the day's journey. But Tarma shena Tale'sedrin suddenly wrinkled her nose as a breeze so laden with a foul odor it could have been used as a weapon assaulted her senses.

"Feh!" she exclaimed, jerking her head back so violently that one of her braids flopped over her shoulder. "What in hell is—"

Her answer came as she and her partners, the sorceress Kethry and the great *kyree* Warrl, came over the crest of the next hill. The unsightly blotch on the grassy vale below them could only have been put there by the hand of man.

Huge open vats and the stack of raw hides piled like wood beside the entrance identified the source of the harsh chemical reek. The amber-haired sorceress curled her lip in a scowl at the sight of the tannery at the bottom of the hill, though her distaste might as well have been for the cluster of hovels around it.

"That's 'progress,' " the sorceress said flatly. "Or so the owner would tell you. Justin warned me about this."

Tarma narrowed her eyes in self-defense as another puff of eye-watering potency blew across their path. "Progress?" she said incredulously, while their dappled-gray warsteeds snorted objection at being forced so close to the source of the stench. "What's progressive about this? Tanneries don't have to stink like that. And that village—"

"I don't know much," Kethry warned her partner. "Just that the owner of this place has some new way of tanning. It takes less time supposedly."

"And definitely makes five times the stink." Tarma would have lifted her lip, but she didn't want to open her mouth any more than she had to.

:*And five times the filth,*: Warrl commented acidly. :*The place is sick with it. The earth is poisoned.*:

Well, that certainly accounted for the unease the place was giving her. All Shin'a'in had a touch of earth-sense; it helped them avoid the few dangerous places left on the Plains, the places where dangerous things of magic were buried that were best left undisturbed.

"If this is change, progress, I don't like it," Tarma said. "I know you sometimes think the Shin'a'in are a little backward, because we don't like change, but this is one reason why we prefer to stay the way we are."

The sorceress shifted in her saddle and shrugged. "Well, that isn't the only thing the man's changed," Kethry continued. "And until just now, I didn't know if it was a good change, or a bad one."

Her partner's troubled tone made Tarma glance sharply at the sorceress. "What change was that?"

"There're no Tanners' Guild members down there except the owner," Kethry replied. "And I thought that might be a good thing, when I first heard of it. Sometimes I think the Guilds have too much power. You can't get into an apprenticeship if you haven't any money to buy your way into the Guild, unless you can find a Master willing to waive the fee. I thought that something like this might open the trades, give employment to people who desperately need it. But that—" she waved at the cluster of shacks around the tannery building, "—that mess—"

"That doesn't look as if he's doing much for the poor," Tarma finished for her. "But there isn't much that we can do about it. We're just a couple of free-lance mercs on the way to interview for a Company." At Kethry's continued silence, she added sharply, "We are, aren't we?"

Kethry smiled a little from behind a wisp of wind-blown, amber hair. "Need isn't complaining, if that's what you're worried about. By which, I assume, Master Karden isn't interested in providing females with employment."

"Possibly." Tarma shrugged leather-clad shoulders. "Whatever the reason, at least we aren't going to have to fight your sword and its stupid compulsion to rescue women whether or not they deserve rescue—or even want rescue."

Kethry didn't even answer; she simply touched her heels to Hellsbane's sides and gave the mare her head. The warsteed, sister to Tarma's Ironheart, threw up her head and moved readily into a canter, all too pleased to be getting out of there. Ironheart was after her a fraction of a heartbeat later.

The stench proved to be confined to the valley. Once they were on the opposite side of the next hill, the air was fresh and clean again. Tarma could not imagine what it must be like to live in that squalid little town.

:Presumably, their noses are numb,: Warrl supplied, running easily alongside the road, his lupine head even with Tarma's calf. His head and shaggy coat were the only wolflike things about him; if Tarma squinted, she would have sworn there was a giant grass-cat running at her stirrup, not a wolf. In reality, Warrl was neither; he was a *kyree*, a Pelagir Hills creature, and bonded with Tarma as Kethry's spellsword Need was bonded to the sorceress.

Once out of the reach of the stench, the horses slowed of their own accord. Warrl looked pleased with the change of pace. He looked even happier with the village built of the yellowish stone of these hills that appeared below them, as they topped yet another rise.

This would be their last stop before Hawksnest, the home of the mercenary company called "Idra's Sunhawks." Tarma had no doubts that between the letters of introduction they carried, letters from two of Idra's former men, and their own abilities, Idra would sign them on despite their lack of training with a Company. After all, it wasn't every day that a Captain could acquire both a Shin'a'in Swordsworn and a Journeyman White Winds sorceress for her ranks. When you added the formidable Warrl to the bargain, Tarma reckoned that Idra would be a fool to turn them down.

And no one had ever called Captain Idra a fool.

But that was ahead of them. For tonight, there would be a good meal and a bit of a rest. Not a bed; that single-storied country inn down there wasn't big enough for that. But there would be space on the floor once the last of the regulars cleared out for the night, and that was enough for the three of them. It was more than they'd had many times in the past.

It was an odd place for a village, though, out here in the middle of nowhere surrounded by grassy hills. "So, did Justin tell you why there's a town out here, back of beyond?" Tarma asked out of curiosity.

"Same thing as brought that slum here," Kethry replied. "Cattle. This is grazing country. There's a real Tanners' Guild House here, that's made leather for generations, and the locals produce smoked and dried beef for fighter rations."

"And sometimes it's hard to tell one from the other," Tarma chuckled.

Kethry laughed, and the sound of her merriment

made heads turn toward them as they rode into the village square. Her laughter called up answering smiles from the inhabitants, who surely were no strangers to passing mercenaries.

Even Warrl caused no great alarm, though much curiosity. The dozen villagers in the square seemed to take it for granted that the women had him under control. It was a refreshing change from other villages, where not only Warrl's appearance, but even Tarma and Kethry's, was cause for distress.

In fact, no sooner had they reined in their horses, than one of the locals approached—with the caution a war-trained animal like the mares or Warrl warranted, but with no sign of fear. "The inn be closed, miladies," the young man said diffidently, pulling off his soft cloth hat, and holding it to his leather-clad chest. "Beggin' yer pardon. Old Man Murfee, he died 'bout two weeks agone, an' we be waitin' on the justice to figger out if the place goes to the son, or the barkeep." He grinned at Tarma's expression. "Sorry, milady, but they's been arguin' an' feudin' about it since the old man died. It ain't season yet, so 'twere easier on the rest of us t' do without our beer an' save our ears."

"Easier for you, maybe," Tarma muttered. "Well, I suppose we can press on—"

"Now, that's the other thing," he continued. "If ye be members of the Merc Guild, the Tanners' Guild Hall be open to ye. Any Guild member, really. Master left word. One Guild to another, Master Lenne says."

That brightened Tarma's mood considerably. "I take it you're 'prenticed there?" she asked, dismounting with a creak of leather and a jingle of harness.

"Aye," he replied, ducking his head. "Ye'll have to tend yer own horses. We don't see much of live 'uns at the Guild. Ye can put 'em in the shed with the donkey."

As the young man turned to lead the way across the dusty, sunlit square, Tarma glanced over at her partner. "Worth our Guild dues, I'd say. Glad now that I insisted on joining?"

Kethry nodded slowly. "This is the way it's supposed to work," she said. "Cooperation between Guilds and Houses of the same Guild. Not starting trade wars with each other; not cutting common folk out of trades."

"Hmm." Tarma held her peace while they stabled the warsteeds in the sturdy half-shed beside a placid donkey, and took their packs into the Guild Hall. Like the rest of the village, it was a fairly simple structure; one-storied, with a kitchen behind a large meeting hall, and living quarters on either side of the hall, in separate wings. Built, like the rest of the village, from the yellow rock that formed these hillsides, it was a warm, welcoming building.

"Ye can sleep here in the hall, by the fireplace," said the young man. "Ye can take a meal when the rest of the 'prentices and journeymen come in, if that suits ye."

"That'll be fine," Kethry replied vaguely, her eyes inwardly-focused, her thoughts elsewhere for a moment, the faint line of a headache-frown appearing between her eyebrows.

"Where's the tannery at?" Tarma asked curiously. "I haven't caught a whiff of it—"

"And you won't, sword-lady," said a weary, if pleasant voice from the shadows of one of the doorways. A tall, sparse-haired man whose bulky scarlet-wool robe could not conceal his weight problem moved into the room.

He's sick, Tarma thought immediately. The careful way he moved, the look of discomfort about him, and a feeling of *wrongness* made her as uneasy as that foul tannery.

"I agree,: Warrl replied, startling her. *:He has been ill for some time, I would say.:*

"No, you will not smell our tannery, ladies," the man—who Tarma figured must be Master Lenne—repeated. "We keep the sheds well-ventilated, the vats sealed, and spills removed. I permit no poisoning of the land by our trade. I am happy to say that tallen-flowers bloom around our foundations—and if we find them withering or dying, we find out *why.*"

Tarma smiled slightly at his vehemence. Master Lenne caught the smile and correctly surmised the reason.

"You think me overly reactive?" he asked.

"I think you—feel strongly," she said diplomatically.

He raised his hands, palms up. "Since the arrival of that fool, 'Master' Karden, and his plague-blotch, I find it all the more important to set the proper example." He tucked his hands back in the sleeves of his robe, as if they were cold. Tarma read the carefully suppressed anger in his voice, and wondered if the real reason was to hide the fact that his hands were trembling with that same anger. "I was not always a Tanner, ladies, I was once a herder. I love this land, and I will not poison it, nor will I poison the waters beneath it nor the air above. There has been enough of that already." He turned his penetrating brown eyes on Tarma. "Has there not, Swordlady Tarma? It *is* Tarma, is it not? And this is Kethry, and the valiant Warrl?"

Warrl's tail fanned the air, betraying his pleasure at being recognized, as he nodded graciously. Tarma spared him a glance of amusement. "It is," she replied. "Though I'm at a loss to know how you recognized us."

"Reputation, ladies. Songs and tales have reached even here. I know of no other partnering of Shin'a'in and sorceress." The Master chuckled at Tarma's ill-concealed wince. "Fear not, we have no women to rescue, or monsters to slay. Only a meal by a quiet hearth and a bed. If you would be seated, I would appreciate it, however. I'm afraid I am something less than well."

The four of them took seats by the fire; something about the Master's "illness" nagged at Tarma. What hair he had was glossy and healthy; at odds with the rest of his appearance. Short of breath, with pallid and oily skin, and weight that looked to have been put on since he first fell ill—his symptoms were annoyingly familiar—but of what?

It escaped her; she simply listened while Master Lenne and Kethry discussed the rivalry between the Guild and the interloper outside of the village.

"Oh, he couldn't get villagers to work there," the Master said, in answer to Kethry's question. "At least, not after the first couple of weeks. The man's methods are dangerous to his workers, as well as poisonous to the land. He doesn't do anything *new*, he simply takes shortcuts in the tanning processes that compromise quality and safety. That's all right, if all you want are cheaply tanned hides and don't care that they have bad spots or may crack in a few months—and you don't give a hang about sick workers."

"Well, he must be getting business," Kethry said cautiously.

Master Lenne sagged in his chair and sighed. "He is," the man said unhappily. "There are more than enough people in this world who only want cheaper goods, and don't care how they're made, or what the hidden costs are. And—much as I hate to admit it, there are those in my own Guild who would agree with him and his methods. There were some who thought he should take over all the trade here. I only hold this Hall because I've been here so long and no one wants to disturb me." He smiled wanly. "I know too many secrets, you see. But if I were gone—well, the nearest Master is the same man who erected that disaster outside of town, and no doubt that those others would have their wish."

"So who *is* doing the work for him?" the sorceress persisted.

"Cityfolk, I presume," Master Lenne said, with an inflection that made the word a curse. "All men, a mixture of young ones and old men, and he works them all, from youngest to eldest. And work is all they seem to do. They never put their noses in town, and my people are stopped at the gate, so more I can't tell you."

At that moment, the young man who had brought

them here poked his head into the hall. "Master, can we schedule in 'bout twenty horsehides?"

"What, now?" Master Lenne exclaimed. "This close to the slaughtering season? Whose?"

The young man ducked his head, uncomfortable with something about the request. "Well . . . my father's. Ye know all those handsome young horses he bought without looking at their teeth? 'Twas like you warned him, within a week, they went from fat and glossy to lank and bony. Within two, they was dead."

Master Lenne shook his head. "I told him not to trust that sharper. He obviously sold your father a lot of sick horses." He heaved himself to his feet. "I'd best get myself down to the tannery, and see what we can do. At least we can see that it isn't a total loss for him. By your leave, ladies?"

Glossy and fat . . . glossy and fat . . . Tarma nodded absently and the Master hurried out, puffing a little. There was something about those words. . . .

Then she had it; the answer. A common horse-sharper's trick—but this time it had taken a potentially deadly turn. Horses weren't the only things dying here.

"Keth," she whispered, looking around to make sure there was no one lurking within earshot. "I think Master Lenne's being poisoned."

:Poisoned?: Warrl's ears perked up. *:Yes. That would explain what I scented on him. Something sick, but not an illness.:*

But to her surprise, Kethry looked skeptical. "He doesn't look at all well, but what makes you think that he's being poisoned?"

"Those horses reminded me—there's a common

sharper's trick, to make old horses look really young, if you don't look too closely at their mouths. You feed them arsenic; not enough to kill them, just a little at a time, a little more each time you feed them. They become quiet and eat their heads off, their coats get oily, and they put on weight, which makes them look really fat and glossy. When you get to the point where you're giving them enough to cover the blade of a knife, you sell them. They lose their appetites without the poison, drop weight immediately, and they die as the poison stored in their fat gets back into their blood. If you didn't know better, you'd think they simply caught something, sickened, and died of it."

Kethry shrugged. "That explains what happened to the horses, but what does that have to do—"

"Don't you see?" Tarma exclaimed. "That's exactly the same symptoms the Master has! He's put on weight, I'll bet he's hungry all the time, he obviously feels lethargic and vaguely ill—his skin and hair are oily—"

Kethry remained silent for a moment. "What are we supposed to do about it?" she asked slowly. "It's not our Guild. It's not our fight—"

Perversely, Tarma now found herself on the side of the argument Kethry—impelled by her bond with Need—usually took. Taking the part of the stranger. "How can you say it's not our fight?" she asked, trying to keep her voice down, and surprising herself with the ferocity of her reaction. "It's our world, isn't it? Do you want more people like Lenne in charge? Or more like that so-called 'Master' Karden out there?"

It was the poisoning of the land that had decided her; no Shin'a'in could see land ruined without reacting strongly. When Master Lenne died—as he would, probably within the year—this Karden fellow would be free to poison the entire area.

And if he succeeded in bringing high profits to the Guild, the practices he espoused would spread elsewhere.

It wasn't going to happen; not if Tarma could help it.

As she saw Kethry's indifference starting to waver, she continued. "You know who has to be behind it, too! All we have to do is find out *how* Lenne is being poisoned, and link it to him!"

Kethry laughed, mockingly. "All? You have a high opinion of our abilities!"

"Yes," Tarma said firmly. "I do. So you agree?"

Kethry thought for a moment, then sighed, and shook her head. "Gods help me, but yes. I do." Then she smiled. "After all, you've indulged me often enough."

Tarma returned the smile. "Thanks, *she'enedra*. It'll be worth it. You'll see."

By the time dinner was over, however, Tarma's certainty that the task would be an easy one was gone. For one thing, both questioning and close observation had shown no way in which poison could have been slipped to Master Lenne without also poisoning the rest of the Guild. They ate and drank in common, using common utensils, serving themselves from common dishes, like one big family. Tarma and Kethry ate with them, seated at the table in the middle of the hall, and they saw that the Master ate exactly what everyone else ate; his wine was poured from the same pitchers of rough red wine as the rest of them shared.

Each member took it in turn to cook for the rest, eliminating the possibility that the poisoning could be taking place in the kitchen. Not unless every Guild member here hated the Master—and there was no sign of that.

It *could* be done by magic, of course. But Kethry was adamant that there was no sign of any magic whatsoever being performed in or around the Guild House.

"In fact," she whispered, as the Guild members gathered beside the fire with their cups and the rest of the wine, to socialize before seeking their beds, "there's a spell of some kind on the Guild House that blocks magic; low-level magic, at least." The fire crackled, and the Guild members laughed at some joke, covering her words. "I've seen this before, in other Guild Houses. It's a basic precaution against stealing Guild secrets by magic. I could break it, but it would be very obvious to another mage, if that's what we're dealing with. That spell is why I've had a headache ever since we came in the door."

But Tarma hadn't been Kethry's partner all this time without learning a few things. "Maybe it blocks real magic, but what about mind-magic? Isn't there a mind-magic you can use to move things around?"

:*There is, mind-mate,*: Warrl confirmed before Kethry could answer, his tail sweeping the flagstones with approval. Kethry added her nod to Warrl's words.

"Ladies, gentlemen," Master Lenne said at just that

moment, calling their attention to him. He stood up, winecup in hand, a lovely silver piece he had with him all through dinner. The glow of the firelight gave him a false flush of health, and he smiled as he stood, reinforcing the illusion. "I am an old man, and can't keep the late hours I used to, so I'll take my leave—and my usual nightcap."

One of the 'prentices filled his cup from the common pitcher of wine, and he moved off into the shadows, in the direction of the living quarters.

"Keep talking, and keep them from noticing we're gone," Tarma hissed to her partner, signaling Warrl to stay where he was. "I'm going to see if anything happens when he gets to his room."

Without waiting for an answer, she melted into the shadows, with Warrl taking her place right beside Kethry. There was no other light in the enormous room besides the fire in the fireplace, and Master Lenne was not paying a great deal of attention to anything that was not immediately in front of him. Still, she made herself as invisible as only a Shin'a'in could, following the Master into his quarters. *Can I assume that if someone used mind-magic around here, you would know it?* she thought in Warrl's direction, as she slipped through the doorway on Lenne's heels.

:Possibly,: he answered. *:Possibly not. I think it will be up to your own powers of observation.:*

She waited at the end of the hallway, concealed in shadows, for the Master to take his doorway so that she could see which quarters were his. When he had, she waited a little while longer, then crept soundlessly on the flagstoned floor after him, opening the same door and slipping inside. She had thought about making some pretense at wanting to talk further with the Master, but had decided against the idea. If this poisoner was using mind-magic to plant the poison, he might also be using it to tell whether or not the Master was alone.

Kethry knew more of mind-magic than she did—but Tarma had a good idea what to watch. That business about a "usual nightcap"—if the poisoner knew about this habit of Master Lenne's, it made an excellent time and place to administer the daily doses.

Then, once he's got the Master up to a certain level, he stops. The Master loses his appetite, like the horses, stops eating, and drops all the weight he put on. And the poison that was in the fat he accumulated drops into his body all at once. He dies, but by the time he dies, there's no external evidence of poisoning.

And of course, everyone would have known that the Master was ill, so this final, fatal "sickness" would come as no surprise.

Once inside the door, she found herself in a darkened room, with furniture making vague lumps in the thick shadow, silhouetted against dim light coming from yet another doorway at the other side of the room. She eased up to the new door, feeling a little ashamed and voyeuristic, and watched the Master puttering about, taking out a dressing gown, preparing for bed. The winecup sat on a little table beside a single candle near the doorway, untasted and unwatched.

Master Lenne entered yet another room just off his bedroom, and closed the door; sounds of water splashing made it obvious what that room's function was.

Tarma did not take her eyes off the cup; and in a moment, her patience was rewarded.

The surface of the wine jumped—as if something invisible had been dropped into the cup. A moment later, it appeared as if it was being stirred by a ghostly finger.

Then Master Lenne opened the door to the bedroom, and the spectral finger withdrew, leaving the wine outwardly unchanged. His eyes lighted on his winecup, but before he could take the half-dozen steps to reach it, Tarma interposed herself, catching it up.

Master Lenne started back, his eyes as wide as if she had been a spirit herself. Before he could stammer anything, she smiled.

"Your pardon, Master," she said quietly. "But I think we need to talk."

The arsenic had not completely dissolved; there was a gritty residue in the bottom of the cup that proved very effective at killing a trapped mouse, eliminating Master Lenne's doubts.

The three of them were ensconced in his parlor; he was wrapped in a robe and dressing gown, looking surprisingly vulnerable for such a big man. There was a fire in his tiny fireplace, and candles on the table between them, and the light mercilessly revealed the shadows under his eyes. "But who could be doing this?" he asked, looking from Tarma to Kethry and back again. "And why? They say that poison is a woman's weapon, but I've angered no women that I know of—"

"Not a woman's weapon, Master," Kethry said, tapping her lips thoughtfully with a fingernail. "Poison is a *coward's* weapon. It is the weapon of choice for someone who is too craven to face an enemy openly, too craven even to come into striking range of his enemy himself. It's the weapon of choice for someone who is unwilling to take personal risks, but is totally without scruples when it comes to risking others."

Tarma saw by the widening then narrowing of Master Lenne's eyes that he had come to the same conclusion they had made.

"Karden," he said flatly.

Tarma nodded, compressing her lips into a thin, hard line.

Kethry sighed and held up her hands. "That's the best bet. The problem is proving it. It's hard enough to prove an attempt at murder by real magic—but I don't think there's anyone in this entire kingdom with enough expertise at mind-magic to prove he's been using it to try to poison you. By the way, where did you get that goblet?"

Lenne seemed confused by the change in subjects. "Every Master has one; they're given to us when we achieve Mastery."

Kethry nodded, and Tarma read satisfaction in her expression. "That at least solves the question of how he knew where the poison was going. If he has the match to that goblet, that gives him a 'target' to match with yours."

"But that also compounds the problem, Greeneyes," Tarma pointed out. "If every Master has one of these, *any* Master could be a suspect. No, we aren't going to be able to bring Karden to conventional justice, I'm afraid."

Master Lenne, sick or no, was sharper than she had expected. "Conventional justice?" he said. "I assume you have something else in mind?"

Tarma picked up the now-empty goblet, and turned it in her hands, smiling at the play of light on the curving silver surface. "Just let me borrow this for a day or so," she replied noncommittally. "And we'll see if the gods—or something—can't be moved to retribution."

Kethry raised an eyebrow.

"This might not work," Kethry warned, for the hundredth time.

"Your spell might not work. It might work, and Karden might notice. He might not notice, but he might not drink the wine in his own goblet when he's through playing with it." Tarma shrugged. "Then again, it might. You tell me that mind-magic is hard work, and I am willing to bet that a sneaky bastard like this Karden gets positive glee out of drinking a toast to his enemy's death and refreshing himself at the same time when he's done every night. If this doesn't work, I try something more direct. But if it does—our problem eliminates itself."

They were outside the protected influence of the Guild House, ensconced in the common room of the closed inn. Just she and Kethry; Lenne was going through his usual after-dinner routine, but this time, he was not using his Master's goblet for his wine. That particular piece of silver resided on the table in the middle of the common room, full of wine. With a spell on the wine. . . .

Not the goblet. Kethry was taking no chances that bespelling the goblet would change it enough that Karden's mind-magic would no longer recognize it. The two of them were on the far side of the room from the goblet; far enough, Kethry hoped, that Karden would judge the goblet safely out of sight of anyone. The inn's common room was considerably bigger than Lenne's quarters.

That *was* assuming he could check for the presence or absence of people. He *might* be getting his information from a single source within the Guild House. But Kethry was of the opinion that he wasn't; that he was waiting for a moment when there were no signs of mental activity within a certain range of the goblet, but that there *was* wine in it. That, she thought, would have been the easiest and simplest way for Karden to handle the problem.

All of it was guess and hope—

Kethry hissed a warning. Something was stirring the surface of the wine in the goblet.

Something tried to drop into the wine. Tried. The wine resisted it, forming a skin under it, so that the substance, white and granular, floated in a dimpled pocket on the surface.

"*Ka'chen*," Tarma said in satisfaction. "Got you, you bastard."

The pocket of white powder rotated in the wine, as the invisible finger stirred. Quickly, Kethry's hands moved in a complex pattern; sweat beaded her brow as she muttered words under her breath. Tarma tried not to move or otherwise distract her. This was a complicated spell, for Kethry was not only trying to do the reverse of what Karden was doing, she was trying to insinuate the poison back into *his* wine, grain by grain, so that he would not notice what she was doing.

Until, presumably, it was too late.

It was like watching a bit of snow melt; as the tiny white pile rotated, it slowly vanished, until the last speck winked out, leaving only the dark surface of the wine.

Tarma approached the cup cautiously. The spectral "finger" withdrew hastily, and she picked the goblet up.

"Well?" she said, "can I bet my life on this?"

Kethry nodded wearily, her heart-shaped face drawn with exhaustion. "It's as safe to drink as it was when I poured it," she replied, pulling her hair out of her eyes. "I can guarantee it went straight into the model-cup. What happened after that?" She shrugged eloquently. "We'll find out tomorrow."

Tarma lifted the cup in an ironic salute. "In that case—here's to tomorrow."

"Now don't forget what I told you," Kethry said firmly, from her superior position above the Master's head, where she perched in Hellsbane's saddle. "I may have pulled most of the poison from you with that spell, but you're still sick. You're suffering the damage it caused, and that isn't going to go away overnight."

Master Lenne nodded earnestly, shading his eyes against the morning sun, and handed Kethry a saddleroll of the finest butter-soft leather to fasten at her cantle. Leather like that—calfskin tanned to the suppleness and texture of fine velvet—was worth a small fortune. Tarma already had an identical roll behind her saddle.

"I plan to rest and keep my schedule to a minimum," Lenne said, as obedient as a child. "To tell you the truth, now that I no longer have to worry about Karden taking my trade and exerting his influence on the Guild as a whole—"

"So tragic, poisoning himself with his own processes," Tarma said dryly. "I guess that will prove to the Guild that the safe old ways are the best."

Master Lenne flushed and looked down for a moment. When he looked back up, his eyes were troubled. "I suppose it would do no good to reveal the truth, would it?"

"No good, and a lot of harm," Kethry said firmly. "If you must, tell only those you trust. No one else." She looked off into the distance. "I don't like taking the law into my own hands—"

"When the law fails, people of conscience have to take over, Greeneyes," Tarma said firmly,. "It's either that, or lie down and let yourself be walked on. Shin'a'in *weave* rugs; we don't imitate them."

"I don't like it either, ladies," Master Lenne said quietly. "Even knowing that my own life hung on this. But—"

"But there are no easy answers, Master," Tarma interrupted him. "There are cowards and the brave. Dishonest and honest. I prefer to foster the latter and remove the former. As my partner would tell you, Shin'a'in are great believers in expediency." She leveled a penetrating glance at her partner. "And if we're going to make Hawk's Nest before sundown, we need to leave now."

Master Lenne took the hint, and backed away from the horses. "Shin'a'in—" he said suddenly, as Tarma turned her horse's head. "I said that poison was a woman's weapon. You have shown me differently. A woman's weapon is that she thinks—and then she acts, without hesitation."

:*Usually, she thinks*,: Warrl said dryly. :*When I remind her to.*:

Put a gag on it, Furface, Tarma thought back at him. And she saluted Master Lenne gravely, and sent her warsteed up the last road to Hawksrest, with Kethry and Warrl keeping pace beside her.

THE TALISMAN

This story sprang out of a complaint that bad fantasy always seems to rely on the magic thingamajig to get the hero out of trouble. Seemed to me that a magic thingamajig could get someone into more trouble than it would get him out of. As always, Tarma and Kethry rely as much on intelligence and quick thinking as magic and swordplay to get them out of trouble.

It was hard for Kethry to remember that winter would be over in two months at the most. The entire world seemed made up of crusted snow; it even lay along the bare branches of trees. From this vantage point, atop a rocky, scrub-covered hill, it looked as if winter had taken hold of the land and would never let go. The entire world had turned into an endless series of winter-dormant, forested hills, hills they plodded over with no sign that there was an end to them. Although the road that threaded these hills bore unmistakable signs of frequent use, they hadn't seen a single soul in the past two days. Kethry stamped her numb feet on snow packed rock-hard and frozen into an obstacle course of ruts, trying to get a little feeling back into them. She shaded her eyes against snow glare and stared down the hillside while her mule pawed despondently at the ice crust beside the trail, hoping for a scrap of grass and unable to break through.

She heard the creaking of Tarma's saddle as her partner dismounted. "Goddess!" the Shin'a'in croaked. "I'm bloody freezing!"

"You're always freezing," Kethry replied absently, trying to make out if the smudge on the horizon was smoke or just another cloud. "Except when I'm roasting. Where are we? Is that smoke I'm seeing out there, or a figment of my imagination?"

There was a rattling of paper at her right elbow as Tarma took out their map. "I could make a very bad pun, but I won't," she said. "Yes, it's smoke, and I'd guess we're here—"

Kethry took her watering eyes off that faraway promise of habitation, and turned to see where on the map Tarma thought they were. It wasn't exciting. If the Shin'a'in was right, they were about a candlemark's ride away from a flyspeck too small even to be called a village, marked on the map only with the name "Potter," and the symbol for "public well."

"No inn?" the sorceress asked wistfully.

"No inn," her partner sighed, folding the map and tucking it back inside the inner pocket of her coat. "Sorry about that, Greeneyes."

"Figures," Kethry said sourly. "When we've finally got the money to *pay* for inns, we can't find any."

Tarma shrugged. "That's fate, I suppose. We'll have to see if we can induce some householder to part with hearth- or barn-space for a little coin. Could be worse. If it hadn't been for everything that happened in Mournedealth, we wouldn't *have* the coin."

"True—though I can think of easier ways to have gotten it."

"Hmm." Tarma made a noncommittal sound, and swung back up into her saddle. Kethry cast a glance at her out of the corner of her eye and wondered what she was thinking.

We're still not—quite—a team. And she worries about me a lot more than I think is necessary.

"I don't regret any of it," she said then, trying to sound as if she had intended to continue the sentence. "It's just that I'm *lazy*. That little set-to with my former spouse was a whole lot more work than I would have preferred!"

Tarma's grating laugh floated out over the hillside, and Kethry relaxed a bit.

"I'll try and spare you, next time," the Swordsworn said, nudging her mare with her heels and sending Kessira picking her way through the ruts down the hill. Kethry could have sworn as they passed that the elegant little mare had her lip curled in distaste. "If you promise to give me a little more warning. This could all have been taken care of quite handily by waylaying Wethes and your brother and—ah—'persuading' them that everyone would be happier if we were left alone."

"I thought you Kal'enedral were bound by honor," Kethry mocked, as Rodi lurched and slipped his way down the hill in Kessira's wake.

"*Her* honor, not man's honor," Tarma corrected, not taking her attention from the path in front of her. "And in matters where Her honor has no bearing, we're bound by expediency. I'm rather *fond* of expediency. It saves a world of problems."

"Except when you have to explain your notion of

'expedient' to the City Guard." Rodi took the last of the slope in a rush that made Kethry grit her teeth and cling to the saddle-bow, hoping the mule knew what he was doing.

"You have a point," the Shin'a'in admitted.

It took most of the remaining daylight—*not* the single candlemark the map promised—to get to the cluster of houses alongside the road. That was because of the condition of the road itself; as hummocked and rutted as the hill had been. Tarma didn't want to push the beasts at all, for fear they'd break legs misstepping. So they picked their way to "Potter" with maddening slowness.

So maddening that at first Kethry did not note the increasing pressure of her geas-blade "Need" on her mind.

She was tightly bound to the sword; as bound to it as she was to her partner, and *that* binding had the blessing of Tarma's own Goddess on it. The sword repaid that binding by healing her of anything short of a death-wound in an incredibly short period of time, and by granting her a master's ability at wielding it—a fact that had saved *Tarma's* skin now and again, since no one expected blade-expertise from a mage. But Kethry paid for those gifts—for any time there was a woman in need of help within the blade's sensing-range—and Kethry had not yet determined the limits of that range—she *had* to help. Regardless of whether or not helping was a prudent move—or going to be repaid.

Hardly the most ideal circumstances for a would-be mercenary.

Need's "call" was like the insistent pressure of a headache about to happen—except when the situation was truly life-or-death critical, in which case it had been known to cause pressure so close to pain as made no difference. Tarma must have learned to read or sense *that* in the few months they'd been together—she suddenly looked back over her shoulder almost as soon as Kethry herself became aware of the blade's prodding, and frowned.

"Tell me that expression on your face isn't what I think it is," the hawk-faced Shin'a'in said plaintively.

"I would," Kethry sighed, "but I'd be lying."

Tarma shook her head, and turned her ice-blue eyes to the settlement ahead of them. "Joyous. Well, at least there shouldn't be much trouble figuring out *who* and *what*. If there're more than a dozen females down there, I'll eat a horseshoe."

Kethry urged her mule forward until she rode knee-to-knee with her brown-clad partner. "I'll say what you're undoubtedly thinking. If there's a problem in so small a settlement, everybody is likely to know about it. Which means everybody may well have a vested interest in keeping it quiet. *Or* may like things the way they are." The vague splotch beside the road ahead of them resolved itself into a cluster of buildings as their beasts brought them nearer. A few moments more, and they could make out the red-roofed wellhouse, set apart from the rest of the buildings.

"*Or* may simply resent outsiders interfering," Tarma finished glumly. "There are times—heads up, *she'enedra*. We're being met."

They were indeed. Even as Tarma spoke, something separated itself from the side of the wellhouse. Shrouded in layers of clothing, for a moment it looked more bearlike than human. But as they neared, they could see that waiting beside the public well was a stoop-shouldered old man, gnarled and weathered as a mountain tree, with a thick thatch of snow-white hair tucked under a knitted cap the same bright red as the wellhouse roof.

"Evening," Tarma returned the greeting, crossing her wrists on her saddlebow and leaning forward—though *not* dismounting. "What kind of hospitality could a few coins purchase a tired traveler around here, goodman?"

He looked them up and down with bright black eyes peeping from beneath brows like overhanging snowbanks—eyes that missed nothing. "Well-armed travelers," he observed mildly.

Tarma laughed, and a startled crow flapped out of the thatch of one of the houses. "Travelers who aren't fools, goodman. And two women traveling alone who *couldn't* take care of themselves *would* be fools."

The old man chuckled. "Point taken, point taken." He edged a little closer. "Be any good with that bow?"

Tarma considered this for a moment. "A fair shot," she acknowledged.

"Well, then," the oldster replied tugging his knit cap a bit farther down over his ears. "Coin we got no use for till spring an' the traders come—but a bit of game, now—that'd be welcome. Say, hearth and meal for hunting?"

Tarma nodded, and seemed satisfied with the tentative bargain, for she dismounted. Kethry was only too glad to follow her example.

"I can't conjure game out of an empty forest, old man," Tarma said warningly as he led them to a roomy shed that already sheltered a donkey and three goats.

"There's game, there's game. I wouldn't set ye to a fool's task. Just we be no hunters here." He helped them fork hay into the shed; for bedding the mare and the mule would have to make do with the bracken already layering the floor.

"Not hunters?" Kethry said, puzzled, as they took their packs and followed their guide into the nearest house. "Out here in the middle of nowhere? What on earth do you—"

The answer to her question was self-evident as soon as the old man opened the door. The house was a single enormous room, combining sleeping, living and working space. It was the working space that occupied the lion's share of the dwelling. In one corner stood a huge sink and pump, several wooden boxes of clay, and a potter's wheel. Various ceramic items were ranged on two long wooden tables in the center of the room according to what stage they were in, from first drying to final glazing. The back wall was entirely brick, with several iron doors in it. It radiated heat even at this distance; it had to be a kiln of some sort, Kethry reckoned. Most of the windows were covered with oiled parchment, but there was a single glass window in the wall opposite; directly beneath that was a smaller workbench with pots and brushes, and a half-painted vase. The rest of the living arrangements were scattered haphazardly about, wherever there was room for them.

It was, to Kethry's mind, stiflingly warm, but Tarma immediately threw off her coat with a sigh of pure bliss.

"Put yer bedrolls wherever, ladies," the old man said. "There's porridge as supper."

Kethry rummaged out a packet of some of their

dried fruit and tossed it to the oldster, who caught it deftly, grinned his thanks, and added it to the pot just inside one of those iron doors.

"Directly supper's finished, we'll be gettin' visitors," their host told them, as they found places to spread their bedrolls on the clay-stained, rough board floor. "I be Egon Potter; rest of the folks out here be kin or craft-kin."

Kethry's curiosity had turned her attention to the half-finished pottery. It was more than simple pots and bowls, she realized as soon as she had a good look at it. It was really exquisite work, the equal or superior of anything she'd ever seen for sale in Mournedealth.

"Why—" she began.

"—are we way out here, back of the end of the world?" Egon interrupted her. "The clay, lady. No match for it anywhere else. Got three kinds of clay right here; got fuel for the kilns; got all winter t'work on the fancy stuff an' all summer t' trade. What else we need?"

Tarma laughed. "Not a damned thing else, Guildmaster." At his raised eyebrow and quirky, half-toothless grin she laughed again. "I've always wondered where the best of the Wrightguild porcelain and stoneware came from—it certainly wasn't being made in Kata'shin'a'in. You think I can't recognize the work of the Master when I see it?"

"Then there be more about you than shows on th' surface, swordlady. But you tol' me that, didn' ye?"

"Oh, aye, that I did." They matched grins in some kind of wordless exchange that baffled Kethry, then the Shin'a'in edged her way past the crowded worktable to the oldster's side. "Here. Let me give you a hand with that porridge."

As darkness fell, Kethry came to appreciate old Egon's craftsmanship even more, for he lit oil lamps around the room with shades of porcelain so thin that the light glowed through it easily. And when the first of the lamps was alight, the rest of the inhabitants of the little settlement began to arrive.

They crowded about the newcomers, treating them with friendly reserve, asking questions, but free enough with their own answers. Fairly soon everyone had found space on the hearth, and Kethry was able to examine them at her leisure. They seemed amiable enough. None of the women seemed to be in *any* distress. In fact, it didn't look to Kethry as if there were anything at all wrong here—and this despite Need's unvarying pressure on the back of her mind.

Finally, while Tarma entertained the company with some Shin'a'in tale or other, the sorceress edged over to where old Egon was sitting alone a little off to one side.

He nodded to her, but waited for her to speak. She cleared her throat a little, then said, trying not to sound awkward, "Egon, is everyone in your settlement here?"

He seemed surprised by her question. "Oh, aye; all but the little ones. Well—barring one."

This sounded a little more promising. "One?" she prompted.

His eyes went wary. "Well—she bain't a guildsman. Stranger. Settled here, oh, three or four winters ago. She don't have much t' do with us, we don't have much t' do with her. Unchancy sort." Egon blinked, slowly. "Trades with us, betimes. I think she be grubbin' about in the ruins, yonder. Bits of metal she trades, old stuff, gone t' powder mostly, but good for makin' glazes."

Something about this "stranger" evidently made Egon more than a little uneasy. Kethry could read that in his shuttered expression, and the careful choice he made of his words.

"Are the ruins forbidden, or something?" she asked, trying to pinpoint his uneasiness.

"Forbidden?" He flashed her a startled glance, and chuckled. "Great Kernos, no! It's just—she seems witchy, like, but she ain't never *done* nothin' witchy." He gave her a sidelong glance, as if gauging her response to that. "It's like she was looking for something out there and mad as hops 'cause she ain't finding it. 'Cept lately she been acting like she had. Her name's—"

The door opened, and a bundled figure half-stepped, and was half-windblown, into the circle of light. She blinked for a moment, her eyes sunken into pale, pudgy cheeks, her flabby arms hugging her fur cloak tightly about her.

She'd put on so much weight since Kethry had last seen her that at first she didn't recognize her former schoolmate.

Then— "Mara?" she said into the silence the woman's abrupt arrival had imposed on the group.

The woman whirled; peered past the heads of those nearest her at Kethry. Her mouth worked soundlessly for a moment; one plump, pasty hand flew to her throat—then she turned and bolted back the way she had come in a clumsy run.

The door slammed behind her. The rest of those gathered sat in embarrassed silence.

Finally Egon self-consciously cleared his throat. " 'Tis a bit late, and we all have work, come the morning light. . . ."

His kin and fellow guildsmen were not slow at taking the hint. Before too very long the house was silent, and empty of all but Egon and the two women.

There seemed no way to break that silence, and after a few halfhearted attempts at conversation, Egon excused himself and went to bed.

Kethry took a long while falling asleep, and not because of the unfamiliar surroundings. Mara Yveda was the *last* person she expected to see out here.

I wondered where she went, after she'd disappeared from White Winds. Poor Mara. She was so certain that we were hiding something from her—that control of magic was just a matter of knowing the right words, having the right talisman. . . .

I'll never forget the night she ran off. Right after she stole Master Loren's staff—then found out the only thing that was unusual about it was that it was cut to exactly the right height to most comfortably help him with his lame leg.

She broke it in two when it wouldn't magic anything up for her. And then—she ran away.

She would never believe that power isn't a matter of "magic," it's a matter of discipline. . . .

She's the one that's in trouble. She's found something, I know she has, and she's gotten into trouble over it. What's more, Egon knows it, too.

So what do I do about it?

She fell asleep finally, without being able to come to any conclusion.

Kethry watched her partner dress the next morning, still in a decidedly unsettled state of mind.

"Swordlady," Egon said hesitantly, as Tarma prepared to set off at dawn to make good her side of the bargain, "there's something I need to tell you. About the game."

Tarma didn't even stop lacing up her boots. "Go ahead," she said. "I'm listening."

"There's a bear about."

Now she left her lacing, to raise her head and stare at him. "A what? Are you sure? That—that's hardly usual."

"Aye," the old man replied, shifting from one foot to the other. "But we've seen it about, not more than a day or two ago."

Tarma took a moment to secure the lacings, and straightened up, her face dead sober. "Do you have any notion what that means, that there's a bear, awake and walking this deep into winter?"

Egon shook his head.

"That is a very *sick* bear, Egon. Either it didn't eat enough to keep it going through winter-sleep, or something woke it far too early, and only illness can do that. In either case, its body is trying to make it go down for sleeping, and it's going completely against those instincts. It's going to die, Egon—but before it does, it'll be half mad with starvation. It could be very dangerous to you and yours."

The old man shook his head. "It's left us alone; we're minded to leave it alone. Don't kill it, sword-lady. Leave it bide. Deer, boar, even a mess of rabbit or bird—just—not the bear."

Tarma checked the condition of every arrow in her quiver before attaching it to her belt. Then she looked at Egon and frowned. "You're not doing that beast any favor, old man."

Egon's face set stubbornly. "Not the bear."

She shrugged. "On your head. By the time it's trouble, we'll be gone past calling us back." She half-turned to face her partner. "I should be back by afternoon. One more night here, then we'll be off in the morning, if that's all right with you."

Kethry smiled. "Who am I to complain about another night under shelter? Good hunting."

"Thanks, Greeneyes." The Shin'a'in slipped out the door, leaving Kethry and the Guildmaster alone, sitting across the worktable from one another. The silence between them deepened and grew heavier by the minute. The sorceress stared at her hands, trying to decide what to say—and whether now was the right time to say it.

Finally, when Kethry couldn't stand it any longer, she opened her mouth.

"About that bear—" she began.

Egon spoke at exactly the same moment. "Lady, be you—"

They looked at each other and laughed shakily. Kethry nodded, gesturing to Egon that he should speak first.

"Lady, I wasn't sure, you wearin' steel and all, but then seemed you know Mara—be you witchy? A sorceress, belike?"

"Yes," Kethry said slowly, wondering if he was going to be angry at the idea of having sheltered a mage without knowing it. There were some who would be. Mages were not universally welcomed.

"Thank the God," Egon breathed fervently—

Oh, terrific. He isn't going to throw me out, but—

"It's that Mara, lady. I tol' you she been pokin' about in them ruins? Seemed like maybe she found somethin'. Them ruins, there's stories that the people there was witchy, too. Shape-changers." Egon swallowed. "We—we think maybe Mara found something of theirs."

Kethry put fact on top of surmise, and made a guess. "You think Mara's the bear."

He looked relieved, and nodded. "Aye. Exactly that. We figure maybe she found some kind of witchy thing of theirs, what let her shape-change, too. Now she's strange, but she bain't *bad*, or bain't been before. But she's got stranger since we started seein' the bear. There be bear tracks about her house—she *says* 'tis 'cause the bear comes to her feedin', that it's harmless if it's left be—but we don' think so. So—I dunno lady, I dunno what t' ask, like."

"You want to know if she's dangerous?" Kethry asked. She got up from her seat and began pacing, her hands clasped behind her. "Yes, dammit, she's dangerous all right. The more so because I don't think she ever really listened to a single word anyone ever told her at mage-school. Do you know why most mages *don't* shapechange? Why they use illusions instead?"

Egon shook his head dumbly, his wrinkled face twisted into a knot of concern.

"Because when you shapechange, you *become* the thing you've changed to. You're subject to *its* instincts, *its* limitations. *Including the fact that there's not enough room in a beast's head for a human mind.* That usually doesn't matter, much. Not so long as you don't spend more than an hour or two as a beast. You don't lose much of your humanity, and you can *probably* get it back when you revert. But it's not guaranteed that you will, and the stronger the animal's instincts, the more of yourself you'll lose."

"She been spendin' whole days as bear, we think. She don' come t' door when a body calls till after sundown," Egon whispered hoarsely.

"And at a time of the year when bear instincts are strongest." Kethry twisted the Shin'a'in oath-ring on her left hand. "No wonder she put on weight. Bears go into a feeding frenzy in the fall—and she *can't* have gained as much as a bear needs to winter-sleep. No wonder she looked like hell." Abruptly she stopped pacing, and went to her bedroll, picking up the sword-belt that held Need and strapping the blade over her breeches and tunic.

"Lady? What be you—"

"Oh, don't worry, Egon." Kethry turned to smile at him wanly. "I'm not going to use this on her."

For one thing, I don't think it would let me.

"I'm going to go talk to her," the sorceress continued. "Maybe, just maybe, I can help her."

She must be being torn nearly in two by now, Kethry thought unhappily, as she, in turn, slipped out into the dawn-gilded, frozen air. *Caught between the bear and the woman—if I can get her to take Need, I think the blade can rebalance her body for her. I hope. I'm no Healer, and that's what she needs most right now. That assumes she'll let me, of course.*

She picked her way across the lumps of frozen snow to the farthest house of the cluster—a cabin, really. It had never been intended to be used for anything more than living quarters, unlike the rest of the dwellings in the settlement. That cabin was Mara's, so Egon had said. It looked deserted.

Kethry pounded on the door for several moments, and got no answer.

With my luck—

She circled around to the back and found what she'd been dreading. The back entrance was unlatched; the cabin was empty. And among the many tracks leaving and entering the cabin from the rear, there were no *human* footprints among them. Only the half-melted and near-shapeless tracks of a small bear.

Damn!

So many tracks suggested that Mara had fallen into a pattern. And that was bad; it meant she wasn't thinking in her bear-form, she was just acting. Then again, that she was following a pattern meant that if Kethry followed the old tracks, she'd probably be able to find Mara along the trail she'd established.

Whether or not she'd be able to reason with her—

I don't have a choice, Kethry decided. *That's why Need's been after me. Mara's going to get trapped in her bear-shape—and she's going to die.*

The trail took her deeply into the woods; without the trail, Kethry knew she'd have been lost. There were no signs of any habitation, no traces of the hand of man in this direction—except for certain rock outcroppings that didn't quite look natural. Gradually, as the sun rose higher and crept toward the zenith, it dawned on Kethry that these outcroppings were becoming more frequent, as if they marked some kind of long-vanished roadway.

She's going out to these "ruins." She must be going there every day. But why? And why in bear-form?

She was never to have an answer to that question, because as she rounded the torn-up, snow-covered roots of a fallen tree, something stepped out of the shelter of a cluster of pines to block her progress.

"You!" Mara spat. "You've come to steal it, haven't you?"

Her eyes were dull and deeply sunken; her hair was lank and unwashed. As she lumbered clumsily toward Kethry, the sorceress got a whiff of an unpleasant reek—half unwashed clothing and stale sweat, half an animallike musk.

"Mara, I—" Kethry swallowed. *If I say I haven't got the vaguest notion what she's talking about, she'll know I'm lying.* "—my partner and I are here by merest chance. We're on our way down to the Dhorisha Plains. Mara, I'll be blunt; you look awful. That's why Egon asked me to follow you. He's worried about you. Are you ill? Can I help?"

Mara's hands came up to her throat. "Liar! *He* wants it, too! He sent you to take it away from me!"

Kethry raised her chin and looked squarely into those mad, glazed eyes. "Mara, Egon is a Master craftsman. He doesn't *need* magic. And *I* don't need some stupid trinket to shape-change; I can do it myself. I don't because it's dangerous—"

"Oh, yes, I remember you! Dear, bright, *pretty* Kethry! You never needed anything, did you? They *gave* you everything you ever wanted—power, magic, secrets—all those old men just fell over themselves to give you what they kept from me, didn't they? And the young men gave you—other things— didn't they?" Mara's face contorted into a snarling mask of hate. "Well, I've got secrets now, secrets *they* tell me. They made me their lover, just like those old men made you—they come to me when I change, and they make love to me, and they whisper their secrets—"

As she babbled on about her "secrets" and her

"lovers," Kethry realized with a sense of growing horror what must have happened. She'd changed, possibly for the first time, during mating season. And now she had convinced herself that the male bears that had mated with her were the long-gone shape-changing builders of the ruins—

Never particularly stable, perhaps it had been the shock of mating as an animal—and being unable to cope with it—that had pushed her over the edge.

"—well, you can't have it!" Mara shrieked at the top of her lungs. "It's mine, it's mine, it's—"

The words blurred, the voice deepened, the shapeless bundle of fur took on a shape. The words were lost in the roar of the enraged bear that balanced manlike on hindlegs, and advanced—no longer clumsy—on Kethry.

"Mara—*Mara!*"

There was an oddly shaped metal pendant slung about the bear's neck on a blackened thong. Kethry *reached* for it with her own magic, to try and nullify it—and met nothing.

This "talisman" was not magic at all! Mara's shape-changing was not the result of some ancient sorcery; it was only that she *believed* the medallion could work the change.

And in magic, as Kethry had often told her partner, belief is the most important component.

"Mara, I don't *want* your talisman! It's worthless—"

The bear ignored the words, dropping to all fours and continuing to advance, saliva dripping from her snarling jaws.

Kethry flung a sleeping-spell at the shape-changer. It was the most powerful spell she had in her depleted arsenal at the moment. She'd used so much trying to escape Wethes' makeshift prison—

The bear ignored the spell; ignored the mage-barrier she tried to erect to hold it off.

She convinced herself she can change shape—she probably convinced herself she can defend against spells, too—

So she really can.

Kethry stumbled backward, stumbled and fell over the blade strapped to her side.

Need!

She tried to draw the sword—

—and discovered that she couldn't. It *would not* clear the sheath. It wouldn't allow itself to be used against a woman.

The bear reared up on hind legs again, as Kethry backed into the tangle of roots and frozen earth and found herself trapped. She drew her belt knife; a futile enough gesture, but she was *not* going to go down without a fight.

And an arrow skimmed over her right shoulder to bury itself in the bear's throat.

The bear screamed, and pawed at the shaft, and a second joined the first—then a third, this one thudding into the shaggy chest.

A fourth landed beside the third.

The bear screamed again, and Kethry hid her face in her hands. When she looked again, the bear was down, its eyes glazing in death, a half-dozen arrows neatly targeting every vulnerable spot.

"Next time you take a walk in the woods, lady," Tarma said harshly, grabbing her by her shoulder and hauling her to her feet, "don't go alone. I take it this isn't what it looks like?"

"It's Mara," Kethry replied, trying to control her shaking limbs. "She learned to shape-change—"

The Shin'a'in nodded. "Uh-huh; what I thought. Especially when you didn't give her the business-end of Need. Hanging about with a magicker taught me enough to put two and two together once in a while on my own." She prodded the stiffening carcass with the tip of her bow. "She going to change back? I'd hate to get strung up for murder."

Kethry held back tears and shook her head. "No. She froze herself into that shape—Goddess, *how* did you manage to get here in time?"

"I got Egon's deer almost before I left cleared lands; came back, and found you gone." The Shin'a'in poked at the medallion around the bear's neck. "What's this? Is this—"

"No," Kethry said bitterly. "It's just a bit of trash she found. She was so busy looking for 'secrets' that she never learned the secrets in her own mind. *That's* what killed her, not your arrows."

"That could be said about an awful lot of people." Tarma cocked an eye up at the sun. "What say we make a polite farewell and get the hell out of here?"

"Expediency?" Kethry asked, trying not to sound harsh.

Tarma shrugged.

The sorceress looked down at the corpse. She'd offered Mara her help; it had been refused. Staying to be accused of murder—or worse—wouldn't bring her back.

Expediency.

"Let's go," Kethry said.

A TALE OF HEROES

(Based on an idea by Robert Chilson)

Rob Chilson and I were in a discussion at a convention about fantasy clichés; he wondered why no one ever bothered to point out the viewpoint of the poor chambermaid in all of the stories about iron-thewed, rock-headed Barbarian Swordsmen. That was an idea I couldn't pass up. And who better to help with the concept than Tarma and Kethry?

As for this particular chambermaid's happy ending—well, *I* wouldn't be particularly suited to Tarma's life either. I hate camping, bugs, cold, and wet; I don't much care for half-burned food cooked over a campfire, and if I didn't have some form of vision correction, I'd be legally blind. My personal idea of "the way things should be" is that all people be allowed the same opportunity for a life that suits them, period. If that happens to be becoming a mother or being an astronaut, both are important.

And if those same people don't make the most of the opportunities that are given them, that's their own problem.

"Miles out of our way, and still not a sign of anything out of the ordinary," Tarma grumbled, her harsh voice carrying easily above the clopping of their horses' hooves. "For certain no sign of any women in distress. Are you—"

"Absolutely certain," Kethry, the swordswoman's partner, replied firmly, eyes scanning the fields to either side of them. Her calf-length buff-colored robe, mark of the traveling sorceress, was covered in road dust, and she squinted in an attempt to keep that dust out of her eyes. The chilly air was full of the scent of dead leaves and dried grass. "It's not something I can ignore, you know. If my blade Need says there are women in trouble in this direction, there's no chance of doubt: they exist. Surely you know that by *now*."

It had been two days since they diverted from the main road onto this one, scarcely wider than a cart track. The autumn rains were sure to start before long; cold rains Tarma had hoped to avoid by getting them on the way to their next commission well ahead of time. Since they'd turned off the caravan road, they'd seen little sign of habitation, only rolling, grassy hills and a few scattered patches of forest, all of them brown and sere. The bright colors of fall were not to be found in this region. When frost came, the vegetation here muted into shades more like those of Tarma's worn leathers and Kethry's traveling robes than the carnival-bright colors of the farther north. In short, the trip thus far had been uneventful and deadly dull.

"I swear, sometimes that sword of yours causes more grief than she saves us from," Tarma snorted. "Magicians!"

Kethry smiled; she knew very well that the Shin'a'in swordswoman was only trying to get a rise out of her. The magic blade called "Need" that she carried had saved both their lives more than once. It had the peculiar property of giving weapons' expertise to a mage, or protecting a swordswoman from the worst magics; it could heal injuries and illness in a fraction of normal time—but it could only be used by a female. And, as with all magics, there was a price attached to Need's gifts. Her bearer must divert to aid any woman in need of help, no matter how far out of her intended way the sword pulled her. "You weren't saying that a few weeks ago, when Need and I Healed that lung-wound of yours."

" 'That was then, this is now,' " her hawk-visaged partner quoted. " 'The moment is never the same twice.' " A bit of fresher breeze carried the dust of the road away, but chilled both of them a little more.

Kethry shook amber hair out of her eyes, her round face full of amusement. "O wise sister-mine, do you have a proverb for *everything?*"

Tarma chuckled. "Damn near—Greeneyes, these fields are cultivated—left to go fallow just this year. I think there's a farm up ahead. Want to chance seeing if the owner'll let us pass the night in his barn? Looks like rain, and I'd rather sleep dry without you having to exhaust magics to keep us that way."

Kethry scanned on ahead of them for possible danger, using magic to smell out magic. "It seems safe enough—let's chance it. Maybe we can get some clue about what Need's calling us to. I don't like the way the air's chilling down, sybarite that I am. I'd rather sleep warm, if we can."

Their ugly, mottled-gray battlemares smelled the presence of other horses, even as the sorceress finished her sentence. Other horses meant food and water at the least, and a dry and warm stable at best. With the year being well into autumn a warm stable was nothing to scorn. They picked up their pace so abruptly that the huge black "wolf" that trotted by the side of the swordswoman's mount was left behind in the dust. He barked a surprised protest and scrambled to catch up.

"That's what you get for daydreaming, lazybones," Tarma laughed, her ice-blue eyes slitted against the rising dust. "Don't just look stupid. Get up here, or we'll leave you!"

The lupine creature—whose shoulder easily came as high as Tarma's waist—gathered himself and sprang. He landed on the carrying pad of stuffed leather just behind her saddle; the mare grunted at the impact, but was unsurprised at it. She simply waited for the beast to settle himself and set his retractile claws into the leather pad, then moved into a ground-devouring lope. The sorceress' mount matched her stride for stride.

Strands of raven hair escaped from Tarma's braid and blew into her eyes, but didn't obscure her vision so much that she missed the sudden movement in the bushes at the side of the road, and the small, running figure that set off across the fields. "Looks like the scouts are out," she grinned at her partner. "We've been spotted."

"What? Oh—" Kethry caught sight of the child as he (she?) vaulted over a hedge and vanished. "Wonder what he made of us?"

"We're about to find out." From the other side of the hedge strode a heavy, muscular farmer, as brown as his fields; one who held his scythe with the air of someone who knew what an effective weapon it could be. Both women pulled their horses to a stop and waited for him to reach the road.

"Wayfarer's Peace, landsman," Tarma said when he was near enough to hear her. She held both hands out empty. He eyed her carefully.

"On oath to the Warrior, Shin'a'in?" he replied.

"Oath given." She raised one eyebrow in surprise. "You know Shin'a'in, landsman? We're a long way from the plains."

"I've traveled." He had relaxed visibly when Tarma had given her pledge. "Soldiered a bit. Aye, I know Shin'a'in—and I know a Sworn One when I see one. 'Tisn't often you see Shin'a'in, and less often you see Swordsworn oathed to outlander."

"So you recognize blood-oathed, too? You're full of surprises, landsman." Tarma's level gaze held him; her blue eyes had turned cold. "So many I wonder if we are safe with you—"

He raised his left arm; burned onto the back of the wrist was a five-spoked wheel. Kethry relaxed with a sigh, and her partner glanced sidelong at her.

"And I know the Wheel-bound," the sorceress replied. " 'May your future deeds balance all.' "

" 'And your feet ever find the Way,' " he finished, smiling at last. "I am called Landric."

"I'm Tarma—my companion is Kethry. Just out of curiosity—how did you know we were she'enedran?" Tarma asked as he moved up to walk beside their mounts. "Even among Shin'a'in, oathsisters aren't that common."

He was a big man, and muscular. He wore simple brown homespun, but the garments were well made. His hair and eyes were a few shades darker than his sun-darkened skin. He swung the scythe up gracefully out of the way, and though he eyed Tarma's beast-companion warily, he made no moves as though he were afraid of it. Tarma gave him points for that.

"Had a pair of oathbound mercenaries in my company," he replied, "That was before I took the Wheel, of course. Brother and sister, and both Swordsworn as well, as I recall. When you held up your hands, I recognized the crescent palm-scar, and I couldn't imagine a Shin'a'in traveling with any but her oathsister. If you've a wish to guest with me, be welcome—even though—" his face clouded, "—I fear my hearth's cold comfort now."

Kethry had a flash of intuition. "Grief, landsman—your Wheelmate?"

"She waits the next turning. I buried what the monster left of her at Spring planting, these six months agone."

Their host walked beside their mounts, and told his tale with little embellishment.

"—And there was no time for me to get a weapon—and little enough I could have done even had there been time. So when the monster headed for the babe, she ran between it and him; and the creature took her instead of the child, just as she'd intended." There was heavily veiled pain still lurking in his voice.

"Damn," Tarma said, shaking her head in awe at the dead woman's bravery. "Not sure I'd've had the guts to do that. What's this thing like anyway?"

"Like no creature I've ever heard tell of. Big; bigger than a dozen horses put together, covered with bristly brown hair—a head that's all teeth and jaws, six legs. Got talons as long as my hand, too. We think it's gotten away from some mage somewhere; it looks like something a nasty mind would put together for the fun of it—no offense meant, sorceress."

"None taken." Kethry met his brown eyes with

candor. "Lady knows my kind has its share of evil-doers. Go on."

"Well, the thing moves like lightning, too. Outruns even the lord's beasts with no problem. Its favorite prey is women and children; guess it doesn't much care for food that might be able to fight back a little."

Kethry caught her partner's eye. *Told you,* she signaled in hand-speech. *Need knows.*

"The Lord Havirn hasn't been able to do anything about it for the time being, so until he can get a hero to kill it, he's taken the 'dragon solution' with it."

" 'Dragon solution'?" Tarma looked askance.

"He's feeding it, in hopes it'll be satisfied enough to leave everyone else alone," Kethry supplied. "Livestock—I hope?" She looked down at the farmer where he walked alongside her horse. He kept up with the beast with no trouble; Kethry was impressed. It took a strong walker to keep up with Hellsbane.

He shook his head. "People. It won't touch animals. So far he's managed to use nothing but criminals, but the jails are emptying fast, and for some reason nobody seems much interested in breaking the law anymore. And being fed doesn't completely stop it from hunting, as I well know to my grief. He's posted the usual sort of reward; half his holdings and his daughter, you know the drill."

"Fat lot of good either would do us," Tarma muttered in Shin'a'in. Kethry smothered a smile.

They could see his farmstead in the near distance; from here it looked well-built and prosperous; of baked brick and several rooms in size. The roof was thatch, and in excellent repair. There were at least five small figures gathered by the door of the house.

"These are my younglings," he said with pride and a trace of worry. "Childer—" he called to the little group huddled just by the door, "—do duty to our guests."

The huddle broke apart; two girls ran into the house and out again as the eldest, a boy, came to take the reins of the horses. The next one in height, a huge-eyed girl (one of the two who had gone into the house), brought bread and salt; she was followed by another child, a girl who barely came to the wolf's shoulder, carrying a guesting-cup with the solemnity due a major religious artifact. The three children halted on seeing the wolf, faces betraying doubt and a little fear; plainly, they wanted to obey their father. Equally plainly, they didn't want to get within a mile of the huge black beast.

Tarma signaled the wolf silently. He padded to her right side and sat, looking very calm and as harmless as it is possible for a wolf to look. "This is Warrl," she said. "He's my soul-kin and friend, just like in the tales—a magic beast from the Pelagir Hills. He's wise, and very kind—" she raised one eyebrow with a comic expression "—and he's a *lot* smarter than I am!"

Warrl snorted, as if to agree, and the children giggled. Their fears evaporated, and they stepped forward to continue their tasks of greeting under their father's approving eye.

The guesting ritual complete, the eldest son—who looked to be no older than ten, but was a faithful copy of his father in miniature—led the horses to the stock-shed. It would probably not have been safe to have let him take ordinary battle-trained horses, but these were Shin'a'in bred and trained warsteeds.

They had sense and intelligence enough to be trusted unguided in the midst of a melee, yet would no more have harmed a child, even by accident, than they would have done injury to one of their own foals.

Just now they were quite well aware that they were about to be stabled and fed, and in their eagerness to get to the barn they nearly dragged the poor child off his feet.

"Hai!" Tarma said sharply; they stopped dead, and turned to look at her. "Go gently, warladies," she said in her own tongue. "Mind your manners."

Landric hid a smile as the now docile creatures let themselves be led away at the boy's pace. "I'd best help him, if you think they'll allow it," he told the Shin'a'in. "Else he'll be all night at it, trying to groom them on a ladder!"

"They'll allow anything short of violence, providing you leave our gear with them; but for your own sake, don't take the packs out of their sight. I'd hate to have to recompense you for broken bones and a new barn!"

"Told you I soldiered with Shin'a'in, didn't I? No fear I'd try *that*. Take your ease inside; 'tis poor enough, and I beg you forgive the state it's in, but—"

"Landric, no man can be two things at once. Better the house should suffer a little than your fields and stock. Clean plates won't feed your younglings," Kethry told him, following the oldest girl inside.

There was a musty smell inside, as of a house left too long unaired. Piles of clean clothing were on the benches on either side of the table, the table itself was piled high with dirty crockery. There was dust everywhere, and toys strewn the length and breadth of the room. The fire had been allowed to go out—

probably so that the two-year-old sitting on one corner of the hearth wouldn't fall into it in his father's absence. The fireplace hadn't been cleaned for some time. The kitchen smelled of burned porridge and onions.

"Warrior's Blade—what a mess!" Tarma exclaimed under her breath as they stepped into the chaotic kitchen-cum-common room.

"It's several months' accumulation," her partner reminded her, "and several months of fairly inexpert attempts to keep up with the chores. Guests or no, I'm not going to let things stay in this state." She began pinning up the sleeves of her buff-colored traveling robe and headed toward the nearest pile of clutter.

"My thoughts entirely," the swordswoman replied, beginning to divest herself of her arms.

Landric and his son returned from stabling the mares to a welcome but completely unexpected scene. His guests had completely restored order to the house; there was a huge kettle of soup on the once-cold hearth, and the sorceress was making short work of what was left of the dirty dishes. Every pot and pan in the kitchen had already been washed and his oldest girl was carefully drying and stacking them. The next oldest was just in the last steps of sweeping the place out, using a broom that one of the two had cut down to a size she could manage. His four-year-old son was trotting solemnly back and forth, putting things away under the careful direction of—the *swordswoman?*

Sure enough, it was the hawk-faced swordswoman who was directing the activities of all of the children. She was somehow managing to simultaneously change the baby's dirty napkin, tickling him so that he was too helpless with giggles to fight her as he usually did; directing the four-year-old in his task; and admonishing the six-year-old when she missed a spot in her sweeping. And looking very much as if she were enjoying the whole process to the hilt.

Landric stood in the door with his mouth hanging open in surprise.

"I hope you two washed after you finished with the horses," Kethry called from her tub of soapsuds. "If not, wait until I'm through here, and you can use the wash water before you throw it out." She rinsed the last of the dishes and stood pointedly beside the tub of water, waiting for Landric to use it or carry it out.

"This was—not necessary," he managed to say as he hefted the tub to carry outside. "You are guests—"

"Oh, come now, did you *really* expect two women to leave things in the state they were?" Kethry giggled, holding the door open for him. "Besides, this isn't the sort of thing we normally have to do. It's rather a relief to be up to the elbows in hot water instead of trouble. And Tarma adores children; she can get them to do anything for her. You said you know Swordsworn; you know that they're celibate, then. She doesn't often get a chance to fuss over babes. But what I'd like to know is why you haven't hired a woman or gotten some neighbor to help you?"

"There are no women to hire, thanks to the monster," he replied heavily. "Those that didn't provide meals for it ran off to the town, thinking they'd be safer there. I'm at the farthest edge of Lord Havirn's lands, and my nearest neighbors aren't willing to cross the distance between us when the monster is known to have taken my wife within sight of the house. I can't say that I blame them. I take the eldest with me, now, and I have the rest of the children barricade themselves in the house until we come home. The Gods of the Wheel know I'd be overjoyed to find some steady woman willing to watch them and keep the place tidy for bed, board, and a bit of silver, but there isn't anyone to be hired at any price."

"Now it's my turn to beg your pardon," Kethry said apologetically.

"No offense meant, none taken," an almost-smile stretched his lips. "How could I take offense after this?"

That night Tarma regaled all the children with tales until they'd fallen asleep, while Kethry kept her hands busy with mending. Landric had kept glancing over at Tarma with bemusement; to see the harsh-visaged battle-scarred Shin'a'in warrior smothered in children and enjoying every moment of it was plainly a sight he had never expected to witness. And Warrl put the cap on his amazement by letting the baby tumble over him, pull his fur, tail, and ears, and finally fall asleep using the beast as a mattress.

When the children were all safely in bed, Kethry cleared her throat in a way intended to suggest she had something touchy she wanted to ask their host.

He took the hint, and the sleepiness left his eyes. "Aye, mage-lady?"

"Would you object to my working a bit of magic

here? I know it's not precisely in the tenets of the Path to use the arcane—but—"

"I'm a bit more pragmatic than some of my fellows—nay lady, I've no objection to a bit of magicing. What did you have in mind?"

"Two things, really. I'd like to scry out this monster of yours and see what we're going to be up against—"

"Lady," he interrupted, "I—would advise against going at that thing. Let the hired heroes deal with it."

"While it takes more women and children?" She shook her head. "I can't do that, Landric—if it weren't against my conscience, I'm geas-bound. Anyway, the other thing I'd like to do is leave you a little help with the children—something like a cross between Warrl and a sheepdog, if you've no objection. It won't be as bright, or as large and strong, but it will be able to keep an eye on the little ones, herd them out of mischief, and go for help if need be."

"How could I object? The gods know I need something like that. You shouldn't feel obligated, though—"

"Balance the Wheel your way, and I'll balance it in mine, all right?" The twinkle in Kethry's eyes took any sting there might have been out of her words.

He bowed his head a little. "Your will, then, magelady. If you've no need of me, I'm for bed."

"No need, Landric, and thank you."

When he'd left, Kethry went to the stack of clean dishes and selected a dark, nearly black pottery bowl.

"Water scrying?" Tarma asked, settling herself on one side of the table.

"Mh-hm," Kethry replied absently, filling it very carefully with clear, cold water, then bringing it to the table and dusting a fine powder of salt and herbs from a pouch at her belt over the surface. "For both of us—you may see what I'd miss."

She held her hands just above the water's surface and chanted softly, her eyes closed in concentration. After a few moments, a mistlike glow encircled her hands. It brightened and took on a faint bluish cast—then flowed down over her hands onto the water, hovering over it without quite touching it. When it had settled, Kethry took her hands away, and both of them peered into the bowl.

It was rather like looking at a reflection; they had to be careful about moving or breathing, for the picture was distorted or lost whenever the surface of the water was disturbed.

"Ugly rotter," was Tarma's first comment, as the beast came clear. "Where and when?"

"I'm past-scrying; all the encounters with the would-be heroes thus far."

"Hmm. Not having much luck, is he?"

That was an understatement, as the monster was making short work of a middle-aged man-at-arms.

"It looks like they feed it once a week," Kethry said, though how she was able to keep track of time passage in the bowl was beyond Tarma. "Oh, this is a mage—let's see how he fares."

"Huh—no better than a try with a sword."

Magics just bounced off its hide; the mage ended up traveling the same road as the fighters.

"It's a good bet it's a magic creature," Kethry concluded. "Any mage worth his robe would armor his own toys against magic."

After watching all the trials—and failures—they both sat silently.

"Let's think on this a while—we've got enough information for now."

"Agreed. Want to build Landric's little shepherd?"

"*That* I could do in my sleep. Let's see—first I need a vehicle—"

Warrl got to his feet, and padded over to Tarma. :*Let me hunt,*: he said in her mind.

"Warrl just volunteered to find your 'vehicle.' "

"Bless you, Furface! I take it there's something within range?"

"He says 'maybe not as big as you were hoping, but smarter.' "

"I prefer brains over brawn for this task—"

Warrl whisked out the door, and was back before a half hour was up, herding an odd little beast before him that looked like a combination of fox and cat, with humanlike hands.

"Bright Lady—that looks like a Pelagir Hills changeling!"

"Warrl says it came from the same place as the monster—when *that* got loose, apparently a lot of other creatures did, too."

"All the better for my purposes—" Kethry coaxed the creature into her lap, and ran softly glowing hands over it while she frowned a little in concentration. "Wonderful!" she sighed in relief, "It's Brightpath intended; and nobody's purposed it yet. It's like a blank page waiting to be written on—I can't believe my luck!" The glow on her hands changed to a warm gold, settled over the creature's head and throat, and sank into it as if absorbed. It sighed and abruptly fell asleep.

"There—" she said, rising and placing it beside the hearth. "When it wakes, all its nurturing instincts will be imprinted for Landric's children; as bright as it is, he'll be able to leave them even with a fire burning on the hearth without them being in danger."

She stood, and swayed with exhaustion.

"That's more than enough for one night!" Tarma exclaimed, steadying her and walking her over to the pallets Landric had supplied. "It's definitely time *you* got a little rest! Greeneyes, I swear if I wasn't around, you'd wear yourself into a wraith."

"Not a wraith—" Kethry yawned, but before she could finish her thought, she was asleep.

They left the next morning with the entreaties of the four youngest children still in their ears. Despite the distraction of the new "pet" they still wanted the two women to stay. None of the six had wanted Tarma, in particular, to leave.

"I'd've liked to stay," Tarma said, a bit wistfully, as she turned in her saddle to wave farewell.

"So would I—at least for a bit," Kethry sighed. "Need's not giving me any choice though—she's nagging me half to death. All last night I could feel her pulling on me; a few more days of that and I'll start chewing furniture. Besides, I had the distinct impression that Landric was eying me with the faint notion of propositioning me this morning."

"You should have taken him up on it, Greeneyes," Tarma chuckled. "You could do worse."

"Thank you, but no thank you. He's a nice enough man—and I'd kill him inside of a week. He has very firm notions about what a wife's place is, and I don't fit any of them. And he wouldn't be any too pleased about your bringing up his offspring as Shin'a'in either! You just want me married off so you can start raising a new clan!"

"Can't blame me for trying," Tarma shrugged, wearing a wry grin. The loss of her old clan was far enough in the past now that it was possible for Kethry to tease her about wanting to start a new one. "You *did* promise the council that that was what you'd do."

"And I will—but in my own good time, and with the man of *my* choice, one who'll be a friend and partner, not hope to rule me. That's all very well for some women, but not for me. Furthermore, any husband of mine would have to be *pleased* with the idea that my oathsister will be training our children as Shin'a'in. I didn't promise the Council, *she'enedra*," she rode close enough to catch Tarma's near hand and squeeze it. "I promised *you*."

Tarma's expression softened, as it had when she'd been with the children. "I know it, dearling," she replied, eyes misting a trifle, "And you know that I never would have asked you for that—never. Ah, let's get moving; I'm getting maudlin."

Kethry released her hand with a smile, and they picked up their pace.

They entered the town, which huddled at the foot of the lord's keep like a collection of stellat shoots at the foot of the mother tree. The ever-present dust covered the entire town, hanging in a brown cloud over it. Warrl they left outside, not wanting to chance the stir he'd cause if they brought him in with them. He would sneak in after dark, and take up residence with their horses in the stable, or with them, if they got a room on the ground floor with a window. Taking directions from the gate-guard, they found an inn. It was plain, but clean enough to satisfy both of them, and didn't smell too strongly of bacon and stale beer.

"When's feeding time for the monster?" Tarma asked the innkeeper.

"Today—if ye get yerselves t' the main gate, ye'll see the procession—"

The procession had the feeling of a macabre carnival. It was headed by the daughter of Lord Havirn, mounted on a white pony, her hands shackled by a thin gold chain. Her face bore a mingling of petulance at having to undergo the ceremony, and peevish pride at being the center of attention. Her white garments and hair all braided with flowers and pearls showed the careful attentions of at least two servants. Those maidservants walked beside her, strewing herbs; behind them came a procession of priests with censors. The air was full of incense smoke battling with the ubiquitous dust.

"What's all *that* about?" Kethry asked a sunburned farmwoman, nodding at the pony and its sullen rider.

"Show; nothing but show. M'lord likes to pretend it's his daughter up for sacrifice—but *there* is the real monster fodder," she pointed toward a sturdy farm cart, that contained a heavily-bound, scurvy-looking man, whose eyes drooped in spite of his fate. "They've drugged 'im, poor sot, so's the monster knows it'll get an easy meal. They'll take milady up the hill, with a lot of weepin' and wailin', and they'll give each of the heroes a little gold key that unlocks her chain. But it's the thief they'll be tying to the stake, not her. Reckon you that if some one of them heroes ever *does* slay the beast, that the tales will be sayin' he saved her from the stake shackles, 'stead of that poor bastard?''

"Probably."

"Pity they *haven't* tried to feed her to the beast— it'd probably die of indigestion, she's that spoiled."

They watched the procession pass with a jaundiced eye, then retired to their inn.

"I think, all things considered," Tarma said after some thought, as they sat together at a small table in the comfort and quiet of their room at the inn. "That the best time to get at the thing is at the weekly feeding. But *after* it's eaten, not before."

"Lady knows I'd hate being part of that disgusting parade, but you're right. And while it's in the open— well, magics may bounce off *its* hide, but there are still things I could do to the area around it. Open up a pit under it, maybe."

"We'd have to—" Tarma was interrupted by wild cheering. When peering out of their window brought no enlightenment, they descended to the street.

The streets were full of wildly rejoicing people, who caught up the two strangers, pressing food and drink on them. There was too much noise for them to ask questions, much less hear the answers.

An increase in the cheers signaled the arrival of the possible answer—and by craning their necks, the two saw the clue to the puzzle ride by, carried on the shoulders of six merchants. It was one of the would-be heroes they'd seen going out with the procession; he was blood-covered, battered, and bruised, but on the whole, in very good shape. Behind him came the cart that had held the thief—now it held the head of something that must have been remarkably ugly and exceedingly large in life. The head just barely fit into the cart.

The crowd carried him to the same inn where the two women were staying, and deposited him inside. Tarma seized Kethry's elbow and gestured toward the stableyard; she nodded, and they wriggled their way through the mob to the deserted court.

"Well! Talk about a wasted trip!" Tarma wasn't sure whether to be relieved or annoyed.

"I hate to admit it—" Kethry was clearly chagrined.

"So Need's stopped nagging you?"

Kethry nodded.

"Figures. Look at it this way—what good would Lord Havirn's daughter *or* his lands have done us?"

"We could have used the lands, I guess—" Tarma's snort cut Kethry's words off. "Ah, I suppose it's just as well. I'm not all that unhappy about not having to face that beast down. We've paid for the room, we might as well stay the night."

"The carnival they're building up ought to be worth the stay. Good thing Warrl can take care of himself—I doubt he'll be able to sneak past that mob."

The "carnival" was well worth staying for. Lord Havirn broached his own cellar and kitchens, and if wine wasn't flowing in the fountains, it was because the general populace was too busy pouring it down their collective throats. Neither of the women were entirely sober when they made their way up to their beds.

A few scant minutes after reaching their room, however, Kethry *was* sober again.

The look of shock and surprise on her partner's face quickly sobered Tarma as well. "What's wrong?"

"It's Need—she's pulling again."

"Oh, bloody hell!" Tarma groaned and pulled her leather tunic back over her head. "Good thing we hadn't put the candle out. How far?"

"Close. It's not anywhere near as strong as the original pull either. I think it's just one person this time—"

Kethry opened the door to their room, and stared in amazement at the disheveled girl huddled in the hall just outside.

The girl was shivering; had obviously been weeping. Her clothing was torn and seemed to have been thrown on. Both of them recognized her as the inn's chambermaid. She looked up at them with entreaty and burst into a torrent of tears.

"Oh, bloody hell!" Tarma repeated.

When they finally got the girl calmed down enough to speak, what she told them had them both incensed. The great "hero" was not to be denied anything, by Lord Havirn's orders—except, of course, the lord's daughter. *That* must wait until they were properly wedded. That he need not languish out of want, however, the innkeeper had been ordered to supply him with a woman, should he want one.

Naturally, he wanted one. Unfortunately, the lady who usually catered to that sort of need was "inconvenienced" with her moon-days. So rather than pay the fee of an outside professional, the innkeeper had sent up the chambermaid, Fallan—without bothering to tell her *why* she was being sent.

"—'m a good girl, m'lady. I didna understand 'im at first; thought 'e wanted another bath or somesuch. But 'e grabbed me 'fore I knew what 'e was about. An' 'e tore me clothes, them as took me a month's wages. An 'e—'e—" another spate of tears ensued. " 'E was mortal cruel, m'lady. 'E—when I didna please 'im, 'e beat me. An' when 'e was done, 'e threw me clothes at me, an' 'e yelled for me master, an' tol' 'im I was no bloody good, an' what did 'e think 'e was about, anyway givin' 'im goods that was neither ripe nor green? Then me master, 'e—'e—turned me off! Tol' me t' make meself vanish, or 'e'd beat me 'imself!"

"He did what?" Tarma was having trouble following the girl, what with her thick accent and Tarma's own rising anger.

"He discharged her. The bastard sent her up to be raped, then has the bloody almighty gall to throw her out afterward!" Kethry was holding onto her own temper by the thinnest of threads.

" 've got nowhere to go, no ref'rences—what 'm I going to do?" the girl moaned, hugging her knees to her chest, still plainly dazed.

"*She'enedra*, get the brandy. I'll put her in my bed, you and I can sleep double," Kethry said in an undertone. "Child, worry about it in the morning. Here—drink this."

"I *can't* go back 'ome—they 'aven't got the means to feed the childer still too little to look for work," she continued in a monotone. "I bain't virgin for two years now, but I been as good as I could be. I bain't no lightskirt. All I ever wanted was t' put by enough for a dower—maybe find some carter, some manservant willin' t' overlook things; have a few childer of me own." She was obviously not used to hard liquor; the brandy took hold of her very quickly. She mumbled on for a bit longer, then collapsed in Kethry's bed and fell asleep.

"I'd like to skewer this damned innkeeper," Tarma growled.

Kethry, who'd been checking the girl for hurts, looked up with a glower matching Tarma's. "That makes two of us. Just because the girl's no virgin is no excuse for what he did—and then to turn her out afterward—" Tarma could see her hands were trembling with controlled rage. "Come look at this."

"Ungentle" was a distinct understatement for the way the girl had been mauled about. She was bruised from knee to neck, ugly, purple things. Kethry took Need from beneath the bed and placed it beside her, then covered her with the blankets again.

"Well, that will take care of the physical problems—but what about the bruising of her spirit?"

"I don't have any answers for you," Kethry sighed, rage slowly cooling. "But, you know, from the way she talked, it isn't the rape that bothers her so much as the fact that she's been turned out. What we *really* need to do is find her somewhere to go."

"Bloody hell. And us knowing not a soul here. Well—let's worry about it in the morning."

In the morning, it seemed that their erstwhile charge was determined to take care of the problem by attaching herself to them.

They woke to find her busily cleaning both their swords—though what she'd made of finding Need beside her when she woke was anyone's guess. Tarma's armor lay neatly stacked, having already been put in good order, and their clothes had been brushed and laid ready. The girl had both pairs of boots beside her, evidently prepared to clean them when she finished with the swords.

"What's all this about?" Tarma demanded, only half awake.

The girl jumped—her lip quivered as she replied, looking ready to burst into tears again. "Please, m'lady—I want to go with ye when y' leave. Ye haven't a servant, I know. See? I c'n take good care of ye both. An' I can cook, too—an' wash an' mend. I don' eat much, an' I don' need much. Please?"

"I was afraid this would happen," Kethry murmured. "Look, Fallan, we really *can't* take you with us—we don't need a servant—" She stopped as the girl burst into tears again, and sighed with resignation. "—oh, Bright Lady. "All right, we'll take you with us. But it won't be forever, just until we can find you a new place."

" 'Just until we can find you a new place.' *She'ene-dra*, I am beginning to think that this time that sword of yours has driven us too far. Three days on the road, and it's already beginning to seem like three years."

Fallan had not adjusted well to the transition from chambermaid to wanderer. It wasn't that she hadn't tried—but to her, citybred as she was, the wilderness was a place beset by unknown perils at every turn. Every snake, every insect was poisonous; she stayed up, kept awake by terror, for half of every night, listening to the sounds beyond their fire. Warrl and the mares terrified her.

They'd had to rescue her twice—once from the river she'd fallen into, once from the bramble thicket she'd *run* into, thinking she heard a bear behind her. For Fallan, every strange crackle of brush meant a bear; one with Fallan-cutlets on his mind.

At the same time, she was stubbornly refusing to give up. Not once did she ask the two women to release her from her self-imposed servitude. No matter how frightened she became, she never confessed her fear, nor did she rush to one or the other of them for protection. It was as if she was determined to somehow prove—to herself, to them, perhaps to both—that she was capable of facing whatever they could.

"What that girl needs is a husband," Kethry replied wearily. "Give her things to do inside four walls, things she knows, and she's fine, but take her out here, and she's hopeless. If it weren't for the fact that the nearest town is days away, I'd even consider trying to get her another job at an inn."

"And leave her open to the same thing that happened before? Face it, that's exactly what would happen. Poor Fallan is just not the type to sell her favors by choice, and not ugly enough to be left alone. Bless her heart, she's too obedient and honest for her own good—and, unfortunately, not very bright. No solution, Greeneyes. Too bad most farmers around here don't need or can't afford woman servants, or—" she stopped with an idea suddenly occurring to her. Kethry had the same idea.

"Landric?"

"The very same. He seems kind enough—"

"No fear of that. He's Wheel-bound. When he took that tattoo, he took with it a vow to balance the evil he'd done previously with good. That's why he became a farmer, I suspect, to balance the death he'd sown as a soldier with life. Did his children look ill-treated?"

"Contrarywise. Healthiest, happiest bunch I've seen outside of a Clan gathering. The only trouble—"

"—is, does she know how to deal with younglings? Let's head for Landric's place. You can talk to her on the way, and we'll see how she handles them when we get there."

Two days of backtracking saw them on the road within a few furlongs of Landric's farm. Landric's eldest spotted them as he had before and ran to tell his father. Landric met them on the road just where it turned up the path to his farmstead, his face wreathed in smiles.

"I had not thought to see you again, when the news came that the monster had been slain," he told Tarma warmly.

"Then you also know that we arrived just a bit too late to do the slaying ourselves."

"If I were to tell the truth, I'm just as grateful for your sake. The hero had a cadre of six hirelings, and all six of them died giving him the chance he needed. I would have been saddened had their fate been yours. Oh—that little pet you left for the children has been beyond price."

"If we'd gone down that thing's gullet, you wouldn't have been half as saddened as I!" Tarma chuckled. Out of the corner of her eye, she saw Kethry, Fallan, and the children entering the house. "Listen, you're in the position to do us a favor, Landric. I hate to impose upon you, but—well, we've got another 'pet' to find a home for." Quickly and concisely she laid out Fallan's pathetic story. "—so we were hoping you'd know someone willing to take her in. She's a good worker, I can tell you that; it's just that she's just not suited for the trail. And to tell you the truth, she's not very flexible. I think we shock her."

He smiled slowly. "I am not quite *that* stupid, Sworn One. You hope that *I* will take her in, don't you?"

"Oh, well, I'll admit the thought did cross my mind," Tarma smiled crookedly.

"It is a possibility. It would neatly balance some wrongs I committed in my soldiering days . . ." His eyes grew thoughtful. "I'll tell you—let's see how she does with the younglings. Then I'll make my decision."

By the look in Landric's eyes when they crossed the threshold, Tarma knew he'd made up his mind. It wasn't just that Fallan had duplicated their feats of setting the place to rights, (although it wasn't near the task they'd had) nor was it the savory stew odor coming from the kettle on the hearth, nor the sight of five of the six children lined up with full bowls on their knees, neatly stowing their dinner away. No, what made up Landric's mind was the sight of Fallan, the youngest on her lap, cuddling him and drying his tears over the skinned knee he'd just acquired, and she looking as blissful as if she'd reached heaven.

They stayed a week, and only left because they'd agreed to act as caravan guards before all this began and would be late if they stayed longer.

Fallan had been in her element from the moment they'd entered the door. And with every passing day, it looked as though Landric was thinking of her less as a hireling and more in the light of something else.

"Are you thinking what I'm thinking?" Tarma asked her partner as soon as they were out of earshot.

"That he'll be wedding her before too long? Probably. There's mutual respect and liking there, and Fallan loves the children. She even likes the little beastie! It's not a life that would appeal to me or you—but it looks like exactly what *she* wants. There've been worse things to base a marriage on."

"Like the lord's daughter and her 'hero'?" Tarma grimaced. "I don't know whether to feel sorrier for him or her or both. From the little I saw and heard, she's no prize, and m'lord is likely to have made an arrangement that keeps the pursestrings in his hands and out of her husband's."

"Which is hardly what he'd counted on when he went to slay the monster. On the other hand, we have reason to know the man is an insensitive brute. They deserve each other," Kethry replied thoughtfully.

"As Landric and Fallan do. There's your real heroes—the people who keep coping, keep trying, no matter how many blows Fate takes at them. Nobody'll make a song about them, but they're heroes all the same," Tarma said soberly, then grinned. "Now, if we're going to get *our* deserts, we'll have to earn 'em. Let's ride, *she'enedra*—before that damned sword of yours finds something else it wants us to do!"

FRIENDLY FIRE

Ever have one of those days?

Sometimes you can get into more trouble just because of Murphy's Law than for any other reason. The problem with heroic fantasy is that very few of the heroes seem to be affected by Murphy's Law.

But very few heroic fantasy heroes are like Tarma and Kethry.

Tarma shena Tale'sedrin, Swordsworn Shin'a'in, was up to her earlobes in a different kind of battle than she usually fought.

A battle with current finances.

Where does it all go? I could swear we just got paid. . . .

Huh. Down the throats of the mares, us, and that eating-machine that calls itself a kyree, that's where.

She and her partner, the White Winds sorceress Kethry, had taken to the marketplace armed with slender pouches of copper coins; no silver there. With luck, they would be able to stretch those pouches of coin enough to cover provisions for the two humans, the two Shin'a'in battlemares, and Warrl, the wolflike *kyree*. Those provisions had to last for at least three weeks, the time it would take them to get to their next job.

There was a certain amount of self-provisioning they could do. Warrl could hunt some for himself, and so could Tarma and Kethry if they were careful. Warrl was quite intelligent enough to confine his hunting to nondomestic beasts, and there were always rabbits living in hedgerows that could be snared. But this was farm country, and there was very little for the warhorses to forage on along the roadside—and if those rabbits proved elusive, any fresh meat would have to go first to Warrl.

It was at times like this that Tarma wished her partner had been a little less generous to her ex-"husband"—or rather, to his other victims. A spot of judicious blackmail or a decision to claim some of the bastard's blood-money for herself would have left them with a nice cushion to get them over lean spots like this one. Granted, once they arrived at Kata'shin'a'in, they should have no trouble picking up a caravan job—and with luck, it might be a very lucrative one. Their friends, Ikan and Justin, had promised to put in a good word for them with the gem merchants whose caravans they habitually guarded, and a good word from them would mean a great deal. *They* did so well over the course of a year that they never had to scramble for work during the lean season; they were able to find a friendly inn and take a rest over the winter, if they chose.

But first, she and Kethry had to get to Kata'shin'a'in, and the start of the caravan routes.

And to get to Kata'shin'a'in, they needed provisions.

They were so short on money that they were not even staying in an inn; despite the bitter, early spring weather, despite the very real threat of sleet and foul weather, they were camped outside the city walls.

Their tent cost nothing, and the walls were over-grown with weeds—dried now, but sufficient fodder for a couple of days, so long as Tarma supplemented their gleanings with a grain ration.

Tarma would be bargaining for the horses' grain; Kethry, with the remainder of their slim resources, was to buy the humans' rations, and Warrl's. The *kyree* himself remained at the camp—between the presence of Warrl and the warsteeds, the camp was safer than if there had been two armed guards there. In a way, Tarma pitied anyone who was stupid enough to try to rob it.

There were at least a dozen folk in the market sell-ing grain and hay, and Tarma intended to check them all before making a purchase. She made her way down the stone-paved street of the beast-market, with the cobbles wet and slippery under her boots, and the calls, squalls, and bellows of everything from huge oxen to cages full of pigeons on all sides. The stalls for the feed-sellers themselves were simple can-vas awnings fronting stables, corrals and warehouses, none of which had anything to do with what was being sold under the awnings. There was a scattering of grain on the cobbles, and a great deal of straw underfoot. The air was damp, chilly, and smelled strongly of too many animals crowded too closely together.

Eleven of the twelve were unremarkable; farmers, and all within a hair of each other so far as price went. Tarma was not in a position to buy so much that any of them were likely to make a special price for her. The twelfth, however . . .

The twelfth was some kind of priest, or so it seemed. He wore some kind of rough brown cassock with an unbleached linen surcoat and a rope belt; with him were two young men in similar robes, but no surcoat.

Tarma had always gotten along fairly well with other clergy, and these folk looked friendly, but harried. The elder of the trio had a frown of worry, and the two younger looked rather harassed. She watched them as she made desultory attempts to bargain with the last of the farmers, a stolid, square fellow, and began to feel sorry for them. It seemed that if it wasn't for ill-luck, the three clergymen would have no luck. Their straw bales would not stay stacked, toppling any time anyone brushed against them. The canvas roof of their stall drooped, threatening to fall at any moment. One of their carthorses had gone lame and wore a poultice on its off-hind foot, and the canvas they had used to cover the hay on the way in had leaked, spoiling half the hay, which had burst its bales and now covered the street and the floor of their stall.

Another customer, more eager to buy than Tarma, engaged the farmer's attention. She made no attempt to regain it; instead, she drifted over to the sagging stall of the clerics.

"Greetings," she said, carefully, for although she got along well with other clergy, sometimes the reverse was not true. This time, however, the chiefest of the clerics greeted her with something like harried enthusiasm.

"And to you, Shin'a'in," he replied in the common Trade-tongue. "I hope your fortune this day has been better than ours."

"I cannot see how it could have been worse," she replied, just as the sagging canvas gave way, and the chief cleric dodged out of the way. The two assistants scrambled to prop it back up again, one of them swearing with a most unpriestly set of oaths and tone to his voice. His superior gave him a reproachful look, and the offender flushed with embarrassment, bending quickly to his work. The elder cleric simply sighed.

Tarma shook her head. "It's hard for the young to adjust," she offered. "Especially under provocation."

The priest only smiled, wearily. Very wearily. "We have been experiencing somewhat extreme provocation lately."

As the canvas gave way a second time, this time swatting the poor young men in the side of the head, Tarma bit her lip, torn between sympathy and laughter. "So I see," she replied tactfully. "Ah—have you any grain?"

Kethry sighed, and told herself to be patient; Tarma never shirked, and if she was late, there was a reason for it. The lot of partnership was to pick up when your partner wasn't there to deal with her share. Tarma had done that in the past for Kethry, and while the sorceress was muscle-sore, hot, and tired, she kept her temper carefully reined in. She simply did the work, and when Tarma finally put in her appearance, the Shin'a'in looked as if she had been through just as much as Kethry. Beads of sweat ran down her temples, bits of hair had escaped from her neat braids and straggled into her eyes. Her shoulders sagged under bags of grain, and she was breathing heavily. "How did you do?" Kethry asked her partner. "I hope your booty was worth the wait."

She had already packed up the tent and both sets

of gear; the horses were saddled and bridled and standing ready. Even Warrl was pacing back and forth under the walls, impatient, ready to go. They had planned to get their provisions quickly and be on their way before noon; it was nearly that now, and Kethry could not imagine what had kept Tarma for so long.

"Yes and no," Tarma replied, frowning a little. "I got the grain at a pretty good price, but—Keth, I swear there's a plague of bad luck going around this town! I'd no sooner gotten the grain and my change, than some damn fool upended a cartload of stable leavings across my path. And from there, things got worse. Everywhere I went, it seemed like there was something blocking the street. I got involved in street brawls, I got trampled by a runaway carthorse—I wound up going halfway to the other side of town before I could get back to the gate. I caught the bags before they were about to split and managed to save most of the grain, but that meant I had to get new bags. I can't wait to get out of here."

"Well, that makes two of us," Kethry replied, with an eye to the gathering clouds. "With any luck, we can beat this storm."

Tarma stowed the grain bags carefully in their packs. Too carefully, it seemed to Kethry, as if she didn't quite trust the sacks to hold. That seemed odd, but maybe Tarma had gotten spooked by all the misfortune in town. *She* was ready to be out of there; the sooner they got to Kata'shin'a'in, the better.

But it seemed that the plague of bad luck that had struck the town had decided to follow them. Already they were half a day late on their schedule; and when they were too far down the road to turn back, the sky opened up, even though it looked as if it was about to clear.

There was no warning at all; one moment the road was dry, the sun peeked through the clouds—the next, a cold, sleet-laden downpour soaked them to the skin.

There was nowhere to go, no place to shelter from the torrent. There was nothing on either side of the road but fields; fields of cattle that had wisely huddled together, fields of sheep who also huddled in a woolly mound, or empty fields awaiting the farmer's plow. No trees, just hedgerows; no houses, no sheds, not even a single haystack that they might burrow into to escape the rain.

So they rode onward under the lowering sky, onward into the gathering dark.

Kethry was chilled to the bone in the first candlemark, so cold that she couldn't even shiver. She simply bent her head to the rain, which penetrated her clothing and plastered it to her skin. The cape she wore, which had been perfectly waterproof until that day, was not proof against this rain.

Warrl paced at the heel of Tarma's horse, head and tail down, fur plastered against his skin and looking just as miserable as Kethry felt. At least she was riding—poor Warrl splashed along the road, ankle-deep in mud.

And even as she thought that, Hellsbane slipped and slid in the mud—and a moment later, so did Ironheart. Kethry clung to the saddle, dropping the reins to let Ironheart find her own footing; for a heart-stopping moment, she thought that her mount was going to go over, falling on her—

Her heart clenched, her throat closed, and her

hands clutched the saddlebow. Ironheart scrambled to get her feet under her again; went to her knees—

And rose. Kethry caught her breath again, as her heart fluttered and slowed. Then her heart dropped into her stomach, as the mare staggered and limped.

She dismounted quickly and felt blindly for the mare's rear hock. Sure enough, her probing fingers encountered an ankle already hot and swelling. She looked up from under a dripping curtain of hair to see Tarma doing the same, and shaking her head.

"Lame," her partner said flatly, when she caught Kethry's eye. "Yours?"

Kethry could only nod glumly.

Just before nightfall, they finally found shelter of a sort. They took refuge in a ruined barn, with just enough of its roof intact to give a place for all of them to escape the rain. By then, Kethry had more bad news. She was not normally prey to female troubles, but the twisting of her guts and a deep ache just behind her navel told her that this session of moon-days was going to be one of the bad ones. . . .

While Tarma struggled to light a fire, she rummaged in the saddlebags for herbs to ease her cramps. And came up with a sodden mess of paper packets. The seam on the top of the bag had parted, letting water trickle in all during their ride.

Behind her, she heard her partner sneeze.

Sneeze? Tarma? She never—

"*Sheka*," the Shin'a'in swore, her already harsh voice with a decidedly raspy edge to it. Kethry whirled, alarmed.

A tiny fire smoked and struggled to burn already wet wood, and the face Tarma turned up to her partner was red-eyed and red-nosed. The Shin'a'in sneezed again, convulsively, and sniffed moistly.

"Oh, *hell*," Kethry swore. "Oh, bloody *hell*."

Tarma nodded, and coughed.

There was nothing for it; wet and sodden as the herbs were, they were all she and her partner had to take care of their ills and the sprained hocks of their horses. She emptied out the saddlebag, carefully; separated the packets of herbs while Tarma tried to find them something dry to change into and started two pots of water boiling on the fire. Herbs for the poultices went right into the wet bandage; for this, at least, it wouldn't matter that they were soaked. As Tarma bandaged the warsteeds' sprains, she made two sets of tea, blessing her teachers for forcing her to learn how to distinguish herbs by taste.

And, given that everything else had been going wrong, Kethry made very certain that the metal pots were no closer to the flames than they had to be— and that they were quite dissimilar.

Eventually, Tarma found an odd assortment of dry clothing, most of which was ill-suited to the chill of the air. Still, it was dry, and with enough clothing layered on, they might pass the rest of the night a little warmer, if not in comfort.

The tea, as might have been expected, was lukewarm and weak, but it was better than nothing. And meanwhile, Tarma's sneezes and coughs grew more frequent, and her guts twisted.

They sipped their tea, nibbled the soaked remains of one packet of their travel bread. Neither of them had the heart to check further to see if the rest of their rations had suffered from the leak.

"Cand you casd some kind ob sbell?" Tarma asked miserably. "Healig, or somedig?"

"Not while I've got—cramps," Kethry replied, pausing for the pain to ease. "Anything I do will backfire. I can't hold the concentration."

"Ad I sbose Need wond do anydig, since id's nod life-threadenig?" Tarma sneezed convulsively, and wiped her nose with a leftover bandage-rag.

"That's right. I can't believe this," Kethry said, teeth clenched against a spasm of her stomach. "It's like everything that *could* go wrong *has* gone wrong! It's like we've been cursed—but who would have bothered? And why?"

"Damn ib I doe, Greeneyes," Tarma said thickly. She turned out her purse on the blanket they shared, and a few small copper pieces chinked together. "Ib we ebber get to a town, is this going to be enough to ged more herbs?"

Kethry reached for the coins, and froze, her hand outstretched. There was something there that was not a coin.

"Where did this come from?" she asked, stirring the coins with her fingernail, and turning up something that *looked* like a coin, but wasn't.

It was about the size of a copper-piece, but was bronze, not copper, and inscribed with odd symbols. Tarma looked at it, her expression puzzled.

"Don'd know," she replied. "Wid da change, maybe. Wad is id?"

Kethry decided that there was nothing more to lose by picking the thing up, and her jaw clenched. "You *must* have gotten this in with your change," she said, angrily. "From those priests. *This* is why we've been having all this bad luck. Dammit! It's a cursed coin;

there's a sect of Lurchan that makes these blasted things.''

Tarma shook her head, baffled. "I don'd unnerstad. Lurchan's a luck-god. Ad those priests weren'd ob Lurchan—''

"They make them for Lurchan's followers to distribute to enemies,'' Kethry replied, realizing that she was adding a headache to her aching guts. "They're—a counter-luck talisman. They make anything that can possibly go wrong, do so.'' She forced down tears; crying wasn't going to help right now, much as she'd like to indulge herself. "Don't think we can just leave it here either,'' she continued bitterly. "It'll just show right back up in your pouch. You can't leave it or force it on someone; they have to *take* it from you. Like you did, taking it with the change.''

Tarma nodded glumly. "Dow I doe why de priests were habing such trouble,'' she said. "Hodestly, I don'd think they eben dew they had this. Or whad id was, anyway.''

"Maybe not,'' Kethry replied with a sigh. "Probably not. They'd have tried to conceal it, or they'd have gotten it back to the Lurchan-priests. They probably didn't recognize it any more than you did. I guess it was probably just a case of 'friendly fire' getting us.''

"Fredly fire idn't. Wad can we do?'' Tarma asked plaintively, her eyes watering, blowing her nose on her rag.

"We'll have to get rid of it somehow.'' Kethry sat back against her packs—but not without first checking, carefully, to make certain that the packs were steady. "It's not going to be easy. Whoever takes it has to want it—and I won't pass this thing off on someone innocent, I just *won't*."

:*Admirable,*: Warrl said dryly. :*Stupid, but admirable.*:

Kethry turned on him. "Don't *you* start!" she snarled. "If you want to do something useful, we should reach Ponjee tomorrow morning. Help me find someone who deserves this damned thing, then help me think of a way to make him take it!"

Warrl recoiled, his ears flattened, and blinked at her vehemence. Tarma made a choking sound.

It sounded like a suppressed laugh and Kethry raised an eyebrow. "What's so funny?" she asked.

"You won'd like id," Tarma said, still chuckling between blowing her nose and coughing.

"If it's enough to make you laugh—"

"He said, 'Mages be glad I'b a neuder.'"

Kethry blinked slowly, then smiled slowly. No point in getting angry—and besides, she had just thought of something useful.

"Well, Warrl," she said sweetly, "It just occurred to me that these things have a range of about ten furlongs. And we need meat. Now obviously, anything *we* do is doomed to failure—but *you* can go out there and catch us all something outside that range. *Can't* you."

Warrl's ears drooped, and he sighed, but he obediently got up and padded out into the wet and dark.

Tarma held her laughter until he was out of range, then chuckled. "Revenge id sweed," she observed.

"And even a neuter should know better than to annoy a female with an aching gut," Kethry agreed. "Now—let's figure out how to subvert this stupid talisman as much as we can. . . ."

*   *   *

The rain stopped before dawn; Warrl brought back two rabbits and only dropped them in the mud once. They had decided that the way to deal with the talisman was to make very certain that there were as few opportunities for something to go wrong as possible. Which meant, *nothing* could be taken for granted. Everything must be checked and double-checked. They were to check each other and remind each other of things that needed to be done, no matter how annoying it got.

And it got annoying very shortly, yet somehow they both managed to keep their tempers, mostly by reining them in.

The village of Ponjee was not terribly prepossessing. A huddle of mud-and-daub huts around a center square, straddling the road. No inn, but careful inquiries brought the name of someone who sold herbs. Tarma kept the talisman in her pouch and waited outside the village until Kethry was outside of the damn thing's range; the mage bought the herbs they needed without incident, and stowed them in the still-waterproof saddlebag before Tarma brought the thing close again.

As if their attempt to get around its powers angered it, before they had a chance to leave the place, Kethry's blade Need "woke" with a vengeance.

Immediately she had a splitting headache—and as if to make certain that there was no mistake about a female in trouble, the sounds of shrieking and a woman being beaten sounded from the last house in the village.

Kethry had no choice; given the way the sword was reacting—and the pain it was putting her through—she wouldn't even be able to get past that hut without blacking out. If then. Need could be very persistent in seeing that her bearer dealt with the troubles of those women unable to help themselves.

The door was open; right up until the moment they reached it. Then it slammed shut in Tarma's face, and Tarma hit it at a dead run, like a comic in a farce. She bounced off it and landed on her rump in the mud of the street; Kethry, several steps behind, prepared to hit it with her shoulder and ram it open—

But it opened again, just as she reached it, and she staggered across the threshold and into a table laden with dirty pots and pans. The table collapsed, of course, and the pots and pans fell all around her.

By then Tarma was up and through the door. The man who had been—quite clearly—beating his woman, stared at her in amazement as she blundered inside.

And slipped on the mess spilled from the dirty pots. And fell again.

Need had, by now, taken over Kethry; she couldn't stop herself. She was on her feet, sword out—

Overreaction, of course, but that was the talisman's doing; it couldn't stop the sword, so it was making whatever it did be the worst possible response to the situation. And as Kethry realized that, she also realized that it had made certain Need was entirely inflamed, so that it took her over completely.

The man was unarmed and unarmored; it didn't matter. Need struck to kill.

At the last moment, Kethry managed to get enough control back to turn the flat of the blade on the man rather than the edge, and to hold back the blow a little.

It hit him in the head like a club, and he went down without a sound. But, thank the gods, not dead.

The moment her man went down the woman screamed with outrage.

Kethry couldn't quite make out what she was shrieking; the woman's dialect was so accented and so thick that she didn't get more than one word in five. But the meaning was clear enough— "How dare you bitches hit my man!" She grabbed crockery and anything else she could reach, hurling it and invective at the two of them. Tarma seized a pot lid to use as a shield; Kethry wasn't so lucky.

That was when the rest of the village decided to get involved.

"Now I know how Leslac feels," Tarma said wearily.

"Leslac doesn't have two battlemares and a *kyree* to hold off the enraged populace while he makes his escape," Kethry replied, blotting at a bruise on her forehead. "*She'enedra*, we have got to get rid of that damned thing. Either that, or we'd better take up living in a cave for a while."

:*Your troubles are not yet over,*: Warrl cautioned them. :*There is a band of robbers on the road ahead. If you wish to avoid them, we will have to go back to the last crossroads and detour three or four days out of our way.*:

Tarma cursed in three languages—then stopped, as something occurred to her. "Keth—how helpless can you look?"

"Pretty damned—" Understanding dawned on the sorceress' face, and she nodded. "Right. *Don't say anything.* I don't know how the curse works except that it doesn't seem to read thoughts. Here—" she unburdened herself of everything except Need and the money pouch, and handed it all to Tarma. "Furball, you follow me on the other side of the hedgerow and call Tarma when the time is right."

Warrl nodded, and wormed his way through a gap in the hedge to the field on the other side. Kethry left her mare with Tarma and trudged on ahead, trying to look as much like a victim as possible.

The road twisted and turned here, and rose and fell as it went over gently rolling hills. Shortly Tarma was out of sight. Kethry might have been worried—except that she was feeling too cold, sore, and generally miserable to bother with something as simple as "worry." Of course, given the way the talisman worked, the robbers would appear at the worst—

Her foot hit a rock, and her ankle turned under her. She yelped with pain—she couldn't help it—and she hit the ground hard enough to add yet more bruises to her already considerable collection.

Her ankle screamed at her. Without a doubt, she'd sprained it, but she felt it gingerly to be sure.

It was already swelling. And she looked up to find herself the focus of five pairs of amused and variously hostile eyes.

"Tain't everyday a cony drops right inta the snare!" one of them said with a nasty chuckle. "Wot a nice little bunny it is, too!"

The half-formed plan she had made was now in pieces; obviously she wasn't going to be able to run—or even draw the sword. There was only one thing she could do.

She snatched the purse off her belt and flung it at them.

Two or three coins spun out of the open mouth; three of the men scrabbled after them and retrieved them, shoving them into the front of their shirts, while the man who had spoken snatched the purse out of the mud. Kethry heard a warning howl and ducked, hiding her head in her arms.

Warrl vaulted over the hedge and over her; a breath later Tarma and the mares charged up the road and leaped over her as well.

The bandits scattered, too taken by surprise to make any kind of a stand. Tarma and Warrl pursued them just long enough to make certain that they weren't going to come back any too quickly.

By then, Kethry had levered herself up out of the muddy road using Need as a crutch, and stood there waiting for them.

Tarma pulled her mare up as Kethry's mount came close enough for the sorceress to pull herself into the saddle. Which she did, with no mishap. Proof enough that the curse was following someone else now.

"That was the last of our money," Tarma said, as Kethry ignored her throbbing ankle in favor of putting as much distance between them and the robbers as she could. "We're going to be spending the rest of the trip sleeping in haystacks and eating half-raw rabbit."

Kethry noticed that her ankle hurt less with every moment—as did her bruises. Need was making up for her misbehavior earlier, it seemed.

And Tarma's nose wasn't red any more either.

"Getting the curse to stick on someone else depends on how much you're willing to sacrifice to get rid of it," Kethry pointed out. "I just threw away all our money. The curse is *not* going to come back. And—" she continued, "—have you noticed that your cold is gone?"

Tarma blinked in surprise, and sniffed experimentally.

"I think," the Shin'a'in said carefully, "that this is a wonderful time of the year for camping out. And rabbit is excellent when rare."

Kethry laughed. And after a moment, Tarma joined her. The mares ignored them, continuing down the road at a brisk walk—

With no signs of lameness.

But behind them, Kethry thought perhaps she heard, faintly, the sound of someone cursing.

WINGS OF FIRE

Speaking of children, here's Kethry with some of her own, at last. If you've read *Oathbreakers* you know where she got Her Man.

Fecund little devil, isn't she?

Personally, I prefer having children with feathers. We have a number of them, cockatoos, macaws, and parrots, most of them about as loud as your average four-year-old, but the advantage is that you can keep them in a cage full of toys without having Child Welfare come after you!

The disadvantage is that they can hang off your collar and try to see why your beak (teeth) is on the *inside* of your mouth, destroy your jewelry, try to take your keyboard apart, and surf in your hair.

Heat haze shimmered above the grass stems, and insects droned monotonously, hidden down near the roots or swaying up near the new seedheads. There was a wind, a hot one, full of the scent of baking earth, drying grass, and the river nearby. Kethry held a half-finished basket in her hands, leaned back against a smooth, cool boulder in the shade of her tent, and drowsed. Jadrie was playing with the other youngsters beside the river—Lyan and Laryn were learning to ride, six-month-old Jadrek was with Tarma and Warrl, who were watching him and the other babies of Liha'irden, sensibly sleeping the afternoon heat away. All four of the children were safe, safer than at home, with all of Liha'irden watching out for them.

Kethry felt perfectly justified in stealing a little nap herself. The basket could wait a bit longer.

Then a child's scream shattered the peace of the afternoon.

"Mama!"

Kethry reacted to that cry of fear as quickly as any mother would—though most mothers wouldn't have snatched up a sword and unsheathed it as they jumped to their feet—

Even so, she was a heartbeat behind Tarma, who was already running in the direction of Jadrie's cry, toward the trees lining the river.

"Mama, *hurry!*" Jadrie cried again, and Kethry blessed the Shin'a'in custom of putting women in breeches instead of skirts. She sprinted like a champion across the space that the herds had trampled bare as they went to and from the waterside twice a day.

As she fought through the screening of brush and came out on the bank under the willows, the first thing she saw was Jadrie, standing less than a horse-length away. The girl was as white as the pale river sand, with both hands stuffed in her mouth—she seemed rooted to the riverbank as she stared down at something.

Kethry sheathed her sword and snatched her daughter up with such relief washing over her that her knees were weak. Jadrie buried her face in her mother's shoulder and only *then* burst into tears.

And only then did Kethry look down to the river

itself, to see what had frightened her otherwise fearless child half out of her wits.

Tarma was already down there, kneeling beside someone. A body—but a wreck of one. Shin'a'in, by the coloring; a shaman, by what was left of the clothing. Tarma had gotten him turned onto his back, and his chest was a livid network of burn lines, as if someone had beaten him with a whip made of fine, red-hot wires. Kethry had seen her share of tortured bodies, but this made even her nauseous. She could only hope that what Jadrie had seen had been hidden by river water or mud.

Probably not, by the way she's crying and shaking. My poor baby—

The man stirred, moaned. Kethry bit back a gasp; the man was still alive! She couldn't imagine how anyone could have lived through that kind of punishment. Tarma looked up at the bank, and Kethry knew that cold anger, that look of *someone's going to pay.*

And *get the child out of here.*

Kethry didn't need urging; she picked up Jadrie, and stumbled back to the camp as fast as she could with the burden of a six-year-old in her arms.

By now the rest of the Shin'a'in were boiling up out of the camp, like wasps churning from a broken nest; wasps with stings, for every hand held some kind of weapon. Kethry waved back at the river, and gasped out something about the Healer—she wasn't sure what, but it must have made some kind of sense, for Liha'irden's Healer, the man who had nursed Tarma back to reluctant life so many years ago, put on a burst of speed that left the rest trailing in his wake.

Kethry slowed her own pace, as the Clansfolk streamed past her. Jadrie had stopped crying, and now only shivered in her arms, despite the heat. Kethry held her closer; Jadrie was both the sunniest and the most sensitive of the children so far. So far she had never seen anything to indicate that the world was not one enormous adventure.

Today—she had just learned that adventures can be dangerous.

Today, she had learned one of life's hardest lessons; that the universe is not a friendly place. And Kethry sat down in the shade of the nearest tent, and held her as she cried for the pain of that lesson. She was still crying when angry and frightened voices neared, passed the tent walls, and continued in the direction of the Healer's tent.

When Jadrie had cried herself to exhaustion, Kethry put her to bed in the tent she and Tarma shared with the four children, gathered her courage, and started for the Healer's tent herself.

There was no crowd outside the tent, and the gathered Clansfolk appeared to have dispersed, but the entire encampment was on the alert now. Though there was no outward difference, Kethry could feel the tension, as if a storm sat just below the horizon, out of sight, but not out of sensing range.

She met Tarma coming out of the tent, and the tight lines of anger around her partner's mouth told her everything she needed to know.

"Warrl can guard the children. Do we stay here," she asked, "or do we ride?"

Tarma paused for a moment, and in that silence, the keening wail with which the Shin'a'in mourned their dead began. Her eyes narrowed, and Kethry saw her jaw harden.

"We ride," the Shin'a'in said around clenched teeth.

They followed the river northward all day, then, when it dived beneath the cliff, up the switchback trail at the edge of the Dhorisha Plains. They reached the top at about sunset, but pushed on well past dusk, camping after dark in the midst of the pine-redolent Pelagiris Forest. Tarma had been silent the entire trip; Kethry burned to know what had happened, but knew she was going to have to wait for her partner to speak in her own good time.

Being an Adept-class mage meant that Kethry no longer had to be quite so sparing of her magical energies; she could afford to make a pair of witch-lights to give them enough light to gather wood, and to light the fire Tarma laid with a little spark of magic. It wasn't a very big fire—in this heat, they only needed it to sear the rabbit they shared—but Tarma sat staring into the last flames after she'd finished eating. Light from the flames revealed the huge trees nearest their campsite, trees so old and so large that Tarma could not encircle them with her arms, and so tall that the first branchings occurred several man-heights above the ground. Most of the time, the place felt a little like a temple; tonight, it felt more like a tomb.

"He didn't tell us much before he died," Tarma said finally. "By his clothing, what was left of it, he was *For'a'hier*—that's Firefalcon Clan."

"Are they—all gone, do you think?" Kethry could

not help thinking of what had happened to *Tale'sedrin*, but Tarma shook her head.

"They're all right. We sent someone off to them, but he told us he was on his own. Firefalcon has always been—different; the Clan that produces the most shaman, even an occasional mage. They're known to roam quite a bit, sometimes right off the Plains. This one was a *laj'ele'ruvon*, a knowledge-seeker, and he had come seeking up here, in *Tale'edras* territory—the shaman of Firefalcon have a lot more contact with the *Tale'edras* than the rest of us do. Whatever happened to him, happened here in the Forest."

"You don't think the Hawkbrothers—" Somehow that didn't ring true, and Kethry shook her head, even as Tarma echoed the gesture.

"No—there's a Hawkbrother mixed up in it somehow, he said that much before he died, but it was no *Tale'edras* that did that. I think he was trying to tell me the Hawkbrother was in trouble, somehow." Tarma rubbed her temple, her expression baffled. "I've been trying to think of a way that a Hawkbrother could possibly get into trouble, and I—"

Something screamed, just above their heads. Kethry nearly jumped out of her own skin, squeaked, and clutched Need's hilt.

The scream came again, and this time Kethry recognized it for what it was; the call of the owl-eagle, a nocturnal predator with the habits and silent flight of an owl, but the general build of an eagle. She might not have recognized it, except that a pair were nesting near the Keep, and her husband Jadrek spent hours every evening in delighted observation of them.

Tarma stood up, stared into the tree canopy, then suddenly kicked earth over the fire, dousing it. When Kethry's eyes had adjusted to the dark, she could hardly believe them. Hovering overhead was an owl-eagle, all right, a much bigger bird than either of the pair she'd seen before—and stark white.

"That's a *Tale'edras* bird," Tarma said grimly. "They say the birds their mages use turn white after a while. I think he's been sent for help."

As if in reply, the owl-eagle screamed once more and flew off to the north and west, landing on a branch and looking back for all the world like it expected them to follow it. Kethry put her hand on her partner's arm to restrain her for a moment. "What are we going to do about the horses?"

"Damn. Release them, I guess. They'll head straight back to camp in the morning." Tarma didn't look happy about the decision, but there wasn't much else they *could* do; they certainly couldn't leave them, nor could they ride them through dark woods when they couldn't see where to put their feet. And leading them would be just as bad as riding them.

On the other hand, walking back to camp across the Plains in midsummer—

"Let's just leave them unhobbled, and try to get back before morning," Kethry suggested. "They won't stray until then." Tarma grimaced, but pulled the hobbles from her mare's feet and threw them on the pile of tack, while Kethry did the same. When she looked up, the owl-eagle was still there, still waiting.

He didn't move until they were within a few arm-lengths of the tree—and then it was only to fly off and land in another tree, farther to the north and west. Kethry had had a little niggling doubt at first as to whether her partner had read the situation correctly, but now she was sure; the bird wanted them to follow.

It continued to lead them in that fashion for what felt like weeks, though by the moon shining directly down toward the tree branches, it wasn't much past midnight. It was impossible to tell where they were, now that they'd left the road; one enormous tree looked like every other enormous tree. For the past several candlemarks, she'd been feeling an increase in ambient mage-energies; her skin prickled so much with it that she felt forced to shield herself, and she wasn't entirely sure that time was passing at its normal rate.

"Where are we?" she whispered finally to her partner.

Tarma stopped for a moment and peered up at the moon. "I don't know," she admitted. "I'm lost. Someplace a lot west and some north of where we started. I don't—I don't think we're in the Pelagiris Forest anymore; I think we're in Pelagir Hills country. I wish we'd brought Fur-face with us, now."

"I hate to admit it, but I agree—" Kethry began.

And that was when an enormous, invisible fist closed around them.

The bird shrieked in alarm, and shot skyward. Tarma cursed; Kethry was too busy trying to breathe.

It's the paralysis-spell, she thought, even as she struggled to get a little more air into her lungs. But she couldn't breathe in without first breathing *out*, and every time she did that, the hand closed tighter on her chest. *That's—supposed—to—be—*

A darkness that had nothing to do with the hour

dimmed the moonlight, and her lungs screamed for air.

—lost—

Blackness swooped in like a stooping hawk, and covered her.

Her chest hurt; that was the first thing she knew when she woke again. She opened her eyes as she felt something cool and damp cross her brow, and gazed with dumb surprise up into a pair of eyes as blue as Tarma's, but in an indisputably male face crowned with frost-white hair.

Indisputably? Not—quite. There was something unusual about him. Not that he was *she'chorne*, that she had no trouble spotting. Something like that, and not even remotely evil, but very, very different.

Beyond the face were bars glinting and shining as only polished metal could; and two light sources, one that flared intermittently outside of her line of sight, and one that could only be a witch-light, hovering just outside the bars.

The stranger smiled wanly when he saw that she was awake, and draped the cloth he'd been using to bathe her forehead over the edge of a metal bowl beside him. "Forgive me, lady," he said in oddly-accented Shin'a'in. "I did not intend to lure anyone into captivity when I sent out my bond-bird."

"That owl-eagle was yours?" she said, trying not to breathe too quickly, since every movement made her chest ache the more.

"Aye," he replied, "I sent her for my own kin, but she saw your magic and came to you instead. Now she is frightened past calling back."

"But I didn't—" Kethry started to say, then saw

the wary look in the Hawkbrother's eyes. *We're being watched and listened to. For some reason, he doesn't want whoever caught us to know his bird can See passive mage-shields, the way Warrl can.* She struggled to sit up, and the Hawkbrother assisted her unobtrusively.

They were in a cage, one with a perfectly ordinary lock. Beside them was another—with no lock at all—holding Tarma. The Shin'a'in sat cross-legged in the middle of the contraption, with a face as expressionless as a stone.

Only her eyes betrayed that she was in a white-hot rage; so intense a blue that her glance crackled across the space between them.

Both cages sat in the middle of what looked like a maze; perfectly trimmed, perfectly trained hedges taller than a man on horseback, forming a square "room" with an opening in each "wall." Beyond the opening, Kethry thought she saw yet more hedges.

"As you see," said a new voice, female, with an undertone of petulance, "I plan my prisons well."

The owner of the voice moved into the pallid light cast by the witch-ball; Kethry was not impressed. Face and body attested to overindulgence; the mouth turned down in a perpetual sneer, and the eyes would not look into hers directly. Even allowing for the witch-light, her complexion was doughy, and her hair was an indeterminate no-color between mouse-brown and blonde. Her clothing, however, was rich in a conspicuous, overblown way, as if her gown shouted "See how expensive I am!" It was also totally inappropriate for the middle of a forest, but that didn't seem to bother the wearer.

"For the mages," their captor said, gesturing grandly, "a cage which nullifies magic, with a lock that can only be opened by an ordinary key." She held up the key hanging at her belt. "And since I am as female as you, the spirit-sword won't work against *me*. Even if you could reach it."

Now Kethry saw the blade hanging just outside the cage door, just out of reach.

Of arms. That's her first mistake.

"For the warrior, a prison that only *magic* can unlock."

She giggled girlishly, without the sneer ever changing. Tarma said nothing; Kethry decided to follow her example. Their jailer posed, waiting, doubtless, for one of them to ask why they were being held. Finally, when she got no response, she scowled and flounced off in the direction of the light that flared and subsided, somewhere beyond the bushes surrounding the clearing where their cages sat.

"When her wits aren't out wandering, who *is* this woman?" Tarma asked, in a lazy drawl. "And what in the name of the frozen hells does she want with us?"

The Hawkbrother crossed his arms over his chest, leaned back against the bars of the cage, and grimaced. "Her name is Keyjon, and all her magics are stolen," he said, an anger as hot as Tarma's roughening his voice. "As for what she wants—nothing from you, except to be used against me. As my friend was, to his death."

The Firefalcon shaman. He knows the lad died. She tried to read beyond the Hawkbrother's lack of expression, and couldn't.

"We're to be used to get what?" Tarma asked.

"Something she cannot steal from me, though she has tried, and blunted her stolen tools on *my* protections." He pointed his chin in the direction of the flaring and dying light. "She has firebirds."

At Kethry's swift intake of breath, he nodded. "I see you know them."

"One of the qualifications for entering the higher levels of a White Winds school used to be the Test of the Firebird." She stared at the light, wishing she could see beyond the bushes. "They're too rare now. I only saw one once, at a distance."

"They are not rare here, only endangered by such as she." The Hawkbrother's face darkened. "She wishes me to make them her familiars. She *also* wishes *me,* and she is as like to get that as the other, which is to say, when the rivers of hell boil."

At that, Kethry laughed in astonishment. "Wind-lady—go *ahead!* Give her the birds! The first time she loses her temper with one of them on her shoulder—"

But the young man was shaking his head. "Nay, lady. She knows that as well as you or I. What she means by 'familiar' is 'complete slave.' I would not condemn any living thing to such a fate, even if the dangers of her having such control over something so dangerous were not obvious."

Kethry thought of the things that could be done with a tamed and obedient firebird at one's command, and shuddered again. The dangers *were* obvious. There was a history of the mage-wars purportedly written by the wizard-lizard Gervase that hinted the firebirds had been deliberately bred as weapons.

She couldn't imagine a circumstance terrible enough to make *her* breed something like firebirds as a *weapon.* Frighten one, and send it flaming through a village, touching off the thatched roofs, the hay in the stables . . .

"She was born of mage-talented parents, and given all she desired," the Hawkbrother continued. "But she came to desire more and more, and her own small talent could not encompass her ambition, until she discovered her one true gift—that she could steal spells from any, and power from any, and use that power to weave those spells at no cost to herself. Thus she enriched herself at the expense of others, and the more power she had, the more she sought."

To shake the thought from her mind, she stood up, slowly, and walked the few steps to the bars of the cage, mentally measuring the distance between the bars and Need. And as she studied the blade and how it was hung, another thought occurred to her. *I'm Adept-class. My power is unlimited, for all practical purposes. Could I become like her?*

The Hawkbrother stole silently up beside her, but his eyes were on the light beyond the hedges. "It is not power and wealth that corrupt, my lady, but the lust for power and wealth. When that lust takes precedence over the needs of others, corruption becomes true evil. That you even consider that you could become like Keyjon is a sign that you are not like to do so. She has never once considered anything but what she wanted."

"Well said," Tarma replied, her expression wary. "I'm Tarma shena Tale'sedrin; this is my *she'enedra*, Kethry."

"Stormwing k'Sheyna," he said, and a little rueful humor crept into his expression. "A use-name chosen when I was young and very full of myself, and now so hardened in place that I dare not change it."

Tarma's expression remained the same. "So how is it that you know this woman?"

"I confess; a dose of the same folly that caused me to name myself for the powerful thunder cloud," he replied slowly. "I thought I could help her, I thought that if she had a friend, she could learn other ways. In short, I thought I could change her, redeem her, when others had not been able to." He shrugged. "I thought, at the worst, I was so much stronger than she that there was little she could do to harm me. I thought I could not be tricked; did not even guess that she was planning deeper than I anticipated, that she was using me to come at my charges, the fire-birds. Now, not only do I pay for my folly, but others as well."

"What happened to the Firefalcon shaman?" Tarma asked harshly.

A muscle at the edge of his eyelid twitched; nothing else moved. "She caught him, coming to see me, and flung him into the cage holding the birds, making certain to panic them. She knew that if I once used my powers to control them, she could steal that control." His eyes were very bright with tears that he was holding back. "He knew it, too, and even as they lashed him with their flame, he told me to hold fast." He looked from Tarma to Kethry and back. "Will you forgive me when I close my ears to *your* cries?"

"Will you be closing your ears?" Kethry asked quietly, staring into blue eyes that seemed much, much older than the face that held them. "Or will you be heeding instead the cries of those who would suffer if this woman got what she wanted?"

He closed his eyes for a moment, his expression

for the first time open and easy to read. Pain—and a relief as agonizing as the pain, if such a thing were possible. Then he opened his eyes again, and took her hand and kissed the back of it, like a courtier. It was in that moment that Kethry identified exactly what it was about him that made him so hard *to* identify. Stormwing was the most uniquely *balanced* human being she'd ever met; so completely accepting of both his own male and female natures that he felt poised, like a bird about to fly—

"But you may not have to worry about it," Tarma said, dryly. "Keth, I don't hear her. You want to try the Thahlkarsh gambit?"

"Why not? It worked before." She kicked off her boots, grabbed the bars and climbed up to the top of the cage; once there (cursing her own laziness, that had let her get so out of shape) she carefully threaded her legs between the bars. As she had thought, her foot just reached the hook Need hung from.

"Get ready," she called down below, grinning a little to see Stormwing's eyes so wide with surprise. "I'm going to unhook the sword-belt and lower it to you."

Stormwing shook his head. "What good will having it do us, if this cage negates all magic?" he asked.

"It won't do *us* any good, but in a warrior's hands she cancels all spells cast against the wearer." Kethry's arms were screaming with pain, and sweat streamed down her face as she inserted her foot in the loop of belt, worked it around to the top of the hook, and lifted, carefully. "Tarma's cage is magicked, remember?"

"I hope that I am as good at throwing as you think me to be," Stormwing replied, straining one long arm through the bars until he caught the tip of the scabbard.

Kethry didn't have the breath to spare to tell him that Need herself would take care of that, once out of the influence of the cage. She simply continued to lower the blade, bit by bit, until Stormwing had it firmly.

Then she dropped to the bottom of the cage, and waited for the pain in her arms to stop. *I hate getting old. Why can't we all stay twenty until the end, then fall over?*

When she looked up again, the sword was sailing unerringly across the space between the cages, and Tarma caught it so neatly the movement looked rehearsed.

And no sooner did she have it in her hands, than the entire side of the cage swung open, like a door.

Just as Keyjon appeared in the gap in one of the hedges, accompanied by two enormous creatures, things that looked like nothing so much as walking suits of armor.

"Sheka!" Tarma cursed, and threw herself out of the cage, did a shoulder roll to cushion her impact, and came up running, heading for Kethry. Keyjon was so astonished that she stood there, mouth hanging wide open, while Tarma grabbed Need and shoved her through the bars at Kethry.

Kethry grabbed it just as Keyjon recovered, pointing at the three of them, and shrieked something foreign even to Kethry's ears. Whatever it was, the two suits of armor at her side straightened, drew their weapons, and headed straight for Tarma.

Kethry had seen spells of animation before; this one was better than she had anticipated. The armor

moved easily, smoothly—and quickly. Tarma escaped being sliced in half by a two-handed broadsword only because she was a hair faster than they
were. She wasn't going to be able to escape two of
them for very long, not out there alone.

Hopefully she wouldn't *be* alone much longer.

Kethry pulled out the little lock-pick she kept in
the side-seam of the scabbard, and set to work on
the lock of the cage. Keyjon seemed to be concentrating on Tarma and ignoring them; she hoped things
would stay that way.

*Now, just so Stormwing doesn't decide that since he's
a man, he can do this better than I can—*

Stormwing pressed in close beside her, and she looked
up, ready to brain him if he tried to take the pick,
and saw that he was clinging to the bars of the cage
with both hands, his body carefully pressed up against
the door so that most of what she was doing was hidden from Keyjon.

"Thanks," she whispered, and then set to work on
the lock, shutting everything out, including the fact
that her partner and blood-bonded sister might die
in the next few moments.

When you work on a lock, she heard the voice of her
thief-instructor say, *Nothing exists for you but that lock.
If you let yourself be distracted, that's the end of it.*

Except that he had never had the distraction of two
magic suits of armor trying to make his partner into
thin slices less than an arm's length away.

She felt the lock give just as Keyjon noticed what
they were up to. She shoved the door open as the
woman shouted another incomprehensible command, and one of the automata stopped chasing after

Tarma, and turned, its blade arcing down over its head—

But not aimed at Kethry.

Aimed at Stormwing.

He couldn't dodge, caught in the doorway as he was. He had no weapon of his own, and no spell Kethry knew could possibly be readied in time to save him.

She watched the blade descend, knowing that *she* would never even be able to get Need up in time— *if only he was a wo—*

CLANG!

When her teeth stopped rattling, her brains stopped vibrating, and her watering eyes cleared, she thought for a moment that she had gone quite entirely mad. For there, with the automaton's blade held a hand's breadth away from his head, was Stormwing, crouched down, one hand raised ineffectually to ward off the blow that hadn't arrived.

For what had interposed itself between him and the broadsword was Need.

They all stood like that for a moment, in a bizarrely frozen tableau—

Then Stormwing dove out from under the arch of sheathed sword and unsheathed, scrambled to his feet as the automaton disengaged and began to turn, and yelled, "Duck!"

Somehow she knew to drop into a ball, and Stormwing dove at the automaton's chest.

The timing couldn't have been any better if they'd practiced it; the animated suit of armor was very heavy and already off-balance, and when Stormwing shoved it, it went further off-balance, staggered backward, and tripped over her, landing with a hollow clangor inside the cage—

The cage which permitted no magic to function within it.

"Move!" screamed another voice from across the clearing; both Kethry and Stormwing scrambled out of the way as Tarma pelted across the intervening space, the other suit of armor in hot pursuit. She fled right into the cage—it had too much momentum to stop.

Kethry heard a strangled croak, and turned to see Keyjon clutching her throat and turning scarlet with the effort of trying to speak. Stormwing watched her from where he sprawled; his finger traced a little arc, and her arms snapped out in front of her, wrists together, fingers interlaced.

Only then did he rise, with a curious, boneless grace, and pace slowly to where the woman stood, a captive and victim of her own greed.

Kethry got up off the ground, wincing as she felt sore places that would likely turn into a spectacular set of bruises. Tarma climbed down out of the cage, favoring her right leg.

"What happened with the fool sword?" Tarma asked, in a low voice.

Kethry shrugged. "I guess when she couldn't identify him as positively male or female, she decided to act first and figure it out later."

Stormwing looked up as they reached his side, but said nothing. "What are we going to do with her?" Kethry asked.

He ran a hand through his hair. "I do not know," he confessed. "I have a feeling that if I tried to harm her, that blade at your side would turn against me."

"Probably," Tarma said, in disgust. "But she's killed at least one person that we know of. A shaman of the Clans, at that, and sacred. Blood requires payment—"

"Would you accept a punishment that left her alive?" the Hawkbrother asked unexpectedly.

Tarma hesitated a moment, then replied with caution. "Maybe. *If* she couldn't get free to try this again. *If* she couldn't even leave here—and *if* it was a living hell for her. My Lady favors vengeance, my friend."

He nodded. "My thought as well. Lady, would you be content also?"

Kethry only nodded; she felt power building, coming from some source she didn't recognize, but akin to the pool of energy available to all White Winds Adepts. She hadn't realized he was an Adept before—

He raised his hands. "All your life, you have sought to be the power in the center of all, to be the manipulator of the fabric of the world around you," he said to Keyjon, solemnly. "So, I give you that; your greatest desire. Control of all you can see, manipulator of the web—"

He pointed; there was a ripple of the very fabric of the place—and a distortion that made Kethry's stomach roil and eyes water.

Then when she looked again, Keyjon was gone. Instead, hanging from a web that spanned a corner between the hedges, was an enormous gray spider, hanging fat and heavy in the center of the pattern.

"Spiders are notoriously short-sighted," Stormwing said, as if to himself. "Now I shall have to see to it that nothing comes here but noxious things, that deserve to be eaten—and old or diseased things, that deserve a painless death."

He looked back at Kethry, and in that moment she knew that not only was he enormously more powerful than she had guessed, he was also older. Much, much older.

"Here is a guide," he said, producing another ball of witch-light. "I have much to do here, and this will take you back to your horses before dawn." Now he smiled, and Kethry felt as if all her weariness and aches had been cured. "I could not have been freed without your aid. Thank you, sisters-in-power. Thank you."

"You're—welcome," Kethry said. She wanted to say more, but the witch-light was sailing off into the darkness, and Tarma was tugging her arm. She followed the Shin'a'in into the maze, quickly losing track of where she was, but torn apart by conflicting emotions. There was so much she wanted to learn from him, so many things he must know—

What have I done with my life? All I have built is one White Winds school. With power like his, I could—

I could make a mess of things, that's what I could do, meddling where I didn't belong. No, I guess that power isn't such a temptation. What would it earn me, anyway, besides envy and suspicion?

If she had Stormwing's kind of power, it would make her a target for those such as Keyjon. Was the knowledge worth the risk?

Risk not only to her, but to Tarma, to the children, to Jadrek?

No, she decided. *And after all, we were the ones who rescued him. Knowledge isn't everything. Sometimes it just takes common sense, good planning—*

A chorus of joyful cries arose behind them; she and Tarma turned as one to see the firebirds rising into the air above the hedge, alight with their own flame. They circled, and dove, and sang; everlasting fireworks that made their own music to dance by. She felt her eyes brimming with tears, and beside her, Tarma gasped with surprise.

The firebirds circled a moment longer, then rose into the tree canopy, still calling in ecstasy to each other. They penetrated the branches, making them glow emerald for a moment, as if each tree harbored a tiny sun of its own.

Then they were gone. And in the light from the witch-ball, Tarma's face was wet with tears. So was hers. She understood, now, the other reason why two brave men had been willing to die to save them from enslavement.

She caught Tarma's shoulders, and held her for a moment.

And this is what's worth having; freedom, and friends, and the ability to see a thing of beauty and not want it all for myself, or because of the power it represents.

Then Kethry let her sworn sister go, as Stormwing had set the birds free.

"Come on, partner, let's go home," she said. "We have a tale to tell."

SPRING PLOWING AT FORST REACH

This is a new short story suggested by Teri Lee of Firebird Arts and Music, who pointed out that on a working farm, such as Forst Reach, most horses would be put into harness in times of heavy workload like planting and harvest. And she noted that, given the temperament of the famous Gray Stud of Vanyel's time (an alleged Shin'a'in warsteed) it was quite reasonable to assume that plowing time (with frisky, hormonal horses) would be rather exciting. She also told me the story of an Amish farmer and his two mares, and his very unique technique for bringing misbehaving horses to see sense.

As for the Shin'a'in technique of taming (or rather, gentling) horses, it is based entirely on fact, and the techniques of a remarkable man named Monty Roberts, who without any form of coercion whatsoever, can take a green, untrained, skittish horse, and have it accepting bridle, saddle, and rider *in thirty minutes*. His technique is based soundly on understanding equine body language and "speaking" to the horse with his own body language, and results in a cooperative partner. His book, *The Man Who Listens to Horses*, is one every horse lover and owner should read.

There was no light but that of the hearty fire in the Lord's Study at Ashkevron Manor, but neither of the two inhabitants of the study needed any other illumination. It was clearly a "man's room," comfortably crowded with furniture that the Lady of the manor deemed too shabby to be seen elsewhere, but too good to be relegated to the rubbish room. Distantly related if one looked back far enough, Lord Kemoc Ashkevron and Bard Lauren would seem unlikely companions to an outsider, and sometimes even seemed so to those who knew them both, but the improbable friendship had prospered for many years and showed no sign of changing. The bard played a soft melody on his gittern as Lord Kemoc seemed to doze, the golden firelight flickering over both of them.

Kemoc opened his eyes and roused, cocked his shaggy-haired head to one side and frowned at something he'd heard that wasn't music. Bard Lauren stopped playing immediately; he'd been trying to soothe Kemoc's aching joints with his Healing-music, and had thought he'd been succeeding. With every passing year, Lord Kemoc's joints hurt more when the cold wind out of the north swept down over Forst Reach at winter's beginning. Even here, in this comfortable wood-paneled room, deep within the belly of the manor, Lord Kemoc could not escape the aching of his bones.

"Is there something wrong, old friend?" Lauren asked anxiously. Kemoc shook his grizzled head ponderously, looking more bearlike than usual, and motioned him to silence.

Lauren held his peace, flattening his palm over the strings of his gittern so that not even a breath of draft would set them murmuring.

"Do you hear that?" Kemoc asked abruptly.

Lauren *listened*, as only a Bard could, taking note of anything that could be termed sound. Past the crackling and hissing of the fire, past the sound of Kemoc's breathing and his own, there was a different note in the sound of the wind about the walls of Forst Reach. "The wind's changed direction?" he replied tentatively.

Kemoc nodded and sighed, both with relief and regret. "It has. It's out of the south, old boy. In a few days, we'll have our thaw, and it'll be time for plowing. And happy as I'll be to see the spring, it's just that much that I dread the plowing. I'm getting too old to cope with it; it's worse than a battle campaign."

Lauren blinked at him in surprise. "Dare I ask, why?"

Kemoc bared his teeth in a grim smile. "Stick around here instead of flitting off as you usually do come spring, and you'll see for yourself."

Now Lauren's curiosity was aroused. "I've nowhere in particular to go," he began, "And if you'll have me—"

"If?" Kemoc's grim smile lightened. "Don't see enough of you, old son. I'll be glad enough to keep you a bit longer—but I warn you, spring plowing around here is not for the weak of heart. I've heard it said that at Forst Reach, 'plowman' and 'wild beast tamer' are considered to be one and the same thing."

Now Lauren's curiosity was more than roused, it was avid. "In that case, I don't think you could be rid of me if you wanted to!"

He attempted to get more information out of Lord Kemoc, but a spirit of mischief—or maybe devilment—had infected the Lord of Forst Reach, and nothing more would Kemoc tell him. Lauren went up to his bed that night with his curiosity completely unsatisfied.

Lauren was happy to spend the winters at Forst Reach—winter being the only season when his services as a Master Bard were not needed at Haven, for *all* the Master Bards that had no families came crowding back to avoid the harsh weather. Kemoc was an old friend from the time Lauren had first gone out on his Journeyman's wanderings, and since he had nowhere in particular to go in winter and no great desire to spend it on the road or in Haven, Lauren welcomed the invitation. In the spring, he would return to Haven bearing all the news of this part of the world back to the capital—and in greater detail than the Heralds of this region did, since he spent more time here than a Herald on circuit could. For his part, Lauren found in Kemoc's household the family he had never known. Perhaps it was easier because he had come into this "family" without any of the burden of childhood memories. *It is easy for parents to pull the strings that make one dance*, he reflected, as he closed his door behind him, *After all, they are the ones who tied those strings in place.* Perhaps it was just that he was familiar enough for the Ashkevron household to be easy with him, yet not so familiar that anyone inflicted family grievances on him.

Or perhaps it is because they know that as a Bard, I might well be tempted to turn an absurd grievance into a comic song.

Lauren knew Lord Kemoc well enough to realize that behind the joking and the grim humor, there was some real worry. But *why* should he be so concerned over a little matter like spring plowing?

Lauren crossed the room unerringly, even in the darkness. There was no doubt that the wind had turned; now it blew full against the shutters of his room, and there was a gentler, wetter scent to it, where it leaked in past the leaded glass windowpanes, than there had been this morning. He put his gittern into the stand by touch and knelt to blow the fire to flame.

In the ten years he'd spent winters here, Lauren had never seen anything to make Kemoc this concerned. Forst Reach was a prosperous and peaceful holding. *Spring plowing*, he wondered again. *Why should he have compared it to a coming battle? Just how difficult could spring plowing be?* He realized that he was not country-wise enough to know *everything* about life on the land, but surely the weather couldn't become that vicious in the spring or he'd have heard something of it by now.

It was as he thought that—though he did not realize it at the time—that he got his first clue. For on the wings of the warming wind came the squeal of an angry stallion from the stable.

Lauren listened to the horse telling the world that he was ready to take on all comers, mare or competitor, and chuckled. No doubt; even the beasts recognized the turning of the season. And since Kemoc had gone coy, he might as well get to sleep; he'd find his itch of curiosity eased all in good time.

Two days later, the last trace of snow was gone, and although the air was chilly and the breeze brisk, it was no longer so bone-chillingly cold. It was time for the first plow to cut the first furrow, while the earth was still damp, but not muddy. Right after breakfast, Kemoc had brought Lauren out to the back of the barns where the harnessing took place, and the sounds of angry horses had rung through the air even before they reached the yard in front of the barn. Now Lauren stared at a pair of fighting, kicking geldings—*geldings*, not stallions!—being dragged to their harness by two sturdy plowmen, and felt his eyes widening.

"Spring plowing," said Kemoc with resignation. "There you have it, the sum and total of our problem."

"But—but—I thought plowhorses were, well, *docile*," Lauren protested, trying to reconcile the fact that he *knew* those horses had been gelded with the fact that they were acting like fighting stallions. The first horse had been dragged to his appointed place and with two people holding his bridle, a third was managing to get a harness on him. The second had already kicked his harness off, and was trying to bite the first horse, whose ears were back and whose yellowed teeth were bared.

"They are," Kemoc replied heavily. "Everywhere but here. Come along, old lad. I'll show you what we're up to here. This is all due to a decision made by one of my ancestors, and the *idea* was a sound one, but—well—there are some problems with the execution, you might say."

Farther along the row of horses being readied for the field, a pair of mares with foals at heel were also being harnessed up. The foals were clever, nippy little demons, who obviously resented the fact that their meal-producers were being interfered with. The men harnessing the mares had to keep them off by main force, and wore leather shirts to protect against bites. "We're famous for our Ashkevron breed of war horse," Kemoc explained. "There was a horse—allegedly a Shin'a'in warsteed—called the Gray Stud. He was the foundation-stallion; we took him to our hunters and plowhorses—in the first generation. He was a fighter and he was smart, everything you'd want in a war horse, but he wasn't big enough to carry a man in full plate armor. We were looking for intelligence and fighting spirit from him, agility and speed from the hunters, and size and strength from the plowhorses. We crossed the sons from the hunters to the daughters from the plowhorses, and that gives us our basic warhorse. We continue crossing the best of the best; geld everything we don't use at stud, and sell the ones we won't breed. Trouble is, we can't afford to keep horses around eating their heads off and doing nothing but breeding, so *everything* is broken to harness and plow except the breeding stallions. Which makes spring plowing time— exciting. The geldings all retain every bit of a stallion's fight. That's why people pay a small ransom for them."

"I can see that," Lauren replied, watching with stunned amazement as a gelding—another *gelding!*— left alone for a moment in a loose box, proceeded to attempt to batter the thing to splinters in an effort to get at the gelding tied to the outside of it.

"The Gray's temper went hand-in-hand with his intelligence and both traits bred true, which makes them finely-honed killers on the battlefield, but no joy in harness," Kemoc continued glumly. "Most of the year you can handle them, but spring brings out the worst in them. There'll be broken bones before the day's over."

And before the day was over, Lauren saw Lord Kemoc's prediction proved true. One pair of geldings decided to go over a stone fence, plow and all, and hung the plow up on the top. A foal ripped out a hank of one plowman's hair (roots and all) in fury when the man wouldn't unharness his dam and tried to separate them. Two more geldings too intractable to be harnessed in a team with anything saw each other and conceived an instant hatred for one another; they dragged their plows and plowmen with them across the width of two fields to meet in the middle in a furious clash that left both plows in splinters. And one of the breeding stallions broke out of his field to get at a harnessed mare, which incident resulted in the first broken arm of the season.

"It could have been worse," sighed Kemoc at the end of the day, as he and Lauren shared a bit of bread, cheese, and beer. "It could have been a broken skull."

"I hope you'll forgive me for asking the obvious, but haven't you tried breeding something with a *good* temper into the line?" Lauren asked.

"Oh, we've tried, but the Gray Stud's temper always comes through." Kemoc shook his head. "I've never seen anything like it. People want the geldings as war horses, there's no shortage of takers for them, but by the gods, it gets hard and harder to survive this season every year! And breeding season's no festival either. The mares fight back even when they're hard in season, often as not, and there's damage all around before they get separated from the stallion."

Lauren pondered this for a moment. "It—really

isn't very funny, is it?" he said. "I mean, it sounds funny at first, but people are getting hurt."

"And it's only damned good luck that no one has gotten killed," Kemoc agreed. "How long before my people start refusing to plow with these beasts? What will we do then? We can't afford to keep one herd of plowhorses and one herd of warhorses, the damned things eat too much."

Lauren didn't say anything then, nor did he mention that he had an idea even when he left Forst Reach to return to his duties at Haven and the Court—but he had made up his mind to try and do something to solve Kemoc's problem before the next plowing season.

Cold rain drummed on the roof of the indoor riding arena, and Tarma shena Tale'sedrin blessed the break in the weather that had allowed her to send her young pupils home for summer holidays before the weather turned this ugly. She'd sent them off a bit early this year, in no small part because they'd gotten an early start last fall, and it hadn't seemed fair to keep them away from home longer than usual.

And besides, she'd had a particular project in mind that she didn't want an audience for—the very project that kept her in the arena at this very moment.

Tarma already had her hands full and didn't really need anything to distract her when one of the servants edged nervously up to the fence intended to keep spectators out of the riding arena. She spared a moment to glare at the hapless servant, silencing him before he had a chance to speak, and turned her attention back to seven-year-old Jadrie, Kethry's eldest.

As blonde as her mother, as blue-eyed as her father, young Jadrie was a pretty child who threatened to become a beauty. Fortunately, it hadn't occurred to her that beauty was a cause for vanity, and neither parent had any intentions of letting her know that fact. Today she wore her oldest, most practical clothing of well-worn woolen tunic and breeches, and scuffed riding boots; she had her hair done up in a practical tail, and looked very much as her mother must have at her age.

This was a special day for her. Tarma had judged her old enough for a horse of her own this year— and in Shin'a'in terms, that meant something of great and specific significance—nothing less than a rite of passage.

Jadrie had been carefully coached for all the winter months in the Shin'a'in art of horse-talking, and now she was putting her new knowledge to the test with an unbroken, green filly, three years old and fresh off the Plains and the Tale'sedrin herds. If she really *had* learned her lessons correctly, the young filly would be carrying her willingly by the end of the day. If she hadn't, Tarma would take over and tame the horse herself, and Jadrie would go back in humiliation to her fat little pony for another year.

A little harsh on the child, maybe—but better that than spoil horse and child together. There's no second chances on the Plains, and it's never too early for a child to learn that.

But things were going very well, so far. The tiny blonde child had the sorrel filly pacing in a circle with her at the center, keeping her going with gentle tosses of a lead rope, making it land just behind the horse's moving feet. As the little girl flicked her soft rope at the heels of the filly, watching the horse with such intensity that her blue eyes shone, the horse turned her near-side ear to catch the girl's murmurs of encouragement.

Another round of the circle, and the filly dropped her head, flicking out her tongue at the same time. Jadrie dropped her eyes back to the horse's shoulders, then to her rump. The filly dropped her head further, chewing at nothing. That was the signal Jadrie was waiting for, and Tarma with her.

Right, girl. Remember your lessons. The filly's saying, "I don't want to run in a circle, I'd like to stop. Can't we eat together and be herdmates?" Don't wait for a second invitation.

Jadrie coiled up the rope and let the filly slow and stop, then walked toward her. The filly started to take a single nervous step away, but before she could, Jadrie looked away from her, then turned away, making chirruping sounds.

Good, good. You're doing everything just right. Keep her soothed, look at her, but not directly. Invite her into your herd.

The filly stepped tentatively toward the little girl, then stopped again. Once again, Jadrie faced her, then turned away, looking back at the filly briefly over her shoulder out of the corner of her eye. This time the filly approached further, one slow step at a time, until she stopped, not quite coming as far as Jadrie's shoulder.

"Good girl!" Jadrie crooned. "That's right, pretty girl! Come on, then—"

Still murmuring, Jadrie walked slowly away. After a moment of hesitation, the filly followed.

Tarma grinned. Jadrie was going to be the envy of her siblings this summer; there was no doubt that she'd mastered all of Tarma's coaching in horse-talk. The Shin'a'in didn't *break* horses, they *spoke* to them, working with their own body language and instincts to convince them that their would-be riders weren't two-legged, horse-eating predators, but were potential partners. With nothing more than hands, mind, voice, a blanket, and a soft rope, any Shin'a'in over the age of ten could have even the wildest horse carrying him willingly in less time than it took to bake a loaf of bread. And since Kethry's children—or, more properly, those who *chose* the life—were to become Shin'a'in in everything but looks, they were going to have to learn horse-talking.

Unless she changed her mind drastically when she grew older, Jadrie would be the first of the renewed Clan of Tale'sedrin. Right now, Jadrie wanted nothing more than to live her life on the Plains; in fact, this last year she'd spent her first autumn fostered with a family of Clan Liha'irden before returning to Kethry's Keep with the first snow, and had gloried in every moment. This little test only proved that she had everything in her to prove to the satisfaction of even the sternest of Clan Chiefs and Shamans that she had the true spirit of a Shin'a'in.

In short order, Jadrie's filly had accepted the rope around her neck, then the blanket on her back, then Jadrie herself on the filly's back with nothing to "control" her but a crude halter made of the rope. As the little girl trotted the filly gleefully around the ring, blonde tail bouncing with the movement of the horse, Tarma turned her attention to the servant.

The man was watching Jadrie with his mouth hanging open and his eyes wide with shock. Tarma snapped her fingers at him to break him out of his trance. "Well?" she said, a little impatient. "What was so important that you had to come down here to interrupt a lesson?"

He stared at Tarma and gulped. "What sorta witchcraft *be* that?" he asked.

"None whatsoever," she countered. "It's nothing more complicated than paying attention." But she really didn't expect the man to believe her, and it was clear that he didn't. The servants that had come with this place were a mixed bag of good and bad, and the bad tended to be ignorant, superstitious, and foolish rather than of ill-intent. Jadrek was gradually replacing the bad ones, but it was slow going. "So?" she repeated. "What sent you down here?"

"There's a man t'see you, m'lady," the fellow said diffidently. "From King Stefansen. He's with Lady Kethry."

From Stef? Huh. She made a shooing motion with her hand. "Well, get back up to the house and tell them I'll be there as quickly as I can."

She pointedly turned her attention back to Jadrie; the servant waited a moment longer, but when it was obvious that she wasn't going to say anything more, he took himself and his message out.

Tarma sighed; the fellow was one of the ones due for replacement, and obviously Jadrek hadn't found anyone with his skills *and* good common sense. It took a certain sturdiness of character combined with a stolid acceptance of anything that came along to work out as a servant at the Keep. As a consequence, they always seemed to be a little shorthanded.

Can't really blame people for getting spooked around here, Tarma reminded herself. *If it isn't the barbarian, raw-meat-eating Shin'a'in leading her pack of male and* female *hooligans in mock wars, it's Lady Kethry's mage-students blowing up storms or setting things afire or conjuring up weird beasts out of the Pelagirs. And if it isn't either of those things, it's Lady Kethry's own brood wreaking some hellishness or other!*

There'd be more mischief, that was sure, now that Jadrie had her very own, grown-up horse. The others would be all over themselves coming up with some prank to counter her new-won glory. Tarma expected to hear tales of woe from the village any day now, of sheep turned interesting colors, or puppies trained to herd chickens, or some strange contrivance powered by a kidnapped and irritated billy goat positioned at the well, a contraption designed to bring up water with no effort. And whatever it was that had happened would all be well-intentioned, meant to *help*, but the end result would be to scare the whey out of the long-suffering villagers.

Eventually, she supposed, they'd get used to it. But the youngsters had only been at this "helpful" stage for a couple of years, and it would probably take a couple more before that happened.

Jadrie, at least, would be well-occupied for the spring, and the first day of summer would be the signal for the annual trek to the Plains, which would at least get the children away from the village for the all-important summer growing season. The Liha'irden found the little ones' pranks amusing, sometimes even hilarious, and were not at all taken aback by them.

They'd howl with laughter at sheep with pre-dyed wool. And it wouldn't matter what mad color the pranksters painted the woolies, there's not a color in the rainbow that my people don't like.

:Feh. I know,: said a voice in her head. *:You'd think that after a few centuries they'd have developed a little taste.:*

Tarma disdained to reply to Warrl's jibe; she had more important things to concentrate on. Jadrie had begun guiding her mare through more complicated moves than simply trotting in a circle, and she wanted to pay close attention to the behavior of both horse and rider.

But there were no problems, none at all. The filly moved well and willingly, head and ears up, tail flagged, and although Jadrie still wore her look of intense concentration, it was overlaid with an expression of intense joy. Tarma knew exactly how she felt; she'd felt that way herself when she'd tamed Kessira. Probably every Shin'a'in child felt that way after taming a horse for the first time—it was a little like magic, and altogether thrilling to have something that large accept you and work with you on its own terms.

Finally Jadrie brought her horse to a neat halt, a few paces away from Tarma, and looked expectantly at her teacher. Tarma gave her a grin of approval, and the smile Jadrie flashed back at her lit up her face.

"Good job, kitten," Tarma approved. "Now, go cement your friendship with a little sweet-feed. You've worked her enough for today, and tomorrow, if the weather's good, we'll move outside."

Jadrie nodded, her tail of blonde hair bobbing with enthusiasm, and slid down off the filly's back with great care to avoid startling her. With a hand on the horse's shoulder, she led her new prize off to the stable, where the filly's good behavior would be rewarded by something the grass-fed beast had never yet tasted—a sweet treat of treacled grain. Then she'd be rubbed down with a soft cloth, although she hadn't been worked up enough to break a sweat—it was the contact that mattered. Jadrie had groomed enough beasts by now to know all the "good spots," and she'd be sure to scratch every one.

"And what do you two think?" she asked the other two spectators, who had remained respectfully silent until now.

Tiny, ice-blonde Jodi, formerly one of Tarma's scouts in the Sunhawks, clasped her hand to her forehead woefully. "Eh now, lady, ye'll be puttin' me an' Beaker out of business here if ye keep trainin' up more horse-talkers!" She imitated Kyra's back-county accent perfectly, Tarma noted with amusement.

Her business partner and mate Beaker, also a former Sunhawk, nodded glumly. He would have been utterly forgettable except for his impressive jut of a nose—and the fact that one of his special messenger-birds, a creature about the size of a crow, with a black body and green head, sat on his shoulder. Tarma laughed at both of their long faces. She'd taught both of them the Shin'a'in ways with horses when they'd come to her asking if she needed instructors at her new school. She hadn't, not yet anyway, but she'd asked them if they had any interest in another trade.

"No fear of that," Tarma replied. "That girl can't wait to get out on the Plains. If her mother would let her, she'd be fostered out at Liha'irden this moment." She was pleased, though, with the implied compliment. "What brings you two out here again, anyway?"

"The usual," Beaker told her laconically. "Still looking for someplace to settle down. Trouble is, nobody in this part of the world needs horsetalkers all year 'round. We're getting a bit long in the tooth for the road life." He looked at her hopefully. "Don't suppose you've heard of anything?"

"Not yet, but—why don't you stick around for a fortnight or so?" she told them. "Maybe something will come up."

"I'd as soon sleep in one of your beds as the floor of an inn," Beaker replied with gratitude. "Thanks."

"No worries," Tarma told him, "You've stayed here often enough; put your mares up, get your gear and find a room, and I'll see you at dinner. Keth'll be glad to see you."

As the two Sunhawks (*former* Sunhawks, she reminded herself) disappeared through the stable door to get their gear, Tarma turned to leave through the outer door. "Coming, Furface?" she asked over her shoulder, as Warrl's great bulk uncoiled from behind the fence.

:*I wouldn't miss this for the world,:* Warrl replied smugly.

Tarma cast him a look of suspicion. Just what did he know about the visitor?

But the *kyree* wasn't talking, so the only way for her to find out what was going on was to get up to the manor.

She found Jadrek and Kethry in the solar, entertaining an ordinary-looking fellow with brown hair, a neatly-trimmed brown beard, and a charming, open face. But it was his clothing that immediately explained the reason for Warrl's amusement. He was dressed in scarlet from his collar to his boots, and there was only one thing *that* could mean.

Oh, gods, she groaned, as Warrl chuckled unmercifully in her head. *Not another bard!*

"Tarma! Just the person we needed!" Jadrek said genially, before Tarma could duck out of sight and hide. "Please join us!"

She sighed, and schooled her face to a pleasant—or at least neutral—expression as she entered the warm, firelit solar. "I really shouldn't," she began. "I've just been in the stables, I smell like horse—"

"But that's precisely why I'm here," the stranger exclaimed, turning toward her eagerly. "Horses! A very dear friend of mine and a *very* important noble of the Valdemar Court is suffering from a rather extreme set of problems with his horses—"

"And you came here?" Tarma allowed one eyebrow to rise quizzically as she chose a sturdy chair and flung herself into it. "Why on earth did a Bard of Valdemar come here for help with horses?"

"Because Roald sent him to Stefansen, and Stef sent him here, of course," Kethry replied, a twinkle in her green eyes. She twined a tendril of hair as golden as her daughter's around one finger in an absentminded gesture Tarma knew meant she was highly amused.

"Ah." Tarma let the eyebrow drop again. "Roald" was *King* Roald of Valdemar, who was Stefanson's friend and had been since the days when they were merely Prince Stefansen and Herald Roald. Jadrek had been Archivist to Stef's father, and he and Tarma and Keth had helped put Stef on the throne of Rethwellan after his brother usurped it, tried to murder him, and succeeded in murdering their sister. She in

turn had been Captain Idra, leader of the Mercenary
Guild Company Idra's Sunhawks—which had em-
ployed Tarma as Scoutleader and Kethry as Company Mage. It sometimes made Tarma's head spin,
what with being a Shin'a'in Swordsworn and simple
trainer of would-be warriors on one hand, and on a
first-name basis with the Kings of two countries on
the other.

"Well," she said, leaning over to help herself to
food and drink with a long arm. "You're a bard, you
ought to know how to tell a tale in a straightforward
manner, so why don't you start from the beginning
and explain the situation to this poor bewildered
barbarian?"

Nothing loath, the young man launched into his
story. Tarma had a difficult time keeping her face
straight when he related the fable of the Gray Stud
being a Shin'a'in warsteed. Nothing was more unlikely, and she said so.

"I can promise you that we haven't lost a stud off
the Plains in our entire history," she told him. "And
it's damned unlikely that your friend's ancestors
even got an accidental halfbreed. Battlemares are perfectly capable of keeping an unwanted male at bay,
and even if one had the poor taste to mate with
something other than another warsteed, I can guarantee you she'd be back *on* the Plains as soon as her
rider knew she was pregnant. We simply don't let
the bloodline out of our hands."

Bard Lauren shrugged. "I'll admit that the story
sounded odd to me," he admitted, "but it's one of
those family legends that no one contradicts." His
face fell a little. "I came here in hope that since the
problem stems from that bloodline, you'd know how

to deal with it," he concluded in resignation. "And since the bloodline isn't what I was told, I won't waste any more of your time—"

"Whoa up, there!" Tarma exclaimed. "I *didn't* say I couldn't help you. As a matter of fact, I'm fairly certain I can."

:*Just what are you up to?*: Warrl asked with alarm.

With no students to train, I was afraid I was going to be bored waiting for the summer trek, she thought gleefully. *This will be a marvelous way to do a little traveling. I'll ask my Hawkbrother friend to magic us up to the north and back, and it won't take any time at all.*

:*You wouldn't!*: Warrl said in horror. He hated the Gates, though he and Tarma had only needed to use them once before, when the Hawkbrother mage she and Kethry had rescued had asked for some assistance in tracking a weird Pelagir beast and bringing it to bay.

Tarma chuckled under her breath.

The Bard's face lit up as brightly as the sun at high summer. "You can?" he exclaimed.

A plan was rapidly forming in her mind, and she turned to Kethry. "You won't need me back here until the trek to the Plains for the summer, will you?" she asked.

Kethry shook her head. "Not that I can imagine— and until then, the rains should keep the childrens' mayhem to a minimum."

"Good! Try and keep them out of the village, will you? They'll probably all try and do something to match Jadrie's new horse if you don't. I've got a notion to see how our old friend Roald is doing, and a run will do Warrl a world of good." She smiled maliciously as Warrl made a sound of inarticulate protest. "I hope you haven't unpacked your things, Bard Lauren; we'll have to leave in the morning if we want to get to your Forst Reach by spring plowing."

The Bard placed one hand over his heart and bowed to her formally. "Swordlady, a Bard can always be on the road at a moment's notice—and if you can solve Lord Kemoc's problem, I will be eternally grateful and at your service for as long as you please."

She chuckled. "Save your gallantries, my friend, and prepare for a hard ride."

Tarma had to give the man credit; he endured the difficult journey without a single complaint. He weathered the passage of a Gate from one Hawk-brother Vale to another farther north, right on the Border of Valdemar, and he put up with the ride by horseback afterward, in spite of the fact that they rose in the dark and didn't look for beds until well after nightfall, or that the rain drenched them every single furlong of the trip eastward. "I've ridden with Heralds a few times," was all he said, and of the three of them, Tarma was the only one who had any vague idea of what that might mean. *She* knew what Companions were—and if they were capable of the sorts of endurance wonders she suspected they were, then the Bard was a tough trooper indeed.

As one of the few Shin'a'in to leave the Plains, Tarma had more contacts among the Hawkbrothers than most of her kin, and partnering with a sorceress had given her a certain stolidity about magic. Her two friends were used to war-magic, and although the Gate excited a little curiosity in them, they weren't terribly startled by it. It was the Bard Tarma expected trouble from—

But strangely enough, it was almost as if his mind went blank from the time they entered the Vale to when they crossed the Valdemar Border. He literally did not remember how they had gotten there. And if Tarma had been inclined to worry about such things, that memory lapse would have seriously bothered her—but knowing the Hawkbrothers as she did, she suspected they had diddled with the man's mind to make him forget them, and she had no particular objection to such meddling.

Beaker and Jodi were looking forward to this job at Forst Reach, and had immediately fallen into the old habit of looking to her as their commander. She had more experience than they did at handling entrenched behavior problems in horses, but she had every confidence, not only in them, but in their mounts. Graceless and Hopeless were as ugly as their names implied, but they were almost as intelligent as a battlesteed, and had been trained for just this sort of situation. What Jodi and Beaker couldn't handle, their mares could.

And for the *really* difficult customers—which would probably be the stud stallions—Tarma had both Ironheart and Hellsbane. She rode the former, and the Bard and his meager pack and hers were gingerly perched atop the latter, though Tarma had to give Hellsbane special commands before the battlesteed would permit a stranger to ride. Warrl rode on his pillion pad behind Tarma.

This strange little cavalcade clattered up the lane to the Ashkevron Manor just as the wind, which had been blowing steadily out of the north, suddenly turned and came from the southwest.

They were met at the door of the Manor by the Lord himself, whose first words were for Lauren, although he couldn't quite keep his startled gaze off Tarma and her companions. "By the gods, Lauren, we missed you this winter, and your mysterious letter was no compensation! Where in all the hells *were* you?"

"Finding you that help for your spring plowing problem, old friend," Lauren said wearily, but with a wide smile at the shock and surprise on Lord Kemoc's craggy face. "May I present to you my friends the Swordlady Tarma shena Tale'sedrin of the Shin-'a'in, and her two compatriots, Jodi n'Aiker and Beaker Bowman, of Rethwellan?"

"A *Shin'a'in*?" Lord Kemoc's eyes nearly bulged out of his face, but he recovered quickly. "You're right welcome to Forst Reach, Ladies, Gents—" He looked somewhat at a loss for something to say, but his lady-wife was under no such difficulty.

"Come in, you're soaked to the skin and no doubt tired to the bone," she said firmly. It was obvious that although she was at a loss as to what their rank and status might be, she was taking them at face value as Lauren's "friends" and ranking them as his equals at least. "You need dry clothing, a good meal, and a warm bed, and anything else can wait until morning," she concluded, with a warning glance at her spouse.

He, wise man, immediately gave way before her; Tarma was not going to argue either.

The lady herself showed them to three rooms, all in a row, with doors on a common corridor. Tarma was in the first, and cheerfully dropped her pack on a bench at the foot of the bed. Neither large nor small, neither luxurious nor sparse, her room had a comfortable-looking bed, a chair, and the bench, with a washstand and a mirror on one wall in the way of furnishings. A fire burned cheerfully in the small fireplace on one wall, and there was glass in the window that looked out over the lane they had just ridden up.

Warrl sighed, and curled up on the hearth rug. *:I wonder how the lady plans to solve the riddle of where to seat us at dinner?:*

"She won't be seating *you* anywhere, Furface," Tarma laughed, just as someone tapped on the door.

Like a miracle, there were two servants, one with covered dishes on a tray—which neatly solved the question of how the lady was going to puzzle out their ranks—and one with water and a bowl of meat trimmings for Warrl.

Tarma was inclined to be more amused than offended at their hostess's neat sidestepping of protocol. She got a dry tunic and breeches out of her pack and changed into them, draped her wet clothing on the mantle to dry, and left her boots off, wriggling her toes in the warm fur of the rug beside her bed as she sat down to demolish the dinner that Lady Ashkevron had supplied her.

"I hate to admit this, but I prefer this to facing two dozen strangers all staring and trying to pretend they aren't," she told Warrl, once a taste had assured her that the savory portion of meat pie would not have to be put to rewarm beside the fire.

:You'll get your staring eyes soon enough. Tonight the Bard will let the Lady know you're fit for the High Table,

and everyone will be able to stare at you as much as they want,: Warrl said, a trifle maliciously. He still hadn't forgiven Tarma for the Gate.

Her high good humor was too strong to let a little jibe like that affect her.

She put her tray outside the door and trotted down the hall to check on Beaker and Jodi. As she had expected, Jodi had simply moved in with Beaker rather than trying to make herself understood, figuring that their hosts would get the correct idea when only one room was in use. Jodi was just finishing her own dinner; Beaker had inhaled his and was examining one of the half dozen books that graced a little desk in their room.

"Wish I could read this," he said wistfully, as he put it down and moved to join Tarma and his partner in the door of his room. "I can speak a bit of their lingo, but the writing's beyond me."

"You aren't going to have time to read," she told him. "At least not for the next couple, weeks. Did you see the size of the stables as we rode in? Figure on the sheer number of problem children they've got!"

While Beaker sat down on the hearth rug beside Warrl, using him as a backrest, Jodi's eyes lit up. Jodi was never happier than when she was working.

"I speak the language pretty well, so just let me translate for now," Tarma went on, sitting tailor fashion on the bed so that Jodi could take the chair. "If we do well here—tell you what, this just might be the long-term position you were looking for. It's obvious they don't know a thing about horse-talking, or they wouldn't be having the difficulty that they are."

Jodi nodded, pursing her lips. "This is all speculation, of course, but I'll bet that though their foundation stud *did* have a miserable disposition, the only thing wrong with their current crop is that they're too intelligent. They *know* they can get away with misbehaving, so they do. These horses are spoiled, that's what's wrong with them."

Beaker snorted. "Hellfires, they're expected to misbehave! Expect *anything* out of a horse, and you'll probably get it!"

Tarma grinned, pleased with herself and them. "The big question is, how do you want to play this? Do we demystify our hosts, or do we play this up as some sort of singular mind-magic?"

Beaker chuckled, and ran his hand through his short crop of graying hair. "We don't demystify them unless we decide we don't want to stay here—and right now, I wouldn't mind settling here for the rest of my life!"

On that cheerful note, the three of them parted company, and Tarma stretched herself out beneath a thick woolen blanket with every feeling of contentment.

But the shrill trumpeting of a stallion woke her at dawn, and sent her tumbling out of that warm, comfortable bed with a great deal more eagerness and enthusiasm than she had expected. She followed her nose to the kitchen, where an intimidated servant gave her hot bread and milk, and then followed her ears to the stables, where a battle royal was in progress. And quick as she had been, Jodi and Beaker were there waiting for her.

So was Lord Kemoc, and she took charge of the situation immediately.

"Whoa-up!" she shouted at the two stablehands

struggling to get the recalcitrant beast into harness. "Leave off!"

Startled, they obeyed; she marched up and seized the reins of the horse, a gelding, looking him over quickly to judge his age and guess at the amount of behavioral damage she was going to have to undo. "Stubborn, aren't you, my lad?" she murmured, seeing that he was no more than three with a touch of relief. "Well, I'm not surprised. But you aren't getting away with this nonsense anymore."

The horse looked at her and snorted, as if daring her to make him behave. She laughed, somewhat to the Valdemaran's surprise. "Lord Kemoc, are these horses ever in harness except at plowing time?"

"No—" came the answer.

She shrugged. "Well, then—what you've got is two problems. The first is that these fellows never get a chance to understand what their job's all about. You shove them into harness, then they get something chasing at their heels for a fortnight or so, then you turn them loose again. The other problem is that you need to speak their language."

Kemoc's mouth literally dropped open. "We— *what*?" he spluttered.

"You need to speak their language," she replied firmly. "You're trying to break them, when they're too spirited and too intelligent to be broken, then when they misbehave, you give up. You just need to talk to them, and make them understand that good things happen when they behave themselves. Beaker, show him how to handle a youngster like this one— I doubt he's got too much to unlearn."

Beaker took the halter of the gelding and led him into a small enclosed exercise yard. Over the course of the morning, he worked what to the Valdemaran probably seemed like a miracle. Using many of the same techniques that Jadrie had used in taming her new filly, he soon had the gelding standing placidly under his harness. But then, instead of hitching him immediately to a plow, Beaker walked behind him, guiding him with the reins as if he were plowing, but without the plow in place; he kept looking back at Beaker in puzzlement, but instead of punishing him for stopping, Beaker simply gave him encouragement. Once the gelding was used to taking his orders from behind, instead of being ridden, Beaker got him accustomed to pulling against a weight— himself, leaning against the harness. Only *then* did he attach a sack full of gravel to the harness and guide him around the yard until he was comfortable with the idea of pulling against something *and* have that "something" right at his heels. Every time the horse began to act up, Beaker went back to the beginning—showing the horse that his behavior was not proper to herd etiquette, rather than punishing him.

Tarma explained what he was doing each step of the way, stressing that it was as important to act on what the horse was trying to tell his handler as it was to get the horse to do what you wanted, but as she expected, the Valdemarans assumed that this was some sort of magic rather than simple common sense and observation. By the time they broke for a little lunch, Lord Kemoc and his stablehands were just about convinced that Beaker was using something akin to a Herald's Gifts. Tarma overheard them muttering about "mind-speech" and "animal mind-speech," and had to stifle her grin.

They took a short break for a little lunch—eaten,

Tarma noted, in a common group that included Lord Kemoc. That boded well for Jodi and Beaker's future. Afterward, she instructed the stablehands to bring in fresh horses two at a time. One by one, Jodi and Beaker took the youngest of the geldings into the exercise yard and ran them through the training routine, only turning them over to the plowmen when they were sure that the horses understood what they were being asked to do. By then, Lauren was nearly beside himself with delight, and Lord Kemoc was eyeing the three outlanders as if he suspected them of far more power than they were demonstrating.

"I still don't understand how you're doing this," he said, "but I'd be a fool to argue with the results. What next?"

"Next, while Beaker and Jodi keep on with the geldings, I deal with the mares with foals—or rather, I deal with the foals," Tarma said firmly.

The mares were easy enough to harness up—they were used to being in harness, since they pulled carts and other farm implements all year long when they weren't in foal. They were also not used to being allowed free rein to their annoyance. It was the foals themselves that were the problem, and that problem was solved rather easily. Whenever one tried to nip, Tarma maneuvered quickly so that it nipped its mother instead of the human. Mother reacted predictably, with a squeal and a lashing hind hoof, or by turning to nip her youngster, and the foal was punished for its behavior by the authority it respected, in a way that it understood, and in a way that did not leave it with a fear of the human.

"Now, let the foals walk alongside while you plow," she instructed the plowmen. "Don't try to separate them from their mothers at this age; they aren't going to trample the plowed earth the way an adult would, and once they understand that mother isn't going to be taken from them, you won't have any more trouble with them. Stop when they need to nurse; they won't take that long. On the whole, I suspect they'll come to enjoy this as a new kind of game."

That brought them to the end of the first day; fully half of the mares and a quarter of the geldings had worked calmly in harness, and although far fewer horses were out plowing, far more had gotten accomplished on this first day than ever had before. Furthermore, no one had been injured! Lord Kemoc was beside himself with joy, and insisted on having all three of them beside him at the head table, displacing his wife and two of his children. Fortunately, those displaced didn't mind in the least and simply added to the chatter; the whole family seemed to be good-tempered and far less concerned with rank than Tarma had expected. When Lord Kemoc learned that the three of them had served in a mercenary company, he was full of questions, and with Tarma translating, Jodi and Beaker soon had the table roaring with laughter with some of their stories.

:*They're doing well,*: Warrl observed, from his place with the family wolfhounds next to the fire at the end of the great hall. :*They're making themselves well-liked as well as respected.*:

What do you think of this place? she thought to him. *Do you think they'd suit here?*

:*I think they'd fit in like a hand into a well-made glove,*: Warrl replied. :*Lord Kemoc's people are well-fed and content with their overlord, and no one here seems to stand too much upon rank and class.:* There was amusement in his next thoughts. *:I did overhear some of the stablehands though—they think Jodi and Beaker had it "easy" today. Tomorrow they'll get the older geldings, the difficult cases, and the ungelded males. They don't think horse-talking is going to work.:*

Well, they're right, but we have more than one trick up our sleeves, don't we? she replied, just as amused as Warrl.

The next day proved the truth of what Warrl had heard. After Tarma reassured the foals that today would be just like yesterday, and Jodi and Beaker coaxed the young geldings into their harness and plows, the first of the "hard cases" was brought out, rearing and kicking. It took two men to hold him, one on either side, and even then he wasn't what Tarma would have considered to be "under control."

Jodi took one look, and turned around and went into the stable, but before Lord Kemoc's men could do more than begin to chuckle at her "cowardice," she had returned, with Graceless and Hopeless in a very special triple harness.

"This lad has a lot to unlearn," Tarma explained, as Jodi and Beaker replaced Lord Kemoc's two men—and Warrl rose up out of the shadows beside the stable to approach the horse from the front. Never having seen a *kyree,* the horse started and tried to shy, all of its attention on the possible threat and none of it on Jodi or Beaker. As Warrl slowly stalked toward the horse, it backed up willingly, and before the gelding knew what was happening, it was between Graceless and Hopeless. Quicker than thought, Jodi and Beaker buckled the gelding into the harness and Beaker took up the reins as Jodi stood aside.

Warrl turned and loped away, out of sight, and the gelding woke to its situation. Predictably, it immediately tried to kick and rear.

Graceless and Hopeless didn't nip and didn't kick—instead, they *leaned*. They were heavier than the gelding and a half a hand taller, and as they leaned toward each other, the gelding was held immobile between them. They remained that way until he stopped fighting, then they shifted their weight again, freeing him.

He seemed very surprised and unsure of what to do; Jodi clucked to the two mares, and they moved forward a few steps, bringing the gelding perforce with them. *Now* he resumed his bad behavior—and they leaned into him again. A little harder this time, squeezing a bit of breath out of him.

Jodi took the three into the yard and put them through the same paces as before, while Beaker watched. The Valdemarans didn't watch, they stared, with their mouths dropping open.

Tarma took the opportunity to get Lord Kemoc aside. "What's the hardest case you have?" she asked.

"A gelding that stood at stud for a while, and thinks he's still whole," Kemoc replied, mopping his brow with a cloth.

"Bring him out," she told him, and went to get Hellsbane and Ironheart.

The chestnut gelding in question needed four men on him; squealing and sweating, he fought every inch of the way.

Bad, or just angry and confused? I can't tell. There was always a percentage of horses in an inbred line like this that were just—crazed. The only way to tell for certain would be to work him with Hellsbane and Ironheart.

"Turn him loose in that yard," she said, pointing to a smaller, ring-shaped exercise yard. The men looked at her as if she was crazy herself, but did as she asked.

The gelding entered the yard kicking and bucking, and soon had rid himself of every bit of harness except his halter. That was fine with Tarma; she didn't want anything getting in the way. She let him run and buck in circles for a while to wear himself out; when he finally stopped, so drenched with sweat he looked black, she whistled softly to the two warsteeds, and calmly walked into the yard while the stablehands hissed in surprise.

As she had half expected, the gelding charged her; it was a sham charge—though if she'd turned to run, he'd have chased her right out of the yard. Instead, she stood her ground with the warsteeds on either side of her, and he stopped short, snorting with surprise.

"Now, my lad," she said calmly to him, "you've been allowed to get away with a lot of bad habits, and we're going to civilize you."

He snorted and danced at the sound of an unfamiliar voice, arrogance in every line of him. *You can't tame me!* his attitude said, as plain as if he could speak. *I'm a Stud! I'm a King! I can do anything I want!*

Then his attention turned to the warsteeds, and his nostrils flared, taking in their scent. They weren't in season, but that wouldn't matter to a gelding who thought he was still potent. His ears came up, and he arched his neck. *Mares!* said his body language. *Girls of my dreams! Don't I impress you? Aren't I won-*

derful? I'm a Stud! Come over here, and I'll show you just how Studly I am!

Ironheart yawned, Hellsbane snorted in contempt. Both looked to Tarma.

"He needs taming, ladies," she told them in Shin-'a'in. "Go give him his lessons."

Ironheart shook her head and ambled forward, with Hellsbane half a length behind. Both of them were a full two hands taller than this would-be stud, and correspondingly heavier, but what mattered to the gelding was that they were mares.

He curveted toward Ironheart, dancing sideways, quite clearly intending to mount. But he kept an eye on her teeth, just in case she took a notion to bite him. Much to his shock, she neither bit nor allowed him to mount her; instead, she sidestepped, neatly maneuvering out of his way.

More determined now, he pursued her, which was exactly what she wanted. After a few feints, she had him positioned right where she wanted him—between herself and Hellsbane.

At that moment, Hellsbane closed in before he could move out of the way, sandwiching him between the two warsteeds as neatly as if he'd been harnessed there.

Graceless and Hopeless could not have maneuvered a loose horse like this, but warsteed mares were quite used to handling herd-studs this way when they got out of hand. This was the way they kept their would-be mates in line when they weren't in season or didn't particularly care for their hopeful mate. This was just as well, given the training that warsteeds had in combat. If they hadn't been able to handle unwanted mates in a nonviolent manner, there would be serious damage done every spring.

This was what Graceless and Hopeless had been *trained* to do with a harnessed horse. They themselves were of Shin'a'in breeding, but from a small herd dedicated to producing working farm horses, a herd carefully preserved as one of the warsteed foundation lines. When problems showed up in a warsteed breeding herd, the stallion was put to one of these mares, and the resulting offspring bred back into the warsteed herd. They weren't as intelligent as the warsteeds, and certainly not as surefooted and quick, but by keeping this herd of foundation-stock intact, the Shin'a'in prevented some of the problems that came with heavy inbreeding.

When the gelding found himself wedged between the mares, he was astonished. *How did this happen?* said his ears and head. *What's going on here? I'm a Stud!* And he tried to struggle loose.

Ironheart flipped an ear. *Oh, really?* said her attitude, and just as Graceless and Hopeless had done earlier, she and Hellsbane *leaned* toward each other.

But they were not just trying to immobilize this importunate young fellow, they were going to teach him a lesson. They squashed him between them so hard he couldn't move at all.

Not that he didn't try, every hair on his body erect with indignation. *You can't do this to me! I'm a Stud! I'm your Master! You were born to serve me!*

Hellsbane twitched her nose. *I don't think so,* said her ears and tail, and she leaned harder.

In short order, the warsteeds had the gelding squashed so firmly between them that they had shoved all the breath out of him, his eyes bulged like a fat frog's, and his hooves no longer quite touched the ground. They let him hang there for a moment, then took some of their weight off him, allowing him to drop down between them.

He stood there, panting, his head drooping, and quite clearly trying to figure out what had gone wrong. By now the yard was ringed with spectators, all of them holding their breath to see what would happen next.

The gelding tried to get away twice more; twice more the warsteeds squashed all the air out of him. Finally, he gave up, and stood between the mares with his head dropped down to his knees. Now it was Tarma's move.

She approached him with a bridle and bit in her hands; when he saw the hated bridle, his head came up and he tried to rear.

But the mares wouldn't let him. Once again they closed in on him, not leaning, not yet, but making it very clear that if he acted in a way they didn't approve of, they would.

Tarma approached his head with the bridle. He tossed his head out of the way. The mares leaned, just a little, then let their weight off him. Tarma tried again, patiently, until once again, he gave up, and she was able to get the bit between his teeth and the bridle on him.

Now was the trickiest part; getting the harness on. She went back to the railing of the yard and collected it, then gave Hellsbane a handsignal. The mare moved out of the way, and the gelding eyed Tarma warily, but with new respect. It was evident now to him that Tarma was a member of the herd, not just one of those annoying two-legs. More than that, by the way that the others were obeying her and cooperating with her, she must be the lead-mare! This was a concept that left his poor head spinning.

Tarma walked calmly up to him, and laid the harness on his back, just as Beaker had done with the younger gelding. He, of course, immediately shook it off. She did it again, he shook it off again. She put it back on for a third time, and his head snaked around to snap at her.

Tried, rather, because before he could move, Ironheart had the back of his neck in *her* strong, yellow teeth, and gave him a good, hard bite. He squealed and tried to kick, but Hellsbane nipped his rump first.

He was every bit as intelligent as Lord Kemoc had claimed for the breed; *this* time, he didn't try to bolt, or bite—he stood there, shivering and thinking.

Tarma laid the harness over his back; he left it there. She buckled it up; he let her.

And now she did something he would never have expected; she praised him, got out a soft cloth and wiped him down, scratched all the places where sweat had collected and dried, and which were itching him like the sting of a horsefly. *Had* he ever been praised and petted before?

Probably not, she decided, judging by the way he started and jumped, then rolled back his eye to look at her with utter bewilderment. But he liked it, oh my yes! He liked it a very great deal, leaning into her scratches, and even rubbing his nose against her tunic.

Spoiled rotten and too full of himself, but not mistrained, she decided with satisfaction. *This won't take long at all.*

She took the harness off him, and the bridle, and let him loose for a moment, then approached him with the bridle again. Of course he wasn't going to let her put it on him now that he'd gotten rid of it! But the warsteeds were ready for that, and quickly had him neatly sandwiched between them again, and this time it didn't take nearly as long to get him bridled and harnessed.

By the end of the day she had him pulling a plow, harnessed between her mares. If he shirked and didn't take his share of the load, they squashed him. If he tried to run away with the plow, they squashed him. If, however, he behaved himself, Tarma was there with a word of praise.

She was concentrating so hard on handling this horse that she completely forgot about her audience, and when she brought the gelding back in to be put up in his stall and fed, the stablehands treated her with a respect verging on awe. "We'll have to work him between my mares for a few days," she told Lord Kemoc, "But after that, he'll go all right for you this spring, and Beaker and Jodi will be able to train him to saddle and sell him afterwards—which I gather you weren't able to do before."

Lord Kemoc could only shake his head in wonder.

She and Beaker and Jodi worked with Lord Kemoc's horses for a week before all of them were working properly in harness. By the end of the third day, Lord Kemoc had voiced delicate hints about their employment status, and by the end of the week, he and Jodi and Beaker had successfully concluded negotiations that gave them equal pay and status with Lord Kemoc's Weaponsmaster. Tarma was completely satisfied at that point; the worst of the horses had learned proper behavior, and with Jodi and Beaker in charge, from now on the foals would never have a chance to learn bad habits. The Ashkevron horses should be the most sought-after in the Kingdom.

She and Hellsbane and Ironheart rode into the gates of their own home just as the spring rains began to break up. Jadrie rode up to meet her on her own sweetly-tempered little mare, full of spirit and impatient to be off to the Dhorisha Plains for summer holiday. Over dinner that night, Tarma had the whole family in stitches over the story of the poor, squashed gelding with his eyes bulging like a frog's.

Kethry wiped away tears of laughter from her eyes with a napkin. "So Jodi and Beaker are safely ensconced, and Lord Kemoc's horses are all going to behave themselves from now on? I'd say that was a successful ending to your assignment! But you still haven't told us what you said to the Valdemarans to explain your training techniques—"

"Well, they probably still think it was magic, Greeneyes," Tarma told her with a chuckle. "But what I *told* them was the truth."

"And what was that truth?" Jadrek asked.

Tarma grinned. "That it was just the proper application of peer pressure."

Oathblood

Here is where I've gotten to put together a bit of what life is like at the schools, and why the partners aren't rolling in gold when their reputation should ensure that they get plenty of clients. Better quality than quantity, as Tarma would say. I'm assuming that the pupils all go home in the summer for a long vacation that corresponds with the growing and harvesting seasons, and take a briefer vacation over Midwinter Holidays, if they live near enough to make it feasible. Obviously, for this story, all of them did.

Tarma watched her two favorite pupils enter the ring—a simple circle of paint on the floor of the salle—with a critical eye. The first, a blonde whose hair was confined in a tail and bound with a bright blue headband, stood about even with Tarma's chin, but the second, whose dark mane was plaited in two braids wound severely around her head, was even shorter. It wasn't often that Jadrie faced off against an opponent smaller and younger than she; at the age of twelve, Kethry's eldest daughter was more likely to find herself paired with Tarma's oldest pupils, two and three years her senior and correspondingly taller. Jadrie was by no means an extraordinary fighter by Shin'a'in standards, but she was quite good, and she *had* been tutored by Tarma from the

279

time she first evidenced an aptitude and interest in warrior-training. That had been at the tender age of four—though naturally she had not been given weapons, even practice weapons, until she was eight and had already demonstrated steadiness and responsibility by taming and training her first horse. Most of Tarma's pupils never had the benefit of such early training, so Jadrie was naturally far in advance of even some much older than she.

Kira was the exception to that; her father, the now-Archduke Tilden, King Stefan's former Horsemaster, gave his children access to some surprising teachers. At the age of three, on the sound principle that taking lessons with a former entertainer would be play rather than work, Kira and her twin sister had gotten a retired professional acrobat and contortionist as a tutor, and at six, along with the usual schooling, lessons given by a professional dancer had been added. At eight, on her own initiative, Kira had begun training with her father's Weaponsmaster, and now, at ten, she and her twin were here, with Tarma, Kethry, and Jadrek.

But Kira and her twin Merili were both extraordinary children, each in her own fashion.

They were not identical twins; in fact, if they had not been born at the same time, their father often joked that he would have suspected his wife of some infidelity. Ash-blonde Merili was as delicate and feminine as her mother, but with her father's eyes, although in Merili the expression was of sweetness and utter innocence—Kira was tough, wiry, tall for her age, with straight brown hair and eyes of an incredible violet that had never appeared in either family to anyone's knowledge.

But unusual things happened in their family; Tilden had seen more than enough not to worry about inconsistency in hair and eye color. Shortly after Kethry and Jadrek had wed, Tilden had married a former bodyguard, who, despite her frail appearance, had more than once broken the necks of assassins with her bare hands. *Her* early training had begun with acrobatics and dance; hence, she had seen to it that her daughters had at least that much in the way of physical schooling.

But Kira had something more than mere training; she was a prodigy, the kind of student every teacher prays to have once in his or her life.

Merili was a graceful dancer and loved the art, was already an accomplished needlewoman, was fascinated with languages and had a strong interest in herbalism. She couldn't have been more unlike Kira, but the bond between them was unbreakable; and where her twin went, there she was. So when the Archduke enrolled Kira in Tarma's school for would-be young warriors, Merili had come along. She worked out in physical exercises with her sister and the rest of Tarma's students, studied nonmagical courses with Kethry's students, and continued other studies with Jadrek, getting as fine an education here as she would with her private tutors. Tilden had *already* had several marriage offers for her, but Merili had already met the eldest son of the Queen of Jkatha, and the two had formed an early attachment so strong that many suspected it to be a lifebond. What with the Archduke's holdings already lying on the Rethwellan-Jkatha border, and the King of Rethwellan wanting very much to strengthen ties between the two countries, the match seemed an ideal one. So although a formal betrothal had not been announced, it was very, very likely that Prince Albayah would wed Merili as soon as both came of age.

"And *I'll* go as Merili's bodyguard," Kira always chimed in, whenever the subject came up.

It seemed to Tarma that there could be no better solution to the Archduke's surfeit of girl-children. There was one older than the twins (already making a name for herself as a scholar) and three younger, one of whom was likely mage-talented, though at the tender age of three it was difficult to say *how* talented.

And why not? Being a bodyguard certainly runs in the family, Tarma thought, as she watched Kira and Jadrie testing each other in the circle. Jadrie was having some difficulty adjusting herself to an opponent so much smaller than she, but Kira far outstripped anyone else her age, and Tarma didn't trust any of the older (exclusively male) pupils to keep their tempers when a child so very much younger scored a touch on them. They could accept Jadrie scoring points; they could always salve their pride by telling themselves that *she'd* had the benefit of Tarma's schooling since the cradle. But Kira (supposedly) had no more advantages than they, and that made losing to her triply painful. The current crop of students older than Jadrie were all noble-born—it would be a lucrative season for the school—and they found it hard to forget that pride has no place in the training-ring.

:*Or outside it,*: Warrl added, echoing her thoughts. :*But this is their first season with us; after the holidays and a thorough lecture or two from their fathers' Weaponsmasters, they'll come back in a properly humble frame of mind.*:

True, Furface, she thought back at him, chuckling to herself. She interviewed the parents of prospective students very carefully, and at holiday time sent home letters of evaluation and instruction timed to reach the parents at about the same time the students did. This year's lot wasn't bad, but the older boys all shared the regrettable certainty that their age and sex meant superiority in the ring over younger, smaller, or female opponents. Tarma's letters of instruction this year carried an admonition about that—and the caution that underestimating a smaller or female opponent could get them seriously dead if they were permitted to hold onto that delusion.

These were all *oldest* sons, extremely precious to their families (or they wouldn't be here), and it was unlikely that the parents would ignore Tarma's admonition.

And if they did—or attempts at correction didn't "stick"—there was always the second season to knock some sense into them. They would be here for at least two seasons, and maybe more, and none of Tarma's pupils ever cherished such ridiculous notions past the second season.

She privately felt that it was doing Jadrie good to have a little competition from someone other than her siblings. It was also doing her good to have not one, but two girlfriends. She'd begun showing more interest in things besides fighting and riding, much to Kethry's relief. Tarma was looking forward to having the twins here for at least another three or four years, and so was Jadrie.

She checked Jadrie, who was about to land a blow, with an admonition of "Jadrie—high." Jadrie flushed, and signaled for a rest. Kira grounded her point, and Jadrie turned to her teacher.

"*Ha'shin*, I'm having a lot of trouble with that," she said, honestly, giving Tarma the Shin'a'in honorific that meant "teacher." "What do you do when your opponent is so much shorter than you are? She's scored five times on me, and I've only managed once!"

"Four—" Kira corrected. "That rib cut wasn't more than a graze; if these had been real, I wouldn't even have marked your armor, so it hardly counts."

Jadrie gave her friend a quick glance of gratitude, then turned her attention back to Tarma.

Tarma looked both girls over, and decided that they'd had a good enough bout that she could legitimately give them a rest. Both of them were panting, and Jadrie's face was sweat-streaked. "Good question, and time for a demonstration," Tarma told them, then raised her voice. "Justin, as soon as you're ready to break, I can use you. Demonstration time."

Justin Twoblade, who was sparring with one of the older boys, waved his free hand in acknowledgment. Three moves later, and the boy was disarmed; as he shook his stinging hand, Justin strolled over to Tarma's ring, waving his hand to summon all of his pupils to come watch the demonstration.

"Jadrie wants to see how someone works against a much smaller opponent," Tarma told him. Justin nodded, and his craggy features showed none of the amusement Tarma knew he felt at the moment.

"As long as we're going at quarter-speed, Swordsworn," he replied, his face as sober as a priest's. "I remember the time three seasons ago when you used

Ikan in the same demonstration. You may be Sworn to chastity, but I've barely begun my family."

Tarma suppressed a grin. "All right, for Estrel's sake I'll spare you," she said, and went down on one knee, then on guard. This put her head just about at Justin's beltline, which should have been a handicap for her—but as she then demonstrated, even at one-quarter speed, she still made Justin work to defend himself and score on her.

But what she wanted her students to watch was what Justin did, not her—for even Kira might one day have to defend against someone smaller than herself. When she grounded her point, signaling the end of the bout, she saw with satisfaction that both girls had their eyes still locked on Justin's hand and wrist.

She wiped sweat from her forehead with her free hand, and Justin extended his to help her to her feet. "Jadrie and Kira, another bout, now that you've seen a demonstration," she directed. "Justin, if you'd supervise them, please, I'll take Larsh, Hesten, and Belton and work on those disarms and counters."

Since Hesten was the young man that Justin had just disarmed, the other instructor let a brief grin flicker over his face when the aforementioned students couldn't see it. That was a common tactic among the three instructors; when one had administered a rebuke in the form of a painful defeat, one of the others would take over that student and work with him, so that the student didn't have the incentive to try and get back at the instructor. She'd seen this one coming for the last few days; Hesten was good on offensive work, but seemed to think that the best defense was a good offense. She judged that he'd need a couple more lessons to get over that particular fault, and she and Justin would have to take turns in administering those lessons.

She'd hired both Justin Twoblade and his partner Ikan Dryvale the second year the school had been in operation. She and Kethry had known the pair for years, and had known that they were steady enough in temper to be trusted with young students. Ikan currently was out running the rest of the students around the obstacle course; he had all of the younger boys today, since he had a knack with the youngest pupils that was only matched by Tarma herself. To avoid creating the appearance of "favorites" and to keep their students on their toes, the three instructors switched pupils on a regular basis and an irregular schedule, just as young Shin'a'in children were taught.

So Tarma resolutely kept her attention on the three oldest boys and paid no heed to what Justin was doing with Jadrie and Kira. Hesten was still smarting from his defeat, both physically and mentally, and she worked to get him and the other two back to the business at hand.

But they were all distracted, and Hesten clearly resented the fact that "his" instructor had gone to help mere girls.

"Look," she finally said with exasperation, "Hesten, just what do you think you're here for?"

The boy looked at her with a touch of arrogance shaded with suspicion. "You're teaching me swordsmanship—" he began, but she cut him off.

"Wrong," she said with finality. "I'm teaching you how to stay alive. So is Justin. There's a difference."

"But—" the boy looked ready to start an argument, but once again Tarma cut him off.

Time for the annual Lecture, I think.

"No 'buts' about it," she said flatly. "I've spoken at length with your parents. I know what they want from me, and I know what I told them, the kind of training that I could give you." She moved in closer with every word. "As a boy, your father had the best training with highly-recommended instructors, and is a fine swordsman—and a rotten fighter. And he knows it. He can perform every pretty move in the catalog, and can't defend himself against a common merc with a pike. *That's why he limps now*, and if he hadn't been lucky enough to get into the hands of a real Healer, he wouldn't have been around to sire *you*."

Hesten's eyes went wide with shock; evidently his father had not discussed that particular moment in his life with his son.

Tarma continued without pity. "I know what happened, because I was there and I saw it happen, when we all put King Stefanson on the throne. He wants you to have the advantage that he didn't—training with real fighters, not sword-dancers—so that if Rethwellan needs your sword, you stand a decent chance of coming home intact. *Do you understand me?*"

That last sentence was spoken from a distance of mere thumb-lengths as she stared down into the boy's eyes, and saw the first flickers of respect—and yes, fear. She backed off a little, and looked at all three of the boys. "Just what do you know about me?"

Hesten looked at his two fellows, and took it upon

himself to answer, putting on a bravado to cover his betrayal of fear. "You're a Shin'a'in barbarian, there's some songs and tales that might be about you, but you never said anything, and neither did my father, but if you really were with the rebellion—"

Tarma smiled crookedly, a smile with no trace of humor. "I was learning swordwork as early as Jadrie, and I'd killed my first man when I was just about your age, Larsh. That, by the way, is *not* a boast, and it was *not* in a fair fight. And someday, if you deserve to hear it, I'll tell you the whole story. I was a free-lance merc from the age of seventeen and a good one, and believe me, the stories you *have* heard about me and Keth aren't but a quarter of the truth. Justin and Ikan have similar histories." Her smile turned feral. "The reason you weren't told is because both your parents and I know you boys would have had one of two reactions—you'd either have disbelieved it, figured it was boasting, and ignored what we tried to hammer into you, or you would have believed it and decided to prove you were better than us. Neither reaction is conducive to learning anything, which is why you are here—*not* to prove that at your tender age you already know better than your teachers."

The boys all had the grace to look ashamed. Larsh looked down at his feet.

"As to why your parents chose me—and *I* agreed to take you as students—it's because they wanted something very specific for their firstborn sons. If you are called on by your King to go to war, if you are forced to lead your own people against brigands or bandits, or if you are forced into a position where you might fight to preserve your own life, you will have the best possible training to meet those situations." She dropped her smile and looked stern. "And do you know why?"

Hesten shook his head.

"A mercenary knows only one trade—killing—and one goal—to stay alive to collect his pay. No matter what you've heard, most mercs don't *like* killing, so they make a point of being very, very good at it, and very efficient, so as to get it over quickly. Most mercs *do* like being alive, so they make a point of learning everything they can to stay that way. That includes a great many things that are not considered 'fair play' by the standards of people lucky enough to have been born in your rank and class." Hesten's mouth firmed in a stubborn line; she knew he was the leader of this group, and she would have to convince him before the other two would see sense. He had unfortunately been infected with that noble nonsense known as chivalry; hopefully not for so long that he couldn't be cured of it.

"If and when you take the field in a battle, or if someone decides he doesn't like you and sends an assassin out after you, *that* is the kind of person you are going to have to defend yourself against. I know that. Justin and Ikan know that. Most importantly, your parents know that, and that is why you are all here. When you go home, you can take all the lessons you want with fashionable instructors, and learn pretty tricks to impress your friends, but when you are here, you'd better keep your mind on the fact that we are going to teach you how to stay alive, even if we have to half kill you to do it!"

Hesten looked even more rebellious. "Oh, really now, lady!" he objected. "*Assassins?* Maybe where you come from, but not here. Things like that just don't happen in civilized lands like Rethwellan!"

She got some unexpected support then, from the hitherto-silent Belton. "Yes they do, Hesten," the boy snapped, then dropped his eyes before Tarma's.

Oh, really?

"Belton is right," she agreed, following up on her advantage, quickly, before Hesten could get over his surprise. "There are a lot of things that go on that Kings and Princes have no idea of. I know for a fact of two people at least *in Rethwellan* who are making a very fine profit from assassination. And when you have bodyguards of your own, I'll make a point of giving them that information so they'll know who to watch out for."

"Why not give it to us directly?" asked Larsh, surprised.

Once again, to her surprise, it was Belton who answered before she could. "Because some day we might be tempted to use it," he said, face totally closed.

Hesten opened his mouth to protest, then stared into Belton's eyes and looked properly abashed. Belton's eyes were opaque, and she couldn't read what was in them—but she had the suspicion that what she had said had struck forcibly home with him. Well, sooner or later he'd tell her; they all did. Kethry might be the more motherly in appearance, but somehow most of the youngsters, the boys especially, came to Tarma when they had fears that needed soothing or confessions to make. Perhaps it was simply because they assumed that she would never be shocked by anything they said.

"And," she added, allowing her voice to soften

with good humor, "if we can possibly do so, we intend to make sure we all have a good time while we're doing this. Now, I just delivered this particular little lecture for a reason. In a couple of days, you'll be going back to your families for winter holidays. If you really and truly don't want to learn what we have to teach, you have only to tell your parents, or us, and you won't have to come back here. I know this is a hard school—but we don't accept just anyone, and we don't want someone here who doesn't want to be here. If you're having trouble wrapping your mind around the idea of being trained like a common—or perhaps I should say, *un*common mercenary, I can understand that. But bear in mind that you are not here as a punishment from your parents; you're all here because they truly, deeply, profoundly care for your well-being."

Hestin bit his lip. "But we aren't exactly being trained like mercenaries, are we?" he ventured. "I mean, we don't spend more than half our time drilling and all—"

Tarma nodded. "Right, exactly right. Your parents want a special education for you, which is why you spend half your time in classes with Jadrek which seem to have nothing to do with fighting. You'll need them, not only to mark you as gentlemen of the highest order, but to make you better-educated than any other boys of your rank. If you stay, you'll not only be trained in personal defense, but you'll eventually be trained in strategy, tactics, and command, with an eye to serving the King as commanding officers, should he need you."

She didn't miss the sudden flash of interest in Hesten and Larsh's eyes.

"You'll also be well-rounded and well-educated *noblemen*, people whose opinions are sought after, and who are taken seriously. People who are given high office and great responsibility. And people who can take care, not only of themselves, but of those who depend on them, no matter what the situation."

Now she had Belton's full and unwavering interest, and the hooded eyes had come alive.

"But before that happens, you have a lot of work ahead of you." She paused, and smiled again. "You might be wondering why I'm giving you this speech now, instead of when you first came here. The reason is—now you've had a full season here, and you know what I mean by *work*. You've had the full experience, as Keth would say. So—are you ready for three to four more years of it? There's no shame in saying you aren't suited to this, not everyone is, and sometimes parents aren't very good at judging what their children are suited to. Hesten?"

"I'll be back," the boy said shortly, but with more than enough determination and respect in his voice to please Tarma.

"Larsh?"

"Absolutely." More anticipation than determination; that was what she had expected. Larsh would have made a good mercenary; he fit in here as well as any boy she'd had.

"Belton?" she asked, turning to the third boy, and was a little surprised at the vehemence of his reply.

"If they couldn't afford to pay you, I'd work in the stable to stay here!" came the fervent answer, and she blinked a little at the passion in his voice.

Interesting. Deep water there.

:As you suspected, there's a tragedy in his background,

mindsib; I can't get anything more specific than that. I suspect a beloved relative may have been the victim of a feud or something of the sort.: Warrl seemed very interested. *:If he doesn't tell you about it before he leaves, he will when he returns. He has just decided to trust you completely.:*

That corresponded with her feelings about the boy; that he had been holding something back until this moment, testing her and his other teachers, looking for—what? Some kind of flaw, she suspected. Whatever it was, only he knew, but she had no doubt she would find out.

"Now, back to work," she decreed. "There's still plenty of time before supper, and you haven't even broken into a good sweat yet!"

Supper was the best time of the day, so far as Tarma was concerned. Her pupils and Keth's generally ate breakfast and luncheon separately, because the mage-students were on a slightly different schedule and menu. *Her* students needed a great deal more to eat than the mage-students, and after rising at dawn for a run and a session of strenuous physical exercise, began the day with absolutely enormous breakfasts, then restoked their furnaces with equally enormous luncheons and afternoon snacks. The scholars and mage-students required far less in the way of fuel, some had decided on a purely vegetarian regime for themselves, and in any case, over-full stomachs often got in the way of mental concentration.

But by the time Tarma's pupils cleaned up, the mage-students were also finished for the day, and everyone met together for supper and study or amusement afterward.

Altogether, there were ten pupils in Tarma's school, a round dozen in Keth's, and two that were pure scholars, being taught by Jadrek. One of those was Kira's twin Merili, the other a "charity student" from their own village, a young boy who lived to learn. Jadrek intended to recommend him as Rethwellan Archivist-in-training when he finished with the child, the current Archivist having no wife or children to follow him. Of Kethry's pupils, one was her own son Jadrek, though it was likely he'd employ his knowledge as a Shin'a'in shaman rather than a White Winds mage—the shamans being the only Shin'a'in permitted to use magic. Only Jadrie was in Tarma's group; the twins Lyan and Laryn were not particularly interested in fighting, and were learning only the basics every Shin'a'in should know. Like Jadrie, they had decided early that they wanted the Clan and the Plains, but they were completely horse-mad. On their own initiative, during the summer that followed the spring that Jadrie had tamed *her* first horse, they had secretly picked a pair of two-year-olds out of the Tale'sedrin herds and tamed them without any help at all. The Liha'irden horse-herders had seen them at it, of course, but since they weren't doing anything wrong, they were allowed to carry out their plan. Tarma privately suspected that the herders were very proud of the audacious young twins, though if they'd begun to ruin the horses, they'd have been punished for their audacity.

It was too soon to tell what the latest baby, Jendar, was going to turn out to be like—Tarma's only clue was that he stuck by his mother's side during every lesson, and only toddled off when she turned her hands to anything other than magic.

But with twenty-seven children of various ages crowded around the supper table, the evening meal was a noisy and amusing affair. No rules of silence were invoked, and the children were allowed to talk about anything they pleased and for this one meal, eat or not eat whatever they liked. At the beginning of each season, there were always a few bellyaches when students stuffed themselves with sweets—one surfeit usually cured them of further foolishness, especially when the next day brought no sympathy, and no break from lessons. The only iron-clad rule was that there were to be no food fights. Tarma and Kethry had both gone without often enough that the idea of wasted food was intolerable. The one and only time that rule had been challenged, Kethry's combined solution and punishment had been swift and effective. The next day, she had scryed out a group of hungry shepherd-children in the hills. When everyone gathered for breakfast, and the savory meal was laid out on the sideboard—when mouths were watering and appetites roused—she transported every bit of that hot, tantalizing meal to those children, and presented the school with what the children would have eaten. Stale, hard bread and cheese rinds came as quite a shock to pampered children of noble houses. She did the same at lunch. At dinner, she made it very clear that she was prepared to continue sending their food "to children who appreciated it" if there was *ever* a repetition of the incident. The story had been passed to every new student since then, by word of mouth, and Tarma had no doubt that it had grown in the telling. It certainly guaranteed that there were *no* food fights again.

She noticed the three older boys had unbent and were treating Jadrie and Kira more as their equals than usual. This meant, of course, that instead of being ignored, the girls came in for teasing and sur-reptitious prodding and poking. For a while, they seemed to enjoy it, but when the sweet was served, they were clearly beginning to lose their tempers. She debated interfering, but Merili beat her to it.

"Weren't there supposed to be some gentlemen at this table, besides our teachers?" she asked Tarma pointedly, after a quick flash of a frown at Larsh.

"I thought so, but I haven't seen any," Tarma replied, hiding her amusement.

"That's too bad," Merili said with a dignity that was so funny Tarma nearly spoiled everything for her by laughing. "If there had been *gentlemen* here, I was going to ask them to come riding with me after dinner." She sighed and looked only at Tarma. "Well, if any *gentlemen* appear, the invitation will still be there."

The three older boys secretly worshipped their "Little Princess," and that put a stop to the tor-menting. All through dessert, they remained on their best behavior, much to the relief of the other two girls. None of them wanted to fall under the Royal Disfavor, for Merili was as good-natured as she was pretty, and never minded helping when one of Ja-drek's lessons proved difficult to conquer, or when something needed mending or embellishing.

As usual, the children inhaled their sweets; before many moments had passed, they had all scattered to the four winds to ride, continue last night's work on a pair of snow forts, or run off the last of their energy in games, until a candlemark before bathtime, when they would be herded to the library for study. That left the adults alone except for the baby, and they looked at each other, heaved a sigh of relief, and laughed.

"Does it get noisier every year, or is it my imagination?" Jadrek asked, prying Jendar's chubby fingers off the handle of a knife, and giving the boy his heavy silver bracelet to play with instead.

"Of course it gets noisier every year; there are more children every year," Ikan Dryvale replied, wriggling his finger in his ear as if to clear his hearing. "Even if you didn't take more students, Kethry would be providing the increase herself!"

"Oh, come now!" Kethry laughed. "You make me sound like a brood-hen!"

"I overheard you delivering the Lecture to the boys, Tarma," Justin interjected. "How did they take it?"

"We'll have them all back after Midwinter," she was able to tell him, with great satisfaction. "We'll still have to pound sense into their heads, but we aren't going to be the enemy anymore."

"Oh, really?" Ikan's eyebrows arched. "I wasn't all that sure of young Hesten. There's a strong streak of rebellion in that one."

"There always is in the smart ones," Justin pointed out, refilling his cup. "It was Belton I wasn't certain of. He hasn't completely trusted us since the day he arrived."

"Warrl says he does now," Tarma replied. Justin glanced over to the fireside, where Warrl was finishing his own dinner, and the *kyree* looked up and nodded in confirmation.

"Well, that's a relief," was all Justin said, and the conversation turned to other topics and other students.

As the servants finished clearing the table, leaving only the pitchers of drink, Tarma sat back in her chair at the foot of the table and pondered her "family" with a feeling of complete contentment.

Justin looked far more prosperous than he had in the old days; there were threads of gray in his blond hair, and his face was craggier, but other than that he carried his age lightly. That might have been due to Estrel, his wife, who sat beside him—their baby Kethren was in the nursery asleep, where Jendar would be shortly. Estrel looked like what she was, a fresh-faced young shepherdess of a mere seventeen. What *didn't* show on the surface was a vast knowledge of herb-healing and midwifery, a very shrewd and clever mind, and an utter devotion to Justin. She first saw Justin at the school, where she and the other village younglings were taking short lessons in reading, writing, and figuring from Jadrek, who gave those lessons gratis. She had also been apprenticed to the village midwife, and had naturally come into close contact with Kethry.

Estrel had fallen in love with Justin immediately, and set about winning him for herself with a determination that surmounted each and every obstacle in her path. She fit in very well here, and was in charge of the nursery when Kethry was busy with her own students.

Justin and Estrel sat in the middle of the table on Tarma's right. Ikan sat across from them on the left.

His amber hair betrayed no gray yet, and if someone didn't know what to look for, he could be mistaken for a plowman. He still had utterly innocent blue eyes, and the face of a country-bred dolt straight out of the fields. That might have been why the younger boys responded better to him than to Justin; he didn't look nearly as intimidating. He had yet to settle down, distributing his favors to as many women as cared to fling themselves at him—and plenty did.

Kethry and Jadrek sat at the head of the table—and equal distribution of teachers ensured that mayhem at supper was kept to a minimum. Since they'd come "off the road" and settled down here, on the estate that King Stefanson had bestowed upon them for their service in getting back his throne, Kethry had allowed her hair to grow, as had Tarma. Kethry's had grown faster though, and it had already been much longer than Tarma's when they retired. Now, if she let it loose from the single plait she wore it in during the day, it would just brush the floor, a glorious waterfall of dark amber with red highlights. There was no sign of gray in it yet, although there were the faint beginnings of crow's feet at the corners of her eyes.

Jadrek's hair had gone completely to silver-gilt, but all of the lines in his face now were those most often associated with pleasure rather than pain. He was both a handsome and a distinguished man, and between them, he and Kethry had produced some incredibly handsome children. Though he still suffered a bit in the winter from his old troubles, Estrel and Kethry kept the worst symptoms of his bad joints at bay.

And me—

:And you, mindmate. You are still as thin and tough as a whip, though a bit creaky in the joints yourself. There's a trace of white in your hair, but no sign of age on your face, and no sign of it in the ring, provided you don't do anything intolerably stupid. And no one would ever mistake you for anything but Shin'a'in, blood and bone. Great beak of a nose, golden skin, blue eyes, black hair, just like every other Clansib I've ever seen.:

She grinned, hiding it behind her cup. *Thank you, Furball, for deflating any vestige of vanity I might have had.*

Yes, the years had been very kind to all of them. About the only thing she could have wished for was that Ikan would settle down himself. Preferably with a spouse with true Healing talent; that was the one thing the school lacked, was a resident Healer.

:Be careful what you wish for,: Warrl cautioned, with a laugh behind his mental voice.

Oh? You know something?

:There's going to be a new Healing Priestess arriving tomorrow in the village. Same Order as Tresti was—so there will be no difficulty at all if she decides to get married. I hear she's very pretty and very, very clever.:

What else did you hear? Tarma asked, sensing that Warrl was much more amused than his simple description would warrant.

:Only this; Father Mayhew has been warning the boys to mind their manners and keep their hands to themselves. He told his housekeeper that her Superior warned him that as a Novice she knocked a man unconscious with a piece of firewood for trying to take liberties. I'd say she isn't going to be the easy conquest the village girls have been.:

Tarma almost choked, and took a quick swallow

to hide it. Well, well, well, so Ikan was finally going
to meet his match!

:*She'll either infuriate him or captivate him.*:

Huh. Probably both.

Warrl yawned hugely and winked at her, then
turned to the fire to warm his belly.

"Jadrek, have you got any word on when their
escorts come to get the children?" she called into the
next break in conversation. "We ought to tell them
at bedtime."

"Your three oldest boys will be leaving in three
days; their escort is due to arrive then. Three of
Keth's children will be staying here over the holidays, and all of the rest with the exception of Kira
and Merili will go out with a caravan coming in tomorrow and leaving the day after. Kira and Merili's
escort will be here in four days." Jadrek sounded
quite sure of himself, as well he should be; he had
messengers traveling between himself and the escorts
every day from the time they left the students'
homes. He was taking no chances on a "false escort"
presenting himself and making off with one of the
children, for all of them were highborn enough to
command significant ransoms.

"That'll cheer Kira up; she was afraid the weather
would keep her here over Midwinter," Tarma said
with satisfaction.

"Oh, but Jadrie will be devastated," Kethry replied. "Would you believe my little hoyden was
looking forward to having Kira do her hair and Merili help her with a *dress* for the Midwinter feast?"

Tarma felt her jaw go slack with surprise. "Jadrie?
A *dress?* Next thing you'll tell me is that she's trying
to snare herself a boyfriend!"

Jadrek laughed. "Just wait until summer, Tarma, I think she's got her eye on that stripling shaman—" he paused for a moment, and his capacious memory supplied the name before Tarma could think of it. "—Ah'kela, that's it. Ah'kela shena Liha'irden. The one two years older than she is."

With the name came the face, and Tarma couldn't help but grin with acute satisfaction. Ah'kela was a handsome, and unaccountably shy adolescent, in training with Liha'irden's Chief Shaman. And if Jadrie did manage to snare him—well, that solved the problem of where the new Clan Tale'sedrin was going to get its new shaman when the time came to form it up. Jadrek the younger certainly wasn't going to be old enough in time.

Ah, but that will give us a shaman-in-training under Ah'kela. Shamans are always in demand as spouses, and the twins will have no difficulty finding mates, not with every Liha'irden girl over the age of ten petting them and admiring their golden hair and green eyes . . . Jadrie was the one that might have been too much for most boys, just as I was. Hah! I should have known she'd solve her own problems!

Justin burst out laughing, interrupting her reverie. "Tarma, you look like the most self-satisfied matchmaker I ever saw in my life!"

"It can't hurt to *think* about these things, can it?" she protested.

"Yes, but you look like a cat who's stolen an entire pitcher of cream," Ikan teased. "You should see yourself!"

"Piff," she scoffed, and glared at Justin. "Just you wait until *your* babies are grown! If you don't turn out worse than me, I'll be greatly surprised!"

Estrel giggled, and Justin turned beet-red. "He already is, Tarma. He already is!"

She didn't elaborate, much to Justin's obvious relief, but Tarma could well guess. Like every male with strong bonds to his children, he was probably planning who was and was not a "worthy" prospective mate for his little boy, and worrying about the possible consequences. "Well, unless you want to lose your son and heir to the barbarians, better not plan on a betrothal to Jadrie—or any other girl-child Keth may conjure up," she teased.

"And have *you* as an in-law?" he shuddered. "Perish the thought!"

She mimed throwing a dagger at him, and the evening broke up in laughter.

After the official "lights out" time, Kira waited until the last sounds of the grown-ups checking on all of the students faded, then for good measure, waited another one hundred breaths, before reaching up with her foot and poking the bottom of her twin's bunk. Merili had been waiting for that signal; she slipped out of bed and slid down to the floor as silently as a kitten, and the two of them wrapped warm robes around themselves and slid their feet into sheepskin slippers, using only the light of the embers in their fireplace to see by. The pockets of both their robes bulged, hinting at something interesting inside. As Merili rummaged a carefully-hidden package out of her wardrobe, wrapped in paper she had saved from lessons and patterned with berry-juice ink, Kira got a similar package from under her bed. With Kira in the lead, scouting every step of the way, they made their way down the dark hallway each with one hand trailing along the wall to guide her. Both of them had made this journey innumerable times before, and they slid their feet soundlessly along the smooth wooden floor.

When Kira's hand encountered empty air, she knew she had come to the staircase, and she warned her twin with the merest thread of a hiss. She bent to pull off her slippers, picked them up, and felt her way down with her bare toes a step at a time, pausing on the landing to put her slippers back on and hiss the "all clear" for Merili. She was glad to get her slippers back on; the floor was icy-cold and she wriggled her toes in the warm fleece while she waited for Merili.

When her twin's hand touched her arm in the dark, Kira led the way out into the second-floor hall, and onto the corridor where Jadrie and her twin brothers had their own rooms. Keeping to the left side of the hall, she felt her way along the wall. When her hand brushed the third door, she stopped and gave three very soft taps.

The door opened, swiftly and silently, and Jadrie grabbed both their hands and pulled them inside.

She had built up her fire to a cheerful blaze, had cleverly shrouded the window in a rug so that no light betrayed her, and had lit a single candle. As Kira and Merili took their places on sheepskin-covered cushions beside the fire, suppressing giggles, Jadrie rolled up a towel and stuffed it against the door sill, sealing off the crack at the bottom so that no light would leak out there either, to show that there was a cozy little clandestine party going on.

Only then did the older girl joined them, taking her own cushion and plumping herself down on it.

"There!" she whispered, looking very proud of herself. "We should be safe as long as the boys don't wake up." Then her face fell a little. "But this is probably the last chance we'll get to be together before you go home."

"Yes, but we'll be back soon enough! Look what I brought for our party—" Merili replied cheerfully, and began pulling handfuls of chestnuts out of the bulging pockets of her robe.

"I got apples," Kira supplied, pulling three luscious fruits from *her* previously-loaded pockets, as Jadrie arranged the chestnuts close to the fire to roast.

"Oh, good! I've got spiced cider, and I swiped some honeycakes from the kitchen before study," Jadrie said with satisfaction, pointing to the foot of her bed, where a jug with water beading up on its sides hid just behind the outer leg, and a plateful of slightly squashed honeycakes resided beside it. "And I've got Midwinter presents for both of you."

"Oh, but you open yours first!" Merili cried, ever generous, although Kira ached to see what *hers* was. "Here—" she thrust the bulky package at Jadrie, who needed no second urging to tear off the paper.

But Jadrie's reaction more than made up for the impatience Kira felt, and she giggled along with her twin at Jadrie's round eyes.

"Oh!" Jadrie squealed, shaking out the folds of silk and leaping up to try the dress against herself. "Oh! It's *wonderful*, Meri! How did you do it?"

The dress probably would have been scandalous by some standards, with its split skirt for riding astride. Merili had used Jadrie's Shin'a'in costumes and her own festival-dresses as patterns, and come up with a dress that combined recognizable facets of both. It was sewn of the pastel-colored silks thought appropriate for young girls in Rethwellan, but the embroidery on the bodice and hems, though executed in pale hues of blue, pink, green and soft yellow, was recognizably Shin'a'in in pattern and execution. The split skirt was a reasonable substitute for Shin'a'in breeches, the huge, fluttery butterfly sleeves were pure Rethwellan, but the sleeves could be pulled up and held out of the way by an embroidered band passed through them and along the inside of the back of the dress, and the "skirt" could be gathered at each ankle with separate embroidered bands. The bodice was low enough to satisfy the cravings of a girl wanting to be thought grown-up without being so revealing that it would arouse the ire of her mother.

"Here's mine," Kira said with satisfaction, handing her a neater, smaller package. And Jadrie exclaimed again, to find it contained a pair of soft, sueded ankle-boots, and a belt and sheath for her knife, all beaded with tiny crystal beads and freshwater pearls in the same Shin'a'in patterns as the embroidery of the dress.

"I—I don't know what to say!" Jadrie said, sitting down abruptly, still holding the dress to herself, with the belt and boots in her free hand.

"It was all Kira's idea," Merili offered, her eyes sparkling with happiness. "I wanted to do the dress, but she told me it would be stupid to make something you couldn't be yourself in, so Estrel helped me do something that was like your Shin'a'in clothes, and when Kira saw the colors I was doing it in, she got the boots and the belt and did the beading to match."

"I'm glad you like it," Kira added softly.

"*Like* it? I love it! I can't believe you did all this just for me!" Jadrie's face shone with happiness, and she put the dress down long enough in her lap to reach behind her and bring out two packages of her own. Hers were wrapped in the thin paper normally used for embroidery patterns, and Kira knew it was meant for Meri when the packages were opened. "This one is yours, Kira, and this is yours, Meri. I hope you like your presents half as much as I like mine!"

Meri looked significantly at her twin, and motioned for Kira to open hers first. Nothing loath, Kira removed the paper from her package to disclose a carved box. She opened the lid to find, nestled into the velvet lining, a very different sort of present in the shape of shining steel.

She gasped, hardly able to believe her eyes. Identical except for decoration to a set that Jadrie owned and Kira had lusted after ever since she saw them, it was a set of matching knives. A long-knife, just a scant thumblength from qualifying as a sword, a belt-knife for less lethal use, a set of throwing-knives and arm-sheaths to hold them, and a tiny boot-knife that slipped invisibly into the side of a riding boot. Jadrie's weapons were undecorated except for the Tale'-sedrin emblem of a stooping hawk carved into the hilts, but Kira's were ornamented with inlaid silver wire in an intricate spiral on the hilt, and had garnets inlaid in the pommel-nuts. Kira's throat knotted up, and tears sprang into her eyes, and when she looked up at Jadrie, she was completely unable to say anything.

Jadrie seemed to understand, and chuckled. "I

asked Tarma if I could—she said you'd earned them. I designed the decoration.''

Now at last it was Meri's turn, as Kira held the precious package to her chest, half afraid they would vanish if she turned them loose. This was more than just a set of weapons—this was confirmation of her dream, for a set of knives like this, with the addition of a sword, was *precisely* what a professional bodyguard would sport. So her teacher Tarma agreed with Kira's dream—and so, presumably, did Kira's parents. There would be no separation from her beloved twin when Meri went to marry the Prince of Jkatha.

Meri's exclamation was as surprised and delighted as Kira's, as she opened her package with far more decorum than Kira had used with hers. Her box would be perfect for storing her embroidery materials, for it was unlined, and it contained fabric. Kira didn't see what it was that merited such delight—it just looked like white silk to her—

Then Meri took it out of the box, and shook it out—and out—and out—

It must have been a dozen ells of silk so thin it was almost transparent, like mist made into fabric.

Then Meri saw what the folded fabric had hidden, and actually wept with joy.

"I can't believe you found it!" she said over and over, fingering the fabric and the embroidery silks of the purest white, a box of tiny freshwater pearls the size of pinheads, and silver thread as supple as the silk. "I can't believe you found it!"

"Found what?" Kira whispered under her breath to Jadrie, mystified, as Meri picked up each skein of thread and examined every strand with delight.

"It's the makings for a traditional Jkathan royal bridal veil," Jadrie replied, eyes sparkling. "The bride's supposed to provide the veil, and it's *supposed* to be of silk so fine the veil can pass through her wedding ring, and she's supposed to embroider it herself. Meri wanted to do things right for her Prince, but silk that fine is hard to come by, as Meri's been finding out." She shrugged, and grinned. "Shin'a'in connections can get you amazing things—would you believe that Tarma got this from the Hawkbrothers?" She raised her voice. "You'll have to start embroidering that right away, won't you?"

"Absolutely," Meri said firmly. "I'll want to set the pattern so Mummy's maids can match it on my dress—and then I'll only want to work on it when the light is good and strong."

"Well, work out the pattern *you* want, and don't worry about using up the pearls and the thread. I've got a good connection, and I can get you plenty more if you need it." Jadrie's grin got wider, if possible. "As you well know, it's the veil that's the hard thing to get hold of."

Meri shook her head, and carefully wiped the tears from her eyes to avoid spotting the silk. "This has been the best Midwinter ever!" she said. "I don't know how anything we get from our parents could be better than this—"

"Then let's celebrate!" Jadrie urged, carefully putting her new outfit on the bed and covering it with the coverlet, just in case. Kira and Meri both put their presents back in their wooden presentation boxes, both with a last pat of satisfaction, and accepted mugs of cider from Jadrie. Kira held hers up in a toast, and they followed her example.

"To the best Midwinter ever," Kira said firmly, "and to more to come!"

"Best friends and sisters forever!" Meri said, touching mugs with her twin and Jadrie.

"*Kal she li de'gande, orm she li de'gande,*" Jadrie said solemnly.

"What's that?" Meri asked.

Jadrie took a sip of her cider before she answered. "It's something best friends swear in the Clans—'I swear my sword to you, I swear my hand to you.' It means that if you ever need me, I'll drop everything to come help you."

"Huh!" Kira said, impressed, and touched her mug again to Jadrie's. "*Kal she li de'gande, orm she li de'gande,*" she repeated, and Meri did the same, making a better job of the pronunciation than Kira had.

They managed to hold the solemn moment for several heartbeats, until one of the chestnuts jumped on the hearth, its shell splitting with a *pop*. That broke the spell, and they dove for the hot nuts, laughing and sucking burned fingers as they devoured their little feast.

Warrl scratched once, very softly, on the door to Tarma's room, and the Shin'a'in left her comfortable chair to let him in. He'd been making his nightly patrol of the childrens' wing, moving as only he could, so quietly they had no idea he was ever lurking outside their doors, listening with both ears and mind. He was in a very good mood, and grinned up at Tarma, tongue lolling, as he passed her.

"So, what mischief are the youngsters up to?" Tarma asked the *kyree*. He only grinned like that when he'd caught one or more of the children having a romp.

:*Everyone is asleep except the girls,*: Warrl replied, curling up on his bed, an enormous, flat cushion near the hearth but out of range of any errant embers. His eyes reflected the flames as he sighed with content. :*As you had thought, they are having a farewell party.*:

Tarma chuckled. "Not exactly a big surprise, with Midwinter Gifts all wrapped up and ready to present. I didn't think they could hold out until departure day. Right, then we'll give them a little longer to gossip and giggle, then I'll go make enough noise that they scatter back to their beds. Whose room are they in? Jadrie's?"

The *kyree* nodded.

"I thought she went to bed a little too easily. She must have hidden some goodies under the bed and she didn't want anyone finding them." There were no rules about taking food from the kitchen at any time—growing, active younglings needed a lot of food. Sweets were generally locked up, but there was always nuts, cheese, bread, fruits and vegetables, and journey-cakes made with enough honey to make the children *think* they were sweets. However, there *were* rules about keeping food in the bedrooms. Once too often in the first year an unpleasant stench or an outbreak of flying pests or mice had been traced to forgotten goodies squirreled away in a chest or wardrobe, or under a bed. Kethry had decided that making it against the rules to have food in the rooms would not stop the children from taking food to their rooms for little "parties," but *would* ensure that all traces would be erased and all food would be eaten before it could become a problem.

"You can't keep them from it," Kethry had said philosophically. "Children just like to have secret social get-togethers, and it's no fun for them if they can't nibble on something. Lock up all the food, and they'll get bitten stealing squirrels' hordes, get scratched and punctured picking wild berries, get sick on sour fruit, and get stung stealing honey from forest hives."

"Or worse," Tarma had pointed out. "Our brood at least is woods-wise and they know what's not safe to eat, but the same can't be said for our students. And the gods only know what sort of things they'd pick to try and eat. You're right; the rule about keeping food should take care of the problem."

And it wasn't really *breaking* the rule if the food was eaten immediately, just bending it a little. After all, the rule specifically said *keeping* food in their rooms, not eating it there.

:I wonder why the older boys aren't having a similar—: Warrl broke off his thought to cock an ear at the door. *:Footsteps on the stair. One of the older boys. Belton, by the footsteps.:*

Since the hallway on which the adults had their rooms was dimly lit with a night-lantern, there was no need for a child to stumble through the dark to find any of his teachers. A moment or two later, the expected tap came at Tarma's door.

She opened it; Belton stood there, with a guarded expression, still fully dressed although he should have been in his nightclothes by now.

"Come to say good-bye privately?" she asked, giving him an easy excuse for his presence, so that he could broach the real reason he had sought her out when he felt a little more comfortable. "Please, come in and share my hearth."

The boy blinked in the fire- and lantern-light, and came hesitantly inside. Tarma waved him to a chair, and took her own seat again. "Tea?" she invited, holding up a pot. He shook his head, and she put it back on the table beside her chair. "I'm glad all three of you boys will be coming back after the holidays," she said, relaxing into the embrace of her chair. "You are all intelligent and quick, and I think you'll be happy here. I'm happy to have you as students. More than that, well, I like you boys for yourselves." She smiled at him. "Even when you're all acting like brats, I still like you."

Belton didn't relax. He stared at his hands, clenched tightly on one knee, then at the fire, then back at his hands, all without saying anything. Tarma waited with infinite patience; she had a fair idea that he was about to tell her the secret she'd sensed in him.

In the meantime, she filled the silence with one-sided conversation, about her own training, about things Belton could expect to learn when he returned, about how *she* had felt at his age when confronted by some of the things she had been expected to learn. Finally, he looked as if he was ready to say something, and she paused to give him a chance.

"Is revenge wrong?" he finally blurted, looking up urgently into her eyes. "Not for something petty, not a stupid argument or something. Serious revenge, grown-up revenge."

Interesting question. "Are you asking the teacher or the Shin'a'in?" she replied.

"Both. Either." He shook his head, clearly confused. "I don't know what I want to hear—"

"Well, the teacher would say—'yes, of course, revenge is wrong, doing something terrible to revenge yourself is creating a second wrong on top of the one that was done to you.' But the Shin'a'in has a different way of looking at things than the teacher who has to live in civilization." She smiled slowly. "The Shin'a'in would say that it depends on what you expect you're going to get out of the vengeance—and it depends on what the vengeance is going to do to you."

"What I'm going to get out of it? Don't you mean, what I'm going to accomplish?" Belton looked puzzled at her wording, and she wasn't surprised. She was about to introduce him to some complicated thinking, but she thought he could grasp it.

"No, that's not what I mean. The Shin'a'in are not at all against vengeance, or against blood-feuds. In fact, I'm here now because of an oath of vengeance." She nodded at his look of surprise. "For us, the key difference is that in order to swear an oath of vengeance, or take on a blood-feud, you have to swear yourself to the Warrior-Goddess, and that means giving up *everything*. Family, Clan, love, marriage—all of it."

"Why?" Belton wanted to know.

"In part, to make sure that revenge is the act of last resort—that it is kept for very specific purposes." She wound a strand of hair around one finger. "We don't allow people to declare blood-feuds just because they can't get along with another person in their Clan, and we don't let Clan declare blood-feud with Clan. Very far back in the past, our people separated into two groups, one of whom became the Shin'a'in, because of a difference of opinion. That separation came out all right, but it isn't something we want to happen again." *How much to tell him? I can't give him the whole history of the Clans in one night!*

But the boy did look intent on her words, so she continued. "That's why someone who needs revenge that badly gives up everything, and becomes an instrument of the Shin'a'in as a whole. The Shin'a'in take revenge *very* seriously, and only someone who is acting for the People of the Plains rather than himself is permitted to take it. We believe that if you aren't serious enough about revenge to be willing to give up everything in order to have it, then you aren't going after revenge for the right reasons."

Belton chewed on his lower lip for a long time before answering her. "What are the right reasons?"

"I can't give you all of them, but I can tell you mine—and as to how I know they were right, well, the Goddess accepted my oath, so they must have been." She took a sip of her warm tea and let the taste of honey and flowers linger on her tongue for a moment. He continued to watch her face intently. "Bandits had slaughtered my entire Clan. I wanted to wipe them off the face of the earth—but not because killing them would bring any of my people back. Yes, I wanted to kill them because they had killed everyone I cared about. But I also knew that if they got away with the murders, others would try to emulate them—and the People *could not* have that happen."

"What if you'd gotten killed yourself?" Belton asked.

"If I had failed, there would have been other Shin-

'a'in who would have come after me who would have succeeded where I failed. I just had the right to try to do the job first." She nodded as his eyes widened. "I also knew that they had probably murdered plenty of other people in the past, and would do so again in the future—and there is one sure thing you can say about destroying a murderer, and that's that he won't be around to kill again."

Belton pondered her words silently; she waited for him to say something, but he remained silent.

"However—" she held up a cautionary finger "—revenge for an insult, for a purely personal wrong—that's no reason for revenge. And I'll tell you why; you don't teach a piece of scum a lesson by serving out to him what he served out to you, all you do is give him a reason to heap your plate with more of the same. Slime doesn't learn lessons; it just stays slime." She took a long, deep breath. "Don't fool yourself, don't try to tell yourself you intend to teach your enemy a lesson. You won't. Revenge on slime is not education, it's got to be eradication—or at the very least it has to accomplish the task of making absolutely sure that the slime can't *ever* commit that particular act again."

The boy blinked at her, as if he couldn't quite believe that she had said that. "But what about—what if someone arranged—hired someone else to do his dirty work for him?"

"When someone is low enough scum to buy a bully-boy to hurt or kill someone you care about, just who do you intend to get your revenge on?" she asked bluntly. "The bully-boy? Granted, *that* piece of garbage won't be taking on any more jobs, at least for a while, but the perpetrator won't care, he'll just hire someone new."

Belton chewed his lip a little more. "No, no—it would have to be the one who did the hiring."

"So, you want to take on the scum himself?" She saw a fire leap into Belton's eyes and again raised a cautionary finger. "Think it through. Can you prove that he bought the bully? Obviously you can't, or you or your family would have brought him up before the King's Justice on charges."

The boy's face tightened up. "You're right," he said harshly. "We can't prove anything."

"I'm going to be saying this a great deal, Belton—*think this through*, every aspect of it. What if he really didn't do anything? What if you're wrong?"

"But—" Belton began. She shushed him. "Humor me. What if you're wrong? You try to hurt an innocent man. Well, maybe not *innocent*, but certainly one who isn't guilty of that particular crime. I don't know what your religion says about that, but I know that the King's Justice will certainly catch up with you, and their punishment here on earth is bad enough."

His face looked like a mask, but at least he was still listening. "Yes, but—"

"I know, I know, it's easier for me to say this, to think about it, because I wasn't the one who was wronged. Belton, your father is powerful, and powerful men have more than one enemy. It is possible that some *other* enemy did this—even deliberately staged things to make it look as if the person you suspect did it, knowing that in seeking revenge on the so-called innocent, you'd get yourselves into even more trouble. Isn't it?"

He paled a little, and nodded. "But—"

"But assume you're right, and he did the dirty deed. *Whether you fail or succeed in killing him, he wins.*"

Belton's mouth fell open in shock. "How can you *say* that?" he cried, his voice cracking.

She spread out her hands. "Simple, friend. *Think it through.* You can't prove that he did the thing, that's a given. So, if you succeed in killing him, since you are *not* going to take your revenge by hiring another assassin—or if you are, you aren't going to be as practiced at it as he is—you're going to get caught. Your family is disgraced, and you die as a murderer, executed, and your family is impoverished in paying the blood-debt to his. Or, if you fail, your family is disgraced, and you die at his hands, or the hands of his bodyguards, which amounts to the same thing. You're still dead, and *he* is still sitting fat and happy on his ill-gotten goods." She cocked her head to the side, and regarded his glazed eyes. "Doesn't seem like justice, does it? You've been wronged, and trying to make things right will only make them worse."

Slowly, he shook his head, and despair crept into his expression. "So what do I do?" he asked bitterly. "Let him go on gloating because he killed my cousin and got away with it?" The pain in his voice tore at her, but she knew that giving him sympathy at this moment would only allow him to wallow in feeling and keep him from thinking.

"Oh, absolutely not!" she replied. "But you have to have an eye to the long view. What's the goal?"

"*Get* him!" Belton replied passionately. "Make him pay!"

"Then plan," she said shortly. "Use your mind—

he's certainly using his against you, and that's the way you can catch him."

"Plan?" he repeated, as if the concept had never occurred to him. It probably hadn't. After all, he was a very young man, and young men tended to act rather than think.

"Planning—that's what will get you what you want," she said firmly. "Every action you take must have sound planning behind it. You don't think that generals just charge out onto the field without first choosing their ground and scouting the enemy do you?"

"Well," he admitted. "No, I guess."

"This is war; think of it that way—not in terms of a single confrontation, but as a campaign. You've got to get on your choice of ground, and you have to know exactly what you're up against." She was satisfied with his initial reaction. His face lost that tight, tense look.

"What do you mean?" he asked very slowly.

"First, you make absolutely certain that he really *did* order the murder, on purpose, with malicious intent." This was going remarkably well, perhaps because the wound was no longer fresh. That was all to the good, since it meant he *could* think as well as feel.

"How do I do that?" Belton asked, losing a little more of the despair.

"Depends on a lot of things, but remember that this is a campaign. Remember the end result that you want. Wouldn't it be best if you could turn this enemy over to the authorities?"

He sat and thought about that, and finally admitted, "Better, I guess. Not as—as satisfying, but better."

"Then the *easiest* is to find a powerful enough mage to scry out the answer for you, and an honest enough one that he'll tell you the truth and not what you want to hear. That's expensive, but it's the cleanest—and any mage in Rethwellan who learns the identity of a murderer is required by law to report it to the Justices." She nodded as he brightened. "This, of course, assumes *he* hasn't hired mages to cover his tracks, which he might have. A sufficiently powerful and persistent mage can untangle all that, of course, but again, it's expensive and time-consuming. And I would be *very* much surprised if your family wasn't already doing that."

Belton opened his mouth to protest, then stopped himself as something occurred to him. His brow creased in thought, and he finally admitted, "You're probably right. Father said the family was doing something, but he didn't say what."

"Then knowing your father, that's probably what's going on." Now she reached out to pat his hand. "Your father is a very intelligent man, and a very caring one. He's too intelligent *not* to take the most obvious route, and too caring to burden you with the knowledge of it until he knows whether or not it will work. Belton, you're supposed to be concentrating on your studies, not on family troubles!"

"How could I not?" he asked, unable to understand that.

She sighed. "Remember how earlier today I said that parents sometimes don't know what suits their child? Well, they often think that they can shelter their children from their own troubles. Parents can be incredibly short-sighted about their children—and their children have to learn to forgive them for it."

He looked a little bewildered now, but he did accept that, and waited for her to go on.

"Now, there's another route you can take, which might not have occurred to him. Informants." She took another sip of her tea. "If this low-life *has* arranged for a murder, he had to go through intermediaries, and every intermediary is potentially someone who knows who ordered the killing. He probably has boasted of it to someone, or more than one, and *those* people know he ordered it. Nothing stays a secret forever, and money loosens even the most reluctant of tongues. So, if the mage doesn't work out, that's the next path to try. And your father has probably already planned that, as well. Ask him; I think he'll probably tell you."

"But what does that leave for me to do?" Belton asked, despair once again creeping into his voice.

"Ah, now that is a good question, and I have an answer for you, but it means being very patient, confiding in your father, and the two of you working together." Tarma was beginning to enjoy herself; it was a little like old times. "Your job will be to learn all you can from me, then return home and convince him that you have learned enough to become a partner in his plans."

"And? What can I do then? What if *he* doesn't have any plans?" Belton asked.

"Assuming he doesn't, I can tell you what I'd do. If I were doing this, I would then pretend to everyone else to have learned nothing," she told him, throwing out the idea that had come to her when he first revealed everything to her. "In fact, you should

pretend to be a very typical young man of your set—
learn the silly sword-tricks and act the complete fop.
Unless I miss my guess, you'll be such an obvious
target that your enemy won't be able to resist going
after you in order to harm your father even more."

Now Belton's eyes were truly shining with excitement. "And when he does—it'll probably be another
assassin, right?"

"Or an assassin in the guise of a street-robber or
even someone who arranges for an insult one way
or the other so that a duel can be set up between
you," Tarma agreed. "And?"

"And I—*don't* kill him? I take him prisoner?" He
looked at her like an eager puppy, and she had to
restrain herself from patting him on the head and
telling him he was a good boy.

"Exactly. *Then* you have the link back to your
enemy; I have no doubt that a skilled priest can elicit
the truth out of your captive. When you've got the
truth and a warm body to confirm it, you let the law
deal with him." She nodded affably. "Chances are at
that point there will be plenty of people ready to link
him with your cousin's death, and he'll be called to
answer for that, too. But it's all going to depend on
patience on your part. Three or four years' worth of
learning and getting ready, knowing that at any time
your parents may take care of the situation through
other means."

"I can do it," Belton said firmly. "I don't think
Hesten could, but I can wait."

"I think you can, or I wouldn't have told you how
to set it all up," Tarma affirmed, and leaned forward.
"Now, feeling better?"

"Better than—in a long time," the boy said, with a slow, shy smile. "I think I can sleep now."

"Then go let yourself out—and do me a favor, go tap on the door of Jadrie's room and tell her I'm about to make a last bed-check, would you?" She leaned back lazily in her chair.

He cast a sharp glance at her, then grinned. "Are you?"

"Not if I don't have to—but it's time they stopped giggling and gossiping and got some sleep." She shook her head. "Sometimes I wonder if we just shouldn't let all three girls bunk together and be done with it."

"Hah. You know girls, they'd *never* get any sleep," said Belton, with the superior air of a boy who has not yet learned the real fascination of the female sex. "They'd spend every night giggling over nothing."

"You're probably right," Tarma sighed with mock regret as Belton got up and went to the door. "Just pass them the warning for me, would you?"

"I'd be glad to," the boy said with a grin, and managed to close the door quietly behind himself.

:That was neatly done,: Warrl observed without raising his head from his forepaws.

"What, getting the lad to scare the brats back into bed, or dealing with the potential avenger?"

:Both.: Warrl sighed, and rolled over so that his belly was to the fire. *:Thank you for arranging things so I wouldn't have to leave the fireside.:*

"Thank you for the compliment, Furball." She yawned, and realized that she had no real interest left in the book she'd been reading, or the tea she'd been drinking. "And since I won't have to go chivvy the girls into their beds either, I'm going to set a good example and go to mine."

It was the usual sort of midwinter day for the south of Rethwellan; gray and overcast, with clouds like long, lumpy serpents packed together so tightly that not a trace of blue showed through. A breeze hissed in the bare branches, but didn't disturb the ankle-deep snow. Kethry, with Jadrek, Jadrie, and Tarma had come down to say their farewells to Kira and Meri; a part of Kethry regretted the need to stand there in the snow waving until the children, at least, were out of sight. Her feet were cold, and breakfast had been a long time ago. Still, Jadrie would have thought it terribly unfeeling of her not to be here.

The last set of escorts finally rode out of sight with Kira and Meri safely in their midst, and Kethry was grateful that there had been remarkably few tears of parting. And, in fact, long before the last speck faded out of sight, Jadrie had left them to go back inside the gates. As the core group of adults walked back through the gates and entered the door of the manor, Kethry cocked her head to one side. Tarma looked at her with a quizzical expression.

"What is it?" the Shin'a'in asked.

"Listen—" Kethry whispered, and grinned at Tarma's quick answering smile. "Silence. Isn't it wonderful!"

"By the end of the month you'll be bored and wanting your students back, and so will Tarma and I," her husband replied knowingly, and took Kethry's arm. Even after all this time, she still got a warm thrill at his touch, and she laid her free hand over his. He had a knowing twinkle in his eyes as she squeezed his hand in response.

"Well, we still have our own younglings, and I'm going to go drill Jadrie and the twins in the riding arena," Tarma replied. "They think I'm teaching them riding tricks and Shin'a'in horseback games to impress their friends. Hah!"

One of these days that trick isn't going to work anymore. Kethry laughed. "Just don't keep them at it too long. It *is* a holiday, and it's not fair for us to give their friends release from study and not give them the same treatment."

Tarma tossed her hair back with a casual flip of a hand. "Oh, don't worry, I'm an old hand at making lessons seem like play."

"At least until they catch you at it," Jadrek warned, echoing Kethry's thought, with a chuckle. "Last holiday within a fortnight they had it figured that your game of 'hide and hunt' was nothing more than practice in tracking."

"Well, that's *your* fault for breeding such clever children," Tarma retorted, as she strode off in the direction of the stables. "You should have been a little more careful."

Kethry laughed, and hugged Jadrek's arm, reminded again how grateful she was that her *she'enedra* and her beloved were as fond of one another as the best of siblings. "To think that I was once worried about how you two would get along!"

Her husband arched a slender, silver eyebrow at her, and she braced herself for something witty, funny, or both. "Do you think that for one scant moment I would even contemplate doing or saying anything to offend our best unpaid child-tender? Perish the thought, woman!"

"I know, how foolish of me." She released his arm with a kiss on the back of his hand. "I am going to go do something nonmagical, frivolous and feminine; I'm going to go brew up some perfume in the still-room. I've spent so much time making bruise-ointment and salve for the little hoydens that I haven't done a thing with the roses I harvested this summer, or the sentle-wood and amba-resin that I bought from that trader this fall."

"Mmm," Jadrek replied absently, as his mind apparently flashed elsewhere. *I think he just realized that he's going to have whole stretches of time without interruptions for the next moon.* "I've got a translation I promised to young Stefansen that's been giving me some problems."

Kethry made a shooing motion with her hands. "Go do it, then but set the candle-alarm for three marks, or you won't remember to eat luncheon, and I'm certain that Cook is already planning something a bit more experimental now that the children are gone."

This would make another pleasant change; on the whole, children bolted food without paying much attention to it, and looked upon things that they didn't recognize with suspicion. It was only when no one was in residence but "the family" that Cook made anything other than good, basic fare. And Cook looked forward to the holidays with some anticipation for that very reason.

"Well, I wouldn't risk my marriage by offending Cook either," Jadrek laughed, and kissed her forehead. "Now don't *you* forget to set your alarm-candle!"

They went their separate ways, and Kethry immersed herself in the intricacies of creating her own signature perfumes—a light floral, rich with roses, and a heavier, more incenselike scent, both with hints of cinnamon. The still-room was one of her favorite places in the manor, pleasantly dim (some essences reacted poorly to sunlight), cool in summer, warm in winter. There was just enough room for one person to move about, so no one came here unless invited. She puttered happily with oils and fixatives, flagons and pestles. When her alarm-candle burned down the allotted three candlemarks and released its little brass ball to clang into the copper basin, she came to herself with a start.

She cleaned up and headed for the table, to find Tarma, Jadrie, and the twins making serious inroads on Cook's latest creation. It involved finely-chopped meat and vegetables, cheese—something vaguely like sheets of pastry—and there Kethry's knowledge ended.

"Pull up a plate and tuck in," Tarma urged. "I haven't a clue what this is, but it's marvelous!"

The twins looked up with full mouths and slightly-smeared cheeks, nodded vigorously in agreement, and dove back in. All of the "home children" were used to eating things they didn't recognize and were prepared to enjoy them, partly because of their cheerful tempers, and partly because they had *always* been used to eating things they didn't recognize. They had spent their entire lives shuttling between the school-manor, with fairly ordinary fare, and the Dhorisha Plains. Shin'a'in cuisine was not something that most

Rethwellans would be at all familiar with, and there often was not much choice in what they were offered when on the road.

Cook came in with a loaf of hot bread and a pot of butter, wearing a look of anxious inquiry on his face. "Tasty dead horse, Cook!" Jadrie called, and ducked as he mimed a blow at her. It was an old joke between them, since the time when Jadrie had pestered him as a toddler, wanting to know what was in each dish he made. He had finally gotten annoyed at her incessant questions and snapped, "Dead horse! Can't you see the tail?" From that moment on, any time Cook presented them with an experiment, Jadrie referred to it as a "dead horse."

"I wasn't certain, before, but I think this would be a good school dish," Cook said to Kethry. "It's easily made ahead and kept warm next to the ovens. Do you think the students would eat it?"

"If they won't, I'll eat theirs for 'em," Lyan said with his mouth full.

Jadrek laughed. "With that kind of enthusiasm before them, I imagine they will, Devid, he replied. "This is definitely one of your better experiments."

Cook beamed his pleasure, and hurried back to the kitchen to supervise the cleaning up. The rest of the meal proceeded in pleasant silence as the mystery dish and the hot bread and butter vanished away like snow in sunshine. Even Kethry, who normally wasn't all that hearty an eater, found herself unusually hungry after her work in the still-room, and was absorbed completely in the meal.

It wasn't until she had eaten the last bite that she could possibly hold and looked up that she realized not everyone had come to lunch—or, apparently, were expected to.

"Estrel and Justin and Ikan went down to the village to meet the new Healer-Priestess and they took Jadrek Minor with them," Jadrie said, as Kethry noticed that the other three places weren't set. "Estrel put the babies down for their naps before she left, and Warrl is watching them. Cook said he'd save them lunch; they expected to be back by the time the babies' naps were over."

"Then I'd better supervise the nursery until they get back, and give Warrl a break," Tarma said, not only willing, but eager. "Jadrie, will you and the twins—"

Just at that moment, Kethry felt the room drop away from under her, a wash of anger threaten to overwhelm her, and a surge of nameless emotions hit her with a force that made her gasp. Unconsciously, she braced herself on the table, as her family turned to stare at her with varying degrees of surprise and concern.

And for a moment, she didn't recognize what had hit her, it had been so long—

"*Need*," she gasped, when she got her breath back. "It's Need! Something's wrong, something horrible has happened—"

"To whom?" Tarma demanded. "Can you tell?" Her face paled. "Dear gods, surely not Estrel—"

Kethry shook her head, both in negation and to clear the tears of shock from her eyes. "Not Estrel, it's not in the direction of the village," she managed to reply. At least in all the time she'd been soul-bonded to the blade, she'd learned to pick out which direction that "trouble" was coming from. "But it

can't be too far away, not more than a day's ride at
most, or it wouldn't be this *strong*—"

Jadrie and the twins stared at her with alarm and
dismay. *Of course, they've never seen me like this before,
Need hasn't grabbed me like this in years*—

"Should we send out a hunter or something—"
Jadrek began, and Tarma snapped her fingers.

"Of course!" she said, then frowned in concentration. "Keth, what direction?"

"North, north and a little east," she replied, as sure
of it as if she was the needle of a compass pointing to
the source that was wrenching at her skull and heart.

A door slammed somewhere, as Tarma said,
"Warrl's on it. He's faster in this weather than anyone, and he'll find out exactly *where* the trouble is.
Can you hold out until he calls me or comes back
himself?"

"I'll have to, won't I?" she replied grimly, for now
the pull that the sword exerted on her had settled to
a painful headache echoed by wire-tight muscles in
her neck, shoulders, and stomach. "This isn't something we can delegate. We'd better get ready to ride.
Jadrek—"

How do I tell my beloved that he'll only be in the way?

"I won't be of much use to you, dearest," he admitted without rancor, a fact that brought tears of
gratitude to her eyes. "Or rather, I will be of *more*
use to you here with the children. What can I do to
help prepare?"

"Travel packs; you know what I need," she said
immediately. The mere thought that *she* wouldn't
have to try and think through this pain to select what
she would require came as a profound relief.

"I'm on it, love." Jadrek pushed away from the table and left the room, as quickly as he could.

Tarma took over, as the three children stared, dismayed and frightened. "Children, you three get Hellsbane and Ironheart ready. Jadrie, you've had lessons in provisioning, you make up the packs for the horses. I'm depending on you to get it right. Boys, saddle and harness the mares, and when Jadrie's put the packs together, bring them to the riding arena. *Go.*"

The children scrambled to their feet and sped out of the room like three hornets from a roused nest. Tarma turned to Kethry, who was taking slow, even breaths, and trying to get a little magical shielding between herself and the pain. "Keth, get to your rooms and get changed. I'll tell Cook what's going on, and he can handle the servants until Jadrek has time to deal with them, I'll get changed and collect the medical kit and traveling cash, and I'll meet you at the riding arena. Good?"

She nodded; in a moment or two she *would* be able to walk. "Right," she replied, and as Tarma left her alone in the room, she began a silent colloquy with the sword hanging on the wall of her sitting room, trying to persuade it that *nothing* was going to happen unless it gave her—not freedom, but a long enough leash to act.

Old warriors never let their fighting gear get out of condition; that is how they *become* old warriors in the first place. Tarma's armor and weapons were always kept oiled, polished, and in a place of honor on the proper stands in her room. When the family made its annual summer pilgrimage to the Plains, she wore it religiously, even though in all the years she had done so, they had never once been set upon.

And I always keep a traveling pack three-fourths complete, just in case. You never know. . . .

So in her case, it wasn't at all difficult to assemble the proper pack and get herself properly arrayed. In fact, the pack was complete and she had just about finished lacing herself into her armor when she heard Warrl's "call" in the back of her head, as if he was shouting from a long distance away.

The *kyree* had awesome speed when he needed it, and was not limited to using roads; he could cover in a candlemark what would take a horse and rider half a day to traverse if it was necessary. He'd pay for it afterward, and be useless for the rest of the day, but if there was ever the perfect scout to send off looking for trouble, it was Warrl.

Between his speed and his nose, he required only a simple direction to find the source of whatever had set Need off. That violent a reaction had to have its cause in further violence, and Warrl could scent blood on the wind a league away. Tarma would have been astonished if he *hadn't* found the source of their alarm.

And she had a horrible feeling, as well, that she already knew who it was that had caused the alarm. *North* was the direction that Kira and Meri had gone. And Need "knew" them, by virtue of being within the same walls for the past four moons.

Warrl was so far away that he was barely at the limit of his range, and his mental voice was faint and thin.

But it was clear enough, and it was exactly what

she had dreaded hearing. :*Kira and Meri. Escort all dead, girls gone. On my way back.*:

Scant information, but enough. He was probably saving his energy for the run. He'd be exhausted when he reached the manor, but that was all right, he could ride pillion on Hellsbane and recover while he guided them.

Worry about them in the back of your mind, Tarma. Concentrate on getting on their track now.

She raised her voice and called out the open door of her room, knowing that Jadrek and Kethry would hear her, reporting exactly what Warrl had told her, and forced her fingers to work faster in the lacings of her armor. When the last piece was fastened, she grabbed her thick, quilted wool Shin'a'in coat and her pack, and ran as fast as the weight of the armor would permit, heading for the still room.

Once there, she made up a medical kit of anything that might be useful—from silk thread and needles to poppy-gum. Ordinarily this would be Kethry's job, but Tarma had seen her do it often enough to know what went into such a kit, and there were special padded leather roll-pouches, each with the appropriate pockets, just waiting for anyone who needed to make up such a kit. That went into her pack, well-cushioned by the bedroll, and she headed for her next destination, Justin's office where the strongbox was kept.

Old habits die hard for former mercenaries; as she had half hoped, there was a full money-belt coiled inside the strongbox, along with the rest of the school's treasure. Justin wouldn't have felt easy unless he knew there was a full money-belt ready in case of an emergency trip. She hefted it, judged it to be sufficient by the weight, and buckled it on over her armor. Later, she could put it on *under* the armor, but she didn't think she had the time to right now. Whoever had kidnapped the girls already had half a day's head start on them—for they must have gotten at least that far from the school before they were attacked. It could snow at any time, and if the kidnappers were intelligent, they would take to the trade roads and trust to the inevitable traffic that moved even in winter to confuse or obliterate their trail.

Thank the gods Jadrek didn't ask why we're doing this, she thought, heading for the stables. There had never been any doubt in her mind that they would do *something* from the moment that Need woke from her years-long sleep. But strictly speaking, she and Keth didn't *have* to go after the girls. *They* weren't at fault, their escort was. They had already relinquished control of the children the moment the escort took them off the property. All they were obligated to do would be to send word to the girls' father of the disaster.

Right, and how do I look Tilden in the face again, if all I do is that? Hellfires, how do I look at myself in the mirror? No way am I going to abandon them, and neither is Keth, and with Need to guide us, we're the best chance those girls have got.

She beat Keth to the riding arena by a few moments, but no more—just long enough to see with relief that Jadrie and the boys had gotten things exactly right—

And that Jadrie and her brothers were sitting on their own horses, with packs tied on behind that were identical in every way to the packs she and Keth were taking.

Her mind hadn't quite grasped that, when Jadrek

and Kethry reached the door of the arena. Jadrek was the first to react in any kind of sensible fashion.

"Just what do you children think you're doing?" he thundered, in his best wrath-of-the-gods voice.

The boys winced a little, but Jadrie was unimpressed. "We're going with you," she stated flatly. "You need us."

Tarma covered the distance between herself and Jadrie in a mere blink of an eye, grabbing Jadrie's ankle and looking into her eyes with a glare that full grown men could not face. "Jadrie," she said, her harsh voice made even harsher with anger. "This is *not* a game. And it's no time for playing stupid tricks."

To her surprise, Jadrie did not back down, though tears of anger and frustration started from her eyes—anger at being misjudged, and frustration at being thought a mere child with no understanding. "Don't you think I *know* that?" she cried. "Don't you think Lyam and Laryn do? They heard you, heard you telling Mummy and Da what went wrong, and they came to tell me! It's Kira and Meri who are in trouble, and I *swore* to help them, Clanmother, I *swore* it, sword and hand!"

The words hit Tarma like a blow to the heart, and she cursed under her breath.

She swore the oath. Damn her, she's of the blood and she swore the oath to her friends. It's sacred; she knows it and I know it and the Star-Eyed knows it. That was the *only* thing that could have persuaded her to allow Jadrie to come within a thousand leagues of this rescue mission—and how had this infuriating little Clanswoman known it? And *why* did she swear the

Oath of Sword and Hand to a couple of outClan children?

Kethry and Jadrek had been among the Shin'a'in long enough to know how serious the Oath was— and what were they supposed to do? Tell Jadrie that she was too young to know what she was doing, when she plainly had? Tell her that oaths sworn by not-so-little girls didn't count? What kind of an idiot would do that to a child?

What kind of idiot would make a child into an oathbreaker?

Tarma turned, and saw the same conflicts warring within Jadrek and Kethry. Finally, it was Kethry who spoke.

"You're her teacher," Kethry said flatly. "*Can* she help?"

Tarma closed her eyes, and tried to forget that the youngster before her was the firstborn of her best friends, the firstborn of Tale'sedrin. Jadrie was no younger than many Shin'a'in children on patrol now at the edge of the Plains, or guarding herds from predators, or performing any one of a number of "adult" tasks. She was as well-trained, or better, than all of them. "Yes," she said finally, flatly. "She has the skills to be very useful."

She opened her eyes, and saw fear and pride warring in her friends' faces, and it was Jadrek who looked up at Jadrie, and said, "Very well. Because you swore an oath, you can go."

Jadrie had the good manners not to cheer, but the twins didn't. And Jadrek cut them off.

"But *you* two didn't swear any oaths, and *you* are staying here!" he barked.

"That's an order," Kethry added in a voice of steel.

"And if you *dare* to try and follow, you lose the use of your horses for the rest of the year."

That was more than enough threat to keep them safely behind, as their stricken looks proved. Crestfallen, the boys slid off their horses, and meekly led them back into the stable.

Kethry turned to her daughter, and still using that same cold voice, addressed her in a way that made her turn a little pale. "I am not pleased with this," she told the girl. "I am not particularly pleased that you decided to use an oath that serious without thinking of the consequences. You have a chance to redeem yourself *if* you follow every order we give you to the letter, with no argument, and no hesitation. If you cannot keep up, you will return home on your own; we won't have time to take you back. This is going to be the hardest thing you have ever done, and there will be no room for thoughtless acts. I am not your mother on this trip; Tarma is not your foster mother. We are your commanders, and if you make a mistake, it could be fatal, not just for you, but for all of us. If there is fighting, you *will* stay clear unless otherwise ordered. If you bring danger on us, we will save you if we can, but it is not only possible but *likely* that we cannot. Is that understood?"

Clearly this was a side of her mother that Jadrie had never seen before. She was as pale as a spirit, but her chin was set firmly, and she replied in a voice that was as steady as Tarma could have wished. "Perfectly, commander."

Now Kethry looked at Tarma. "Let's get in the saddle and get moving; we'll meet Warrl on the way, and save him a little running. We need all the daylight we can get."

"Right." Tarma heaved herself up into Hellsbane's saddle, and Kethry got herself in place on Ironheart, leaning down to kiss her husband when she was secure.

"Go—" he urged. "I'll take care of things here—as soon as the rest get back, I'll send Ikan up to Tilden; better this comes from a friend than a strange messenger."

She needed no more urging than that, and neither did Tarma; lifting the reins, the two battlesteeds loped out into the gray light of afternoon, followed by a much subdued Jadrie on her mare.

Kira had created plenty of daydreams about bandit raids and kidnappers, and had imagined herself being heroic and triumphant in all of them, but when attackers really struck, it wasn't *anything* like her daydreams.

It was all so sudden she barely had time to react, much less act in a heroic fashion. The guards were all calm, talking and joking, and no one was at all wary and watchful. She had the impression that this had been considered a "soft" job, and the men with her were very much envied by their peers. There was no indication that there was anything to be worried about.

The very first sign that something was wrong was when one of the more nervous horses stopped, snorted, and twitched his ears forward.

There was no other warning. Before even the horse's rider had a chance to do anything, a guard at the front of the escort suddenly screamed and fell off his horse.

For all of her reading, this was the first time that

Kira had ever seen a man die, and this one was dying right in front of her; at first, it didn't seem real. Before she could do more than stare stupidly at the arrow in his back and the spreading scarlet stain in the snow as he writhed there, two more of the guards made horrid gurgling sounds and fell off, too, with arrows sticking out of their throats.

She sat there on her fat little pony, paralyzed with a mixture of fear and horror, wanting to throw up and run away at the same time. The only thing that came into her mind was that there was never any blood in her daydreams. . . .

Meri screamed, startling her out of her shock, at about the same time as chaos erupted all around them.

Their ponies were shoved aside by more of their guards, as the men made a wall of themselves around their charges. But that wall didn't last long; ignoring armored men, the attackers cut down the horses with their arrows, sending screaming animals to drop under their riders. Behind the volley of arrows came a charge, then there were frantically running men and horses, screaming and shouting, and swords cutting everywhere. Confused and frightened, the pony only thought to flee; he bolted between two screeching, bleeding horses into the first open space he saw.

Suddenly she was sitting on her pony in the middle of the open road, and there wasn't anybody standing protectively between her and a rough-clad man who was riding straight for her.

She thought, belatedly, of her knife at her belt—her pony tried to bolt as she gave him confused signals—then the stranger was right on top of her. He snatched her out of her saddle with an impact that drove all the breath out of her and made her see stars.

He paused just long enough to rob her of her knife, then dumped her across the front of his saddle, face-down—as the horse galloped off, she thought she was going to be sick. The pommel of his saddle jolted into her stomach, and she had a terrible time just getting a full breath between jolts. The whole world was reduced to lashing hair and snow-covered ground, and the pain of an ever-increasing number of bruises.

The next thing she knew, he'd stopped as abruptly as he'd started. He grabbed her under the arms before she got a breath, and threw her toward a—wagon? Whatever, she was flying through the air, straight for it. Before she had time to brace herself, she landed inside a darkened boxlike structure, and hit her head against the wooden floor. Meri landed on top of her in the next moment, then something bulky and heavy flew in after them. The door they'd been tossed through slammed shut, there was the sound of a bar dropping in place over the door. Before either of them could move, the box began jolting around, bouncing and bruising them both unmercifully to the sound of wheels and galloping hooves.

We're in a wagon. A prison-wagon, or a treasure-wagon, they're about the same—

That was all the tiny, still-sane part of her could think, as she and Meri clung to each other, and screamed and cried until they were hoarse, sore of eye and of throat, as well as battered and bruised.

Eventually they managed to brace themselves so that they weren't bouncing around quite so badly,

and long after they'd cried themselves out, the
wagon finally slowed to a reasonable pace.

"What happened?" Meri asked tearfully, in a
hoarse whisper.

"I th–think we've been kidnapped," Kira stam-
mered back.

"But—*why?*" Meri wailed. "Who would want to
kidnap us?"

Kira ignored that question; obviously their father
was under the impression that *someone* would want
to, or he wouldn't have sent guards to escort them
home for the holidays. She knew, beneath her own
fright and nausea, that somehow she would have to
come up with better questions than that. You had to
have questions before you could have answers—and
oh, she needed answers now!

A voice out of memory interrupted her chaotic,
fear-filled rambling.

"Think things through."

She started; for a moment the memory of Tarma's
voice was so clear that it seemed as if she'd really
heard the words.

"We have to *think*, Meri," she whispered fiercely.
"Like Tarma always says." She screwed up her face
in concentration, and tried to dredge up other memories that might help.

*"Start with what you know, and go on to what your
resources are. Don't waste the first few moments on
speculation."*

She licked her lips. What she knew—well, they'd
been kidnapped. They were in a wagon, being hauled
rapidly away from where they'd been taken. And
she knew that sooner or later, someone would come
looking for them.

How soon? No, that's a speculation.

There was nothing to tell her who it was that held them captive. But at the very least, she should begin by examining their prison.

There wasn't much to examine; there was enough room on the floor for both girls to stretch out at full-length, but not much more than that. The walls were straight and unadorned, and would permit an adult to stand erect. There were no windows, no benches to sit on, but light did leak in through a couple of chinks and knotholes.

No help there.

She examined the bulky objects that had been tossed in after them by touch, and discovered to her joy that it was their packs! But it was obvious that they'd been opened, and a quick feel through both proved that nothing in the way of a weapon had been left to them, not even a pair of Meri's scissors.

She still had the tiny knife in her boot, but it wouldn't be of much use.

Resources. Clothing, Meri's embroidery, beads and jewelry they didn't steal, and my journal. I suppose we could use drawstrings to strangle someone, provided he held still and cooperated—

She stifled a hysterical laugh. Concentrate! What came next?

"Father will send someone to find us, won't he?" Meri asked, her voice trembling just a little.

"Once he knows we're gone. *If* he can find us." There didn't seem any point in telling her twin less than the truth. "That could be hard. I don't know where they're taking us, but it's probably far away. And they've got us locked up in this wagon, I bet, so we don't attract attention. If they get onto a trade road, it's going to be awfully hard to track us."

Meri took a shuddering breath, but kept herself under control. "Couldn't we—leave a trail of something? Like the goose-girl and her pocket of pebbles?"

Kira almost dismissed that as desperate babbling, but something in her seized on the idea. A trail—maybe that wasn't such a bad idea. There *was* a chink in the floor, and they could drop something small out of it without much trouble. But what? And how could they keep what they dropped from being seen by their captors? Almost anything they dropped would stand out in the snow—

—snow. White snow. White *silk!* Silver *beads!*

"Meri, I need the white silk you got from Jadrie, and the silver beads," Kira said urgently. "Can you find it in here?" She shoved Meri's pack over to her, and hoped that the silks hadn't been looted.

"I think so." Meri rummaged around in her pack in the semidarkness, and finally came up with a handful of skeins of thread that shone pale as moonlight in her hand, and a little box that rattled. "Here. What are you going to do?"

"Leave a trail for people to follow," Kira replied, carefully finding the end of one of the skeins, then snipping off a short piece with her tiny knife. "They should have dogs. They might have Warrl! When they find this silk, they'll *know* it's us."

Carefully, she fed the silk through the chink, doing her best to keep it from snagging on a splinter. It took three tries, and three pieces, before she hit on the idea of making a funnel with a piece of paper from her journal, but at last she got one to drop all the way through.

Meanwhile, she kept thinking. "We've got to figure out a way to slow everything down," she said, as she continued to thread bits of silk through the wooden floor, alternating the silk with silver beads. "Think, Meri! What can we do to make it hard for these people?"

"Should we try to run away when they take us out?" Meri asked doubtfully.

"They're a lot bigger than we are, and there's more of them," Kira reminded her. "And I don't think they care if we get hurt a little."

Or even a lot.

"Besides," she continued, "If we try to run away, they won't ever let us out again."

"Could we do something to the horses?"

"Only if they let us get near them." Kira thought about it a moment, pondering the possibilities of burrs under saddles, or crystal beads lodged in hooves, then shook her head regretfully. "I don't think they're going to do that. If we were bigger, we could probably loosen the wheels on the wagon or something—if we had wine we could get them all drunk—"

Meri thought for a while longer, then said, reluctantly, "What if we got sick? Wouldn't they have to stop so we wouldn't die?"

"They'll know if we aren't really sick, and anyway, they could just leave us in the wagon."

"Not—" Meri bit her lip, and Kira could tell her twin was blushing by the tone of her voice. "Not if it's—stomach troubles. And lower."

"Stomach grippe? What are you thinking of?" Kira asked sharply.

"Remember my black beads? The ones Kethry told me never to let the baby play with, because they'd make him sick? They took my good jewels, but not those." Meri rummaged in her pack again, and came up with three long ropes of small, dark beads. "They're not really beads, they're seeds, and Jadrek helped me to find out what they were. They don't taste like anything, and if we eat three or four, we'll get sick. Then they'll have to stop to let us—be sick. Won't they?"

Kira looked at her twin with sudden admiration. *I would be willing to get sick to slow everything up—but I wouldn't have thought Meri would!* "I think so," she said, with another thought coming into her mind— but one she would save, until she had a better idea of what their situation was. "It's worth a try."

Blood everywhere. I'd thought I would never have to deal with a situation like this one again. Tarma surveyed the carnage impassively, but with a sinking feeling in her heart. The bodies of the ten guards that had lately left the school with Meri and Kira now sprawled in ungainly poses over about a quarter of an acre of trampled snow. Three were down on the road itself, four lay in a ragged line under their dead and fallen horses and had clearly never gotten the chance to struggle free before they, too, were killed, and the remaining three were in a line behind them, where they had made a final stand afoot. Blood stained the white snow red everywhere, and liberal trails of more blood heading off to the south and west showed that the kidnappers had not gotten away completely unscathed.

But there were no dead that were not of the guards in Tilden's livery, so if any of the attackers had died, their bodies had been carted away. A bad sign. *Whoever planned this was well organized, well armed, and with a lot of men. And it wasn't a simple bandit-raid.* Not one guard had been left alive to send word of the massacre. Those horses that weren't dead were grouped together, heads down, exhausted—not carried off with the bandits. The two ponies that Meri and Kira had ridden out on stood under a tree beside the road, sadly nosing through the snow and biting at the withered grass they found there.

Nobody actually stopped to loot either, not even the gear on the dead and living horses. All the arms and armor, all the packs that belonged to the dead men, it's all still here. Just the girls and their packhorse, that's all that were taken, and I have to wonder if the packhorse wasn't grabbed just because they didn't want to take the time to unload the girls' stuff off him. If we hadn't had Need, nobody would have known this happened until some trader or farmer stumbled over the bodies—and even then, no one would know that the girls were missing. Until Tilden came looking for them, that is.

"Where now?" she asked Kethry.

"South and west," she replied immediately. "More west than south."

Well, that certainly corresponded with those telltale blood trails.

Tarma sucked on her lower lip, and glanced up at the sky to the west. Behind the gray pall of clouds, the sun shone feebly, no more than a finger's-breadth above the horizon. The air was sharply cold, too cold for snow at this point, so for a while they could follow the clear trail left by the kidnappers. It would be dark soon—and no time to act on her hunch that the kidnappers were about to drive straight south. At least, not in time to cut them off.

"Stay on the pillion, Furball," she told a weary Warrl behind her. "I'll track them as long as I can see, then you take over until we can't ride anymore."

But just as twilight faded, that became easier to do, for the tracks of the running horses in the unbroken snow were joined by the tracks of wheels. Warrl raised his nose for a quick investigation, as Tarma read the churned-up snow. The blood-trails ended where the wheel marks began, so the kidnappers had paused long enough to rough-bandage their wounds.

:New men, here. They waited for some time while the others created their ambush and sprung it.:

"So they had a wagon ready and waiting, and that's where they put the girls." She gritted her teeth. "Smart. You keep them completely under control and you don't have to worry about someone accidentally seeing them. Hard to explain a little girl trussed up like a chicken for the pot, but *no one* is likely to be curious about a prison-wagon. I wish to hell I knew who these people were! It would tell me a lot about why they've done this and what they want."

"Surely ransom," Kethry ventured, but Tarma shook her head.

"Not necessarily, *she'enedra*. This could be political, an attempt to force Tilden into a position he wouldn't otherwise take by holding his girls." She used a little mental discipline to keep herself calm so that she could think properly, as her battlemare responded to her unease by shifting her weight and looking

around for the danger. "It could be political in another way, to make an example out of the girls, to
show how ruthless these people can be. Hellfires, if
there are still any of Char's old allies around, I'd
count on them to be that ruthless. It could be religious; the Triune Goddess Priests have been getting
their noses out of joint since there isn't an official
state religion anymore."

"It doesn't even *have* to have anything to do with
Rethwellan," came the small, uncertain voice from
behind her. As she turned to peer at Jadrie through
the gloom, the girl swallowed but looked straight
into Tarma's eyes and bravely continued her thought.
"Merili is supposed to marry the Prince of Jkatha.
And the kidnappers *are* going south. Maybe someone
wants to force Queen Sursha to do something to get
Meri back safe. You *know* she'd have to do something, especially if it's Jkathans that took Meri and
Kira."

"Damn. Out of the mouths of babes. Good thinking, kitten." *And maybe I ought to be grateful that she's
along. . . .* Tarma shook her head, then tried to visual-
ize where they were on a map. With a sinking feeling, she realized that if the kidnappers continued
southward, they would quickly strike a major trade
route, and the odds were high that they would be
able to muddle or hide their trail there in the tracks
of ongoing traffic.

Which meant that the odds were high that they
would strike straight south soon. Going across country to try at least to catch up was a better plan than
it had seemed a few moments ago.

*Plots on plots—what if someone wants the boy to marry
his girl? Getting Tilden to forbid the marriage in order*

to get the girls back would do that, and Sursha doesn't even have to enter into it. What if they want to make a political incident out of this, between Jkatha and Rethwellan? Making it look as if Sursha is behind it could easily do that. The trouble is—the trouble is—a lot of these plots end in murders.

"Warrl, we need you now," she told the *kyree*, and with a groan, he jumped down off the pillion-pad behind her into the ankle-deep snow. "We'll keep going as long as we can, then we'll stop for a rest and start as soon as there's light."

"Footing?" Jadrie said hesitantly. "For the horses? Shouldn't we have some light?"

Tarma followed in Warrl's wake before she answered, but this was practical knowledge for Jadrie. "If we didn't have Warrl, or if he was fresh, or if we were on anything but Shin'a'in horses, I would agree. Warrl is too tired to make more than a walk," she pointed out. "At that pace, we let the horses feel their own way. I don't want to advertise our presence with a light—in conditions like this, you could see a light for leagues. Plus if the kidnappers have a mage, he might be able to sense a mage-light."

There was no more comment from Jadrie, so Tarma put the child out of her mind, and let Warrl lead them all onward, as the horses placed their hooves with deliberate care.

At this point, she wasn't anything more than a passenger; she folded her arms and tucked her hands into her belt, let her head sag, and dozed. If the damned sword wasn't making life too difficult for Kethry, she knew her partner was doing the same. *Catch sleep whenever you can.* The mares and Warrl would warn of danger long before it was visible, and they were too far behind the kidnappers for there to be any likelihood of stumbling into their camp. Of course Jadrie wasn't going to nap, and *shouldn't*, because she didn't have a battlemare, only a Shin'a'in-bred saddlemare. But Jadrie also had two advantages over her elders—the first, that she wasn't expected to fight or track later and didn't need the extra sleep, and the second that she was decades younger than either Tarma or her mother and could go longer on less rest.

The horses plodded on into the thick darkness, as Tarma roused herself roughly every candlemark or so to check their bearings by Kethry and Need. As she had expected, some time within the first candlemark after darkness fell, the kidnappers turned south, and were probably on the trade road into Jkatha right at that moment. *Probably camped. I hope the girls are all right, at least for now.* It was some comfort to know that they were in a wagon, probably locked in there, and that the people who'd taken them were trained and disciplined. If all they were was terrified—well, they could get over simple terror. There were other things that could happen to little girls that were harder to get over.

Including being murdered.

It was just after midnight that Warrl stumbled over a snow-covered branch, and admitted, :*I'm done in, mindmate. We have to rest now. The track still says nothing has happened to the girls, and I can't go any further.*:

Both mares stopped when Warrl did, and Jadrie's horse only went another pace or two further than that. "Right. We're stopping, Keth," Tarma called.

Kethry grunted a vague reply, and shook herself awake. As she and Tarma slid stiffly out of their saddles, Kethry kindled a very dim mage-light and Tarma looked around for a suitable campsite. There wasn't much, out here in an area of rolling hills mostly covered with scrub and very rough grasses, but a half-circle of snow-covered bushes gave a certain amount of protection from wind and watchers. She got Jadrie to help set up the tiny tent, and Kethry got out grain for the horses and took over the three packs and extinguished the light. Then, while Kethry laid blankets down on the floor and tucked their packs inside for safekeeping, Jadrie and Tarma unsaddled the horses, rubbed them down, and gave them their rations. She didn't need to hobble the battlemares, for they wouldn't wander, and to keep Jadrie's mare from strolling off, she simply fastened her halter to Ironheart's.

The tent was very small, but big enough for all three of them to lie down together, with a little room to spare for luggage. As Tarma had known she would, Kethry had set up a spell to keep it warm all night long, without a fire. She'd also done something to make the tent poles glow faintly (a glow that couldn't be seen from outside through the canvas) so that they could see to keep feet out of faces. Their blankets were to pad the tent floor beneath them, and to keep the cold from seeping into their bodies from below, not for warmth. It *was* possible that a mage could sense all this, but these were very minor magics, and well within the scope of just about any earth-witch or hedge-wizard.

Without being asked, Jadrie brought in a leather pail full of snow, and tucked it into the corner to thaw, then took one of the outside positions. Tarma took the other, putting Kethry into the "protected" position between them—but then Warrl wriggled into the tent, somehow getting into the available space (what there was of it) and put himself between Jadrie and the tent wall. Kethry gave each of them a strip of dried meat and a piece of hard journey bread; they ate in silence and warmth and passed the waterskin back and forth until the thirst roused by salt-dried meat and bricklike bread was gone. Kethry extinguished the glow of the tent poles, and the silence seemed even deeper.

Then Kethry took a deep breath, and Tarma knew she was going to say something.

"You've been quiet, you've kept up, you've obeyed orders, and when you've said something, it's been sensible," the mage said softly into the darkness, and all of them knew which "you" was meant. "You've been a help instead of a hindrance."

"Thank you," Jadrie said in a small voice.

"I'm not *glad* you're here, kitten—and all you have to do is think back on the ambush to know why." Her voice broke a little. "The idea that something like that could happen to *you* has me in knots. *You're only a child.* You aren't supposed to be seeing things like that."

Tarma heard Jadrie swallow, then she said, "But— I already have. How can we be sheltered when we're *your* children?"

"She's got you there, Greeneyes," Tarma said dryly.

"I promise, I *promise*, that unless you tell me to do otherwise, when we find these people, I'm going to stay far enough behind that I can run if I have to." Jadrie paused and then said, in a new and tearful voice, "But you have to promise that you won't let anything like that happen to you!"

It was almost a wail, and Kethry caught her daughter up in her arms, as Tarma grabbed a free hand and squeezed it.

"I can promise we'll try, kitten," Kethry said, in a voice nearly as hoarse as Tarma's.

And with that, they all sought uneasy sleep, and were exhausted enough to find it.

When you're sick, riding in a wagon is really a bad idea. By the time darkness fell, the seeds they'd eaten had taken full effect, and Kira really *did* feel sick; her stomach churned, there was a fat lump in her throat that kept making her gag, and her mouth felt sour and dry. In fact, she wasn't sure now that she could manage to keep her nausea under control much longer, which could make things really nasty in there. When the wagon stopped, she pounded on the door, and put desperation into her voice.

"Please!" she wailed, and fought back the nausea. "Let us out! We're sick!"

Footsteps creaked on snow just outside the door. "What do you mean, sick?" asked a suspicious voice from the other side.

"Please! I'm going to *throw up!*" she gulped, beginning to retch a little in spite of herself, and the door opened immediately.

"If you're faking—" the man began, but had no further chance to say anything, for Kira couldn't control her heaving stomach anymore, and threw up at his feet. He jumped back just in time to avoid being splattered, cursing.

"I'm—sorry—" She clapped her hand over her

mouth, as tears rolled down her face from the pain of her bruised stomach muscles. He kicked snow over the mess and lifted her and Meri out with surprising care, seeing as she'd almost thrown up on *him*. Maybe he just didn't want to have to dodge the mess again.

I don't think he's angry, though. . . .

"Please—" Meri gasped. "—where?"

He pointed, and they ran for the bushes at the side of the camp, where they rid themselves of the dreadful little seeds, and everything else that was in their stomachs. Both of them were chilled, shaking and weak when they finished. Kira filled her mouth over and over with snow, spitting it out again to rid herself of that awful taste, and Meri did the same. Her hands shook, her head ached, and her stomach muscles were so sore she wanted to just lie down in the snow and never get up again. But she did, even though her knees threatened to collapse as she helped her twin to her feet. No one asked if they were all right, or came to help them.

But no one kept them from going to the fire instead of the wagon either, and they huddled together as close to the warmth as they could, eyes half-closed, holding hands. Surely the way they looked now would keep anyone from thinking they had it in them to try and escape. But now that the seeds were gone, every passing moment brought a little more relief and strength.

In spite of the—now ebbing—nausea, Kira saw quite a bit behind her eyelashes. They *were* on a road, or rather, in a camp just off of a road, so it was a good thing that she'd been dropping silk and beads all along. And there were about twenty men in this group, which seemed like an awful lot to kidnap two little girls.

The man who'd let them out came over and poked Kira with his toe. "Hey, why're you sick?" he asked gruffly. He didn't seem unkind; in fact, there was some concern on his unshaven face. Although he wasn't anyone she would have picked for a friend, she sensed they might have a reluctant ally.

It was Meri who answered. "A lot of the students were sick before we left," she replied in a thin and weak-sounding voice. "I didn't think we'd get it, but I guess we did." She shivered and said in a half-moan, "I feel *awful*. I want to go *home!*"

"I told you there was nothing to worry about. It's just some childish ailment, and it will pass off in a day or so." The irritated voice out of the dark beyond the fire was a new one, and had an odd accent. Kira didn't place it, but Meri did.

She put her head down on Kira's shoulder, and pressed her mouth up near Kira's ear, as if she couldn't hold her head up any longer. "*Jkathan*," she whispered, a mere thread of sound.

The man who'd helped them seemed to feel a little sorry for them now; he hovered over them both for a moment, then went a few paces off and returned with a huge fur rug—a bit motheaten and bare in patches, but warm. He wrapped it around both of them, and actually tucked it in awkwardly.

"I don't s'pose you want anything to eat?" he asked. "Beans ain't done, but they're cooking in broth, you could have a bowl of that an' bread."

Kira's gorge rose at the mere thought of eating, and she shook her head as violently as she dared. Right now, though, she'd have traded every valuable she had ever owned for a mug of willow tea for her aching head.

"Just sit there an' get warm, an' when you wanta sleep, take the rug into the wagon with you. I don' need it," he said gruffly, and left them alone.

There was a pot on the fire in front of them, which Kira's nose told her was the one that held the broth and some simmering beans; next to the fire was a stack of journeybread, and a stack of bowls beside it. Good; the little seeds wouldn't stand out in a pot of beans. Hopefully, before they got chased into the wagon, her stomach would settle and she could slip the seeds into the pot under cover of getting bowls of broth for herself and Meri. If this was a camp like any other, the beans were for breakfast, as it would take that long for them to soften in the cooking enough to eat.

Meanwhile, she and Meri pretended to doze as sick children do, and she watched as much of the camp as she could see without moving her head. Slowly, her stomach settled; slowly her headache went away. The cold air helped, and so did the fact that they weren't moving anymore.

Although these men were dressed roughly, they didn't *act* like anything other than a well-trained group, accustomed to working together—so the shabby clothing they had over their armor must have been a disguise. Three of them quickly put up a small but luxurious tent, got coals from the fire for a brazier to heat it, and brought in a generous amount of bedding, before arranging their own bedding beside the fire. Kira got a brief look at the tent's owner before he went inside and laced the door shut; *he* wasn't shabbily dressed, and she thought he was the owner of the Jkathan accent.

The rest of the men seemed to relax a little when he went inside his own little quarters, though they studiously ignored the girls' presence. Some of them had been hurt in the fight, and they took this opportunity to get each other bandaged properly. Kira was obscurely grateful that she hadn't known any of her own guards; it would have been horrible to sit there watching these people patch themselves up, while wondering which of them had been the murderer of someone she knew.

Some of the men went out of the camp and didn't come back—they had gone out on guard duty, Kira was fairly certain, which made it less likely that she and Meri could slip away under cover of darkness. *And even if we did, where would we go? I don't know where we are, and neither does Meri. You've got to know your territory before you can hide easily, or find help.*

Some of the men dipped out bowls full of broth to soak their bread in and sat down on their bedding to alternate broth-dipped bread with bites of dried meat. They didn't seem inclined to talk much, not even with their fellows; as soon as they finished their abbreviated meals, they crawled into their bedrolls and were soon snoring. Kira wondered how they could sleep so easily after the awful fight, after killing and being wounded. Shouldn't they be staring up at the sky, sleepless, or haunted by nightmares?

Maybe they don't care anymore.

The thought was too horrible, and she resolutely put it away. Feeling bad wasn't going to fix anything right now. What she and Meri needed do was to get their own plan in motion, to slow their captors down.

Maybe in the process, they'd find an opportunity to escape. "Want to go back to the wagon?" Kira whispered. "I'm feeling better."

"I could eat broth and bread—if you were thinking of that." Meri squeezed her hand to show that she remembered the plan for Kira to doctor their kidnappers' food. "I'll take the robe back to the wagon, if you can bring food for both of us."

One of the men roused from sleep and watched them as they got up, but lost interest when they crept about with all the symptoms of still being ill and weak. Meri dragged the heavy robe back to the wagon and climbed inside; Kira feigned equal weakness and wobbled toward the fire.

She was afraid that the helpful fellow would show up and dip out the broth for her, but evidently he was on guard duty, and the only men still awake looked pointedly away from her. Maybe their consciences were bothering them—here were these two poor little girls, obviously sick, who should have been at home in bed, not dragged about in a prison-wagon. That only made her subterfuge easier, and she whispered a little prayer of thanks as she made the most of her opportunity. The seeds were in a drawstring bag that matched one of Meri's dresses and had been meant to hang on her belt. The bag was up her sleeve, and she'd already unfastened the mouth of it. As she dipped out the second bowl of broth, a steady stream of seeds poured out of her sleeve into the pot, the splashing they made covered neatly by the noises she made dipping out the broth. She made sure to take enough bread to hide in the wagon for breakfast—they would *not* want to share those beans, and could easily feign an attack of nau-

sea to cover their disinterest in food. Once the caravan got back underway, they could eat the bread
without fear of discovery.

She handed the food to Meri and climbed into the
wagon herself, pleased to discover that Meri had
taken the clothing in their packs and made a kind of
nest out of it. "Hide most of that bread," she whispered, as she got in beside her sister and took back
her bowl. "We'll need it for tomorrow."

She tasted her broth, and wished for Devid Cook;
it wasn't horrible, but it was very flat, unseasoned,
probably made by boiling unsalted dried meat. The
journeybread wasn't any better, but when the bread
was soaked in the broth it made a palatable mush
that was warm, and it was probably better for their
tender stomachs than real food would have been.

After that, there didn't seem anything more to do
but sleep, so they curled up around each other to
share the warmth of their bodies, and somehow, in
spite of all the horrible things that had happened to
them, they fell quickly and dreamlessly into sleep.

It wasn't even dawn when the camp roused and
the men began packing things up, and not at all quietly either. There was a lot of cursing, groaning—
wounds had probably stiffened in the night, and so
had muscles. Horses stamped and complained, harness jingled, but all of the sounds were very brisk
and businesslike. *They probably aren't taking any
chances that someone might follow,* Kira thought muz-
zily. *They want to get as far away from the ambush as
possible. The farther they are, the less likely that anyone
will connect them to it.*

Their helper poked his face into the wagon door

just at that moment. "Need the bushes?" he asked. He looked friendlier today, and Kira found herself hoping he hadn't been part of the ambush. She didn't want to hate him.

They nodded, and he helped them out of the wagon again, then took them over to the side of the camp and pointed to some very thick evergreen bushes a little shorter than they were. "Keep your heads in sight, one of you, anyway," was all he said; they took the hint, went to the other side and relieved themselves quickly. At least he hadn't made them take care of it while he watched.

They continued to feign weakness and sickness as he escorted them back to the wagon. "Want breakfast? You won't get another chance till we stop, and that won't be until dark," he told them, and both of them shook their heads violently. "Right, then. In you go." Rather than wait for them to climb into the wagon, he picked each of them up in turn and left them on the floor. "Here—" He dropped in a waterskin beside them. "Got stomach troubles, you can't let yourself get all dried out. Drink that a bit at a time. Try and sleep; the less noise you make, the better off you'll be. *He* doesn't want any trouble, and *he's* not one to cross."

Then he closed the door, and once again, closed in the cold darkness, they heard the bar drop across it outside.

Well, this time at least we have food and water, that nice fur robe, and we've padded the floor. She didn't want to risk making any conversation that might be overheard, so she curled back up in the still-warm fur robe and after a moment of hesitation, Meri curled up beside her. She shoved their padding aside until she found the chink in the floor by the thin, weak light that came up through it, and got the knife, the paper cone, the bits of white silk, and the silver beads out of hiding.

Then they waited, listening to the sounds of the men moving around the camp outside. Some of them were speaking a language Kira didn't know, but Meri nodded when she looked askance at her sister. *Jkathan, then. So why have Jkathans kidnapped us?* It was all a frustrating puzzle.

Finally there were the sounds of jingling harness and horses' hooves, and the wagon moved as at least two horses were hitched up to it. There hadn't been a driver's seat on the front of what was essentially a plain box, so Kira decided that the kidnappers must be controlling the horses with one man riding on the near-side beast. That was the way that prison-wagons were often harnessed so that the prisoners inside would not get a chance to kill the driver; it would make sense for their kidnappers to use a prison-wagon to hold them. There was no chance they would be able to break out of it, and nothing for them to use as a weapon inside. As for getting attention or help from strangers, most people avoided prison-wagons like a curse, and if anyone *did* hear screaming and calling from one, they'd ignore it, even if it sounded like children were doing the screaming. There were plenty of ways a child could end up in a prison-wagon, all of them perfectly good reasons to lock such a child up. Madness, for one, which would make it highly unlikely that *anything* they shouted would be heeded or believed.

Well, she didn't need to make any trouble for their captors in here—she'd already made enough out there. If everyone ate at least some of the beans, in a couple of candlemarks, they'd start to feel the effects.

We only ate two seeds each, and there must have been dozens, maybe hundreds, in that bag. But they were cooking all night, and that might have weakened the brew. Or would it have concentrated? I wish I knew more about these things.

Finally the wagon lurched forward and bumped onto the frozen surface of the road. Meri got the journeybread out of hiding and offered her some. They shared the waterskin between them, but drank sparingly; neither of them doubted that their captor had been telling the truth, and that there would be no stops until nightfall.

Well, no planned *stops.*

When she'd finished her tasteless chunk of bread, she laid the patch of floor bare, and under cover of the fur, began dropping beads and bits of silk to the road below. If the seeds affected their kidnappers at the same rate she and Meri had been affected, right about noontime things would start to get interesting.

In the uncertain light of false dawn they woke and packed everything up hastily. Warrl had recovered his strength completely, and was ready to go before they were, so he took the opportunity to run down a bunny for his breakfast. They were back on the trail before true dawn.

As Tarma had bleakly expected, the trail dead-ended on the traderoad, which had thawed and refrozen, leaving an unreadable, hard, rutted surface. There was no trace of the wagon or the horses they'd been following. Even Warrl couldn't get a scent on a surface like that.

That would have been all right, since with Need to guide them, they knew which direction to go, but they hadn't gone a league before the road split into three, all of them going south. Pick the wrong one, and their quarry would get so far ahead they'd never catch up. She sat and swore, silently, staring at the damned triple-fork, as Warrl scouted ahead on the frozen surface, hoping for a trace of scent or some other miracle to give them a clue.

Then, beyond expectation, the miracle occurred.

:Mindmate!: the *kyree* called excitedly. *:Here, the middle road! I have a patch of Kira's and Meri's scent!:*

Now Tarma swore *happily.* "Warrl has a scent!" she called to the other two, and sent her mare loping down the uneven surface as they followed the *kyree.*

Warrl went on ahead, reporting tiny patches of scent at uneven intervals, confirming that the first patch wasn't a fluke.

"What is he picking up?" Kethry asked, wonderingly. "What could he possibly be picking up?"

"I don't know," Tarma began, "Maybe one of them managed to rub a hand on a wheel, but you'd think he'd have picked that up before this—"

"I think *I* know!" Jadrie suddenly said, and urged her horse ahead of theirs. She dangled down from the saddle in a trick Tarma had taught her and snatched something tiny off the top of a rut without pausing, then turned her horse and came back to them. "Look!" she said in triumph, holding up a tiny thread of white. It didn't look like anything.

"What in—" Tarma went cross-eyed trying to look at it.

Jadrie grinned. "It's the white silk embroidery thread I gave Meri for Midwinter. Remember, you've trained Kira, and she knows she has to leave us something to follow. I bet they're cutting it up and dropping it out of the wagon."

"I bet you're right." She turned her attention to the *kyree* and *thought* at him. *Warrl, if you lose the trail, check to either side of the road. You're following bits of silk, and they might blow off the road itself.*

:Clever girls!: was his comment, and with that sure guide, they were able to increase their pace to the ground-eating lope that best suited the *kyree,* even when the road branched, and branched again.

By midmorning, they came upon the kidnappers' camp, with the scent of the girls all around it. The ashes of the fire were cold, but Tarma knew the kidnappers couldn't have increased their lead by much, if anything. Warrl reported that the girls had been sick, which didn't surprise Tarma at all, and didn't worry her too much. That was a natural reaction to what had happened to them, and it was encouraging to know that Warrl reported no signs that the children had been mistreated in any way—no blood, no torn-out hair, the scent of fear but only what he would have expected. He would be able to scent a drop of blood too small to see; even bruised flesh would leave a "different" odor to his keen senses. And as for other kinds of abuse—well, those would have left clear scents as well, and Warrl found nothing of the sort.

They didn't spend too much time at the campsite; there wasn't much it could tell them that they didn't already know. The snow was too trampled to tell how many men they were facing, though Warrl's guess was around twenty. There *was* one place where a small tent had clearly been set up, and that meant these kidnappers had a leader, someone who considered himself too superior to the others to sleep beside the fire with the rest of them. There was no scent of the girls at that spot, and it wasn't likely they'd be allowed out of their prison, especially at night, so the tent had to belong to the leader.

They set off in much less than a candlemark, and when the road forked again, Warrl ranged up both forks until he found another bit of silk, giving them the right direction. But it wasn't until they came across a horse-dropping that was still faintly warm that Tarma knew for certain that they *would* be able to catch up to the kidnappers.

Twenty men against the two of us? Well, I'm sure Leslac would assume it was no contest, but I'm not that sanguine. Still, if they'd camped last night, they would probably do the same tonight; they could stay out of spotting range with Warrl to scout, and creep up on the camp tonight.

"We're catching up—which means we'd better think of something. Keth, I don't suppose you could cast some sort of magic that would put them all to sleep, could you?" she asked, a little doubtfully. After all, she'd never seen Kethry do anything of the kind—but it was worth asking about.

Beside her, the sorceress tucked her hair under her hood as she replied, moving easily with her horse. "That only happens in childrens' tales and bad melodrama," Kethry said, then shrugged an apology. "Sorry, but that's how it is. Even if I could, it would be a sure bet that men as organized as these are would have a countering magic in effect. I see your point, it would be convenient if we could put the whole encampment to sleep and just pluck the girls out of it." She chewed her lower lip. "Let me think about it, and I'll tell you what I *can* do, other than call lightning down on them, or something equally spectacular and dangerous."

"Spectacular would be a bad idea," Tarma agreed, and Jadrie nodded, so she added for Jadrie's benefit, *"Because—?"*

"We don't know who these people are or where they're going; we don't know who is watching for them or coming to meet them. Doing something spectacular could bring down more trouble than we can deal with." Jadrie had *that* lesson by heart, at least.

"The ideal thing would be to draw them out of the camp, one at time, and pick them off that way," Kethry mused. "But we'd have to do it quickly enough that they wouldn't notice until we'd whittled their numbers down to a manageable size."

"We'd need something to draw them out," Tarma pointed out. "As fast as they're trying to go, I doubt that they're going to stop to hunt, no matter how tempting the game looks. I just can't think of anything likely to bring them out one at a time."

"Maybe something will occur to us." Kethry dismissed all speculations, and glanced up at the overcast sky. "Maybe I can do something with the weather. Or maybe I could cast a glamour to make them think they are under attack by a large force,"

:Mindmate—: Warrl's "voice" was attenuated by distance. *:I believe you had better stop now and come in carefully. They've been forced to camp.:* There was savage good humor in his thoughts. *:Evidently whatever made the children ill is . . . contagious. Or it has been made to seem so. I'll come back and meet you halfway.:*

* * *

When the effect of the seeds struck, it was fortunately quite gradual, so it didn't look like the mass poisoning it really was.

Just about noontime, the men who had eaten the most began to sicken. Although the girls couldn't make out exactly what was happening, Kira heard voices strained and distressed, then sounds she thought meant that riders were dropping back for a moment, then returning—and each time that happened, the wagon slowed a little more. The leader was annoyed at first, then angry, but there wasn't anything he could do about it—the men weren't in control of their stomachs anymore, their stomachs were in control of *them.*

Kira and Meri exchanged grins in the semidarkness of the wagon; after all, only one of the men out there had offered to help even a little when *they* were sick, and it seemed fitting revenge that no one wanted to help the kidnappers now.

"They probably don't even have any herbs or anything to make them feel better," Meri whispered, in ill-concealed glee.

"Probably not, or I bet they'd have drugged us to keep us quiet," Kira agreed.

Finally the wagon stopped altogether, and Kira definitely heard a rider slide off the near-side horse and make a stumbling run for the bushes. At that point, the leader roared some angry commands and when the wagon moved again, it was only a short distance.

Someone unbarred the door, but didn't open it. When Kira pushed on it tentatively, it moved, and she cautiously stuck her head out.

From the look of things, virtually every man in the

group was suffering, but not all of them were hit as badly as the others. The healthiest three were guarding the wagon, looking pale and unhappy. The worst off could not be seen at all, but from the sounds of it, they were off in the bushes, throwing up everything, including their toenails. A couple, including their lone ally, had collapsed on hastily-spread blankets beside a small fire. *They* looked absolutely green, and Kira didn't think that a single gut-wrenching purge was going to help them get over the effects of the seeds. No, they were going to be visiting the bushes quite frequently, until every bit of the poison worked itself out of their systems.

The only man totally unaffected was the leader, probably because he had his own private stock of food, and now Kira got a good look at him. There wasn't much that was memorable about him; of average height, weight, and coloring, brown hair and brown eyes, and only his air of authority and the fine cut and fabric of his otherwise plain garments marked him as different. Even so, there was no way to tell that he wasn't what he seemed, either a prosperous merchant, or some other well-off professional, such as a sheriff or an alderman. At the moment, he scowled so furiously that Kira was very glad *she* wasn't under his command. He was taking the illness of his men very personally, as if they were doing it to make trouble just for him.

She looked around, making certain that she didn't attract attention to herself by moving too much, but there wasn't much that was memorable about this place. Just like the last spot, they had stopped in a cleared place at the side of the road, this time in a little depression between two hills. She had no idea where they were, and there was no sign of any habitation, not even a thin stream of smoke rising from some far-off farmhouse chimney. There were low, scrubby trees and thick bushes, a thin cover of ankle-deep snow, and not much else. The hills themselves were bare of significant cover, which would give anyone atop one a good view of the countryside. She wondered if any of the men would have the strength to climb up there to stand sentry, and privately doubted it.

If I just had some idea where to go, we might be able to get away tonight, she thought with rising hope. *Maybe if we just stuck to the road, we'd be able to find an inn or a farm or something. . . .*

A hint of movement atop the hill to their rear caught Kira's eye, and she withdrew a little into the wagon so the leader of their kidnappers wouldn't see her interest. She waited to see if something appeared again. She tried to tell herself that it was only a far-off animal, perhaps a wild cow or donkey; tried not to get her hopes up too much. But she *thought* there had been something familiar in that half-seen shape and the way it had moved.

Would it appear again, or was it just a trick of her eyes and the hope that someone would come to save them? As she watched, holding her breath, that half-familiar silhouette did appear, just for a moment, leaping up onto the top of the hill and back down again. Her heart jumped into her throat, and when it happened a third time and she was sure of what she'd seen, she stuffed her fist into her mouth to stifle an inadvertent cry of joy that would surely have betrayed them.

No sound escaped, but Meri grabbed her shoulder,

seeing her excitement. She motioned for silence, curled up into the fur and Meri cuddled up with her, then she pulled the fur over their heads to muffle her whispers. She didn't dare take a chance that there might be someone near enough to the wagon to overhear them.

"Warrl's out there," she hissed. "I saw him."

That was all Meri had to hear; she knew what it meant. Warrl meant Tarma, and Tarma meant Kethry. If *anyone* could get them out of this, it would be their teachers! Meri hugged her hard in a fit of repressed excitement.

"Let's see if they'll let us use the bushes," Meri hissed. "That way you-know will see us and know we're all right, and they'll know we're in the wagon. If we get locked in tonight, they'll know where we are."

Now that was a good thought, and after a moment or two to make sure she wasn't going to betray herself by looking healthy and excited, Kira went to the door of the wagon and slowly lowered herself to the ground. Actually, her stomach muscles still ached, and she was so stiff from being cramped up on the floor of the wagon that she didn't have to feign that much.

No one said anything, and Meri followed her. Holding onto each other like a pair of feeble old women, keeping their eyes on the ground and avoiding looking at anyone or anything, they moved cautiously toward a stand of the thick evergreens they'd used this morning. They stayed there just long enough to seem convincing, then, with their heads still down, plodded wearily back to the wagon.

We're such meek, obedient little things—and sick, very sick. We're no threat, we'll be no trouble, we're harmless, absolutely harmless.

Suddenly there was a pair of shiny, expensive black boots between them and the wagon.

Kira raised her eyes, slowly. In the boot were legs, clad in fine woolen trews of charcoal gray. The legs merged into a torso wrapped in a handsome fur-lined cape of matching wool. Her eyes traveled slowly up the chest to the face, a face with angry eyes and a bitter mouth, wearing a scowl that froze the blood in her veins.

The man who was responsible for their current predicament had taken an interest in them, and it wasn't out of concern for their health.

She felt blood draining out of her face, and had the irrelevant thought that at least she wouldn't have to try and feign being pale and ill. Her knees shook so hard that she was afraid they might to go jelly at any moment. What did he want? Why was he looking at them like that? Surely he didn't suspect that she had poisoned the food! After all, she and Meri had been the very first to be ill, and their "symptoms" were the same as the men's.

She felt herself starting to shake as those eyes, so full of anger, looked her over as if she was a particularly shabby bit of merchandise that he might keep or might discard.

She didn't want to move, didn't want to do anything that would cause him to focus on her. Nevertheless, she had a duty; she interposed herself between the man and Meri, and met his cold, cold eyes.

He spat something that could only have been a curse, though it was not in a language that Kira knew. She stood her ground, still looking up at him, but doing her best to look fragile and pathetic, rather than combative. "Fragile and pathetic," wasn't her strong suit, but she leaned heavily on remembering times when Meri had managed to get out of trouble by doing just that. How had she looked? What had her expression been? Meri was better at this than she was. . . .

She opened her eyes as wide as they would go, let her lower lip pout out a little and tremble, and thought desperately sad thoughts—that they might never see home again, or the school, the horrible fight, how afraid she was. The last wasn't very hard to do, with that awful man glaring at them as if he held them personally responsible for everything that was going wrong.

Of course they *were*, but that was beside the point. *I need to cry, but not blubber. A runny nose and red face is just going to disgust him. Tears, but artistic ones.* She wasn't sure how she knew that, but she was certain of it. By widening her eyes and tilting her head so that the dry breeze hit them, she managed to get them to water, which would pass very nicely for tears.

One huge, fat drop rolled down her right cheek. Two more followed, one on the left and another on the right.

He was unmoved. She sniffed delicately, and another couple of tears coursed in the paths of the others. He was never going to feel sorry for them, but maybe, *maybe*, she might awaken a tiny twinge of shame for picking on two little girls and making them miserable. She let the tears flow, keeping her eyes glued to his the entire time.

It seemed to work. He cursed again, and looked away—then angrily turned and stalked toward one of his men that was still standing. For a moment Kira couldn't move, and shook all over. In his anger at being delayed, he was looking for some ready target to discharge that anger on. And she sensed that he might be rethinking his plans to match the current conditions.

He was thinking about doing something awful. To us. Oh, Goddess, that was too close. . . .

From the way her twin sister was shivering, Meri also knew how close it had been.

Finally, when she figured she could make her legs move without collapsing, she led Meri back into the wagon and they climbed slowly in, to hide in their fur robe. Maybe if they stayed out of sight and completely quiet, he'd forget about them for now.

The view from the top of the hill was excellent, and it was even possible to hear a certain amount of sound from the camp below. Scrubby brush made fine cover to a pair of experienced (if out-of-practice) scouts. "They aren't going anywhere," Tarma said at last, as she watched the leader pitch his *own* damned tent. "Whatever's made them sick, it's keeping them here until tomorrow at best, and their commander is furious. And look at those three—" she pointed her chin at three recumbent forms wrapped in sleeping rolls. "They haven't moved at all since their last bout. I think they're going to need to sleep until noon tomorrow at the earliest."

"Mmm," Kethry agreed, watching the activity below. For two former scouts of *their* experience, this surveillance was routine; although a civilian would have said that these hilltops were barren, there was more than enough cover for *them* to hide in.

Everything was going exceptionally well, all things considered. The twins had seen Warrl, as Tarma had hoped they would when the door of the wagon eased open. Smart of them, to go out as if they needed to relieve themselves, but do nothing. That was as clear a sign that they knew help was out here as if they'd shouted and waved.

Now—how to separate out the kidnappers? Warrl's estimate appeared to be correct, and twenty was far too many for two women and a *kyree* to take on. No matter how sick they appeared to be, most of them were not as depleted as the three comatose beside the fire. If they thought they were under attack, it would be amazing how quickly they would recover.

"If this was anywhere near a city, I'd be tempted to send you down there to shake your hips at them and lure them into the bushes one at a time, Keth," she murmured.

Kethry snorted. "At my age? I'd need a hell of a glamour to pull that off," she retorted. "You'd better think of something else to lure them off. Even at my youthful best, I was never so stunning that men would chase after me with all the blood gone from their brains into their—"

She stopped, and something in the silence made Tarma turn her head the little it took to see her face.

It was dead white.

What would turn her that white? There's nothing going on down in the camp . . . it must be what we were talking about. How to lure the men out one at a time. And—oh—

"You know what will get them to hare off," Tarma said instantly, as she saw the thought, too. "We'd have to wait until after dark, though."

Kethry closed her eyes and clenched her jaw; this

had to seem like one of her worst nightmares come true. But Tarma didn't see that they had any better options.

"Warrl will be with her," Tarma reminded her. "You don't think I'd send her down there without him, do you? And she won't be that far from you—*and* she's not only female, she's your daughter. If Need won't fight for her, I'll eat her scabbard without sauce."

By now Jadrie must have known something was up, but she hadn't translated it for herself. It was a wonder she wasn't fidgeting right out of her clothes.

"And that's the *only* reason I'd let her." Kethry let out the breath she'd been holding in a long hiss, and opened her eyes again. She looked at Tarma, doing her best to mask her fear, and failing completely. "You tell her; you're her teacher, and her commander."

"Tell me what?" Jadrie whispered, a whisper as tense and electric as a shout.

"You have a task, and it isn't to go back up the road and wait," Tarma said evenly, without removing her eyes from Kethry's. "We're going to need you to do something only you can do. We *have* to lure the men down there out one at a time, and for that we'll need bait. You're the bait."

"Me?" Jadrie squeaked, her eyes huge and round. "What about an illusion? Can't—"

"I think the man leading this group is a mage," Kethry said evenly. "And we don't want to give our presence away by using magic unless we absolutely have to."

Tarma nodded. "You're going to make them think that either Kira or Meri is trying to run away. In the dark, none of those men will realize that you're bigger and older than the twins. All they'll see is a child trying to sneak through the underbrush." She saw the reasonable doubt in her pupil's eyes, and was pleased with it. "I'll explain later in detail why we think that the men will just chase after you instead of shouting for help; just trust that we're sure enough to bet *our* lives on it. It has to be you; neither of us is small enough to pull off a convincing imitation of a child."

There was a long silence, then Jadrie nodded. "All right," she whispered. "Tell me what I'll be doing."

Kira and Meri stayed hidden in the wagon as their kidnappers slowly recovered. By nightfall the worst of their sickness was over, and although they probably felt weak as kittens and wanted to sleep for days, they weren't losing everything they put into their stomachs. The leader stopped cursing, and someone managed to get a pot of broth started. Both girls sighed, and relaxed a little.

Kira had been afraid that their plan was going badly awry; after that single encounter in the snow, she had known beyond a shadow of a doubt that if the kidnappers' plot looked in danger of falling apart, the leader would never hesitate to kill both of them.

But now it was getting increasingly urgent that they actually do what they'd pretended to earlier. Finally, a long, weary time after full darkness fell, they couldn't wait any longer.

No one stopped them, no one said anything to them—in fact, as they crossed the snow, hand in hand, the camp seemed far too quiet.

It made Kira, at least, very nervous, and if she hadn't had to go so badly, she'd have turned around and scuttled back to the dubious safety of the wagon. When they'd finished, they moved off a little deeper into the bushes, reluctant to traverse the dangerously open ground of the camp again. The darkness and the concealing brush were very tempting, as was the knowledge that there was help waiting out there.

"Twin—" whispered Meri, "I wonder if we could get away while they're so sick—"

"*That*," said a Jkathan-accented voice, "*would be a very bad idea, little child.*"

They whirled as one, and a shadow separated itself from the darker shadows behind them, taking on man-shape until it moved to where light shone on its face. Kira's face burned at the notion that he had been watching them all this time.

"Then again," the leader continued, "if I were to rid myself of you troublesome little creatures right here, no one would ever know what I had done until spring. And by then, of course, it would be too late, I would be well away, and at least part of my plans would have been salvaged."

Once again, Kira interposed herself between the man and her twin, although this time she made no effort whatsoever to look frail and pathetic. She felt detached from herself, and she watched everything he did as well as what he said, trying to predict what he was going to do in the next moment. What could she say or do that would make him leave them alone? She *knew* that all she needed was to buy enough time—

"You won't get a ransom without us alive," Kira said, trying to keep her voice from shaking. "Father isn't stupid, and he isn't going to send ransom money without seeing us alive. You know that if you get rid of us, your men will know that, too, and they'll figure there's nothing to get a share of. They won't like that, and there's twenty of them and only one of you, and you've been awful mean to them."

"Threatening me with the revolt of my own men?" The man sounded surprised, and his voice lost that faint trace of cruel amusement. "You're more dangerous than I thought." His tone hardened and took on an edge Kira would only recognize later, much later, when she encountered another man the world called "fanatic." "As it happens, ransom is the least of my interests. My intention is to prevent your filthy outland sister from sullying the purity of the Blood Royal by wedding the Prince of our land. Ransom is secondary, and always has been, a mere convenience to offset certain expenses. If I need to change my plans to exclude the ability to ransom you, I would not hesitate to do so."

"You can't—" Meri began, then clapped her own hand over her mouth.

He leveled his gaze on her and she shrank to hide behind Kira. "I can, foreign child of a foreign whore," he said conversationally. "And although I would prefer to do so without taking your lives on my soul, I am beginning to think you are too dangerous to leave on this side of eternal judgment."

Jadrie moved in past the man relieving himself, creeping along on her belly like a rabbit under cover of the brush, freezing every time she heard a twig snap or thought she might have disturbed a branch. The hiss of liquid on snow covered her little mistakes, though, and it probably didn't hurt this man was still thinking more about the state of his stomach than about possible enemies. Now she was grateful for all of the hours spent learning to do this very thing, grateful that Tarma had taught her so well she could creep up on a dozing deer without waking it. Only when she was past the kidnapper and between him and the camp did she stand up.

Then she began sneaking through the scrub the way a common child would—moving slowly, but not slowly enough, and disturbing plenty of twigs and branches on the way. Sure enough, the man saw her movement, then saw only a child trying to escape, and cursed, leaping to exactly the conclusion they wanted.

"Get back here, you brat!" he spat—but not so loudly that he would alert anyone else. Jadrie knew why, another lesson in reading the state of an enemy camp. The leader of these men tolerated very little in the way of weakness, and nothing in the way of failure. This man and his fellows were already in disgrace because of their illness, and the leader's temper was in no fit state to be disturbed. The men were afraid of incurring further wrath, sick, and not thinking very clearly. This man, confronted by a harmless child running off, would not admit that he could not catch her himself. He would not raise a hue-and-cry, because that would cause the leader to punish all of them for allowing the child to escape in the first place. He would not want to waste time going back quietly for help—time in which the child *could* escape. He was like a coursing-hound with a rabbit starting up just under his nose; all of him focused on pursuit to the exclusion of everything else.

And *that* was what made this whole plan possible. Tarma and Warrl had already taken care of the sentries, but there was a camp full of men to be eliminated before the partners could effect a rescue. Jadrie had already played this ruse twice; this was the third time, and it continued to work.

At the first word, she looked back over her shoulder, and broke into a run. Reacting just like a hunting hound, the man remembered only that if the leader discovered the girl had slipped past him, he would be in horrible trouble, and sped after her.

She led him on a path she had already scouted, and to a destination of her own choosing, over the hill and into the valley on the other side. She looked back over her shoulder from time to time, but he wasn't putting on any unexpected bursts of speed.

Even if he does, she thought, panting, *there's always Warrl.* Warrl, who was running alongside him, invisible in the darkness. Warrl, who could make a single leap and tear out his throat before he could shout. . . .

But that wasn't where she was leading him; Warrl was only her backup. When he was far enough from the camp that no sound he would make could alert the other kidnappers, he learned that it isn't wise to run into unknown territory after even the most tempting of targets.

It was a lesson he would never profit by, however, though perhaps his ghost would be comforted by the fact that his teacher was the famous Need.

While her mother cleaned Need's blade, Jadrie went back in search of another victim, glad that it had been too dark for her to really see the end-game of each stalk. She wasn't—quite—ready for that. Better not to think about it for now.

Better concentrate on narrowing their odds. At some point—soon—the odds would be with them. She went back into the scrub and headed for the welcome yellow eye that was the campfire.

As she slipped through the brush, Warrl appeared beside her. She didn't start, perhaps because she had attuned herself so closely to these scrubby woods and her erstwhile partner that she had anticipated him before he actually arrived.

:*Another,*: he said in her mind. :*This way.*:

She followed him, as she had done the last two times. She suspected that he might be fiddling with the minds of their enemies, too subtly for detection. They certainly were drinking an awful lot of water, with the attendant requirement to go rid themselves of it. And they weren't thinking, either—or they would have noticed that three of their number had gone out and not come back yet.

But maybe Warrl wasn't doing anything. After being so sick, the men were surely very thirsty. Maybe it was just sheer luck.

Maybe she wasn't going to argue the point.

This time she lured her quarry to Tarma; that was her choice, when she had one. Tarma was only braining the men with a stout log; it was her mother, under the influence of Need, who was wreaking sheer havoc on the hapless enemy. Now Jadrie really understood some of the comments that Tarma had made in the past about the sword, and she was altogether glad that *she* wasn't going to inherit such a troublesome treasure. Granted, Need's abilities could come in handy, but the idea of an inanimate object that was so downright *bloodthirsty* made her feel more than a little sick herself.

The man looked up as she deliberately broke a twig, and sighed instead of cursed. "Little one—don't run," he said with weary patience as she looked back at him. "There is nowhere to go, not even a shepherd hut for leagues and leagues. You are sick, you will die of cold. Come back to the wagon—"

She ran, glancing back. He shook his head and lumbered after her, still calling to her.

"I will catch you sooner or later," he promised. "Then I will have to carry you back and lock you in. Do you truly wish to be locked in?"

She was a little ashamed at leading this fellow to an ambush, even if he was an enemy. He seemed to be the only one who was treating her friends with any sort of kindness.

At least it'll be Tarma, and the worst he'll have is a horrible headache—

Her thoughts were interrupted by a dull *thud* and the sound of someone crumpling into the brush and hitting the ground.

"Hated to do that, but better me than Keth," Tarma whispered. "At least we know we saved the one decent one. Now go get me another, kitten, you're doing fine."

Kira swiftly drew her tiny knife from her boot, and stared at the leader, menacing him as best she could. He looked down at the slender blade in mild surprise.

"Stay away from us," she told him. "I don't want to hurt you."

"What a pity I need to kill you, child," he said. "You prove more entertaining by the moment." He regarded her as he would have examined a particularly interesting insect, and she felt very much like a poor little bug that was about to be squashed.

I can't kill him—maybe if I hurt him, Meri can get away— But she knew with a sudden sick feeling that she couldn't even manage that; maybe if she'd been older, bigger, maybe if she'd seen and done more, but not now. Not when she was too small to take him bare-handed, not when it wasn't a daydream, not when she *knew* what human blood looked like. Her hand started to shake.

I'll just keep him occupied long enough for Meri to run. That was all she could manage.

He stepped toward her a pace, with his hands spread wide. He wasn't holding his own knife; he wasn't even trying to grab her. What did he think he was doing?

His next words told her. "So—let me see what you are made of. Let me see if a foreign child has half the courage of a Jkathan child." His sardonic smile told her that he really didn't expect her to show even an ounce of courage. "Come at me! Do what you will! I will not even stop you! A child of *my* people would be at my throat like a mad dog by now!" His eyes taunted her. "What? Have you no stomach to make good on your threats?"

She brandished her knife at him, backing up into the brush, which crackled beneath her feet. Meri backed up with her, crazily staying behind her, even as Kira screamed silently at her to run while she had the chance.

He advanced, another slow step, then another. He laughed. "Use that little blade, girl!" he taunted.

She tried—she tried to force herself to stab at him, and she couldn't. She just couldn't.

Why is he doing this? To get me to come within reach so he can just break my neck? She continued to back up, as he loomed between her and the camp, dark and menacing against the glow of the distant fire.

Why is he playing with us like this?

It struck her that he was enjoying himself. He *liked* seeing the terror on her face, liked feeling so completely in control of the situation.

"You're nothing but a big bully!" she shouted angrily at him. "You just want people to be afraid of you so you can feel important!"

"Little girls should not taunt their elders," he admonished her. "And there are plenty of people who will fear me in the days to come. Think how privileged you are to be the first to taste that terror!"

In answer, she made an abortive rush at him, slashing her knife toward his face, but darted back when he reached out to seize her as she had expected he would.

At this point, she really wasn't thinking anymore. She was observing and reacting, at a level of analysis that was almost instinct, knowing that if she did *this*, he would respond with *that*. As long as she could keep this game going, they would live a little longer. As long as she could observe and react, she wouldn't crumble under the weight of her fear.

But it seemed that he was getting impatient, tired of the game, wanting to bring it to its conclusion.

"What? You dare not strike, even when you know I will kill you? Even when I swear not to defend myself?" A cruel chuckle emerged from his lips. "What a pity; I had even come to like you, a little. Oh, it would not have *saved* you, but I would see that you were properly buried and not left for scavengers. But since you haven't the courage of a jackal, it is fitting that you go to feed them. It is too bad that you have no stomach to use a weapon against another—"

He broke off his sentence to stare stupidly at the length of shining, pointed steel protruding through his chest.

"Fortunately," Kethry snarled, "*We* don't have that problem."

And as he fell, Meri and Kira ran to Tarma's outstretched arms.

"Come on, kittens," she said as she gathered them up. "Let's go home."

Children, kittens and puppies tumbled over one another in a shrieking, joyful mass in the middle of the nursery, a large room lined with shelves upon which resided the battered but beloved toys of a houseful of children. It was just as well that the toys had all been put away, for no doll or wooden horse could ever survive the melee of bodies in the middle of the room. At the moment, it was difficult to count how many there were of each species, but there was no doubt of how happy they all were. Warrl reclined at the sidelines, an indulgent and benevolent presence standing in for adult authority.

"Well, I don't think they're going to kill each other, and I *do* think your Midwinter present is a success, Tilden," Kethry laughed, as three of the mastiff pups together broke from the mass and attacked Warrl's tail. Warrl ignored them, and after a few futile attempts to make the tail do something, the pups galloped back to the larger pile. Even the Archduke's eldest girl, the quiet scholar who considered herself an adult at thirteen, had joined in the romp.

"I was afraid you might be annoyed when I descended on you with more livestock," their old friend replied, eyes twinkling. "But I could hardly have given the girls their pets and not have brought identical offerings for your brood."

Tarma laughed, and slapped him on the back. "You show a fine grasp of diplomacy in your old age," she told him. "And since the manners and morals of the nobility often resemble those of children, I predict you are going to go far in your political career. Let's go off to somewhere where we can talk without having to scream at each other. We can leave Warrl in charge of maintaining a pretense of order and let them sort out which animal belongs to who by themselves."

Tilden's chief Midwinter presents to all of the children consisted of one Brindle Mastiff puppy and one Arborn Hunting Cat kitten for each child old enough to appreciate and care for their pets. With sound judgement, he had left the animals in the nursery and brought in the children, but had not parceled out particular animals for each. Hunting Cats and Mastiffs were about the same size and strength, were often kenneled and trained together and would be perfectly happy paired up together.

"Good idea," seconded Jadrek, who winced as a particularly piercing shriek split the air.

The adults returned to Kethry's solar, which was just large enough to seat all of them without anyone feeling crowded rather than cozy. The furniture was of good quality, but with the touch of shabby comfort about it that furnishings often acquire in a house

where there are many well-loved children. Tilden
looked around and nodded—with satisfaction,
Tarma thought.

"You know," said the Archduke, when they were
all settled—and in some cases, sprawled—comfortably in front of the fire, "this has been such a pleasant Midwinter, I'm tempted to ask you to invite us
again next year."

"In spite of the circumstances?" Tarma asked,
arching an eyebrow at him.

"Absolutely." Tilden nodded his handsome head,
and his wife gave silent agreement. "The twins have
no real friends at home, and to be brutally frank, I
dread Midwinter Court—it's when every social-
climber and bore in the Kingdom shows up to rub
elbows with the great and the pretenders, then goes
home to drop names to impress his provincial
friends. I'd be just as happy to have an excuse to
come here instead of bringing the twins home for the
holidays every year. It wouldn't be any more difficult
to get up a caravan for us to come here. Easier, in
some ways—my guards would only be making one
round trip instead of two."

Unspoken was the clear and obvious fact that no
one in his right mind, however bold and fanatic,
would attack the Archduke and his retinue. Not with
Tilden's reputation as a warrior.

"Tilden!" his wife laughed. "How can you say that
about our worthy peers?"

"Our worthy peers are so preoccupied with sucking up to the King that he could set them on fire
and they'd thank him for the honor," Tilden replied
brutally. "And I'm glad to be among friends with
whom I can speak my mind for a change, instead of

mouthing polite idiocy and trying not to feel as if I ought to be scraping them off my boots." He turned to Tarma, and she shrugged.

"Don't look at me," she declared. "I'm just a barbarian nomad with no sense of rank or decorum, remember? You can keep your Courts; I don't want any part of them."

"You're well out of it, and I wish I'd had your sense and declined the damned title," Tilden grumbled, yet with a smile. "You have no idea what those of us who actually do some work have to put up with from the drones. Listen to this, will you—"

She sat back and enjoyed Tilden's witty, acerbic commentary on the current crop of Rethwellan nobility, as his wife added sweetly pointed asides and Jadrek commented on the lineage (or lack of it) where each was concerned. It was wonderful to have Tilden and his family here; she'd forgotten how much she enjoyed his sharp tongue and razor wit. And of course, Jadrie was thrilled, for she not only had her best friends here for the holiday, but she had a new friend in the shape of Tilden's eldest daughter Arboli. However scholarly Arboli might be, she was also the daughter of a bodyguard and a Horsemaster—she rode like a Shin'a'in and could hold her own in rough games and contests. She couldn't match even Kira in swordwork, but she was wickedly accurate with a snowball and was endlessly inventive in coming up with new amusements to act out.

As for Kethry's twins, they were overjoyed at having a whole new set of playmates, even if those playmates were girls. Even the two youngest played happily together—insofar as any two strange toddlers could play together. At least it was with a minimum of squabbles.

There was never any question of Kira and Meri going back to their father after their ordeal—they were still sick from the effects of cold, fear, and the seeds they'd eaten, and the new Healer in the village insisted they remain in bed at the school so that she could make certain there would be no lasting effects from their experience. They ate as if they were hollow, and slept when they weren't eating, for three days straight.

Meanwhile Kethry had gotten messages to their father telling him what had happened. While the twins were recovering, Tilden had made his excuses to the King, packed up the entire family, and headed at top speed for the school, with the baggage train following at an easier pace. And when he and his retinue appeared on the doorstep, Tarma wasn't at all surprised to see them. She'd expected him to do exactly that—and if he had been hesitant, his wife Diona would have overcome that hesitation.

The first day was spent with Tilden and Diona closeted with the twins, not even coming out for meals. The other children circled each other like wary dogs for half a day, then made up their minds to be friends and went out for snowfights. When Tilden and Diona emerged, they didn't say anything, but they spent part of the second day closeted with Kethry, then joined the rest of the company and acted as if they had come here only for the pure pleasure of the trip.

Today was Midwinter Day, and with it the start of three days of gift-giving and feasting, which thus far had managed to keep everyone off of serious subjects. The one surprise Tilden *had* managed to pull off was the magical production of the litter of kittens and puppies. Tarma *still* had no idea how he'd managed to keep their existence a secret.

Then again, in a baggage-train the size an Archduke has, I suppose you could probably keep just about anything secret for a few days.

Still, the one subject that had not been broached was the kidnapping, and Tarma was waiting. They were just about due for it now.

The same thing seemed to occur to everyone else in the room at about the same moment, for an awkward silence fell, and Tilden cleared his throat carefully.

"I want to thank you," he began, a bit stiffly, as if he wasn't quite sure what to say. "Although thanks is inadequate—"

"Tilden—" Kethry began, but he hushed her rather fiercely.

"*I* made mistakes. I knew about the fanatics and I didn't take them seriously. I certainly never thought they would dare to strike inside the borders of Rethwellan! I sent green untrained men instead of experienced men, and I gave them the impression that this would be more of an excursion than a serious duty." He shook his head. "Those were all my mistakes, and if it hadn't been for your quick thinking and quick action—well, I don't know what would have happened, but I can't imagine anything good coming out of this disaster."

"The twins are as much responsible for their rescue as we are," Tarma pointed out. "*They* were the ones who thought of slowing down their kidnappers, and they were the ones who laid a clear trail for us to follow."

"Because they were well taught," Tilden insisted. "Because of that, they didn't panic, and they didn't assume they were helpless because they were children in the hands of adults. *You* taught them to think that way."

"You can't teach that," Kethry replied. "That's something a child learns from the way she is treated, and it begins in infancy. No, Tilden, be as grateful to your own sense in raising and teaching your girls as you are to us."

"Have you informed Sursha about this yet?" Jadrek asked shrewdly. "I know Kethry has sent off a report to the King, and I expect that you have as well."

"I was waiting to talk to the girls and get Kethry's description of the leader before I sent word to Sursha," Tilden replied grimly. "I think now that this should be delivered by someone I can trust completely, but I don't quite know who—"

"How about me?" Ikan offered. "I know my way around down there; I could go and be back again before spring thaw. Sooner, with a change of horses. Justin and Tarma can handle the boys without me for that long."

Tarma laughed. "I might accuse you of trying to get out of some hard work if I didn't already know how miserable winter is in Jkatha; you're going to be in for a cold, soppy ride. Of course we can spare you; this is too important to be left to an ordinary messenger."

Tilden sighed with relief. "Thank you, and now I'm further in your debt. I suppose I'll have to put up the money to build a dormitory for the school or something of the like."

"Actually—" Kethry got a thoughtful look on her face. "Why don't you hunt up some mage-gifted children from impoverished families and sponsor them here? There's a limit to the number of charity students a school can afford, even ours."

Diona's eyes brightened, and Tilden nodded decisively. "Good plan, I'll see to it." His face clouded a little. "I have a real concern though, about these fanatics. Are there more of them? Would they consider coming *here*, do you think?"

Tarma looked to Kethry, who shook her head. "Not as far as my sources have been able to discover," she told him. "And believe me, I have been very, very thorough. I intend to fortify the warning systems I've put in place as well; right now nothing larger than a sheep can get onto our property without my knowing it, and when I'm done, nothing larger than a rabbit will."

Tilden relaxed, and his wife patted his hand. "I told you," she said in a whisper that was audible to Tarma, at least. Tarma repressed a smile.

"I have to admit that I've learned a lesson or two from this myself," Tarma said slowly, and traded glances with Kethry and Jadrek. "And maybe not the ones you're thinking."

"Oh?" Diona said, her tone inviting further elaboration.

"It was a given that Keth and I would go after the kidnappers—there was never any question of that," Tarma told them. "But the only reason we brought Jadrie along was because she'd sworn a sisterhood-oath with your two—it's a Shin'a'in thing, a serious oath, and it meant that if she didn't help, she'd be forsworn. Keth and I were both fit to be tied."

"I can imagine," Diona said with sympathy. "There was never any question of you forcing her to that, of course." She made it a statement, and Tarma felt her own bit of relief that the lady understood what was involved; she'd known Tilden would, but not necessarily his wife.

"Not a chance. Mind you, we were initially afraid that all she thought was that it would be a big adventure and hadn't any notion how serious a situation it was—and I think there was some of that there, at least until we got to the place where the ambush was sprung. But she didn't *have* to tell us about the oath; all she would have had to do was keep quiet about it and no one would have known. Certainly your girls had no idea how serious it was." Tarma paused, and rubbed her eyebrow with a knuckle. "But it's occurred to me that the first thing I've learned from her is that we're bringing the younglings up right. They take their responsibilities as seriously as we could want."

Kethry nodded emphatically. "I'll admit I was furious that she'd sworn that kind of an oath without asking permission—*I* thought that she had no right to do so without asking me first—and that if she'd asked, I would have told her she was too young to do so, too young to know what she was doing. And there might very well have been a grain of truth to that, but the point is that when she *did* know what she was in for, she didn't try to back out. And as for being too young—well, Tarma and I weren't *that* much older when we swore oaths that were just as serious, mine to White Winds as a novice, and hers to her Clan." She sighed. "I think I've just had a mother's hardest lesson brought home—no matter how young I *think* they are, they're older than I be-lieve, and they aren't going to do anything *except* keep getting older. And sooner than I think they're ready, they're going to need to make their own lives."

Diona winced. "I learned that one when Meri an-nounced that she was going to marry her Prince and that it was a lifebond and no one was going to stop her. Granted, that all might very well have been a children's fantasy—but it wasn't. There are times when they deserve to be taken seriously."

"When they themselves are serious, yes, they do," Tarma agreed. "And that's what we all have to watch for, and not just dismiss it out of hand because we don't think they're old enough to understand a seri-ous situation."

"And when they make a serious decision and want to stand by it, it is our duty to them to help them do so," Jadrek added softly, a gentle smile on his lips. "I must tell you that I am very proud of my firstborn. I don't care if no one ever writes a song about her, or tells a tale about her—but I *do* care that she is already honorable and responsible, and I have no fear that she will ever be less so."

Tarma picked up her mug of mulled ale and raised it in a salute. "Here's to them and to us, then. And may we as parents remember this the next time somebody breaks a window and needs a tanning!"

"Here here!" Tilden seconded, as they all joined her in the toast and the laughter.

Mercedes Lackey

The Novels of Valdemar

KATE ELLIOT

CROWN OF STARS

"An entirely captivating affair"—*Publishers Weekly*

☐ **KING'S DRAGON**   UE2771—$6.99
In a world where bloody conflicts rage and sorcery holds sway
both human and other-than-human forces vie for supremacy.
In this land, Alain, a young man seeking the destiny promised
him by the Lady of Battles, and Liath, a young woman gifted
with a power that can alter history, are about to be swept up
in a world-shaking conflict.

☐ **PRINCE OF DOGS**   UE2770—$23.95
Return to the war-torn kingdoms of Wendar and Varre, and
the intertwined destinies of: Alain, raised in humble surroundings but now a Count's Heir; Liath, who struggles with the
secrets of her past while evading those who seek the treasure
she conceals; Sanglant, believed dead, but only held captive
in the cathedral of Gent, and Fifth Son, who now builds an
army to do his father's—or his own—bidding in a world at war!

Prices slightly higher in Canada.   **DAW 211X**

FIONA PATTON

In the kingdom of Branion, the hereditary royal line is blessed—or cursed—with the power of the Flame, a magic against which none can stand. But when used by one not strong enough to control it, the power of the Flame can just as easily consume its human vessel, as destroy whatever foe it had been unleashed against. . . .

☐ **THE STONE PRINCE**   UE2735—$6.99
Crown Prince Demnor, struggling to master the power of his birthright and to escape an unwanted political marriage, must put aside his personal conflicts when the eternally rebellious Heathland plots a bold new campaign of war.

☐ **THE PAINTER KNIGHT**   UE2780—$6.99
Two hundred years before the events of THE STONE PRINCE, Branion is besieged by a civil war, and only Simon, Court Painter and closest friend to the kingdom's ruler, can find the courage to rescue a young child—the heir to the Flame—from becoming a victim in the family power struggle!

Prices slightly higher in Canada.   **DAW 212X**

Tanya Huff

THE GOLDEN KEY
by
Melanie Rawn
Jennifer Roberson
Kate Elliott

In the duchy of Tira Virte fine art is prized above all things. But not even the Grand Duke knows just how powerful the art of the Grijalva family is. For thanks to a genetic fluke certain males of their bloodline are born with a frightening talent—the ability to manipulate time, space, and reality within their paintings, using them to cast magical spells which alter events, people, places, and things in the real world. Their secret magic formula, known as the Golden Key, permits those Gifted sons to vastly improve the fortunes of their family. Still, the Grijalvas are fairly circumspect in their dealings until two young talents come into their powers: Sario, a boy who will learn to use his Gift to make himself virtually immortal; and Saavedra, a female cousin who, unbeknownst to her family, may be the first woman ever to have the Gift. Sario's personal ambitions and thwarted love for his cousin will lead to a generations-spanning plot to seize total control of the duchy and those who rule it.

- Featuring cover art by Michael Whelan